I0761902

Orcblood Legacy: Honor

BERNARD BERTRAM

Book One of the Orcblood Legacy Series:

-Honor-
-Madness-
-Book Three Coming Soon-

Acknowledgements:
Sergio Salvador [kuyaserge] (Cover Artist)
Jaclyn Schickling (Map Illustrator)
Todor Hristov (Emblem Design)

2nd Edition

ISBN: 1-7327607-3-X
ISBN-13: 978-1-7327607-3-8

Please visit https://bernardbertram.com for additional stories regarding the champions of Orcblood Legacy, updates, and more!

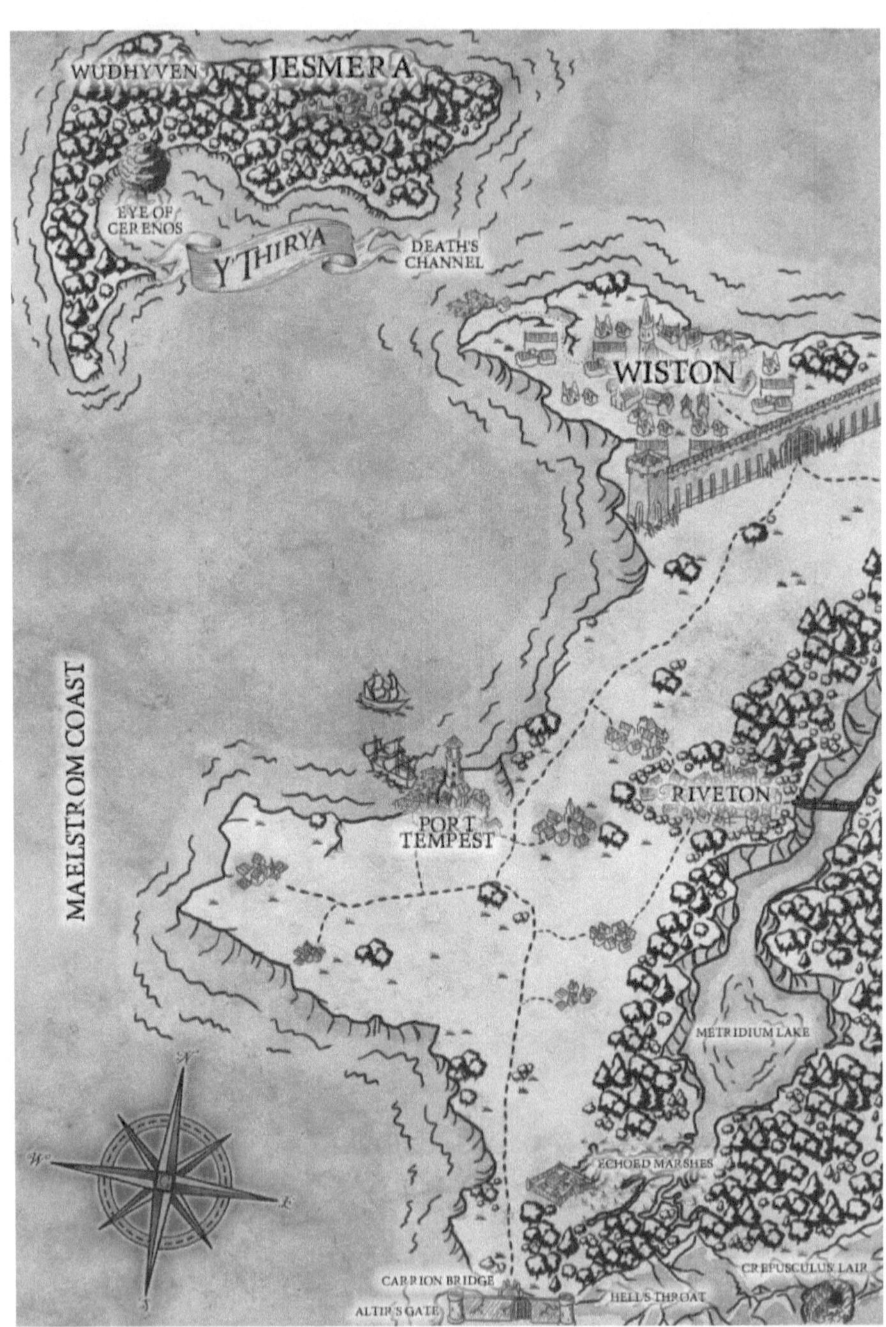
WUDHYVEN
JESMERA
EYE OF CERENOS
Y'THIRYA
DEATH'S CHANNEL
WISTON
MAELSTROM COAST
PORT TEMPEST
RIVETON
METRIDIUM LAKE
ECHOED MARSHES
CARRION BRIDGE
ALTIR'S GATE
HELL'S THROAT
CREPUSCULUS LAIR

CREIN
1.5 in.
20 leagues
MONSTROUS SEA
BEAST'S TEETH
ADDER'S TONGUE RIVERS
LITHE FOREST
TARABAR
ADDERHAVEN
ZHARNIK CLAN
TUSK MOUNTAINS

DEDICATION

To my wife, for giving me everything Fangdarr sought and understanding that the words on these pages can't compare to the ones I don't say.

PROLOGUE

Brutigarr silently passed through the brush toward the encampment. He slowly raised his fist and his raiders' weapons unsheathed from their scabbards. Grins cracked their sinister faces as they crept closer to the gruff sound of snoring dwarves. Pausing to ensure his raiders were primed, the chieftain howled a brutish war cry and charged into the camp. Shouting and growling, the other orcs in the war party sprinted headlong into battle behind their fearless leader.

Fifty bloodthirsty orcs headed straight toward the snoozing dwarves at the fire, hoping to cleave them before they even knew what was coming. But just as Brutigarr and his clan had come within striking distance, their prey vanished from sight.

Astonished, Grazmung, the chieftain's younger brother, growled, "Find me dwarves!" growling out each word.

Uneasy, Brutigarr cautiously searched one of the blankets the dwarves had been sleeping under. Beneath the crumpled fabric stood a dwarf, tucked safely within a pit. As he growled at the creature in the trench below, Brutigarr saw a giddy smirk spread across his enemy's cheeks.

"So, yer thinkin' o' eatin' me up, eh?" taunted the dwarf. "Looks to me like ye got yerself in a wee bit o' a pinch. Bahaha!"

The orc chieftain spat insult after insult, only amplifying the dwarf's laughter. "Bring spear!" shouted Brutigarr, his words dripping with rage. If there was one thing the orc chieftain hated, it was a dwarf that escaped his mighty axe, Driktarr. The eerie moonlight caught the nicked edge of the blade as Brutigarr planted the head of his axe into the ground, outstretching an open hand toward an approaching orc.

Taking care not to impale himself on the hooked blade on the back of the chieftain's marvelous weapon, the raider handed over a spear.

Brutigarr's rippled muscles tensed as raised the shaft high above his head, measuring the throwing angle he would need to exploit the small opening. Now, it was the chieftain who smirked, as the pit that had saved the laughing dwarf from the rampaging orcs would now become his tomb. "What funny now, dwarf?" The mighty chieftain howled a guttural laugh before sucking in breath and retracting his arm. Just as he was about to launch the spear, a small bolt lodged into his other forearm. Brutigarr glanced around puzzled, as did the rest of his raiding party. A moment of silence passed. Then, as sudden as the bolt came, so, too, did scores of dwarves. The stout warriors rushed in from the brush, the trees, under rocks—everywhere it seemed. Within seconds, the orcs were surrounded.

CHAPTER ONE
NEONATE

Vrutnag stared at her newborn son, watching as her labored breaths met his before melding together in a fog against the cool morning air. The babe opened his eyes and looked up at his mother. She smiled back, a shadow of the joy the orc felt in that moment. Then, the child did something so unexpected, the shock nearly made Vrutnag squeal—he smiled back. This was no ordinary smile either. As the tiny orc spread his lips, two small teeth could be seen poking through the red line of his bottom jaw. Such a thing had never been heard of before, a newborn with teeth, even among orcs. His mother stared at him as only a mother could, and lightly said, "Fangdarr. That is your name, child. Fangdarr." As if he understood, the babe gave a slight grumble of approval. Vrutnag laid back, relieved to have completed her labor. There she slept with her newborn son, Fangdarr, the newest member of the Zharnik clan.

Later, a young female orc hesitantly entered the tent. "Vrutnag Chief-mate, where chief?" Her words woke Vrutnag and broke the baby's slumber, causing Fangdarr to writhe and whimper.

Vrutnag rose, clearly aggravated. "The chieftain is with his war party. What is it you require?" The eloquence of her words irked the maiden, as it did every other orc. None could understand how she had learned to speak like the races they so hated. Normally, an orc would be cast out by such talk—or executed. However, as Vrutnag was the chosen mate of Brutigarr, the greatest of chieftains, none dared reproach her.

Shrugging off her discontent at the chief-mate's pronunciation, the visitor continued. "We have problem. Caged peoples."

"Which one, young orc?" spoke Vrutnag clearly, piqued at what could be the problem with the chieftain's prisoners that he liked to 'collect' from his raids. They were in a cage after all.

"Human girl, Chief-mate."

"And what precisely is the issue?"

The maiden looked around outside the tent to be sure none could hear. "Make youngling. Not human."

Vrutnag's eyes burst open. She had not heard the female prisoner had been pregnant. Why had no one informed her? She knew it was best to leave the prisoners to Brutigarr. But, having just gone through the trial herself, if she had known one was pregnant, she would have demanded slightly better conditions for the woman—prisoner or not. Struggling to stand from her exhaustion, Vrutnag placed Fangdarr, thankfully asleep once more, gently in a bundling of blankets before turning to the maiden. "Take me to her at once."

They walked at a brisk pace across the village to the makeshift underground prison. Descending the steps, Vrutnag pulled a torch from the wall and walked the path between the cages. Dwarves, humans, elves, and even an ogre sat in their respective cells, lifeless eyes fixed on an unchanging floor. All the prisoners exuded shame and hopelessness to match the stench of living among their own excrement for months on end. Brutigarr's reputation for his conquests spread far through Crein, but few knew of his torturous methods. Part of the chieftain's success was owed to his acknowledgement that information of your enemy would only serve to benefit his campaigns. So, information was pried out of his captives until the well ran dry—soon followed by their blood.

As the woman's cell came into view, Vrutnag's mind raced. She knew this prisoner had been held captive for over a year, and that a human child took no longer than an orc's to be born. The paired reached the cage and the young orc fumbled with the keys as Vrutnag nervously peered through the iron bars. She glanced at the rusted structure, pleading to herself that an adjacent cell holding a male prisoner would be found with the wall broken through between them. But as the door swung open and she entered, her hopes faded. All that lay in the room was a torn blanket covered in blood, a pillow, and a small bundle of clothes with a child wiggling within its folds. The chief-mate went to retrieve the child, but her attendant reached out to stop her.

"Sure want to do that?" the younger orc asked, a concerned look on her face. "We should wait for chieftain."

Vrutnag growled angrily, causing her attendant to shrink back. "Where is the woman?" Vrutnag asked, reaching again for the child.

"Dead. No survive birth," the orc replied obediently.

Vrutnag seemed to not notice the maiden's reply and pulled the child closer while peeling back the clothes covering its face. As the cloth slipped away, Vrutnag almost gasped as her suspicions were confirmed. The child was half-orc! No orcs were prisoners, and none of the clan would dare touch a prisoner of Brutigarr's. No, this could only be one orc's doing.

CHAPTER TWO
TREACHERY

For the next few days, Vrutnag had remained in her private tent, secretly caring for the half-orc child along with her own. She didn't know what to do or think. Her supposed life-mate had betrayed her. For a *human*! But she couldn't leave Brutigarr. He was the chieftain, and in orc culture, he was above all law. She knew she could not leave him and remain in the clan. This was her home. Despite orcs' general lack of emotion, she loved him. Nevertheless, his betrayal stung, and she wanted to tell him so.

Unfortunately, there was still no sign of Brutigarr and his warriors returning from their raid. They had gone to a nearby dwarf encampment on the eastern edge of the Lithe Forest and should have been back days ago. On top of that, Brutigarr had his son, Fangdarr, to return to. While an orc chieftain is expected to remain indifferent to such emotions, Vrutnag knew he genuinely wanted to see his first child. The news it was male would make him a proud father, having a lineage to carry on his name. But he hadn't returned. She sighed and slumped back into her chair, staring down at both Fangdarr and the half-orc child as they fed. With nothing to do but wait, Vrutnag slowly drifted to sleep.

The next morning, she awoke to a sudden uproar in the village. Vrutnag hastily checked to ensure the two newborns were still asleep. They were, right next to each other, as they had been since the night they were both born. She took a moment to trace her finger along each child's cherubic face. Side-by-side, the contrast between Fangdarr's blackened skin and the other's tanned hue was evident, and already her son seemed a head taller. With gentle touch, she tucked the blanket beneath each babe before turning away.

Vrutnag threw on her robe and stomped out of the tent to see what had the entire village hollering. Grazmung, her mate's younger sibling, had come through the front gate. Bloodied and battered, he shouldered his way through the crowd with a destination in mind. As he saw Vrutnag, he headed her way, and she clambered over to him, wondering where the rest of the party was when she saw it—Driktarr slung across his back.

Grazmung slowly covered the distance to the wide-eyed, halted chief-mate. "Vrutnag, brother-mate."

"Grazmung, where is Bru—" she couldn't even finish the sentence for fear of breaking down. It would be terrible for her status if the entire village saw her emotions on display.

"Me brother dead. Me warriors dead. We trapped. Barely leave alive." Raspy breaths caught between his words and he looked down in shame. "But save the chief-weapon!" The orc's eyes lit up with pride as he pointed a thumb toward the weapon on his back.

"So, you saved his *axe*, but not him?" She gave him an angry glare of disbelief.

"Me try! He kill many dwarves. He not leave. I got stucked," he said, leaning over to expose a small wound in his side. "Then dwarves take him down . . .." At that he dropped his head again.

Fuming, Vrutnag looked at the axe's shaft as Grazmung hunched over in his supposed shame. Taking the opportunity, she wrapped her hands around Driktarr and raised it high over her head. "Coward!" she yelled, her emotion-fueled adrenaline granting her the strength to lift the axe that was nearly half her weight. Grazmung's face turned to shock as Vrutnag planted the nicked edge of the blade in his skull. Blood showered over her, painting her crimson as she howled in rage. The eyes of the villagers were all upon her, but none questioned her. For them, bloodlust is second only to honor within the clan. Every onlooker understood that the chieftain's sibling had run from battle and dishonored himself and the clan. If Vrutnag hadn't been the one to deliver the blow, another would.

Vrutnag looked around at her followers, knowing they expected her to say something. She blinked away the blood that had splattered into her eyes and ripped Driktarr free from Grazmung's corpse before turning to address those gathered. "The war party has been decimated. Our chieftain is dead. Tomorrow, we will hold the Ring of Challenge for any who wish to take his place. Until that time, I remain in charge."

At the notion that a new chieftain would be chosen by feat of strength, the orcs created an uproar of approval. Almost immediately, brawls of excitement and competition broke out in the center of the village, granting Vrutang the opportunity to take her leave.

As she returned to her tent, Vrutnag thought about what she would do. As the mate to the current chieftain, she held power and security. Now that Brutigarr was gone, she and her sons would no longer be safe. Most likely, they would be executed to avoid a power struggle with the new chieftain. The matron slipped through the entryway to her tent and looked down at the two children, now awake and poking each other in their crib. She smiled quizzically. Orcs and half-orcs were known to utterly detest each other. Yet, there they were, playing as if they were one and the same.

Vrutnag brushed her hand along the half-orc child's nose. "It seems I won't be able to ask your father about your mother, little one." As she spoke, she realized that *'your father'* applied to both of them. Whether she liked it or not, they were kin. "Well, it seems I will need to give you a name as well." She pondered for a moment, then came across an idea that seemed so fitting that none other needed be considered. The child her mate secretly had with another woman before being abandoned by his brother. "I think I'll name you Bitrayuul."

CHAPTER THREE

LINEAGE

Vrutnag looked out of the cave, listening to the stillness of the woods. It had been ten years since she left the Zharnik clan and still the sounds of birds singing blissfully in the morning seemed so odd compared to the bustle of the village. She thought back to the fateful night of her departure, now little more than a faded memory. A part of her wished her sons could have grown up among the clan, learning their traditions. Though, if Brutigarr had survived, Vrutnag realized she likely would never have taken Bitrayuul as her own. The boy might not have been hers by blood, but she had learned to love him no less than Fangdarr. As she stared into the forest that was now their home, she could feel the breeze of move across her face, still a hint of chill clinging from the winter. Vrutnag was glad she had raised her brood here.

As if on cue, a clatter of approaching footsteps announced the boys' return from their hunt. At only ten years old, they had grown well. Yet with each passing year their physical differences had become more apparent. Fangdarr was the stamped image of an orc, bald and a head taller than his adoptive brother and with twice the strength. Though still larger than a human child, Bitrayuul always looked so small in comparison. The half-orc's eyes were unmistakably human and blue as the sky, unlike Fangdarr's beady yellow orbs. The small tuft of black hair that Bitrayuul kept tied in a small bunch only added to the list of contrasting traits. Even so, no matter their differences, the boys were inseparable.

The boys chatted together excitedly as they approached the cave, dragging a large boar behind them. Being raised in a forest with no other means to obtain food, the pair had become effective hunters. Though, while Fangdarr was no novice with a bow, he often let Bitrayuul lead the hunts with his favored greatbow the half-orc had named Kwip. Fangdarr was much keener on fighting up close.

The orc took pride in his heritage. He loved hearing stories of his ancestral berserkers. His mother often told him of the feral warriors of his race; how they adorned minimal armor and were lust-driven soldiers of battle, who, no matter how many wounds they received, slaughtered as many as they could until they died a glorious death. Fangdarr wished to be a berserker one day. He often chattered excitedly about how he would be the greatest warrior the world had ever seen.

Bitrayuul, though half-orc, didn't feel as connected to the heritage as his brother. He would always smile and listen along to the stories they were told, though, in truth, the boy felt a keen disconnect. It wasn't that he shied from fighting or killing—he was an excellent shot and loved to hide out in the woods hunting animals for his family to eat. He also wasn't afraid to get up close, donning a pair of makeshift gauntlets with sharpened bone spikes on each knuckle half a finger-length long. It wasn't often that he got to use them on real targets, but a myriad of trees in the area were marked from continuous raking. Nevertheless, Bitrayuul secretly felt as if he didn't fit into orcish ways. But he always felt connected to Fangdarr, at the least, and that was enough.

The young half-orc waved and smiled at his mother as she looked down at them from her overhang. "Got a big one, Mother. First shot!"

"Bring it in, little warrior. I'll prepare dinner," she replied as the boys heaved the fattened boar over the rock face that led to their den's mouth and clambered up after it. "Put your weapons down, rest a while."

"Yes, Mother," Bitrayuul replied.

Vrutnag had taught both her boys to be as equally well-spoken as she was. Bitrayuul was a natural, and each of his words rolled out with ease. Fangdarr, however, avoided speaking properly on purpose. His mother had told him that the way she spoke didn't match the way of their kind, and Fangdarr wanted to be like them. Whilst living in the woods their whole life, they rarely encountered other orcs. And, at Vrutnag's instruction, remained hidden when the trespassers happened by. But Fangdarr would study them from afar, learning how a typical orc acted and spoke. Despite his mother's modeling—which did influence his dialect to be at least a bit more eloquent than a normal orc's—he was becoming more and more like his father.

"Mm, rest," affirmed Fangdarr, a bit of a grumble in his voice. "Then food." He slid his tongue over the pair of thick fangs that protruded from behind his lower lip and now reached the sides of his small nose.

As the boys entered the den, they placed their weapons in their respective rooms. Bitrayuul was always careful to place Kwip against the wall with its quiver and tidily set his gauntlets on each side to keep the bow from falling over. Fangdarr, on the other hand, removed his father's old axe, the mighty Driktarr, from his back and planted the blade into a crevice in the stone haphazardly.

Vrutnag prepared supper as the boys rested. When she called to them to go wash, they headed down the rock face outside to the stream running along the base of the cave.

"Want to brawl after meal?" Fangdarr asked.

"You always want to fight, Fang. What good is it fighting someone you know you can beat?" Bitrayuul knew he couldn't beat his brother in hand-to-hand combat. It wasn't for lack of trying. The half-orc's strength was just no match for Fangdarr's.

"How you get better if you no try?" questioned Fangdarr. He knew Bitrayuul disliked being underestimated—and that it often resulted in being persuaded.

"Fine, fine, after dinner," the half-orc resigned.

Fangdarr grinned, knowing he had won.

CHAPTER FOUR
GUEST

After eating the meal Vrutnag prepared, the boys went down to the woods to spar. "Be careful, you two!" their mother called to them. It wouldn't be the first time one of them had come home with a broken bone or two.

Waving away their mother's concerns as if they had heard them a thousand times—in reality, they may have—the boys continued their path to their crudely built sparring ring. The area was nothing more than a section of forest cleared of leaves and sticks, lined by a roughly-lain circle of rocks. Taking position within the ring, Fangdarr cracked his knuckles as Bitrayuul tightened the straps on his leather tunic. Once ready, the orcs nodded, then began to circle each other with fists raised.

In every previous bout, Fangdarr was quick to charge in, putting himself in a trance-like state of pure aggression. However, it was Bitrayuul who struck first this time. And it worked! Taken by surprise by the half-orc's unusual offensive tactic, Fangdarr took a hard hit to the chest. He staggered back a few steps, flustered. "Good hit," he grunted at his brother, who appeared scared as to what reaction he might get in return.

"Thanks . . ." Bitrayuul replied. The muscles in his calves tightened as his anxiety grew.

The orc rubbed his chest and chuckled. "My turn," Fangdarr stated before he swung full-force at his brother's head. Bitrayuul ducked under the blow by just a hair. Fangdarr's fist collided with the tree behind his brother and a handful of bark exploded from its trunk. The adolescent orc roared and spun around with another fist in the air. Single-minded lust for battle blocked out all other thoughts. Fangdarr's fury and desire for victory became an intense flame within, consuming all. Blinded by his rage, he didn't even see what happened next. All the orc noticed was that he found himself lying on the ground trying to catch the breath that had been knocked out of him. He rolled onto his side, coughing, and saw Bitrayuul squatting in a defensive crouch staring back at him in blank amazement. "What you do, Bit?" Fangdarr asked, groaning to his feet.

"I tripped you and then you fell." It was clear Bitrayuul was just as shocked by what had happened.

"Not think you do that," grumbled the orc, his discontent showing plainly. "Good fight, Bit. You win."

A playfully smug smile spread across Bitrayuul's lips. "I guess, once in a while, tactics beats raw strength."

Fangdarr rubbed his head awkwardly. "I just like to crush first."

The boys stared at each other then laughed. Then, they heard a rustle among the brush near them. Instinctively, they crouched low, expecting it to be some sort of animal. They glanced at each other as their ears remained perked. For many moments they waited, watching the brush intently. But no further sounds came, nor any movement beyond the gentle sway from the breeze.

Fangdarr shrugged and stood up. "I go check."

Bitrayuul watched carefully as the orc approached the foliage. Just as Fangdarr peeked in, a hand reached out to grab his wrist. The boy tried to jump back and retracted his other arm, ready to strike at whatever had taken hold of him. But the hand clenching his arm slipped away weakly. Still on alert, Fangdarr cautiously spread the bush again, though this time the hand didn't reach out. He considered whether to proceed or simply run away. Looking back at Bitrayuul, Fangdarr shrugged and reached through the brush with both arms. The orc's expression turned to shock, quickly overtaken by curiosity as his hands met with unexpected material. Closing his grip around the object, Fangdarr pulled back hard. Straining with effort, the orc heaved as hard as he could, falling back as the object freed from the brush.

The boys gasped in unison. It was a sort of stout being wearing thick steel armor, bloodied and bruised. Neither of the brothers had ever seen a creature such as this before, though they could make an assumption based on the stories their mother told. It was roughly the same height as them, though the creases on its face made it seem rather old.

"Uh . . . think it small dwarf," stated Fangdarr.

"Yes, I see that," replied his brother.

"What we do?"

"Not sure, he seems hurt. Should we leave him here? Or take him to Mother?"

Pondering their options, the pair eyed the unconscious dwarf. It was obviously equipped for battle, and their gaze fell upon a pair of hammers tucked into the creature's belt. Making a decision, Fangdarr reached down to grab the dwarf's thick wrist and started to drag him toward home. Bitrayuul, still not certain it was the best choice of action, wished for his curiosity to be sated as well and grabbed the dwarf's other wrist to assist. Dragging their find back to their den, the boys were certainly concerned about the dwarf, but even more nervous as to how their mother would react.

As they entered their home, Vrutnag was still clearing the makeshift table of their dinner and wrapping the leftover boar meat in wetted cloth. She could hear the boys huffing excessively, much more than was usual. With her interest piqued, she turned her head and was shocked to find the bloodied dwarf sprawled out on the ground.

"Fang! What happened? Were you attacked? Did you kill that dwarf?" she pressed franticly.

"No, Mama, we found him," Fangdarr replied as best he could through the bombardment of his mother's questions.

"He was lying in the brush," added Bitrayuul. He could see the trepidation on his mother's face remain.

"Was he alone?"

"Yes, and he is in the exact shape we found him in." At that his mother seemed to ease slightly. He realized that she was worried they had harmed the small creature. Fangdarr dragged the dwarf by his foot into the main chamber of the den near the fire. All three hung their faces over the being, inspecting it thoroughly. "Will he be alright, Mother?"

"I'm not sure. Help me take off his armor." As they slowly removed each piece, they noticed intricate matching emblems on each one. Once the dwarf was stripped down to just a cloth tunic and leggings, Vrutnag rolled him from side to side searching for wounds. A finger-deep cut ran the entire length of the dwarf's right thigh. And his left shoulder had been dislocated, with a black bruise discoloring the area from bicep to collarbone. The matron pondered, glancing between the wounded dwarf and out the mouth of their den. By then, she had few options, and each came with its risks. Letting out a sigh, Vrutnag looked toward her sons. "Bit, fetch a bucket of water please. Fang, bring some linen and a knife. And add another log to the fire."

Off the boys went at a quickened pace. Neither understood why Vrutnag had chosen to aid the dwarf—one they knew was an enemy of their kind and likely would not have returned the favor. Yet they, too, felt compelled to help him. They returned with the requested items and took a seat nearby. They watched carefully as their mother placed the blade of the knife in the fire and started to remove the dwarf's leggings. The deep gash in his thigh was still slowly bleeding but seemed to have avoided any arteries. He must have been in the woods for a while as an infection had already taken root, causing it to fester.

Vrutnag took the blade from the fire, needing to cut away the pus-covered scab. She slowly pressed the edge against the dwarf's skin, expecting a reaction. None came. She could feel that the creature's skin was much thicker than an orc's, so she pressed down harder. Finally, the blade pierced through and made a light sizzle as it passed beneath the crust of the scab.

Slowly, the knife made its way around the wound, clearing away the infectious parts and causing a steady stream of fresh blood. It wasn't long before two blood-soaked rags had been tossed aside. With a deep sigh, Vrutnag wiped off the knife and placed it back in the fire. Then her gaze drifted to her sons, intently fixated on the dwarf.

"Boys, are you alright?"

They blinked to stop staring and turned to her. "Yes, Mother," Bitrayuul started, "just watching. Are you going to stitch the wound?"

Vrutnag took another look at the wound. "It will be difficult. I had to cut away a lot, widening the gash. Stitching may pull some of the wide parts too tightly. I will need to burn the rest."

"Burn?" Fangdarr chimed in.

"Yes, burn. It is a useful way to seal a wound, but it can be dangerous. And obviously very painful." Her head turned to the dwarf, "Hopefully, he'll stay unconscious."

Vrutnag turned back to her patient and tied one end of a string of cloth around a thick needle-like thorn and formed a knot at the other end. Despite the dwarf's tough hide, the spine held up firmly while piercing through. Concentrating, Vrutnag steadily threaded the thorn and twine through the slimmer portions of the gash. After stitching about half closed, the remainder was left to be burned.

By then, the knife blade was screaming yellow within the fire. Fangdarr and Bitrayuul looked on eagerly as Vrutnag retrieved it. They had been mended by their mother at least a dozen times, but never did they suffer so grave a wound as to have it cauterized shut. They watched as Vrutnag pressed the flat of the blade down onto the wound. Instantly the room smelled of burning flesh and hair. A sizzling high squeal echoed in the chamber, then slowly died down as the knife blade remained in contact. After a moment, their mother removed the knife.

The boys shifted closer to inspect the result. A gnarly melted combination of skin and muscle had fused together beneath the knife blade. The wound had been sealed, but the sight was sickening. Vrutnag placed the knife back into the fire, and the boys watched as flecks of skin and sinew slowly melted off the metal. After the blade was once again gleaming, she pressed it to the next portion of the wound.

In rapt silence, the boys watched their mother continue through the rest of the dwarf's thigh. Finally, she set the knife on the ground. "Bitrayuul, the bucket of water please."

The half-orc reached for the bucket, as well as a spare rag, and passed them to his mother.

"Thank you, dear." She wiped the sweat from her brow, dipped the rag into the lukewarm water and wrung out the excess. Lightly, she laid the rag over the closed wound on the dwarf's thigh, allowing it to cool the severely inflamed skin. "Now for the shoulder. I would like you two to do this one. Don't worry, I will guide you."

"You want *us* to do it?" Bitrayuul asked apprehensively.

"Yes, but it is a bruise, much easier than an open gash. A bruise is just internal bleeding. You have had many, remember? His shoulder is dislocated as well. It is an easy thing to fix and happens to warriors often, so I want you both to know how to fix one."

Fangdarr inched closer. "I do it!"

She handed him the knife, now cooled down to a dull heat. "First, you will need to puncture the area to allow the blood to drain. Make sure you don't go too deep, just enough for the blood to leave his body."

Fangdarr lightly held the knife tip against the dwarf's shoulder. The skin was much tougher than he thought, causing him to push harder. He grew frustrated. "Mama, I will hurt dwarf if I push too hard."

She smiled at his uncharacteristic tenderness. "Don't worry, he can't feel anything. As you can tell, his skin is thick, so you have to press hard. But once you do, the knife will go in easily and you risk cutting too deep. But trust your instincts will tell you when to stop."

Fangdarr steeled his resolve and firmly pushed on the hilt of the knife, waiting for the skin to give way. He felt a quick *pop* as the knife plunged through the flesh. His mother was right. As soon as he felt the knife sink in, his grip instinctively retracted the blade. A steady stream of blood began spilling out onto the ground.

"Good job, Fang. Bitrayuul, your turn. We need to set his shoulder back in its joint."

Bitrayuul crept up to the patient. "What do I do?"

"Grab his arm above the elbow with one hand and his wrist in the other. Hold his elbow down against his body firmly. Lift his forearm up to point to the sky. Then, use both hands and slowly pull down on his wrist *and* his elbow at the same time. Keep going until you hear a 'pop'. That will be his shoulder joint setting back in place. After that, very slowly push his arm back toward his shoulder to push it deeper into the joint. Do you understand?"

The young half-orc nodded hesitantly. "What if I mess up?"

"You'll be fine."

Her assurance did little to calm Bitrayuul's nerves. But he trusted his mother. He set the dwarf's arms into the proper position, then slowly tugged downward. The half-orc's face tensed fearfully as he could feel the resistance as bones dragged across each other. Still, he continued to pull.

Pop.

Bitrayuul's expression lit up. "I did it, Mother!"

"Yes, you did. Now don't forget to push the joint in deeper," she added.

Soberly, he remembered the task at hand. Just another bit forward was all that was needed to set the joint in fully. He sighed as his task was completed.

"Nice job, Bit," Fangdarr commented.

"Yes, both of you," Vrutnag smiled. "Now, we need to tie his arm down to ensure it doesn't fall back out, and put a light wrapping on his burn to avoid irritation."

As the moon ascended the night sky, the boys aided their mother with the last of the tasks, bringing the ordeal to a close.

"Is there anything else, Mother?" Bitrayuul asked.

"Now he needs rest," she answered. "We will check on him in the morning."

CHAPTER FIVE
TORMAG

The next morning Vrutnag woke to the sound of the boys jumping around as if they had found a dragon's hoard. She giggled at their eagerness and said, "Alright, alright. I'll go check on him. Stay in here please." With that, she headed out to the chamber she had set up for the injured dwarf.

Vrutnag slowly entered the dwarf's chambers and noticed that the bed was empty. She quickly scanned the room. As she turned, Vrutnag noticed a small figure huddled under a boar-skin blanket in the corner. "Are you alright, dwarf?" No reply came. She hesitantly reached out for him. When her dark-skinned hands pressed against the bundle, it shook violently in surprise. The dwarf, fully entangled in the blanket, struggled until he spilled free onto the cold stone, falling flat on his nose.

"Oof, reckon that'll hurt in the mornin'," he groaned. Rolling to his back, the dwarf's hands drove the long, black strands of his unkempt beard and hair out of his face. He tilted his head to see Vrutnag standing above him. "Well, if that ain't an orc then I should stop drinkin' with me kin." He lifted his hands again to give his eyes a solid rub. "Yep, that's an orc. Say, orc, what're ye about?"

"Good morning, dwarf. My name is Vrutnag. How are you feeling?" she asked.

The dwarf raised an eyebrow. "Ye sure yer an orc? Ye talk funny." An awkward pause followed, but the orc only offered a light smirk in response. Rolling over onto his good elbow, the dwarf started to rise. "Me name's Tormag Double-Hammers. Where are we?"

"Oh, dear dwarf, be careful," Vrutnag started, grabbing Tormag's shoulders to stabilize him. "You've been injured."

Tormag gave a solid pause as he got his feet beneath him. "Hmph, so . . . let me get this clear and fixed. Yer an *orc* and ye saved *me*?"

"Yes, Master Tormag. My sons found you in the woods and brought you here, to our home, where we dressed your wounds."

"Aye, took a notice t' me linens. Suppose I owe ye some thanks." With that, he bellowed, "BAHAHAHA! Sure never thought t' see the day me skin was saved by orcs." Tormag followed with another outburst of laughter, which drew quick footsteps from the boys approaching. The dwarf hopped to a defensive stance and raised his good arm in a fist.

Vrutnag patted the air calmly. "That would be my sons, Tormag. No need to worry."

The dwarf quickly eased and fell back onto his rear. "Eh, that's good. Standin' hurts worse than bein' clubbed by an ogre, bahaha!"

Seeing her sons peer around the corner, Vrutnag beckoned them over. "Come in boys, everything is fine. This is Tormag Double-Hammers."

Fangdarr approached first. "I, Fangdarr," he stated proudly, clasping his fist to his chest in greeting.

"Bothain's beard, ye sure are a big one, ain't ye?" said the dwarf, needing to look up at the young orc. Fangdarr beamed with pride as Tormag looked toward Bitrayuul, still cautiously a few steps away. "And what be yer name, son?"

The half-orc approached slowly. "I . . . I am Bitrayuul, Master Tormag."

Tormag couldn't help but notice the boy's heritage. He cast a brief sidelong glance at Vrutnag, but politely ignored any pursuit of the subject. "Suppose I owe ye all for patchin' me up. Thank ye, truly. I was one for the crows had ye boys not come along," the dwarf stated, drawing smiles from the boys.

"Your armor and weapons are in the other side of the cavern," Vrutnag explained. "They were moved, just in case, but you are welcome to them at any time." Despite her mate being killed by dwarves, Vrutnag held no animosity. Since leaving the Zharnik clan, it had been her goal to raise her sons to be more than just unthinking savages. She truly believed her sons could do great things for the race of orcs one day if they could learn to be different; to know that there was more to life than endless war. "Speaking of armor," Vrutnag continued. "Why were you fully suited in the middle of the forest, especially with no other bodies around?"

Tormag looked at her plaintively, pondering his choice of words. "I was part o' a caravan that came out o' Tarabar. We were raided . . . by orcs. With only five guards, ain't much we could do, no matter how seasoned. I was able t' slip away through the forest. They chased me for two days before I finally lost 'em. It pained me t' leave without finishin' the fight, but as the general o' the Dwarven Regime, I'm knowin' when me odds are impossible. I kept goin' 'til I collapsed, by the looks o' it."

A confused expression showed on Fangdarr's face. "You kill orcs? *Zharnik* orcs?"

"Aye, lad. I can't lie t' ye. I been fightin' the Zharnik orcs for hundreds o' years," Tormag replied. He shared a worried look with the boy's mother.

"Fangdarr, you know how the world is," Vrutnag explained. "War, fighting, killing, these are all too common, especially between our kind. Tormag was in a small party that was ambushed. The orcs he killed were out of necessity to survive. That is just the way it is. Until there can be peace." Her explanation didn't help. Fangdarr still seemed upset, but he held his tongue and only let out a mild groan of disapproval.

Bitrayuul stepped in to divert the awkwardness that had crept into the room. "You said you were the general for the Dwarven Regime? What is that?"

Grateful for the change of topic, Tormag responded, "Aye, I *am* the general. The Dwarven Regime is the primary army o' Tarabar. We were on leave o' duty for a moon's cycle, so I decided t' join up with me cousin's tradin' caravan. Mainly for the good company and t' stretch me legs, but also t' give protection. Not that it mattered . . ." his voice trailed off somberly.

"Anyways," he continued, shaking off the haunting memories, "hate t' ask, but do ye have anything t' eat around here? Me belly could fit a baby dragon, bahaha!"

Bitrayuul gave an uneasy smile at the dwarf. "Uh . . . Tormag, what is a dragon?"

"Surely ye must be jokin', wee orc," said the dwarf, clearly confused.

"N-no, sir. I have never heard of it."

Fangdarr grunted in confirmation.

Tormag's hand disappeared beneath the tangled sea of black hair to scratch his chin. "Well then, I suppose I'll be needin' t' tell ye about 'em over breakfast—if it be alright with ye," he asked Vrutnag. She nodded in reply before exiting the chamber to fetch some food. Tormag slowly got to his feet. Inspecting his shoulder in the sling, he slowly pressed around the joint with his free hand. Satisfied it had been set properly, he removed the sling and stretched the arm upward. "Ah, that's better."

Vrutnag returned soon after, carrying a slab stacked with boar meat. "Glad to see you are feeling better, Tormag. How is your leg?" she asked, handing him a lump of meat.

The dwarf graciously accepted, digging in ravenously. Tormag looked down at his wounded leg and lifted the edge of the bandage. "Eh, that's one nasty wound, sure as stones. Looks like ye sealed it up pretty well." He took another mouthful of boar, unconcerned. "Not me first wound, nor me first burnin'." Tormag turned his back toward the group and moved his hair to expose a dozen scars of various shapes and sizes. "Warrior's life, eh? Bahaha!"

Vrutnag and her boys just chuckled along politely, unsure of what to say. At the least, it seemed their guest would recover well from their care. Before the boys could ask more about dragons, their mother spoke out. "How long would you like to stay and rest, Master Tormag?"

The dwarf stopped eating. "Hmm. That's a good question." Moments passed with him deep in thought. "Well, ye saved me life. A debt is owed. Rest of me kin think I'm orc food anyways. Might be time for a vacation, if ye'll have me for a few days."

Vrutnag nodded in response. "You may stay as long as you like. But no debt is owed. My boys learned a valuable lesson on mending wounds and we—"

"Can you teach us to fight?" Fangdarr interrupted.

Tormag looked to Vrutnag for an answer. She sighed but nodded once more. The dwarf took another bite and smiled at the eager boy. "Aye, lad. I can teach ye t' fight."

CHAPTER SIX
MENTOR

After waiting another day for Tormag to rest, the boys excitedly led him to their sparring circle where they had found him. This time, though, the boys brought their weapons, hoping the dwarf could provide direction. Their mother had seemed a bit concerned, but Tormag assured her that they would take care. Surprising even herself, she trusted the dwarf would honor his words.

As the trio walked to the arena, Tormag eyed their gear. From what he could tell, they had quite different combat styles. Bitrayuul carried a large bow over his shoulder and a pair of gauntlets on his hands, each with three sharpened bones poking out. On the other hand, Fangdarr fit a typical orc berserker, donning nothing but a short leather kilt and an axe that seemed much too large. Tormag tried to inspect the weapon more closely. The smaller curved blade on the back of the axe looked as if it would make even his thick dwarven armor seem meaningless—if the hefty steel of the front blade didn't already finish cleave through. The dwarf could see the quality was far superior to the typical crudely-forged iron blades he was used to seeing on orcs. Tormag hoped the boy had at least learned how to swing it without letting go, otherwise his promise to Vrutnag may be difficult to keep.

Once they reached the ring, the dwarf pulled the pair of runed hammers from his belt. "Alright, lads, here's what we're goin' t' do. The both o' ye are gonna fight me, ye know, t' size ye up; see what yer made o', aye?"

Fangdarr and Bitrayuul looked at the hammers resting easily in Tormag's hands, the sign of a truly seasoned warrior. Each of the identical weapons displayed perfectly flat faces of such toughened steel that, despite their obvious use, no mars could be seen. Like Fangdarr's axe, the backs came to a point for piercing through armor. Even more brilliant were the intricate runes inscribed along the sides, emanating a dull blue glow. The boys seemed awestruck. In his full set of armor,

Tormag seemed a grand creature. Each piece of silvery steel was masterfully crafted to fit the dwarf's frame perfectly and emblazoned with a matching symbol.

"So, which o' ye be up first?"

Fangdarr proudly stepped forward, ready to prove himself. "I fight first."

"Aye, figured as much."

The large orc child approached, looking down at Tormag—Driktarr at the ready. "What if dwarf get hurt?"

"Don't ye be worryin' about me, boy. Just try t' keep up, eh?"

Fangdarr growled in contempt. He was confident that he could pose a challenge for a creature so small, even if Tormag's thick muscles matched his. The orc gave a vicious roar, tensed his legs, and sprang forward, axe cocked back for a powerful swing. If Tormag had any concern, he hid it well. Fangdarr crashed down, sending a torrent of dust into the air. As the dust cleared, Driktarr's blade was buried a full finger's length into the earth—not the dwarf. He squinted his eyes in search of Tormag through the dust. As he turned his head, the orc felt a quick shove into his hip and fell onto his side.

"Yer a strong one, don't ye doubt. But strength don't win every battle, son," the dwarf stated firmly. "Ye need t' pay attention t' yer opponent, sure as stones. Yer lettin' yer bloodlust get the best o' ye."

Fangdarr grumbled. He had shamed himself. Heavy footsteps dragged across the arena as he went to sit next to his brother. He gave a slight nod to Bitrayuul, "You turn, Bit."

The half-orc, having seen his brother so easily beaten, swallowed his trepidation and rose uneasily from his seat. "I guess I'll try . . .."

"Aye, lad, don't ye be worryin' about the fight. Everyone loses fights. It be best t' lose ye fights right here, in this wee circle, than out there in battle. Yer ol' pal Tormag is just tryin' t' get ye fightin' smart, eh? Now, let's have it."

The orc raised his gauntlets and squared against Tormag. But he didn't charge in as his ferocious brother did. Instead, he cautiously circled his opponent..

As he watched the dwarf pivot with him, Bitrayuul saw a slight limp in Tormag's wounded leg. Bearing that in mind, the boy continued to circle, making the dwarf constantly shift his weight to the weakened leg. Then, just as the dwarf seemed to grow bored of the turning, Bitrayuul exploded into motion, cutting back in a counterclockwise spin toward the left side of the dwarf's body.

Tormag knew that the half-orc might try something deceptive, but he didn't account for the severity of his injury. As the short dwarf pivoted to parry the attack, his left knee buckled and he toppled awkwardly to the ground. By that time Bitrayuul was already standing behind him with both gauntlets poking into the dwarf's neck. A wave of astonishment passed over the young half-orc. "Bahaha! A fine move, lad. Always seek out yer opponent's weak spots. Well done, boy! Ye see Fang? Size and strength ain't squat without some wits."

Fangdarr grimaced in anger at the dwarf. "Fangdarr not stupid."

"Oye, don't ye be mopin' about. If ye pay attention, I'll teach ye t' fight with yer head and use yer strength for more than swingin' that axe o' yers. I was just like ye, Fang. But every warrior needs t' learn t' *win* fights. And I'll teach ye, orc, just give it some time. Ye'll be a legendary warrior someday if yer taught right."

Still offended, Fangdarr considered Tormag's words. It was true he loved to fight and wanted to be the best he could—an impossible task just by swinging his axe at trees. He needed a proper teacher to guide him. He needed Tormag. The orc let out a defeated sigh. "Teach me."

CHAPTER SEVEN

VENGEANCE

Tormag helped Vrutnag down the rocks cautiously, just as he had done each morning for the last year since she had fallen ill. Despite the dwarf's protests, Vrutnag told him the routine kept her body moving though her growing weakness was evident. Waving her off as she disappeared through the brush with her empty basket, Tormag struggled with the thought to bring her back and keep her bedridden—as he did every day.

Six years had passed since the orcs had found Tormag. Even he thought he would have only remained in the cave until his wounds had a chance to heal. But that time came and went, and the old dwarf found himself unable to leave. For each day he had spent with the orcs, training them, telling them stories, their bond deepened. Over the years, Tormag had filled the role of a father, and, in truth, it brought the dwarf much joy. So, with each morning that he was forced to watch Vrutnag stubbornly struggle to make her voyage to gather food, Tormag couldn't help but feel pained as she left.

That morning, Vrutnag slowly walked toward an apple tree half a league from the den. Despite her fatigue, she hummed tunes happily as she progressed through the forest, listening to the birds mimic her songs.

In her trance, the orc failed to notice a group of men on horses only a few paces ahead. When she saw them, her eyes grew wide in shock. "Oh! Umm, excuse me, sirs," Vrutnag flustered fearfully. Trepidation tickled the hairs on the nape of her neck.

The men looked at each other in uncertainty from the unexpected eloquence of her words. One of them slid from his horse and approached. His eyes seemed plain but vicious as they locked onto Vrutnag. "What are you doing out here, orc?" he spat in disgust. The smell of alcohol poured from the man's mouth with each word. "You don't belong in these woods. Where did you come from?"

Vrutnag's fear grew as the man continued to look her up and down. "I-I'm just gathering apples, sir."

"You hear that, Radley? I think we've just found out who's been taking all your apples." The man pulled his sword free from its scabbard and poked the tip into Vrutnag's arm.

Another man dismounted, assumed to be Radley. He didn't seem drunk, but his guise was much more sinister. Scraggly and unshaven, the man's dirty face twisted into a menacing grin as he approached the orc. "So, my favorite apples are being eaten by a degenerate orc, eh? Well, that won't do, will it boys?" Radley asked rhetorically. The men all cackled in response.

Every grin and chuckle was another blade ready to sink into Vrutnag's flesh, only amplifying her fear. The horses circled around her, hooves stamping the ground, simply waiting for their master's call.

"I . . . I'm sorry, sir. I was not aware they were yours," she replied sheepishly.

"Eh, don't worry, orc. It's alright. It's not as if my children need to eat or anything." Radley's sarcasm summoned more laughter from his companions. Vrutnag shrank back, frightfully lowering her gaze. "Hey now, look *here*, orc," the man said, forcefully grabbing her chin. "It's polite to look at someone when they speak to you!" His other hand slapped hard across her face, knocking her prone.

Vrutnag gasped, trying to reclaim the breath gone that had been knocked from her lungs. Her head pounded. She could hardly think straight, but knew she had to run. As all the men laughed at her, Vrutnag slowly stood, still dazed by the blow. Their mocking tones filled the woods, swallowing the songs of the birds. The orc clumsily took a step away from Radley as if reeling. Then, she took off running.

"Oye! She's getting away!" shouted one of the men, whose chorus of laughter quickly turned to anger. Radley and the inebriated man leapt back onto their horses and spurred them in pursuit, followed shortly by their comrades.

Hearing the thunderous hoof beats behind her, Vrutnag sprinted as fast as she could. In her withered state, she knew she couldn't outrun horses—even through the layers of trees. Her advantage dwindled with each step. If only she could make it to her den. Laborious pants erupted from her lungs. It had been decades since she had run like this. The backs of her legs burned; nevertheless, they propelled her forward until her home came into sight. Feeling the breath of the horses on her neck, Vrutnag screamed for her family.

* * * * *

Fangdarr and Bitrayuul arose from their cots. They cast a curious glance at each other, noting they had each been startled by the same barely heard noise. Before they could get up, Tormag burst into the room. "Get up, lads! Yer mother needs help!" Hearing the frantic concern in his voice, both orcs instantly sprung to their feet and grabbed their weapons. Exiting the cave, their eyes nearly jumped from their skulls. They could see Vrutnag sprinting toward them as fast as her legs could carry her, five men on horses on her heels.

With hope finally in sight, Vrutnag felt a horse push her forward. She crashed hard, screaming in agony as the bones in her arm shattered against the ground. The blood-curdling howl caused Fangdarr and Bitrayuul to leap down from the cave wall and break into a sprint, leaving Tormag to descend alone.

Radley and his companions dismounted and circled Vrutnag again, oblivious to the orcs charging toward them. "You really shouldn't have run from us, orc," the man growled. "Though it did make for good sport." This time, the men didn't laugh, too intent on their hatred. Tears filled Vrutnag's eyes as she looked up at them, begging for mercy.

The horsemen all drew their swords. A quick flick of Radley's wrist left a line of blood on Vrutnag's arm. Then, each man took turns slashing at her flesh. They wanted to draw out her pain. She had stolen *their* fruit. Walked *their* land. Delayed *their* fun. It was all her fault. The orc had impeded their greed and when the greed of men is threatened, they become ten times the beast of any orc.

Vrutnag's lifeblood spilled from dozens of gashes before the men finally stopped. Radley bent down and grabbed a clump of her hair, glaring into her half-closed eyes. "Next time, find your own damn apples," he spat through gritted teeth. His hand clenched tighter around her blood-stained hair. Then, with a single, hard slice, the man's sword cut through her neck, his gaze never leaving hers.

Nearly upon the men, Fangdarr and Bitrayuul saw their mother's head separate from her lifeless body. A primal rage ripped through them, sending a roar through the forest that echoed off the trees and drew the band's attention.

Radley dropped Vrutnag's head and quickly arranged his fellow horseman into a small formation. "Looks like we pissed off some of her friends, boys!" Radley chuckled. This time, his companions didn't join in the revelry. "Aww, what's the matter, eh? You don't mind chasing down a defenseless whelp, but armed orcs get you scared? Get ready to fight, you dogs!"

The man's words did little to assuage the band's fear. The others watched in horror as the ferocious pair, orc and half-orc, charged toward them with abandon, an insatiable lust in their eyes. The drunken man who had first confronted Vrutnag ran off in the opposite direction, tripping over himself as he went. Radley spat a curse at the cowardly man and turned to face the orcs.

Closing the distance, Fangdarr's enormous axe raised, ready to cleave downward at the closest man. Radley grinned at the orc's predictable blind assault, preparing his own attack in response. But, at the last moment of his charge, Fangdarr planted his heel hard, redirecting his momentum and sweeping Driktarr from the side in a spinning whirlwind of steel toward the group. Fangdarr's weapon sheared through the first man's awkwardly raised forearm and on through his torso. A piercing shriek erupted as the man's two halves fell to the ground, painting the area in a spray of crimson.

The other three men barely managed to bring their weapons up in time to intercept the attack. But their relief was short-lived as Fangdarr raised his mighty axe high above his head. Radley stabbed forward, driving his sword into the orc's thigh as Driktarr slammed down through another man's skull, crumpling him beneath the weight. The orc howled as a fountain of blood shrouded him. Radley and his companions watched in horror as the orc's wound stitched itself closed, leaving only a scar in its place.

Upon seeing the orc heal himself in an instant, the two remaining men's resolve broke. They fell to their rears, terrified as Fangdarr dislodged his axe from the ground beneath his most recent victim. The two vertical halves of the corpse rolled toward Radley and the other man, only adding to their horror as their companion's open eyes stared emptily at them.

Fangdarr leveled his grim gaze on the stunned pair as Bitrayuul approached. The half-orc was dragging the drunken man who had escaped behind him, two feathered arrows sticking out of the man's back. "Mine is alive. I see you've disposed of two of them already," Bitrayuul stated, inspecting the bloody mess his brother had made.

"Two left, Bit.," Fangdarr grumbled.

The half-orc turned toward the shivering men, then back to his brother. They both recognized which of the men had killed their mother and instinctively decided to save him for last. Bitrayuul grabbed the man next to Radley by his hair and drug him a short distance to a clearing.

"P-please don't kill me! I'm sorry!" desperately yelled the man, tears filling his eyes.

Bitrayuul dropped him to the ground and looked at him, emotionless. The man continued begging and whimpering, but the half-orc simply looked at him and raised his boot.

Before Bitrayuul acted, Tormag finally caught up to them. "Oye, what've ye got, Bit?"

Bitrayuul looked at the dwarf with a hollow visage. Then, still watching his mentor, the half-orc slammed his boot down onto the man's face. There was a muffled crunch and Bitrayuul raised his boot again. And again. His eyes remained empty, but his mind played out the horror of watching his mother being decapitated. The man was dead by the third stomp, but Bitrayuul brought his boot down a dozen more times until the man's face—by then a mash of blood and bone fragments—merged with the forest floor. Life returned to Bitrayuul's eyes as he looked down at his work. His shoulders slumped low. The half-orc fell to his knees, and he began to cry.

Fangdarr looked at his brother. To be sure, he felt the same temptation to weep as Bitrayuul did, but stubborn pride held back his tears. Fangdarr turned his attention to Radley. "What we do with him, Tormag? He kill Mama."

Tormag had grown especially close to Vrutnag in the passing years, and he understood the pain of the boys' loss. They had more right than he to take vengeance upon their mother's murderer. But still, the dwarf felt his stomach drop as he looked at her headless corpse. "Well, lad, he took yer mother. Take his."

Fangdarr beamed proudly at Tormag's unexpected response. The dwarf had certainly taken many lives before. But that was war; this was vengeance. Merciless and without repent. Fangdarr bent down over Radley, his terrible breath blowing into the man's face. "Where you live?"

Radley gave a horrified expression. "No! Please, I beg you, I have children at home!" The man knew his mistake just as he said it, for Fangdarr looked at Bitrayuul and the half-orc nodded.

"Seems only fair." Bitrayuul said, wiping the wetness from his face.

"No! No! You can't! Take me instead! Please!"

Fangdarr and Bitrayuul looked to Tormag. The dwarf knew it wasn't his place to intervene, so he stepped back with a shrug. Fangdarr picked the man up by his tunic and roared into his face, sending spittle flying into his eyes and gaping mouth. "You take ours, we take yours!" Radley only continued to cry out in response, causing the orc to drop him to the ground in disappointment.

Bitrayuul stood and put a hand on his brother's shoulder. "Fang, he'll never tell us where his family is. I have an idea, though." He walked over to the man with arrows in his back. With ease, Bitrayuul grabbed the man's ankle and dragged him over to Radley. "You, where does this man live?" he asked of the injured man, pointing to Radley. The man gave a horrified glance at his pleading companion. The orcs saw the connection and Fangdarr kicked Radley in the face, drawing a groan and a flow of blood. Bitrayuul started again more slowly. "If you tell us where this man's home is, we will let you live. If you don't, we will rip off your limbs one by one."

The man whimpered, then began to sob. "I don't want to die . . . but I can't have another die in my place."

The brothers looked at each other and Fangdarr nodded. Bitrayuul stepped up to the man, clasped his hands firmly around the man's head, and broke his neck. The man's body fell heavily to the ground. The brothers then returned their gaze to Radley, who was covered in tears.

Tormag stepped over to the boys. "Lads, this be yer quarrel. Whatever ye do, ye do. But, surely ye be thinkin' about how yer mother would love t' be proud o' yer actions." The boys stared at Tormag, catching his meaning. Always teaching them whatever he could. Mercy and forgiveness—those were his next lessons.

Fangdarr let out a sigh. Even if the man deserved such horrid grief, his children were blameless. The orc turned to Radley and pointed toward the man Bitrayuul had just killed. "He save your family. You get his punishment."

The horror renewed in Radley's eyes. He quickly tried to scurry toward his sword, but Fangdarr grabbed his arm. Scowling at the man's defiance, the orc gripped the man's wrist and planted a heavy foot on his chest.

Radley started to scream as he thrashed about helplessly beneath Fangdarr's foot. The orc's grip tightened around the man's wrist as he pulled with all his might. Fangdarr grit his teeth, causing Radley's screams to amplify as the arm came free from its socket. Wails of agony growing even louder, the man's torment continued for what seemed an eternity. Then, finally, the muscle and skin tethering the arm ripped loose. Radley convulsed violently on the ground as blood shot out from the empty socket. His mouth was agape, but no sounds escaped. Fangdarr grinned sinisterly at the severed arm and held it over the man's face, wringing the blood out.

Dropping the limb to the side, Fangdarr turned to his brother. "You turn, Bit."

Bitrayuul stared in shock at the gruesome scene. Moments passed without him moving, barely hearing the orc urge him onward again. His heartbeat quickened, and the half-orc glanced around at their surroundings with uncertainty. Blood painted nearly everything around them. As his eyes darted around, they fell upon one corpse in the middle of it all, it's unmistakable black skin a stark contrast to the rest. Bitrayuul felt nauseous as his mother's head sat facedown in the mud. He choked back the bile rising in his throat before finally pulling his gaze from Vrutnag. The half-orc returned to reality as Fangdarr repeated his statement once more, still pinning Radley with his foot. Bitrayuul looked down at the man, heart thumping relentlessly in each of their chests.

For the briefest of moment's Radley's eyes locked with the half-orc's and it seemed as if he would be spared. Then, the man felt Bitrayuul grab hold of his remaining wrist.

CHAPTER EIGHT
CLOSURE

Fangdarr and Bitrayuul searched among the gory chaos for Vrutnag's body and carried her back to their den with Tormag trailing behind. Bitrayuul couldn't hold his tears as their mother lay limp in their arms. Fangdarr, ever prideful, still refused to let his emotions slip from his control. But no amount of corded muscle could prepare him for such a battle. His abdomen tightened as he drove away the feelings, giving everything he had to not show weakness.

Once they had reached their home, the family carefully set Vrutnag's body on the cold stone. Bitrayuul's sobs slowly turned to whimpers. He removed his unblemished gauntlets, realizing he hadn't utilized them during the skirmish. The bones clanked against the ground as the half-orc carelessly let them fall. Then, he leaned over his mother's body as Tormag draped a light sash over her, kissing her forehead lightly—the closest thing he could offer to a final parting.

Bitrayuul rose to his feet and cleared his throat. "I will gather firewood," he choked out.

"Aye, I'll help ye, lad," Tormag offered. Bitrayuul didn't reject him.

"I stay here, look after Mama," Fangdarr said. His eyes were fixated on the cloth-wrapped face of his sweet, loving mother.

Bitrayuul and Tormag nodded back at the orc. They could tell he needed to grieve in his own way. The pair exited in silence, heading back into the woods. As they gathered wood, Bitrayuul could just barely hear muffled sobs escaping from the cave. Trying to drown out Fangdarr's sobs, knowing his brother wouldn't wish that his vulnerability be heard, the half-orc kept his mind on the task. Bitrayuul bent down, grabbing another stick and adding it to the small pile in his arms. As he looked down, he could see the splash of red blood on his boots. He thought back to what they had done and turned to Tormag.

"Tormag . . . did we do wrong?"

The dwarf stopped and let out a knowing sigh. "Ye did what ye had t' do, sure as stones. And ye didn't let yerselves get lost from honor. Ye killed what needed killed. Ye lads made me proud t' see that ye showed the other fella a wee bit of mercy."

"But we killed them all. Viciously. We acted just like how Mother wished we wouldn't." Bitrayuul averted his gaze in shame.

Tormag dropped his sticks and stepped over to the half-orc. His expression was soft, full of understanding. "Aye, ye killed 'em all." The dwarf put his hands on Bitrayuul's arms, bringing the half-orc's attention to the black blood smears covering them.

Bitrayuul noticed his mother's blood on his clothes and arms for the first time. He tried to pull away from Tormag but the dwarf held him in place.

"They put ye in a situation yer never prepared for. Yer mother wanted ye and Fang t' be better—and ye both *are*. Ye showed mercy, Bit. Take it from me, that be a trait that don't exist in orcs. Those men took yer mother from ye," Tormag said somberly, tearing up as his hands brushed against the dark stains. "She may be gone, but she lives through ye and yer brother. Her lessons, her kindness, her *love*, lad. And no one can take that away from ye."

* * * * *

Fangdarr's hand entwined in his mother's. He lamented at how cold her touch was, lifeless and empty. All the love and goodness that she was now gone. Still, he knew she would remain a constant in his memories. The lessons she taught, the compassion she showed. Fangdarr gripped her hand tightly, hoping that he would feel her gently squeeze back.

Nothing.

Fangdarr steadied himself with a deep breath as he heard Tormag and Bitrayuul return.

Later that night, Vrutnag lay burning on a pyre of branches. Bitrayuul and Fangdarr said their final farewells and listened to an old dwarven prayer cast by Tormag. Afterwards, the unlikely family ate dinner in silence before each returning to their respective rooms.

Tormag shut the drape to his room as he entered. Finally having a moment to himself, the dwarf slumped heavily onto his bed as the weight of the day dawned on him. Neither of the boys knew of it, but he had developed quite an intimate relationship with Vrutnag over the course of their time together Therefore, he too had lost someone dear to him on that day. With her gone, Tormag didn't have the stomach to tell her sons of the relationship. Instead, he resigned to simply lock the loss away in his heart. He lay on his bed, remembering the last few years of cherished memories he had built with Vrutnag and her sons, only driving the knife deeper knowing she wouldn't be there to make more.

While reminiscing, Tormag recalled a conversation he had with the boys' mother when her illness had first taken root. Vrutnag had told him of the things she wished for the boys to know, were she to pass, and that she wanted Tormag to do so. They were conversations that Tormag hoped to never have, at least not while the boys were still so young. But a promise was made, and he wouldn't disregard Vrutnag's wishes, no matter how hard. Sitting up, the dwarf donned the façade of strength that he felt the boys needed. He slapped himself in the face with both hands, trying to force away his sorrow. When he felt ready, the dwarf beckoned the boys out of their rooms.

After a long pause, Fangdarr and Bitrayuul pulled aside the drape to Tormag's room and stepped inside. Each wore an expression of weariness, obviously still mourning. But they sat dutifully on the ground and looked at Tormag.

"Boys, this ain't a good time, don't ye doubt. But there's things ye need t' know," Tormag said somberly. "Things yer mother asked me to tell ye, should she not get the chance." The boys continued to stare at him curiously. Tormag gave a reserved sigh. "It's about yer father."

Fangdarr and Bitrayuul's expressions turned to shock, and they inched closer, fully riveted.

"As you know, yer father's name was Brutigarr, and he was the greatest chieftain yer clan had ever seen. I know yer mother told ye that ye were both born on the same night." Tormag paused. "And did she tell ye that ye weren't hers, Bit?"

Bitrayuul looked away. "Yes, she told me. And obviously I am half human."

"Right ye are, lad. The night ye were born, after yer mother had Fang, she heard one o' yer father's prisoners had given birth. The woman died in the process, but ye were born healthy and right. Didn't take yer mother long t' know that yer father had raped the poor girl. O' course, yer mother didn't take it too well. She had planned on givin' him a stern talk, if ye catch me meanin'."

The boys were intently glued to their seats. Tormag noticed their longing looks, knowing that their innocent curiosity may soon sour, and carried on. "So, anyways, yer mother waited fer him t' get back from his raid. But he never made it home. Turns out he died from an ambush. He killed many good dwarves that day . . .." The dwarf's voice trailed off before Bitrayuul asked a question.

"Wait, how do you know how many dwarves he killed? Did anyone survive the raid and talk of it?"

"Hold on, lad. First, only one orc made it back t' the village. Yer uncle, Grazmung. But he abandoned yer father so he could steal yer axe, Fang, and become the new chieftain."

"Uncle betray father for Driktarr?" asked an astonished Fangdarr. He growled angrily.

"Yep, he sure did. But don't ye worry, son. Yer mother killed that dog right when he walked into the village. And, obviously," Tormag pointed to Driktarr, "got yer axe back too. So, after yer mother's mate fell and she killed yer uncle, it wasn't safe for ye t' stay in the village. She grabbed both o' ye boys and headed out, t' keep ye safe."

The boys gleamed with pride at their mother's courage. They knew their mother had left the clan to keep them safe, but never the actual events that had transpired. "Wait, you never answered how you knew about the ambush," Bitrayuul pressed. "It seems our uncle didn't have a chance to recount the battle before he was killed. You said there were no other survivors, so how did you know?"

Tormag gave one final sigh and looked at the ground. A great deal of weariness seemed to show under his old eyes. He seemed pained as he said what he never wanted to say to the boys he had come to love as sons. "I know because I was there. I know because . . . it was me who killed yer father."

CHAPTER NINE
EXODUS

The boys stared at Tormag in disbelief, completely at a loss. Fangdarr's eyes darted over the dwarf, as if he didn't recognize the creature before him. All the years past under Tormag's tutelage and guidance seemed to have been erased in an instant. Bitrayuul opened and closed his mouth repeatedly, trying to find the words to speak, only for none to answer his call. Finally, after the tense silence grew unbearable, the half-orc managed to choke out, "Why didn't you tell us before?"

Tormag looked up at the young half-orc, grateful that Fangdarr hadn't been the first to speak. He wasn't confident that the orc's temper wouldn't get the better of him—could the boy be blamed? Tormag picked his response carefully, not wanting to start a dispute he would be afraid to finish. "Didn't know 'til yer mother and I spoke o' yer father's raid when she fell ill. Didn't know the orc I killed was her mate 'til then. All me eyes saw was another orc killin' me friends. Like I said before, yer father did slay many o' me kin that day, sure as stones. But I be makin' no excuses. After we found out the truth, I was ashamed o' takin' yer mother's mate from her. But she knew that I was only doin' what me people needed me t' do. I was the commander o' the Dwarven Regime and he was the biggest threat. Sure enough, I had t' fight him, or me allies would've fallen by the dozens under his mighty axe."

"What about Fangdarr's axe? Wasn't our father wielding it? You didn't recognize it while you were here?" Bitrayuul asked.

"There be lots o' axes, don't ye doubt, lad. Hard t' look at the details when it's swingin' fer yer head. It be a fine weapon, but in the heat o' combat, just looked like another big slab o' steel."

Fangdarr listened closely. "How you kill father?"

Tormag hesitated. "He underestimated me, just as ye did in our first fight. Yer father was the greatest warrior me eyes had ever seen. It was my honor t' fight him."

The orc scowled. "*Honor*? Honor! You kill father! On day we born! Father never meet us because of you!"

Tormag sighed hopelessly. "Lad, ye have t' understand, I did what I was needin' t' do. Yer own mother, the mate o' the orc I killed, knew that and she forgave me for what I done." He looked into Fangdarr's eyes as he spoke, searching for any glimpse of understanding. "I was hopin' ye could, too."

This time it was Bitrayuul who spoke. "I understand you, Tormag. It wasn't your fault." His brother shot him the most distasteful glare he had ever seen.

"No betray me, Bit. We brothers. We stick together."

Even before he finished his sentence, the half-orc was shaking his head. "I would never betray you, Fang. But you must see the rationality behind Tormag's story."

"No! He kill father. You no care? Our father dead now. Where your pride?"

"My pride is in the acceptance of what's happened, as it should be for you. Who was it that trained you, taught you to be the orc you are today? It wasn't our father; it was our mother and Tormag."

Fangdarr growled, fists clenched as he rose to his feet. "I leaving now. You follow, or you stay, Bit?"

Bitrayuul's gaze lowered to the floor. He thought of his home—how this had *always* been his home. They belonged there, together. He knew it was what his mother would have wanted. The half-orc looked to Tormag for help, but the dwarf only sat in silence, allowing Bitrayuul to make his own decision. He already knew it, but he was afraid it was one he would regret for the rest of his life. The half-orc sighed. "I'm staying, Fang."

A deep grimace appeared on Fangdarr's face. Silently, he left the room, retrieved Driktarr and a pouch of leftover meat, and made his way to the mouth of the cave. He gave one final look back at his brother. Then, for the first time ever, Fangdarr left Bitrayuul's side.

CHAPTER TEN
UPHEAVAL

Another four years went by since Fangdarr had set out on his own. Over that time, he had many uneasy nights in which he regretted leaving and missed having Bitrayuul by his side. Forced to survive alone, Fangdarr had become more savage. In the first days, the orc had barely survived. He had been starved, ambushed, attacked, sleep depraved and more. But each trial made him stronger, wiser. It wasn't long before Fangdarr started to wander the forest, testing his strength on any who crossed his path—ogres, trolls, bears, and especially humans. His axe cleaved through any obstacle indiscriminately, healing the many wounds he suffered along the way.

Upon reaching his second decade, Fangdarr traveled to the village of orcs on the southern edge of the forest. Heads turned as he entered through the wooden gate. To them, he was a stranger. But the weapon he carried, they knew well, even after twenty years. This was his father's old clan, the Zharnik orcs. Orcs gathered behind Fangdarr, following his progress through the village until finally he slowed to a stop in the center. He scanned the mob circled around him, all eyeing him in curiosity or concern. A slight smile spread over Fangdarr's lips. The gathered orcs waited in silence, some clutching their weapons in anticipation. Fangdarr pounded his chest with a fist, the sudden movement causing some of the crowd to take a step back cautiously. Then, Fangdarr exclaimed in a booming voice, "I come to challenge chieftain! *Ortuk Malid*!"

Gasps erupted from the crowd. Some roared in outrage, others hollered in joy. As the clamor was at its peak, an orc exited from a large tent in the center of the village. It was undeniably the clan's chieftain, coming to see what had caused the uproar. Fangdarr almost laughed at the sight of him. The orc was hardly muscular and wielded an iron mace and shield. *Coward*, Fangdarr thought. Orcs didn't carry shields. How this orc had managed to become the chieftain to a tribe of bloodthirsty orcs who thought cowardice in battle was punishable by death was a mystery to Fangdarr.

The chieftain stepped closer, looking out at the crowd from atop his raised platform. With each step, the bones of his necklace and many other jewels clinked together. Though it was obvious, the orc called out, "Who challenges Vrik?" His tone had the hiss of a snake to it. As one, dozens of orc hands pointed to Fangdarr. Vrik looked at his challenger with disdain. It was obvious that Fangdarr was abnormally large and strong for an orc, standing a whole head higher than the rest of the village. But if the chieftain had any concern, he didn't show it. "What your name, orc?"

"Fangdarr, Brutigarr-son, chieftain of Zharnik clan!" A cheer rolled through the crowd at the mention of their fallen chieftain. Brutigarr was a legend among the clan, and by appearance alone, his son seemed to be capable of following in his footsteps.

Vrik's eyes narrowed. "Mighty Brutigarr perish. Battle many years ago. How we know your claim true?"

Fangdarr grumbled at being doubted, baring his teeth. His beady yellow orbs remained fixed on the less-imposing chieftain as he reached behind his back. With a single hand, he hoisted the giant greataxe slowly over his shoulder and let the blade wedge into the cold ground in front of him. The crowd hushed.

The chieftain gave a disrespectful clap. "So, maybe you lost son of Brutigarr. Maybe you find weapon on a corpse. Last seen with Brutigarr-mate—any orc could take from her. You think this mean you chieftain?" His tone grew more condescending with each word.

Fangdarr's anger boiled. It was obvious that was the purpose of Vrik's insults, but the mention of Vrutnag caught the orc off-guard. "I fit to lead. I *big enough* to lead."

The chieftain's gaze narrowed dangerously at the mention of his diminutive stature. "We begin, then."

Both orcs and their entourage of followers headed to an opening in the camp where the contenders would have room to fight. Nearly every member of the tribe huddled in a ring around them. It wasn't often a chieftain was challenged. As they prepared for the conflict, Fangdarr watched as the chieftain removed at least a dozen different accessories—rings, necklaces, charms, everything you could think of. It all seemed so pointless. Nevertheless, Fangdarr could see seasoned warriors in the crowd, all stronger than the current chieftain. Yet, none had challenged him. There must have been more to Vrik than his size.

The combatants stood poised in the center of the ring as a drum sounded signifying the duel was about to begin. In *Ortuk Malid* a challenger had to fight the challenger in hand-to-hand, unarmed combat. It was no merciful fight, though. Orcs were relentless in their challenges. To be named champion, one must kill the other. The victor would then claim all that the defeated owned.

The pounding beat of the drum changed to a rapid pace, indicating the duel had started. Eager for bloodshed, the crowd rampaged in response, stomping along with the rhythm. Vrik lunged forward with a leading fist, and Fangdarr stood perfectly still as the chieftain's attack landed squarely on his abdomen. Not even a flinch. Vrik didn't slow, launching a flurry of punches at his torso. As before, each seemed to be of no concern to the challenger. However, unbeknownst to Fangdarr, the small orc had been quietly chanting with each blow, almost too quiet to hear. Just as Fangdarr caught on, Vrik reeled back his fist and it swirled in a greenish-yellow, wispy glow.

Vrik's eyes widened in glee. He knew his feeble stature gave his opponent a false sense of confidence, enough to give Vrik the time to compel the power of his gods. The shaman's fist became imbued with magical strength as it soared, escalating his elation. As his fist made contact, Vrik closed his eyes and laughed, knowing Fangdarr would be defeated by the sheer force of his divine attack.

A loud gasp came from the crowd. Vrik opened his eyes, expecting their stunned reaction to be from seeing his fist embedded in Fangdarr's lifeless abdomen. The chieftain's eyes widened, realizing his folly. Fangdarr had Vrik's fist clasped tightly in his own. He had completely halted the chieftain's enhanced attack, overcoming the strength the gods had granted him! Mouth agape, the shaman shuddered as he looked at Fangdarr's grin spread widely on his face.

Vrik, informed of his impending doom, frantically tried to back away from Fangdarr. The challenger released his hand, allowing the chieftain to scurry away in fear. Vrik knew his clan would never tolerate surrender, but survival was his only thought. He scrambled to his feet and backpedaled toward the edge of the ring. As the crowd roared angrily, threatening to kill him themselves, Vrik realized he had to give the impression that the fight would carry on. He had to hope, against all odds, that he could win. The chieftain slowly circled the large orc, though he was mentally frozen in fear.

Fangdarr stood still as rock, simply waiting. Spectators watched him, perplexed; however, he didn't keep them waiting for long. As the chieftain danced around him, Fangdarr walked toward the smaller orc in powerful strides. Vrik yelped in terror as he tried to pick up his pace, but the challenger pursued.

In no time, Fangdarr caught up to his frantic opponent and placed a hand firmly over his head. The chieftain cried out in surprise and started kicking about rapidly, hoping to break the orc's strong grip on his face. But it was no use. Fangdarr lifted the orc high into the air, a single hand still planted over Vrik's face. His mighty grip tightened. The chieftain's muffled screams amplified beneath Fangdarr's palm.

Then, with a loud crunch, Vrik's skull shattered beneath his grasp, sending a burst of black blood into the air.

All fell silent. Not even Brutigarr had the strength to crush the thick skull of an orc. Within moments of entering the village, Fangdarr had already proved himself capable of surpassing his father's formidable shadow and birthing his own legacy. The young orc roared vigorously.

The silence broke as every orc cheered for their new chieftain. Though it was unspoken, they knew he would lead them to glory and conquest. Fangdarr raised his blood-soaked arm triumphantly, still holding Vrik's lifeless form. Another roar, another cheer. He didn't even need to speak; his actions spoke loud enough.

The mighty orc walked toward the embellished tent in the center of the camp as chieftain of the clan. He entered alone, the continuous uproar of orcs blasting at his back, and looked around. What he saw inside his new chamber irked him more than a bit. In every corner sat a severed dwarf head on a pike, still bloodied from the day it had been obtained. He respected—even adored—his heritage's barbarism and savagery, yet, seeing the trophies reminded him of his mentor. A pang of guilt cut into the pit of his stomach.

Fangdarr was aware he could never show any weakness if he wished to remain in such high regard. But he also knew he wouldn't be able to look at the dwarves' disembodied heads for very long. He collected the four trophies and threw them through the flap of his tent. Curious onlookers looked up at the platform, waiting for an explanation. Fangdarr walked out of his dwelling, a scowl on his face. "Me orc! Dwarf company forbidden!" he exclaimed to the gathered crowd. At that, a howl of laughter and applause came in reply. He had managed to appease his new followers, but internally his gut sank as he watched the heads of those who reminded him of his adoptive father roll through the muck.

CHAPTER ELEVEN
CONQUEST

For two years, Fangdarr's led his clan on a campaign of conquest, raiding as many settlements and unsuspecting caravans as they could sink their teeth into. In that short time, the Zharnik clan's dominance had every human from Adderhaven to the dwarves of Tarabar afraid to step foot in the woods.

The Lithe Forest stretched from the base of the Tusk Mountains—named so for their infestation of trolls —all the way to the northern cliffs of Crein. The thick layer of trees blanketed all the land between Tarabar, which was built directly into the face of the Tusks lining the east, and the human's capital, Wiston, to the west. Before Fangdarr's ascension to chieftain, many small human villages called the Lithe their home, safely too far north from the orcs that roamed the south. But the distance served meaningless once Fangdarr took over. Within the first year, most of the humans that dwelled within smaller encampments within the forest were forced to flee to the larger towns.

The dwarves, on the other hand, simply remained safely in their cavernous home and stopped their trade with the humans. Dwarves and orcs had always had their disputes—a byproduct of proximity and a deep historical enmity for one another. Orcs knew that dwarves were both masterful craftsmen and living beneath the mountains gave them a nearly unlimited supply of material to forge their weapons with, all the motivation the ferocious clan had needed to try to intercept their caravans. But Fangdarr's aggression kept the dwarves behind their walls. As such, it wasn't long before the path between Tarabar and Wiston had been deemed too great a risk for trade.

Growing up away from his clan, Fangdarr had much to learn about its tradition, but he did so very quickly. The orc relished at the opportunity to follow his birthright. For the first time, Fangdarr felt as he thought he should feel. He felt like an *orc*. With each foe he felled, he could feel the surge of adrenaline, the insurmountable thrill of bloodlust. With each village he raided, Fangdarr got to prove his strength. But his strength was only half of the reason for his success. His mother and Tormag had taught him to fight with his head first. So Fangdarr decided to do something that no other orc chieftain had dared to do—he recruited. The determined orc knew that more numbers meant he could target more settlements. As a result, Fangdarr had joined forces with Raz'ja, the leader of the trolls.

When Fangdarr had first made his way into the mountains, he wasn't daunted by the thousands of trolls watching him. Trolls and orcs shared a deep loathing for humans and dwarves, so Raz'ja needed no coercion to join Fangdarr's campaign. Likewise, the orc knew the powerful asset he was gaining with the alliance. Trolls were agile and brutal. But their true strength was in their massive number, hidden within the dark recesses of the Tusks.

Trolls were also very hard to kill. Their race was blessed with a distinct ability that—when paired with their overwhelming numbers—could best almost any foe. Trolls regenerated monstrously fast. Grievous wounds that would fell even the sturdiest of warriors healed almost instantaneously on their own; even completely severed limbs grew back within moments unless burned with fire.

The alliance with the trolls is what allowed Fangdarr to expand his territory and creep ever closer to the dwarves and humans until one day, he thought, he could overcome them both. He wasn't yet ready for a war. But his numbers were growing, and his troops were growing more and more eager to be rid of their despised adversaries.

Fangdarr sat in his chambers studying maps and devising strategies to attack either race. As he pored over every detail, looking for some weakness his forces could exploit, he sighed. Raiding isolated settlements was simple enough, but attempting to pillage a capital city with proper defenses seemed an impossible task.

Tarabar was closer with nothing but forest between, which would allow his army to remain well-supplied for a siege. Yet the city was entirely underground, an impenetrable fortress hidden within the mountain. There was only one way in, a grand gate made of solid steel with dozens of guards and mounted ballistae. A simple battering ram could never hope to pose any threat.

Therefore, the human capital seemed a better approach—though not by much. Wiston was comprised of a large castle, behind a large gated wall and with a dock in the rear. However, that city, too, had been built in a defensible position. The capital lay on a peninsula among the Maelstrom Coast with the sea at its back. Neither orc nor dwarf had access to water routes, so the humans had used the sea to form a trade alliance with the elves of Jesmẹra, an island not far off the coast. As such, attacking the humans could draw retaliation from the elves. Fangdarr had bested plenty of humans, but he had yet to even see an elf. Others within his clan had not been as fortunate, and they recounted their experiences with the mystical folk with both horror and shame.

Fangdarr sighed and dropped the maps. He was stuck. His people expected conquest from him, especially after the profound success of the last two years. All that was left to do was conquer a race. Yet, it was much more difficult than any of his followers could imagine. Stress bit into his shoulders and Fangdarr closed his eyes to settle his mind. Then, just as he had started to relax, the orc heard screams outside his tent. Fangdarr rose from his seat and raced outside, grabbing Driktarr along the way. At first, he couldn't tell why his people were screaming. Seeing orcs cower in fear, occasionally glancing up at the sky, the chieftain followed their eyes upward. Fangdarr's jaw fell open. High in the clouds, a dragon flew toward the village.

CHAPTER TWELVE
CREPUSCULUS

Circling the village, the drake roared at the scampering and screaming orcs below. A thick smog of dark smoke trickled from the sides of its gaping maw, darkening the sky around it and obscuring the creature. Then, the dragon tucked its ebony wings and dove toward the village and swirling the black smog in its wake. A moment before it crashed into the ground, its wings spread wide. Up close, the beast was enormous. Its wings cast a shadow over almost half the village and its head rose higher than even the tallest tower. Its menacing jaws opened, and a vibrant purple liquid spewed forth, showering a dozen orcs. Once the ooze connected with their skin, flesh and muscle began to melt away. Shrieks of pure agony and terror wailed from each as they helplessly watched their own bodies drip to the ground. Slowly, the tantalizing plague crept further and further along their extremities, eating away and leaving naught in its wake.

Fangdarr watched in horror as the mighty beast liquidated his companions. For the first time in years, the chieftain felt fear. His mind flickered to the tales Tormag had preached to him about the mystical drakes, recalling the havoc they could wreak. Now, he watched as his people faced that very devastation. He steeled his resolve. Amidst the chaos, he shouted, "Archers! Bows!"

A group of orcs started frantically firing arrows at the drake. They each watched helplessly as their missiles bounced harmlessly off the tenebrous scales. One of the archers shouted the obvious to his chieftain, "Arrows no work!"

Fangdarr gripped Driktarr tightly in his hand. "Get inside!" The villagers shoved and trampled each other amidst the chaos before all managed to scramble inside their homes—as if fur-covered tents would protect them. Fangdarr watched from the village center as the dragon eyed the orcs scamper away in their terror. The creature seemed more amused than anything.

Fangdarr started walking slowly toward the foreboding beast. The orcs peeked from their hidden shelters at their leader trudging forward, seemingly devoid of fear. Fangdarr eye's locked with the dragon. He raised his heavy axe at arm level.

Slamming the blade of his weapon into the earth, the orc's visage turned fierce as he roared as loud as he could. The dragon's bright, purple eyes became dangerously thin as it hissed in response. Fangdarr caught the threatening glare and roared once more in defiance. He would not be subdued.

Black scales glimmered in the dull light as the dragon jerked its head toward the chieftain, spewing a beam of its plague-like breath toward the orc. Fangdarr didn't even flinch as death came toward him through the air. The purple, gelatinous liquid fell just short of his position—clearly a warning shot. The drake's eyes narrowed once more. It gave another deep hiss of annoyance. Then, to everyone's surprise, the creature pumped its giant wings twice, taking to the air once more before turning toward the mountains.

Before the dragon had even gone from view, the chieftain was being swarmed from all sides. His people flooded out from their holes to praise their fearless leader. Fangdarr remained stoic, but pride swelled within his chest. He had become akin to a god amongst his clan. Surely his feats would be spoken of through the ages, long after his bones had faded to dust. After finally getting his admirers to return to a state of calm, the chieftain instructed his followers to observe the damage that had been done. At least thirty orcs had fallen, as far as could be told—some had become nothing more than disgusting puddles of ooze.

Fangdarr ordered for the streets to be cleared of the dead and to fetch the clan's shaman before turning into his tent. Shortly after, an aged orc donned in tattered robes affixed with the skulls of at least a dozen different species entered his chambers. "You ask for me?"

The disgruntled chieftain looked at the shaman expectantly. "What was that, Vruul?" Fangdarr asked, pointing in the direction of the mountains where the dragon had gone.

Vruul seemed confused over Fangdarr's ignorance. "That Crepusculus, chieftain. Shadow dragon. Attack every few years. Sometimes more. Sometimes less."

Fangdarr glared at him. He stood in silence, considering what to do next. In truth, the chieftain was almost grateful for the beast's unexpected arrival. It may have been just what he needed to deflect from the impossible tasks his clan expected of him. Though, the new alternative seemed no less daunting. Fangdarr nodded, more in confirmation to himself than to Vruul. "We kill it."

The shaman looked up incredulously. "Y-yes, chieftain. But how?"

Fangdarr paused, weighing the choices one final time. Finally, he grunted out, "Me brother."

CHAPTER THIRTEEN
ACCUSTOMED

Bitrayuul stood at the window within the diminutive, yet luxurious, stone cabin shared between Tormag and himself, staring into the empty darkness of the cavernous city. Six years with no sign of his brother, though Fangdarr's conquests didn't go unnoticed. By then, nearly all the realm muttered fearful whispers of the Zharnik clan and their ferocious leader's growing presence. Tucked safely within the depths of the mountains, the dwarves waved away the threat. But Bitrayuul couldn't help but feel responsible, in part, for the suffering the humans who were settled within the Lithe had been through. After Fangdarr had left their home, Tormag had decided to return to Tarabar with Bitrayuul. Alone, the half-orc would have surely been rejected, but with their lost commander to vouch for him, Bitrayuul was reluctantly granted entry. Over time, he had earned the respect of the dwarves and had even become a general in the Dwarven Regime, under Tormag's command.

That night, an outlandish nightmare found its way into the mind of the half-orc. In the throes of sleep, Bitrayuul dreamt that his brother's campaign for conquest had come to the gate of Tarabar—a horde of bloodthirsty orcs in tow. However, it wasn't the war he feared. Rather, Fangdarr's reckless hand extending too far for him to survive.

He sat entranced at the window, reminiscing on the haunting illusions. The nightmare remained imbedded in his shrouded mind, taking hold of every thought. Vivid images of waves of orcs crashing into the impenetrable gate of Tarabar and the inevitable slaughter to follow.

In the midst of battle, he saw Fangdarr standing in the center of his horde, barking commands. Bitrayuul watched in horror as the mass of orcs slowly pushed open the gate that protected the city he had come to love. Warriors poured in like water breaching a dam. First, a trickle, then a stream, then an endless flow of enraged beasts cutting down any dwarf unfortunate enough to get in their way.

The scene of the fictitious battle raged on. Orcs and dwarves lay lifeless amongst each other. Some say that, in death, all races are equal, and from his vision, Bitrayuul understood what they meant. As the bodies piled, they began to blur together in a single mesh of gore. Bitrayuul watched as his dwarven allies cut down his own kind, as he himself was forced to do for the sake of his friends.

In the chaos, Bitrayuul became separated from Tormag and hoped for his safety. However, all thoughts of others instantly fell silent when he saw Fangdarr approaching him, blanketed in dwarven blood. "Brother, it been too long," the orc growled.

Too stunned to move his lips, Bitrayuul just stared hopelessly as his lost brother drew closer, donning a malicious scowl. It wasn't long before Fangdarr stood at arm's length, weapon raised.

Just as their inevitable fight was to begin, Bitrayuul caught a sudden intense expression cross Fangdarr's face. His brother's glowing yellow eyes flicked from wickedness to confusion, then to agony. The chieftain's mouth opened wide for a soundless scream as a pair of daggers protruded from the center of the orc's chest. A moment later, a small dwarf followed, blasting through Fangdarr's body.

Gore exploded over Bitrayuul. He could only watch in bewilderment as his brother dropped to his knees, a gaping hole in his chest. The light in Fangdarr's eyes slowly dimmed as the orc's head slumped lifelessly. A feeble, trembling hand extended toward the fallen chieftain. Tears welled in Bitrayuul's eyes, and his mouth quivered. His gaze drifted to the assailant who had massacred his kin.

The dwarf didn't have a drop of blood on him. Not a single hair was out of place. In fact, he seemed quite tidy. As he looked up at Bitrayuul, he spoke to him clearly. Yet, it was not the gruff voice of a dwarf; it was the gentle voice of his mother. "Wake up, Bitrayuul. Your brother needs you."

CHAPTER FOURTEEN
REFLECTION

Fangdarr glanced around his tent considering what else he would need for his journey. He hadn't seen Bitrayuul or Tormag in over six years, but that didn't mean he had no knowledge of their whereabouts. It had always been a possibility that he might return to them, so the chieftain made sure to find out what he could. A half-orc living amongst the dwarves wasn't exactly common.

Vruul reluctantly helped Fangdarr prepare, laced with uncertainty. "Great chieftain, what if you no come back?"

"Then *you* be chieftain." Fangdarr responded nonchalantly.

The elderly shaman seemed a bit uneasy but nodded obediently. "Y-yes, great chieftain." Watching Fangdarr continue to rummage through supplies, Vruul still couldn't understand the orc's motives. "You at least take raiders with you?"

Fangdarr placed a final item in a pouch at his waist and turned toward the shaman. Placing a hand on the orc's shoulder, Fangdarr responded, "No. I go alone." With all the preparations made and his axe strapped across his back, the mighty orc proceeded out of the tent and toward the village gate, leaving a horde of confused onlookers at his back. Before the gate had even closed, Fangdarr could hear arguing and shouting as orcs fought over his exodus and what it meant. He turned his head back to see the chaos that was growing and wondered if he had truly made the right decision. But in that moment, all he longed for was to see Bitrayuul again. Taking in a steadying breath, Fangdarr took another step into the forest.

*****

Fangdarr had forgotten how much he loved the calm of the forest. As streams of light pierced the veil of the trees, he cursed himself for having remained cooped up in the confines of his tent for the better part of the past two years. Even while traversing the same beaten path leading raids, he never truly felt the sense of freedom that trekking through the woods alone provided. Fangdarr took in the sway of the leaves, the songs of the birds. It all reminded him of his mother and Bitrayuul. With each eastward step he took toward Tarabar—and closer to the cave he had called home for so long—Fangdarr felt his heart grow heavy. He couldn't help but wonder how his life may have been different, had he not left two years ago. He was proud of what he had accomplished with his clan, but at what cost? His mind began to numb, and each step blindly pressed on of their own accord.

When the sun had faded beneath the horizon, Fangdarr considered whether he should keep going. He had already covered a lot of distance that day, with nothing but dense woodlands around him, but his destination was still days away. Deciding there was no sense in making a decision at day's end, Fangdarr broke for camp to rest. With the strain of his options weighing down on him, little sleep came that night. However, when he awoke in the morning, the orc felt renewed and mind cleared. Rising to his feet, Fangdarr stretched away the weariness and took one final look back to the west before setting off once more toward Tarabar.

Time drained by with the sun pounding on his back. Beads of sweat rolled down his body, sliding through the crevasses of his muscles. Fangdarr continued walking; it seemed that was all he could do. The feelings of freedom and longing had begun to dampen, replaced by the arduous task of putting one foot in front of the other endlessly. And his ears no longer caught the sounds of the woods, but only the patterned stomps of his feet.

As the sun set on the second day, Fangdarr stopped to set up camp. He chomped on a piece of dried meat as he calmly gathered kindling for a fire. With half his journey behind him, he was on the very edge the portion of the Lithe claimed by his clan—the "Orclands", as humans deemed them. Humans used to claim much of the woods before Fangdarr's aggressive leadership had driven them out. Now, half of Lithe Forest was recognized as his domain. Standing so far from his clan's home and still knowing he was within their territory brought a smile to the chieftain's face. He finished setting his camp then lay on the ground next to the fire. With the crackle of flames and smell of burning wood setting him at ease, he drifted off to sleep.

Normally, Fangdarr's dreams were lustful remembrances of battles won and foes slain. But that night his illusions were full of peace and gentle memories of his childhood—playful days with Bitrayuul, sparring, hunting, and swimming. It had been so long since these memories of his past graced his sleep. His dream-self embraced his mother with vigor, as if he knew he would never see her again. The details of her face had blurred ever so slightly. He looked at her with tears in his bright, yellow eyes, only making his vision more hazy. Vrutnag's image grew increasingly muddied with each passing moment, and Fangdarr squeezed her more tightly as if to hold on to the memory. She spoke reassuring words to him with crystal clarity. That was something he would never forget—her soft, eloquent dialect so contrary to their race. Fangdarr's spine tingled as his mother's hand ran over his head.

The sound of a twig snapping ripped the orc from his bliss, and his hand instinctively reached for Driktarr's shaft. His eyes darted in every direction, scanning the darkness. Whatever had made the noise—if indeed there was something out there—seemed to have been gone by then. Fangdarr cautiously lay back down with his axe handle in his grip and an ear perked.

Just when the orc's head hit the ground, a loud rustle came from a nearby bush. As Fangdarr sat up, a large black bear lumbered on top of him. Not caught fully unaware, he lifted his arm in defense and growled as the bear's strong jaws clamped around his left forearm. The pair made eye contact with each other, and Fangdarr scowled at the beast. "No bite me, bear," he grumbled. As if it understood the orc's meaning, the bear clamped its jaw down harder.

Fangdarr stood up, tugging the bear onto its hind legs. The orc shook his arm violently, hoping to shrug the beast off. But all he got for his efforts was more shredded flesh and muscle. The bear offered its own growl in response, whether from the shaking or the taste of Fangdarr's arm, the orc couldn't be sure. With his previous attempt failing, he raised his right fist and began pounding the creature in the face.

After a few strong blows, the bear finally released its hold. It sat glaring at Fangdarr, left eye full of blood. "I said 'No bite me'," the orc repeated accusatorily. The beast's snarl started to fade, and it moaned in pain but didn't run. Fangdarr looked at his mangled arm, and then back at the bear. "Strong bear," he said, lifting his axe. He lifted his axe and reared it back to swing at the beast so that his weapon would heal the wounds it had caused. Once again, their eyes met.

Fangdarr saw the same emptiness in the bear's brown eyes that he hid within his own. He lowered Driktarr to the ground and approached the bear. As he stepped toward it, the beast growled and began backpedaling slowly. Fangdarr reached his hand out and rubbed the top of the bear's furry head. It retracted from his touch immediately and snapped its jaws at the open air. But the orc simply reached out again, this time more slowly. The bear's eyes narrowed as it bared its teeth. Yet, this time, as Fangdarr's hand met the thick, black fur, the beast didn't shy away. It stayed on edge as the orc's fingers ran back and forth. After a while, the bear's snarl began to fade and eventually it seemed to calm.

The orc stopped petting the beast's head and pointed to his damaged arm. "No bite."

The bear lifted its eyes from the torn arm and back up to Fangdarr. Lowering its head, the bear licked the wound a few times then took a step back. A hearty chuckle rolled through the orc's mouth. Lightly grabbing the beast's head, Fangdarr looked at the eye he had beaten. It was still covered in blood, and the skin had started to swell. He produced a knight from a loop on his leather kilt then looked at the bear.

"No move," he said softly. The bear relaxed, allowing Fangdarr to take control. Remembering what his mother had taught him, the orc brought the knife to the bruise and cut a line underneath it. The bear whimpered at the pain, but after the blood within the bruise began to drain, it blinked open its eye and energetically shuffled forward, nuzzling Fangdarr's face with its wet nose.

The orc laughed aloud and happily took the nuzzling. Fangdarr looked around the darkened forest. "Bear have family?" he asked, almost expecting an answer. He laughed again as the bear remained silent. Fangdarr rubbed the beast's ears as he pondered. He looked the bear in the eyes and said, "You come with me, bear. I take care of you." The beast just pressed its nose into the orc's cheek again and licked his cheek. Fangdarr smiled. "You need a name." He thought to himself, thinking up possible choices for his new ally. His mind shuffled through typical barbaric names. Ripper, Gouger, Shredder, all the names in the book for something that had just mangled his arm. Then he laughed out loud and said, "Eh, I call you 'Bear'."

The bear didn't seem to understand anything Fangdarr was saying, but it graciously accepted the attention it was receiving. Then it lay itself down on the patch of ground where the orc had been sleeping and began to doze off. Fangdarr laughed at the ridiculousness of it all. He looked at the resting bear and then again at his wounded arm. "I be back, Bear," he said and started off into the woods.

Bear woke up first the next morning, and walked over to its new ally, thinking to clean the orc's wound. Yet, when it looked at Fangdarr's arm, all that remained was a horrendous maw-shaped scar. The beast sniffed at the scar in confusion. Fangdarr rolled over with a groan. "Bear, your nose cold." He slowly got to his feet and rustled the bear's head in greeting.

Fangdarr felt Bear nudge his forearm again and understood that it couldn't understand how his wound had healed. "Oh," he chuckled, "axe heal me when I kill." He pointed to the edge of their tiny encampment where a young deer lay crumpled and bloodied. The orc chieftain walked over to the dead animal and used Driktarr to cleave it in half. Tossing his axe aside, he scooped up the back half of the animal and dropped it in front of Bear. "This for you," he said, a smile creasing his lips. His companion chomped down merrily on its meal and Fangdarr watched with a smile.

CHAPTER FIFTEEN
REUNION

After two days of uneventful traversal, Fangdarr and Bear stood at the edge of the woods. The orc's gaze shifted between the flickering steel of dozens of dwarves lining the massive gate embedded in the base of the Tusk Mountains. Fangdarr's mouth fell open at the sight of the intricate golden runes etched into the thick, steel doors ahead. By all the accounts he had heard, the dwarves believed the barrier to be protected by the magic of their deity, Bothain. Every time he had heard such telling, the orc scoffed at such a ridiculous notion. But seeing the imposing craftsmanship, even he started to wonder if the tales were true. Fangdarr lifted his eyes to the vigilant sentinels atop the towering structure. Each dwarf adorned an identical suit of armor that seemed sturdy enough that even his axe may not be able to penetrate.

Fangdarr looked down at Bear and let out a sigh before rubbing its head, reassuring himself more than his companion. Sucking in air, the orc passed through the last layer of trees at the forest's edge and stepped into the open. Immediately, the dwarves atop the gate raised alarms and pointed heavy crossbows down at the intruders. Fangdarr slowed his approach, fighting his instinct to reach for his weapon. As he inched closer, he could see the guards all stared at him with hate and confusion.

When Fangdarr had reached the base of the massive gates, one of the dwarves leaned over the edge to get a better look at the curious orc and his pet. "Say orc, what're ye about?" the guard asked.

"I come for Bitrayuul and Tormag," the orc stated firmly.

"Oh? Who be askin'?"

"Fangdarr."

At the sound of the intruder's name, the guards seemed to immediately tense. The dwarf who had called out to Fangdarr disappeared behind the barrier and the sounds of frantic whispers tickled his ears. Many moments passed before the guard returned with another dwarf at his side.

Unlike the others, the new dwarf's head was bald, contrasting with his neat, unbraided beard. He had an intimidating presence with an eye patch covering his left eye, though his stare seemed nonchalant rather than suspicious. The dwarf called out to Fangdarr, "Me name's Cormac, I be the captain of the Shield. What's yer business here, Master Fangdarr?"

"I here to meet brother, Bitrayuul," the orc repeated.

"That's a mighty big axe ye got with ye, orc. Surely ye know that orcs don't like dwarves. Ye willing to give it up if we let ye in?"

Fangdarr growled quietly. He wasn't fond of the idea of a dwarf carrying Driktarr. "Bitrayuul likes Tormag . . . so not all orcs bad."

"Aye, that he does. Do they know yer comin'?"

"No," he replied, then added with much reluctance, "I need help."

The captain's gaze continued to stare down at Fangdarr, unwavering. Then, he disappeared behind the walls.

The large orc sighed as he waited for a long while, all with the guards still pointing their crossbows at him—looking for any reason to release their knocked bolts. Suddenly, the enormous steel doors groaned with protest as they began spreading, and Cormac walked through the opening. Even from a distance, Fangdarr could tell the dwarf was a bit taller than most other dwarves. Once the captain had closed the distance between them, their gazes met as they sized each other up more closely. The captain seemed odd to Fangdarr. Two large shields were buckled to each of Cormac's forearms, with the steel curving from over his shoulders and contouring around his body to reach past his hands, ending with a blade protruding at the bottom. A thousand miniscule scratches could barely be seen along the gleaming silver.

Cormac broke the silence and drew Fangdarr from his inspection. "Well, if ye won't give up yer axe, ye'll need to follow me. I'll take ye to yer brother."

Fangdarr nodded. While he was glad to not be stripped of his beloved weapon, the orc couldn't help but feel the tug of interest at the thought of squaring off against the unique dwarf. But he pushed the thought aside and fell in line behind Cormac. The pair, with the addition of the orc's animal companion, headed into the great city of Tarabar, home of the dwarves. Once past the barrier, the large doors closed behind them. His eyes shifted to adjust to the darkness as the last light of day dissipated with the booming *thud* of the doors. Thankfully, orcs—like dwarves—had excellent sight in the dark. An occasional torch sprouted outside many of the carved-stone dwellings, illuminating the city just enough for Fangdarr to bear witness to the grand spectacle of the entire city buried within the mountain.

Cormac noticed the orc's expression. "Spectacular, isn't it?"

Fangdarr's mouth had fallen open as he continued to scan the vast cavern. It was unlike anything he had ever seen. From their vantage point, he could see a bustling market in the center and huge structures made of stone, steel, and gold all throughout the city. "It marvelous," the awed orc replied.

"Indeed, it is lad. But I've always liked the outdoors, meself. There be times when I'm jealous of ye orcs livin' out in them woods."

That drew the chieftain out of his trance. "Really?"

Cormac simply nodded and continued leading the orc down the path. All the dwarves in the city were surprised at Fangdarr's appearance. The citizens' reactions ranged from suspicious murmurs to straight panic as the trio passed by. By the time they had arrived at Tormag's home, a small crowd of dwarves had collected around them. Most were yelling for the orc to leave, others raised their weapons and seemed as if they'd cut Fangdarr down without hesitation.

The captain simply pushed aside his fellow dwarves and stepped up to the door, pounding his fist against the stone loudly to be heard over the commotion. Tormag came to the door and nearly fell out of his boots when he saw over fifty dwarves, an enormous orc, and a large black bear waiting outside. "What in the name of stones!" he started, not recognizing Fangdarr due to his age and the hundreds of scars he had received in the past six years. "Just because I live with an orc don't mean I'm fer takin' in every stray ye find!" A smile came to Fangdarr's face as he recognized the thick accent of his old mentor.

The commotion drew Bitrayuul to the door behind Tormag. Seeing the orc peering from above the crowd, the half-orc's eyes lit up in shock. "Fangdarr?"

Fangdarr nodded, meeting his brother's gaze. "Bit." He glanced over Bitrayuul's body to see how the years had changed him and almost scowled in response. His brother's appearance had changed little other than he was much cleaner and well-kept. A long black ponytail hung neatly over his broad shoulder, and resting on a glittering gold-laced tunic. Worst of all, there wasn't a single scar scratched into his skin.

Tormag seemed to go unnoticed as the estranged brothers reunited. He looked from one orc to the other then back to the crowd. "Oye, get out o' here, ye nosy pups! I'll be keepin' an eye on the orc." The gathered dwarves offered disgruntled groans and shouts in protest, but Tormag waved them away. "Come inside, lad."

Fangdarr finally acknowledged Tormag and stepped inside behind him, followed by Bear, who remained concealed behind the large orc. Fangdarr silently looked around the small stone house, filled with luscious furniture. As Tormag went to close the front door, the large orc turned to his old mentor, who didn't seem to have aged a day since his departure. "Good home," he stated to be polite.

"Aye got meself a three-room—extra high ceilings too—in case ye ever changed yer mind."

Bitrayuul seemed uncertain of what to feel after seeing Fangdarr. "What brings you here, Fang?"

"I need help."

Bitrayuul looked at Tormag. They knew Fangdarr would never have asked anyone for help unless it was dire. "What happened?" As he spoke, Bear, whom had somehow gone unnoticed to Tormag, appeared and rubbed its face against the dwarf's back.

Tormag yelped in surprise as he spun toward Bear. "Oye! There be a bear in me house!" Bear simply looked at the bewildered dwarf and nuzzled his arm. "And his nose is cold!"

Fangdarr laughed. "Bear nose always cold."

Bitrayuul grew agitated. "Fangdarr. What's happened?"

The orc grumbled slightly. "I chieftain of Zharnik clan. Two years now. Shadow dragon, Crepusculus, attack village. Need to kill it." He averted his eyes shamefully.

Bitrayuul looked to Tormag, who only shrugged in response. The half-orc avoided his brother's implied request and said, "I see you have a few more scars." With that statement much of Fangdarr's pride returned.

"Many battles," stated the chieftain gleefully, spreading his arms wide to display the hundreds of white scars he had earned. He pointed to the maw-shaped marking on his left forearm. "Bear did that," he laughed. Tormag took an uneasy step away from the beast. "So, you help?" Fangdarr asked as he lowered his arms.

Bitrayuul moved to the window, looking out to the inner city. His breathing was steady and calm, but his thoughts were racing. He truly liked the idea of an adventure, as he was sure Tormag did. But to fight a dragon? It seemed hopeless. While in the dwarven city, he had learned much about the outside world—including the nature of dragons. No amount of armor would protect them from the acidic breath of a shadow dragon. He sighed. "No, Fangdarr. We're staying."

Jumping to his feet in shock, Fangdarr shouted, "You no help your brother!?"

"No. This is my home now, Fang. Tormag and I have duties here."

Fangdarr pounded a fist against his chest. "I have duties! Chieftain protect our clan!"

"*Your* clan! Not ours, yours!" Bitrayuul replied angrily, spinning to face his brother. "Don't you understand, Fangdarr? This," he opened his arms toward the city, "is my clan. I have been accepted here as one of their own. Tormag is once again the commander of the Dwarven Regime, with me as a general. The council has taken note of your expansion, Fangdarr. They need us here to protect the city from *your* greedy fingers!"

Fangdarr's eyes narrowed. "Then I go alone."

This time Tormag spoke. "Lad, ye can't take on a shadow dragon by yer lonesome. Just leave the drake t' its hole."

The orc sighed. "No. My clan expect war with Tarabar or Wiston. We not have the strength. Dragon attack give excuse not to pursue war. I do not want to fight you."

Tormag and Bitrayuul looked to each other again. They realized the orc's plight, and that he still loved his family. "Fangdarr, I cannot go. But I beg you not to. Why not stay here with us? Become a general in the Regime," Bitrayuul suggested.

Fangdarr's bellowed in laughter. "Give up chieftain to be general? I am greatest orc chieftain of Zharnik clan; greatest orc ever! I brought glory to our kind. Why throw away to be servant? No. I must kill dragon, with or without you."

Bitrayuul just nodded in silence, knowing any words he offered would fall on deaf ears.

Tormag placed a hand on Fangdarr's arm. "Lad, ye be careful. If yer thinkin' o' takin' on the drake, best ye should be knowin' that shadow dragons have a weak spot. Right in the back o' their blasted head. Ain't much, but their scales will shrug off even yer axe. No scale on the back o' their head."

"Thank you, Tormag," Fangdarr said with a smile. He placed his own hand on the dwarf's shoulder before moving toward the door. "Come, Bear." His companion obediently got up from in front of the fireplace and followed its master through the doorway. Bitrayuul and Tormag watched as their kin walked away from them, again, revitalizing the memories of their last parting.

CHAPTER SIXTEEN
PRIDE

Fangdarr grumbled to himself as he trudged through the torch-lit streets. He barely even noticed the deadly glares cast in his direction from the dwarven citizens as he put one foot in front of the other.

Cormac sat patiently waiting for the orc at the gate, six armored dwarves by his side. In Fangdarr's distraction, the large orc nearly walked right into the captain. "Oye! Watch yer feet, lad."

Blinking in confusion as his mind caught up to reality, Fangdarr looked at Cormac. "Sorry, dwarf," the orc replied softly.

Cormac let out a gentle sigh. "Son, ye follow me for a bit."

Fangdarr cared too little at that moment to reject the command. He and his furry companion slowly followed the captain along the stone wall of the cavern before stepping into what seemed to have been the dwarf's home. Cormac opened the door and bid the pair inside.

When Fangdarr crouched through the stone entryway, he felt slightly more relaxed. Unlike Tormag's finely furnished home, everything was made completely of stone—even the chairs and bed. It reminded the orc of the cave his mother had raised him in. His eyes scanned the room, letting his memories take over. The abode was dwarf-sized, forcing Fangdarr to hunch over until he could place himself in a stone chair before Bear lay comfortably at his feet.

Closing the door behind him, Cormac entered and sat down in the remaining chair. "Ain't much, but its home."

"It perfect," the orc replied, still peering around the room.

"Well, suppose it'll do compared to livin' outdoors. Dwarves belong to the stone, lad. I ain't one for havin' no silks and cushions."

Fangdarr nodded with a brief smile.

The dwarf relaxed into his seat and crossed his arms over his chest. "So, it seems yer meeting with yer kin didn't go as ye planned. Sure as stone, it be written all over ye face."

Had Fangdarr not been raised by Tormag, he likely would have replied with rage at the dwarf's observation. But the orc could tell that Cormac seemed genuinely interested. Fangdarr shrugged. "Bit won't help me."

An awkward silence followed as Cormac waited for further elaboration, but it never came. The dwarf leaned forward and looked intently at Fangdarr. "I was like ye once. Full of life, a taste for battle, don't ye be doubtin'. I lost me boy and love in a raid many years ago. Long before you were even born. Orcs, like yerself. After their passing I became known for me lust for orc blood. I thought the more orcs I killed, the less pain I'd feel. But, I was wrong. Me pride wouldn't let me heal, lad. And it'll do ye the same if ye let it. Ain't nothin' shameful about it."

Fangdarr's brow furrowed. But after a moment, he sighed and let his shoulders drop. He found it hard to form words. "I left Bit and Tormag six years ago. Found out Tormag kill my father. Wanted Bit to come too. He chose Tormag. Fangdarr roam the land, alone, for four years. Return to clan, become chieftain. My village attacked by shadow dragon, Crepusculus. Fangdarr came to dwarf city for brother to help kill dragon," he paused, visibly upset. "He refused."

Cormac sat in silence then let a slow exhale pass through his nose. "Aye, it ain't easy when yer kin turns their back on ye."

"No. It hard." The orc stood up as best he could in the small shelter. "I must go, Shield-Arms. My clan need dragon dead." While Fangdarr had enjoyed the dwarf's company, his fondness for exposing vulnerability was nonexistent.

"Ye know ye can't hope to kill a dragon by yer lonesome," Cormac replied, almost as if pleading.

Fangdarr shrugged. "If I die, it is with glory. This the only way to avoid war. Have to try."

Cormac stood up as well, leading the way to the door. It was clear the orc's mind was made up. With a heavy silence between them, the dwarf led Fangdarr and Bear back toward the main gate.

When they had reached the tunnel leading up to the city's steel doors, Cormac turned to Fangdarr, offering a final nod. The orc clasped his large hand on the captain's shoulder and provided a grateful smile. As the gates ahead began to spread, Fangdarr walked up the path with Bear at his side.

Once the pair had passed the threshold, the orc sucked in a deep breath through his nose, grateful to be back in the open air with the sun on his skin. Fangdarr looked back as the steel behind them groaned shut, a lasting reminder that he was leaving without his kin. He rubbed Bear's ear. "Just us, Bear." The beast licked his hand in reply, then took off toward the woods at a gentle gallop, leaving Fangdarr chuckling behind. He looked out over the tree line to the sharpened stone of the mountains beyond where he knew the drake waited patiently in its pit. He took a steadying breath then pressed on toward the woods.

Fangdarr caught up to Bear, who lay sprawled out on the ground playfully at the edge of the Lithe. As the orc beckoned for his companion to follow, a faint shout could be heard. Fangdarr looked around, searching for the source.

Another exclamation, closer than the last. The orc spun toward Tarabar and saw that the gates had been opened once more. Fangdarr's hand wrapped around his weapon, expecting a hunting party of dwarves. His grip tightened as a small figure ran to him, continuing its shouting.

Fangdarr started to relax his shoulders, not worried about a lone dwarf. The orc felt a small bit of hope that it was Tormag but quickly dismissed the notion. If it was his old mentor, his brother surely would have followed.

The large orc turned to his companion, who had taken to sniffing the air. "Bear, why dwarf so small? Can't see who it is." Bear continued its nasal scan, then just leaned back and sat against a tree, hindquarters splayed out. The orc laughed at the sight. Fangdarr shook his head. "You funny, Bear." His attention turned back to his pursuer who now seemed to be walking. Confident he could handle the possible threat, the orc walked toward the unknown dwarf while Bear remained at its tree, enjoying the rugged bark against its back.

Fangdarr's eyes narrowed with each step lessening the distance between him and the dwarf. The orc tried to focus on the figure's equipment but all he could identify was the reflection of the sun off a suit of steel armor. A dozen strides brought the orc closer until he could finally make out a distinct characteristic of the pursuer: the dwarf had an eye patch.

CHAPTER SEVENTEEN
PARITY

Cormac looked at Fangdarr, who stared directly back. It was the dwarf who began, owing an explanation for his pursuit. "Ye know, I've always wanted to kill me a dragon."

Fangdarr smiled at the small dwarf. "I know where one is."

The dwarf gave a short chuckle. "Well then, what're we standin' here for?" He tossed the chieftain a large pouch. The orc looked inside to see salted meat and bread. Cormac knelt beside his pack, producing a map. Unrolling it on the ground, he looked up to the towering orc. "C'mere, lad."

Cormac chuckled again as Fangdarr knelt beside him, noticing that the orc still towered above him. He simply shook his head and redirected his attention to the map. Cormac pointed to their current position along the edge of the Lithe. "We're here, lad, just outside the woods." The dwarf's finger slid to the southern section of the forest. "This be where yer clan sits. Now, ye could've gone through yer clan's territory, but now ye got a dwarf with ye. Yer kin won't be takin' too kindly to a dwarf walkin' along yer side, don't ye be doubtin'."

Fangdarr nodded his agreement. He knew he could never be seen with a dwarf by any of his clan members. If he did, it would be impossible for him to remain chieftain. He might as well never return home.

Sliding his finger further down the map into the southern span of the Tusk Mountains, Cormac continued. "So, we're needin' to go around. Leaves us with two choices. First, we can go straight south o' Tarabar and hug the Tusks all the way across, or we can go through the center of the forest, then south and try to avoid yer clan."

Fangdarr considered both choices. He was a bit apprehensive about letting the dwarf know he had allied with the trolls who inhabited the mountains. "No mountains. Path too treacherous." He pointed to the far south-western edge of the mountain range, just beyond his clan's village. "Dragon around here." He then traced his gigantic finger along a path from Crepusculus' expected pit west through the mountains to a river inlet that led to the farthest western point of the Tusks, a small distance from the drake's location. "Hell's Throat the way in. Can't go through mountains."

The captain cast a curious gaze Fangdarr's way. "Who's to say an orc can't go through the mountains?"

Fangdarr sighed. "Zharnik clan allied with Raz'ja, chieftain troll. Those troll's mountains."

Cormac nodded, knowing what the alliance meant. He cast the issue aside, knowing it wasn't the time to create problems. "Alright then, so we go through the heart of Lithe Forest, around the land o' yer clan. We'll try to stay between the Orclands and the human settlements in the woods. They extend all the way to the coast. It'd be best to avoid them, if we can. They ain't ones for orcs, sure as stone. I may need to drop in to Riveton for supplies, but we'll see how long the journey be. It'll take a while to reach the mountains by the coast, but there shouldn't be too much hassle compared to a route through the Tusks."

The orc was grateful Cormac didn't bring up his allegiance to the trolls. Grunting his approval, Fangdarr rose from his crouch as the dwarf placed the map back in his pack and slung it over his shoulder.

"Where's yer bear, orc?" Cormac asked.

Fangdarr smirked and pointed to a tree behind him. The dwarf squinted to see the beast in the distance and laughed aloud. "Bahaha! Never thought I'd see a beast sit like a man, sure as stones." The pair walked over to Bear, watching it sleep with its back still against the tree, its bottom paws clenching and unclenching with each satisfied breath.

"Bear, up," Fangdarr said to his furry companion. The large creature simply yawned and rolled over on its side.

Cormac let out another round of laughter. He stepped up to Bear and poked its face. The disgruntled creature awoke abruptly. Teeth bared, the beast growled at Cormac and looked to its master. Fangdarr patted the air, calming the bear. He turned to the small dwarf, and chuckled. "No poke Bear."

"Aye, took a notice to that one, bahaha!" the dwarf's humored response came. "Sorry, bear, didn't mean to offend ye." Cormac stuck his hand out to let the beast sniff him. Bear approached cautiously, running its nose along the captain's hand before letting the dwarf rub its ears. "What's yer name anyway?" he asked Fangdarr more than the bear.

"Bear," the orc replied.

The dwarf nodded, clearly attempting to hold his laughter behind his lips. After a few moments, his resolve deteriorated, causing an outburst of laughter that startled

Bear again. Fangdarr shook his head and smiled. It was going to be an interesting journey.

After the trio concluded their brief preparations, they set off into the forest. They made steady progress, though they were in no rush to reach the dragon. As the sun faded below the horizon, the party stopped for the night and set up camp.

Cormac pulled a small bow and a bundle of arrows from his pack. The dwarf handed it to the orc. "Ye know how to shoot?"

Fangdarr nodded, accepting the bow. "I go hunt, you watch Bear."

Cormac laughed aloud at the absurdity of keeping an eye on a beast that was larger than he was. His cheerful mood was welcomed by the orc, who had already disappeared behind the brush. The dwarf laid out some blankets in the small camp, even one for Bear. Then, he walked around the encampment, gathering branches to start a fire.

After a while, Fangdarr returned to his companions, carrying three small critters, each impaled with an arrow. He tossed them to the ground in front of Cormac who began removing the arrows from the carcasses. The dwarf tossed a rabbit to Bear, who needed no prompting to begin eating.

With a pair of squirrels remaining, he looked at Fangdarr. "Er . . . say orc, how do you like yer squirrel?"

The chieftain laughed. "We don't eat like Bear."

"Aye, wasn't sure. Bahaha!" He skinned the pair of animals and began cutting out what meat he could. The resourceful dwarf grabbed a nearby stick and began jamming it through the small pieces of meat. After the skewer was prepared, he handed it to Fangdarr who held it over the fire. The dwarf prepared his own and began cooking it next to his ally's.

The pair sat next to one another, thinking to themselves as the crackle of flames filled the silence. As their meals began to sizzle, Cormac's expression seemed to change as if realizing something. "Oye, Fang?"

Fangdarr looked at the captain over his skewer. "Mm?"

"What do ye want in yer life?"

The question caught Fangdarr off guard. It was the first time anyone had ever asked him something like that. As such, he had never given it much thought, at least not in a way to put into words. As he pondered his answer, Bear had wobbled over to the orc and rested its head on his lap. He dropped a hand over his companion's ears, rubbing the nooks the animal could not easily scratch. Fangdarr stared at his hand, riddled in scars, and a sigh slipped through the orc's lips.

"Never wondered that. Used to want to be great warrior with glorious tale. So, fought many battles. Killed dozens, hundreds. Carry scars to prove it," he said, raising his hand from the bear for Cormac to see. "Became youngest chieftain of clan. Led my people proudly. But, now, want something else."

The fire cast glimmering shadows on the orc's dark skin, shaping around his mouth as he continued speaking. "Bitrayuul gone." His voice was full of sorrow and his yellow eyes gleamed in the twilight, hiding their own emptiness. "Want him at my side again. Join me in battle. Chieftain expected to conquer dwarf and man. But I do not *want* to conquer them. Mother knew I loved battle but wanted me to fight right ones.

"Sometimes I want to leave clan, explore world, meet humans and elves. I am not normal orc. Mother raised me and Bit different. Different than orcs who only live for war. I want a mate and be accepted for orc I am."

There it was. The proud orc, so full of life and bloodlust, only wanted peace.

Cormac nodded as Fangarr's speech concluded. "Lad, I see meself in ye, sure as stone. I've seen me family killed, me friends pass, me enemies die. These old eyes have seen all ye have seen, and I know the demons that be hauntin' ye. But ye stick to yerself and keep searchin' for that peace. Ain't sayin' it'll be easy. Promise ye it'll be the hardest damned thing ye'll ever do. But if ye want acceptance ye just need to prove ye deserve it."

Fangdarr listened to his dwarven friend, hoping he was right. Already he had made a new dwarven ally by being himself. The realization that he could still be a mighty warrior and not bring harm to innocents was a truly life-altering perspective. The Zharnik clan had pushed Fangdarr to kill humans and dwarves who wanted nothing more than to live in peace.

Cormac clasped the orc's tense shoulder. "Ye'll get yer peace. Ain't a doubt in me mind."

Fangdarr slumped in response. Moisture collected in his bright eyes, and a single tear broke away and rolled down his black face. Peace would come.

CHAPTER EIGHTEEN
EXPOSURE

The piercing sunlight stung the sleeping orc's eyes, rousing him from his rest. Fangdarr groaned, rolling to his side and raising a hand to shield himself from the harsh rays. He scanned the small encampment, but his two companions were nowhere to be seen. A frown tugged at his lips as he considered where they might have gone. They were still only a day's walk from Tarabar, and the chances of an attack this close were slim. With a stretch that eased his stiff muscles and a yawn that pushed the last vestiges of sleep from his mind, Fangdarr finally pushed himself up from his makeshift bedding.

Birds sang in the cool morning air, offering the orc a fleeting sense of tranquility. He doubted anything was amiss, yet a quiet realization tugged at him—he cared for his companions more than he had expected. A slight chuckle hummed in his throat. Much had changed since he'd left his clan's village.

Nearby commotion broke the chieftain from his stupor. Barefoot, Fangdarr padded his way through the dense brush toward the disturbance. Despite his large frame, he moved through the undergrowth without a sound. As the noise grew louder, Fangdarr peered out from behind the trees, searching for the source. Years of battle had made him wary; his guard never fully lowered. But his tension eased as soon as he spotted the cause of the ruckus.

Cormac floated on a small lake, disrupted by Bear's continual splashes as it stomped around the shallow water. A devious grin found its way to the hidden orc as an idea formed.

The stark-naked dwarf remained floating lazily on the water, sunlight gleaming off his bare skin. Fangdarr gave a minor look of disgust as he tiptoed closer through the foliage. Blissfully unaware, Cormac began singing an old dwarven folk song, pushing his voice loudly to carry out over Bear's splashing. Fangdarr concealed his laughter as he snuck out of the brush and crept along the shore where the dwarf's clothes lay in a heap. Bear caught its master sifting through the sand, clearly trying to remain unnoticed. The orc silently raised a finger to his mouth, motioning the bear to keep quiet. Bear cocked its head in confusion, then went back to its merriment, interrupting Cormac's song when the dwarf had to spit out a mouthful of water.

"Oye! Ye keep splashin' me, Bear, and I'll dunk yer head in the lake!" Cormac yelled, muttering curses at the beast.

Another splash.

The dwarf sputtered, sinking below the surface for a moment. "Damned beast! Don't ye know to never get a dwarf wet?" he shouted, glaring at the bear, who had no regard for the dwarf's temper.

After a few more moments of angry shouting, Cormac noticed an unmistakable figure moving along the shore. "Oye! Fang! C'mere lad, water's cool against yer road-weary skin it is! Bahaha!"

Fangdarr froze, cursing Bear for bringing the dwarf's attention. He slowly turned to face Cormac, who stood naked in the shallow water. The orc held the pile of clothes in his hands, suddenly unsure of how to proceed.

Cormac raised an eyebrow, suspicion creeping into his expression. "Say, orc, what're ye hol—" he started before noticing the pile of clothes in his friend's hands. The dwarf let out a long, drawn out sigh, steadying himself. "Drop 'em, son."

Fangdarr looked at the bundle of clothes in his hand, then back to Cormac. He could think of no plausible excuse. So, he did the only thing that came to mind—he flashed the dwarf a grin and bolted into the woods, clothes in tow.

The dwarf's eyes widened. With a yelp, Cormac leapt up out of the water, sending water flying. "Ye yellow-eyed, thick-skulled, hairless, stink-breathed, too-tall orc! Ye best turn 'round and bring me clothes back!" spat the enraged captain. He continued to mutter curse after curse as he trudged toward the shore.

By the time Cormac had left the water, Fangdarr was already back at their small encampment, a hundred bounding strides away. His long legs carried him effortlessly, and he knew the dwarf wouldn't be able to catch him. He sat down with a smug grin, waiting for his furious friend.

Angry and naked, Cormac stomped through the brush, his anger only growing with every step. Behind him, Bear had just started to rouse from its lazy slump in pursuit. But it stopped, sniffing the air as the faintest of scents drifted by. Bear froze, its head lifted and nostrils flaring.

Cormac, meanwhile, was already halfway back to the camp, tracking the orc's trail through the dense forest. Though most dwarves preferred stone to forest, Cormac was no typical dwarf. As captain of the Shield, the elite guardians of Tarabar, he had spent plenty of time outside the stone halls, honing his skills as a tracker.

But in his furious pursuit of Fangdarr, Cormac let his guard slip. His foot landed on a patch of grass that shifted unnaturally beneath him. In a heartbeat, a rope snare tightened around his ankle, and a nearby log fell free, hoisting the dwarf into the air with a startled yelp.

Suspended upside down by the trap, Cormac's beard hung stiffly over his face as he cursed loudly. He wiggled as hard as his stout limbs could muster, hoping to break free of the snare.

Five black-skinned orcs emerged from the brush, hooting and shouting at their prize. The orcs were lightly armored, each carrying a crude spear. Clearly, they had set the trap in hopes of capturing something edible, but now they seemed more excited by the prospect of a dwarf.

Cormac began to wonder if Fangdarr had set him up. He cursed himself for letting down his guard. Still dangling helplessly, the dwarf lifted his head and called down, trying to stay calm. "Oye, what're ye orcs up to?"

The orcs exchanged grins, their jagged jaws clicking as they laughed. One of them replied, "We catch dwarf." A bellow of amusement emanated from the hunting party.

The dwarf sighed, his frustration growing. "Aye, took a notice to that one, I did. But what do ye mean to do with what ye caught?"

The same orc shrugged, as if the answer were obvious. "We set trap for food. You in trap. Guess *you* food!" The others bellowed with laughter at the remark, clearly delighted by their good fortune.

Cormac, though exposed and enraged, kept his cool. "Ain't yer fat-headed mothers ever tell ye not to play with yer food?" he called down, hoping to provoke them.

The shortest of the orcs rammed the butt of its spear into Cormac's side. "Mama no hang food from tree."

Denying his captors the satisfaction of seeing him in pain, Cormac paused before erupting in laughter. "Bahaha! Suppose that be true!"

Baffled by their prey's humor, the orcs exchanged confused glances. One of them raised their spear with a sinister grin. The others followed suit, stepping in closer and forming a circle around the helpless dwarf.

Cormac closed his eyes, ready to face whatever fate awaited him.

CHAPTER NINETEEN

ACCEPTANCE

Fangdarr sat in the brush, observing the altercation as Cormac hung helplessly. The gathered orcs prepared to plunge their weapons into the dwarf's flesh. Fangdarr's gut twisted with a feeling he had no name for. As an orc and chieftain of his clan, he couldn't interfere with the killing of a dwarf without needing to slay his own kind. As the orcs closed in, Fangdarr's mind wavered, but in the end, his body made the decision. Before he even realized it, he was on his feet and out of the brush.

The smallest of the orcs, startled by Fangdarr's sudden appearance, jumped back and pointed his spear a finger away Fangdarr's heart. The orc's eyes widened in horror as recognition hit him. There was no mistaking the chieftain. Standing a head taller than any of them, Fangdarr was a creature of sheer force—a living statue, as if sculpted from stone.

At just twenty-two winters, his body was a canvas of battle. Scars crossed his skin, each with a story to tell—so many Fangdarr barely remembered any of them. As he wore no armor, his flesh had long since become the shield, soaking every blow. In battle, the frenzy consumed him. Pain, fear, all forgotten in the lust for blood.

The small orc trembled. In a frantic movement, he dropped his spear and fell to the ground, bowing low. "I-I-I sorry, chieftain. . ." he stammered, eyes wide with fear.

Fangdarr's gaze burned through him, as cold and unyielding as a mountain. One scowl, and the orc shrank back, lowering his head. The rest of the party, sensing the shift in the air, followed suit. Fangdarr's stare shifted to each of them in turn, his silence like a storm gathering. "What you doing here?" he growled, his voice low and dangerous.

The orc closest to Cormac stepped forward, his hands shaking as he tried to remain composed. "Fangdarr Great-One, we find dwarf in trap. We going to bring back to you as gift, Chieftain!"

The lie hung in the air, thick as smoke. Fangdarr's eyes narrowed and his lips curled into a snarl. "Cut him down," the chieftain commanded, his voice quiet but full of menace. The orcs hesitated, looking at each other. Fangdarr's patience snapped. "CUT HIM DOWN!"

The smallest orc scrambled to the anchor point, hands trembling as he fumbled with the rope that held Cormac suspended. Fear made him clumsy, but at last he managed to loosen the knot. The dwarf dropped hard to the ground with a *thud.* The orc released the rope, then darted back toward the others. They each stepped forward with their crude iron spears leveled at the seated captain, as if ready to strike.

"Stop!" Fangdarr roared, irritation flaring hot in his chest. "I say attack?"

The orcs shook their heads, refusing to meet his gaze.

"Leave him be," the chieftain said, his voice flat but edged with warning.

Confusion rippled through the group. Their grips tightened around their spears, uncertainty giving way to something darker. Each exchanged a glance, silent questions turning into a single agreement. It was time for a stronger chieftain.

The five lunged forward, charging their leader in a reckless burst of defiance. But Fangdarr had watched them closely, noting every conspiratorial nod, every flicker of mutiny in their eyes. Before the first foot even struck the ground, Driktarr was already in his grasp.

Fangdarr's eyes shined brightly, the fires of combat swirling inside him. He was outnumbered, but not a shred of fear lay in the seasoned warrior's body or mind. As the group charged, a hulking black form came loping in from their flank, barreling over the farthest orc. Bear, like Fangdarr, had watched the whole encounter from a nearby bush, waiting for when its master needed it most, and it had come out at the perfect time.

Taken aback by the grizzly bear's sudden and aggressive appearance, the remaining four orcs slowed their charge to watch their fallen companion struggle with the frightening beast. In the takedown, Bear had managed to get its maw over the right shoulder of the doomed orc. The animal clamped tightly down on the squirming monster, its claws raking at the lightly armored chest of the orc. Flesh ripped with its strong swipes, rending deeper gouges with each pass of its long nails.

The remaining four advanced on Fangdarr, odds still in their favor. The chieftain laughed aloud at them. "You think you stand chance?" he asked tauntingly. "Against *me*? Fangdarr, greatest of our kind. *Fangdarr*, who have slain *hundreds*! **Fangdarr**! Who could shatter giant! Who are *you* to fell *me*!?" he roared to them, pride and bloodlust growing with each proclamation. The first of the group raced ahead, challenging his leader. He tried to create enough of a distraction for his allies to surround the chieftain.

Fangdarr smiled at their stupidity. As the orcs split their assault, each of his foes were now on their own with no possibility of support from their allies. On came the first orc, approaching directly with spear raised high, crudely attempting to crash the weapon down onto the large, broad shoulder of his chieftain.

Fangdarr never even flinched. The spear cut deep into his shoulder, lodging itself into the mighty orc's right breast. A victorious holler escaped from the orc, thinking he had scored an easy kill. However, he—and the other three orcs for the matter—froze in place when they saw that the blow did not even cause Fangdarr to recoil. Instead, his smile spread ear-to-ear, relishing in the horror he had instilled in his enemies.

With his foe making a new mistake of trying to dislodge the embedded weapon, Fangdarr pulled back his arm, Driktarr fully extended. A sinister growl slid from his grinning mouth. "My turn," he stated coldly, and down came his enormous axe, the gleaming blade cutting cleanly through the orc. His strike was in the exact position the smaller orc had struck him but his blow cleaved the lesser orc entirely in half. "Mine no get stuck," said Fangdarr to the others as their companion fell to the ground lifeless, blood pouring freely from his exposed innards. The three orcs who had hoped to encircle the gigantic orc were immobilized in terror. Their legs refused their mind's commands to move. Never had such fear been instilled in such creatures. Fangdarr could see it in their awe-filled eyes. His bloodlust only increased.

They watched as Fangdarr gripped the crude spear with his large, black hand, ripped it free from his chest, and threw the feeble weapon to the ground. His grin never left his face. Driktarr had already fed on the life-force of the fallen orc and began fully healing his wound. He looked down at the fresh white scar that remained. Another failed attempt to end his legacy.

Fangdarr turned to face his remaining foes. One orc, losing his will to fight, turned and sprinted in the opposite direction. Fangdarr looked over at his beast companion, who had already disposed of the first orc and was now sitting watching its master with not a care in the world. Its thick black coat was covered in blood, drawing a laugh from its onlooking master. Another bath at the lake was needed, it seemed. "Bear, chase orc," Fang said and pointed at the fleeing orc. Bear gave a whiny yawn, slowly rose from its seat, and started after the orc its powerful legs ensuring it would easily outrun its prey. Fangdarr grinned at his companion, never regretting sparing the beast.

The intimidating chieftain spun back on the remaining two of his minions—former minions, it seemed. "So, you want to kill chieftain?" smoothly stated

Fangdarr. He knew they were afraid and wished they had never provoked combat with their leader.

"No, no, Chieftain! We made mistake! Please, spare us!" begged the small orc, tears of fear welling in his eyes.

Fangdarr spat on the small orc, disgusted at his weakness. Seeing his companion get spat on for begging, the last orc—to his credit—decided against joining in. Instead, while Fangdarr was distracted with the diminutive creature, the lone orc decided to attempt a sneak attack. Ever the ready warrior, Fangdarr was ready for the strike, and just like before, he let it come.

Fear and joy lit up the attacking orc's eyes as the blade sunk deep into Fangdarr's back. It punctured through, poking out of his abdomen in front of the begging orc's nose. The success of his attack catching him by surprise, the foolish orc thought the day won. However, he quickly recalled the fate of his former ally and in trepidation, slid the blade out of Fangdarr's back and let it fall to the ground, now covered in blackened blood.

The assailant took a step back. Then another. He hoped to keep as far away as possible from the threatening force that was Fangdarr. A heavy sigh came from the leader as he looked down at his bloody abdomen and turned back to the cowering orc. Again, he lifted his mighty axe, still dripping with the blood of his previous foe. A light swing of Driktarr removed the left arm of the orc.

His victim screamed in agony, and a pang of guilt ran through Fang as he remembered these were his clan members. His kind. But the light strike had healed the grisly wound to his back and abdomen. Fangdarr, renewed, bent down and retrieved the severed arm of his foe.

Puzzlement crossed the armless orc's face. What could his chieftain be thinking? What purpose could his arm serve? The orc found his answer shortly as Fangdarr pried open his foe's mouth with his left hand and, with his right, slammed the dripping arm fist-first into the orc's gaping mouth. The victim's eyes grew impossibly wide in shock and agony as his own severed arm choked him. The vicious chieftain released his grip on the arm and firmly seized the struggling orc's chin to stabilize him. With his right arm free, he raised it high into the air, his hand clenching into a tight fist.

Down came Fangdarr's fist. The brute force plunged the severed arm into the orc's throat, splattering blood everywhere. Tears streamed down his victim's overextended face. Blood seeped from the orc's sockets, mixing with the moist tears. The blackened skin of the dying victim's cheeks stretched past their limits. Tears formed along the sides his mouth, drowning him in unbearable pain. Down came Fangdarr's fist again and deeper went the arm. Again and again until the arm was elbow deep inside the orc. It mattered little. He was dead by the second blow.

Finally, Fangdarr turned to the small orc, spittle still on his face, and smiled. The orc obediently handed his spear over to his chieftain, hopeful that the act would spare his life. Indeed, Fangdarr turned the other way and began walking.

Just as the minion was about to flee through the woods, away from his old leader, Bear emerged from the brush, dragging the other escaping orc. Now all that remained of the party of orcs were the two that had spoken and toyed with Cormac—just as Fangdarr had wanted.

Blood trickled from three separate bite marks on the first orc and the surprise of the bear's presence halted the small orc in his tracks, fearful that he, too, would be chased down. He tried to focus on the hope that Fangdarr would let him go, but he knew it was a longshot.

Fangdarr continued his steady walk away from the pair of orcs. He stopped in front of Cormac, who had remained on the ground watching his new friend mete out justice.

"Cormac," said Fangdarr, drawing the dwarf's attention. "These ones who prod you?" The dwarf nodded his reply, and Fangdarr growled lowly. "Then they up to you."

The dwarven captain looked up to the mighty orc who had single-handedly saved him from his doom, and appreciation and trust came over his rugged face. Stern determination drove the dwarf to get his feet beneath him as he started toward his harassers. While upside down, locked in the snare's unforgiving grip, Cormac had thought of various—appropriately barbaric—ways to dispose of his captors should he ever get down alive. Now, thanks to his trusted companion, he had his chance to enact them.

The exposed dwarf approached his prey. Oh, how the tables had turned. The stout dwarf had no weapons, no armor, and no clothes—nothing but the body he had sculpted through countless hours of training and combat. Cormac could tell the orcs were less frightened now that their challenger was a naked, unarmed dwarf rather than Fangdarr and his lethal axe. Nevertheless, the enraged dwarf had all he needed to kill these two. Slowly.

As if the two remaining orcs of the party suddenly realized just how furious they had made the stubborn dwarf, they shrank back, hoping to crawl away from the rapidly-progressing captain.

"Ye know," the dwarf coldly started, "ye really, really, REALLY shouldn't have poked and prodded me with yer damned sticks." The pair crawled back more quickly now. Pure rage filled the dwarf's gaze. This time, however, he was careful not to become too blinded by it, as that had been the cause of the entire dilemma in the first place. He held no malice toward Fangdarr for his playful ploy, though. No, this dwarf's rage was fully directed at those who had tried to deprive him of an honorable death.

Cormac halted, finally having reached the injured orc that Bear had hunted down. "Ye were the first one, I remember," said the dwarf, the calm in his voice betraying his murderous intent. His grin widened as he bent to face the first target of his fury, nearly touching nose to nose.

The dwarf captain's stubby, strong hands found their way around the horrified orc's thick neck. He could not quite get both his hands around it, but his grip remained tight enough to effectively seal off the gasping orc's windpipe.

Many heartbeats passed with no sounds except the restricted gasps of the dying creature and the sound of his legs kicking into the ground from convulsions. Just when the orc was in its last moment of life, the dwarf let go. Frantic wheezes came from the desperate orc, struggling to hold on to the last bit of life he had left.

"Didn't think I'd let ye pass that easy, did ye?" asked the dwarf. He stepped away from his first victim, confident he would think of some other way to finish him off after the other orc.

The smaller orc noticed the dwarf's change of target and tried to scamper backwards on his elbows, all the while whimpering pleas to the advancing dwarf, tempting him to relent from his wrath. It was all to no avail.

Cormac picked up the rope with which he had been caught, his grin never leaving his sinister face. A few flicks of his wrists and dexterous fingers, and he had the thick twine secured around one of the helpless orc's ankles. The dwarf turned toward the tree, and once under the thick branch, he threw the other end of the rope up and over, catching it as it fell.

His thick, corded muscles tensed as he pulled on the tether. The whimpering orc scratched at the dirt before ascending into the air, just as Cormac had been. As the dwarf tied off the rope, his naked body now speckled in beads of sweat, the orc continued his pleas to be released.

With his prey hanging above him, Cormac retrieved a nearby spear. It was time for reciprocation. As his captors had done, the captain flipped the spear over in his hands and rammed the butt-end into the hanging orc. Cormac's enraged state caused his pokes to grow more furious, getting increasingly harder and harder as he went.

"Say, this *is* fun, bahaha!" laughed the dwarf in a mocking tone. "Oye, not so fun on that end, eh, orc?" asked Cormac in response to a series of yelps and whines from his captive.

His rage and retribution nearly played out, Cormac grew bored with his victims. Neither were dead, and if he so desired they would be perfectly fine by nightfall. Of course, that was if he so desired. Cormac approached the hanging orc once more.

Without even a blink of consideration, the captain reached up and snapped the neck of his victim.

The deceased orc's lifeless body hung limply on the end of rope, swaying in the light wind. Cormac gave a gruff nod of approval and promptly spit on the corpse. With that, the dwarf turned toward the final foe. He had wondered how to kill the captor who had so toyed with him, but with his rage now diminished, he simply had no desire to hold on to his former barbarism.

The dwarf stood in front of the orc he previously choked to the very brink death, just watching it carefully. A dark shadow had formed around the neck of the orc, further darkening its already black skin. Even in the short time that had passed since the dwarf's hands had forced the orc to the edge of consciousness, this orc—this disgustingly, vile creature—was still trying to catch its breath.

Blood continued to pour freely from the bites the orc had suffered from Bear, who now was napping at the base of a tree, fur still covered in blood from the day's chaos. As the dwarf looked upon the dying victim's wounds, he came to pity the creature. Cormac had been treated unjustly by the villain, yet, with the roles exchanged, the sympathetic dwarf felt it proper to end its suffering.

Cormac half-turned to Fangdarr, who was still watching his friend from a few strides away, leaving the dwarf to enact his desired revenge. The twist was halted abruptly, however, as Cormac felt a sharp pain in his back under his shoulder. Curious, he reached behind his thick shoulder to feel a deep cut. Apparently, in his stupor of rage, he failed to notice the grievous puncture he had suffered from one of his assailant's spears.

"Fang, could I trouble ye for yer axe?" he asked.

The request did not come as a surprise to the orc. Fangdarr noticed the wound long before Cormac had, and he had already been grappling with the dilemma of whether or not to hand over his axe.

The orc felt as he did that fateful day with his brother, all those years ago, when he left his kin for solitude. It seemed he was torn between two worlds, each taking an arm and pulling with an unrelenting tug. He had killed orcs. His own kind—from his own clan! For what? A *dwarf*?

Before this day, the only orc Fangdarr had killed was the former chieftain, Vruk, in the *Ortuk Malid*. He had justified that act with the thought that ridding his clan of the weak orc would be the best for his people. But now, with four of the five orcs dead—three by his own hand—what was his justification?

One thing was for certain. He had crossed a line of self-proclaimed morality he would never have dared to cross, and he had done it for this dwarf. This *friend*. For the first time since it met his hand, he handed over Driktarr.

Cormac knew how attached Fangdarr was to his magnificent weapon. So, when it was handed to him he bowed in gratitude, acknowledging the great trust his friend was exhibiting. Trust he felt himself. In the short time he had known Fangdarr, he and the orc had developed a deep bond—one that ran deeper than any of the mines of his homeland.

Holding the giant axe in his two hands—it was as tall as the dwarf and nearly half his weight—Cormac steadily approached the tormented orc. A look of pity entered the dwarf's face as he raised the axe. There was no relish in his swing. No glee in the kill. But once done, his wound knit itself together creating a fresh pink scar over his thick skin. Cormac looked back at the creature and watched the life drain from his eyes.

The dwarf's blow had been true, and Fangdarr was glad his friend had been merciful to his old subordinate, even if he was not. Fangdarr looked around at the aftermath. Five orcs lay dead and blood covered the area, staining the once pristine nature. He looked at the bodies of his fallen minions and back to the naked dwarf. Fangdarr did not fully understand his allegiance to the gruff captain. Nonetheless, he realized he would do anything for his friend. Even kill his own.

CHAPTER TWENTY
AMALGAMATION

Fangdarr approached Cormac after his rampage had dwindled to an end and clasped an enormous hand on the back on the dwarf's broad shoulder. Cormac raised his eyes to his friend and gave a nod of approval. Both scanned the forest floor around them, surveying the carnage. Deep red stains adorned the nearby bushes and grass. The familiar iron smell of blood greeted their nostrils—a scent they had grown accustomed to long ago.

Cormac rubbed the fresh scar on his shoulder, awed at the healing power of the orc's mystical instrument. His stubby finger traced the line from the top of his shoulder down to the crevice in his back. He was certainly grateful the wound would not be stretched open with every step. His hand still gripped the axe that had cut through the last orc as easily it would animal fat.

The dwarf held it out to Fangdarr, a grin on his face. "Mighty fine axe ye got yerself, orc. Ain't many weapons like this here in the realm."

Fangdarr reached out and took it, glad for the dwarf's understanding of his attachment to the heirloom. He grunted, "Never giving away until Fangdarr die in battle. Hope I will have son to pass it to, as it passed to me."

Cormac smiled. "Both me shields belonged to me father, and his before him." There was an awkward silence between the two for a few heartbeats. Luckily, the dwarf resumed the conversation. "Me life is owed to ye today, Fang. Reckon I should be lookin' a bit more carefully next time I chase ye through the woods for me clothes. Bahaha!" the dwarf laughed. "All the same. Ye risked yer neck against five of yer own kind to save an ol' dwarf. I'm happy to name ye me most dear friend, orc."

Fangdarr was grateful for the acknowledgment of his sacrifice. He wondered out loud, "Would you fight five dwarves if Fangdarr captured?"

"Before today, don't reckon I'd know the answer to that question, lad. But, after all ye did with savin' me hide, I'd stand by yer side in the cave of a dragon if need be," replied Cormac, sarcasm slipping into the end of his statement. After all, they both knew their path was to Crepusculus' lair, high in the Tusk Mountains, and their alliance in that matter had been well-secured.

After a quick cleanse in the pond where the game had begun, the trio prepared to depart. Within the hour, the three started back on their path westward, Cormac now fully clothed and with renewed ease in his stride.

Despite their delay from that morning, they made good progress through the forest. But as they trekked forward, Fangdarr continued to lament the killing of his own race. In truth, it irked him more than a bit. Against his pride's disapproving voice, he chose to speak to his colleague about it.

"Cormac," the orc started, his voice just a whisper in the breeze, "you ever kill dwarf?"

Cormac never took his eyes off the grass-covered road. It was clear he was trying to force back emotions from actions of his past. Yet, the bond between them had strengthened to the level of kin. He owed support to Fangdarr's tormented mind.

"Aye, Fang, me shields have bashed more than just orcs and trolls." A drawn-out sigh escaped the old dwarf as he stopped his feet. "I felled one dwarf, just the one."

Fangdarr stopped his stride as well and looked curiously at Cormac, begging for more detail.

"Me older brother is the only dwarf I've ever killed," added the dwarf, his voice a murmur of dread. "He killed me parents, long ago. Of course, after that, he left Tarabar, having committed a crime and all. I didn't see him for a long while, sure as stones. He was a hundred and eighty-two when I was born, and by the time I found him he was comin' up on his fourth century.

"I was just a young pup, only on me second. Don't know if yer knowin', but dwarves can sometimes see a millennium. So, anyway, I wasn't a part of the Shield yet, and I had set out to find him. Took me fifty-seven years of searchin' every blasted edge of the forest and mountains I could traverse 'til I found him. He was surprised to see me, don't ye doubt."

Fangdarr listened intently to the dwarf. He passed no judgment on Cormac for killing his own kin, his blood. Silently, he knew he would have hunted Bitrayuul to Jesmera and back if his half-orc brother had killed his mother.

Cormac pressed on, this time with more steadiness in his words. "Turns out, he had taken up with a group of ogres in the north-most corner of the mountains. Right at the edge of the Monstrous Sea. Many a dwarf named me stupid as a gnome for goin' after him alone. But, it was me quest. Me family. So, it was me who was needin' to go."

Fangdarr turned to regard him. "How you able to kill brother and ogres?" he asked, astonished of the feat. Even he may have had trouble with the same accomplishment.

"Well, dwarves and orcs are similar, Fang. We both let our pride and stubbornness get in the way of our plights in battle, ye know it be true. We both tend to charge in headfirst when we're angry. But, I knew in me bones I couldn't hope to fight them all head on. So, I waited around outside the camp for a few days, pickin' off the ogres one by one. Me mind was too focused on me traitorous brother that I'd forgotten about food and water. All I needed was him. Knowin' he was within grasp was all the sustenance I needed, don't ye doubt.

"After the damned, filthy ogres were out the way, it was just me and me kin. Bothain's truth, I hadn't seen him in such a long time, I barely recognized the bastard. At the time, he held me two shields, stolen from me father's still-bleedin' corpse. A treacherous thing. To be the one to kill yer own father and steal his heirlooms without earnin' them through proper rites of passage."

The orc cast a curious glance to Cormac. "If you did not have shields, what weapon you use?" he asked.

A smile found its way to the dwarf's face. "Well, Fang, I had used nothin' but the dagger me brother used to kill me parents. No more, no less. Sure as stones, he was shocked to see me, and with the dagger in me hand, he knew I'd come with a debt owed."

At the irony of Cormac's brother's treachery being redeemed by his own blade, Fangdarr couldn't help but grin. "Fine tale, dwarf. Must not be easy to kill brother, even after what he did."

Cormac nodded. His past was hard to deal with, to be sure, but he knew he did what he had to do. "Me parents didn't deserve a traitorous son, and me brother didn't deserve peace after the war he'd created between him and me." It seemed as if the words he spoke were more of a reassurance to himself than an explanation to his curious companion.

The pair—ever growing closer—started back on their journey, a new respect for each other in hand. Fangdarr laughed in his head at the absurdity of it all. Befriending a dwarf as his brother had done. Forsaking his own. But Cormac seemed even more accepting of the union, giving Fangdarr the belief that perhaps others may come to accept him as well.

He hoped to himself that Cormac and Bear would be there with him in creating future tales.

As Bitrayuul was not.

CHAPTER TWENTY-ONE
PURSUIT

The dwarf knelt down, causing the war hammers strapped to his waist to scrape against the hardened dirt of the forest floor. He rummaged through the chaos, taking in the scene. Five orcs lay sprawled lifeless around him, each killed brutally and with the same barbarism that the orcs themselves used. As he rested a hand on the nearest orc, he concluded they had passed less than a day before.

"Bit, come and have a look at these here orcs, will ye?" Tormag asked, standing as he spoke. The strong, stout dwarf adorned his typical, shining silver armor to match his twin hammers. Each weapon carried runes of the ancient dwarven language etched into the large steel heads. It was said that such carvings had the power to grant weapons various effects to increase their value in battle, and Tormag's war hammers contained that magical essence. The runes bestowed by his god, Bothain, upon his hammers were those of retrieval. He could throw his instruments as far as possible and still they heeded his call and returned to his waiting hands. His weapons were formidable, especially in the hands of Tormag Double-hammers. They now swung easily as he backed out of the way, allowing Bitrayuul to get a clear view of the culled party.

The half-orc would have been unrecognizable to Fangdarr while out in the field. In their time together, Bitrayuul had preferred the attire of a ranger—light leather armor that favored his great-bow, Kwip. Now, six years since his separation from his kin, Bitrayuul had taken on an entirely new style of combat.

Kwip remained strapped across his back. However, his back was no longer covered in worn leather. Rather, Bitrayuul was covered head to toe in thick steel armor, where at nearly every finger-width protruded a sharpened spine, hundreds in total. It seemed as if the half-orc had been dipped in molten steel. None of his tanned skin was exposed, safely hidden beneath the threatening carapace.

In addition to his deadly armor, Bitrayuul's helmet sported two large, bladed horns. One lay directly behind the other, beginning with the largest at the peak of his forehead. The next stood half the size of the first. Each of his horns—and all the armor's spines—had seen more blood than most warriors' swords. His position as a general in the Dwarven Regime was a position he earned by blood in short time. The armor that imprisoned Bitrayuul still displayed many blood stains from recent skirmishes, causing it to emit a rather distasteful smell. He presented quite the contrary visage to his lush and clean appearance at his recent reunion with Fangdarr.

Bitrayuul no longer favored picking away targets at a distance. Instead, he now preferred a brutal, yet fluid, close quarters combat. Bitrayuul continued using spiked gauntlets as he had when growing up with Fangdarr. However, thanks to the dwarves' his weapons were now enchanted—blessed by Bothain. Bitrayuul was the first of orcish blood to ever receive such a gift from the dwarven deity. Truly, his life among the dwarves was more than just one of convenience. The half-orc had adopted their culture as his own, including their religion and traditions. His faith in Bothain had been rewarded by the generous god, proving his path was supported.

Just as each of Tormag's war hammers had their own specialty, so, too, did Bitrayuul's gauntlets. The weapons' enchantments turned the steel on his body weightless and provided him the strength of an ogre. Both weapons fit the half-orc's hands perfectly. He could move free of any resistance, making him one of the direst threats on the battlefield. As such, the relentless warrior charged into the midst of encounters, grappling foes in order to shred their flesh against his bladed shell.

Bitrayuul looked down at the orcs, gathering what information he could. After Fangdarr had visited them in Tarabar—and received their refusal to assist—the half-orc and his elderly dwarf ally had set out to follow him. Despite Bitrayuul's initial rejection, he could not help but feel an incessant guilt. The night of their reunion, the half-orc had been tormented with nightmare after nightmare. He watched helplessly in his mind as his bull-headed brother suffered one excruciating death after another, all at the hands of the threat he now sought. Bitrayuul was certain he would be so afflicted forever if he did not act, and it took no convincing for Tormag to join him. After preparing for their pursuit and ensuring coverage of their duties in their absence, the pair had set out late the following day after Fangdarr's departure. Now, they tracked the chieftain through the Lithe, and luckily, it seemed Fangdarr had left a trail, though the current markings of the trail were surprising.

"It's Fangdarr," said the half-orc, seeing how cleanly two of the orcs had been cleaved apart by a large weapon. *Driktarr*, Bitrayuul knew.

Tormag nodded in agreement. "Aye, but there's another set of tracks. Dwarf tracks, no boots. Slave, perhaps?" the dwarf asked.

Indeed, a small pair of bare feet could be picked out among the bodies, indicating more than just Fangdarr's presence. They had not heard of the Shield's captain joining the orc's journey.

"Oye, this one here's got some bite marks," Tormag said, pointing to a fallen orc's three wounds.

Bitrayuul looked carefully at the grievous gashes. "Fangdarr's bear," he sighed.

"Well, surely we're on the right track, eh? Bahaha!" laughed the dwarf.

The pair searched the nearby woods in hope of finding where the orc and his company had gone. It did not take long before a clear path that Fangdarr had blazed with his abnormally large body could be seen. They set off to continue their search.

Tormag lead the pair out of the bloody field, the barbaric spectacle weighing on both their minds. Bitrayuul and Tormag couldn't believe how the kin they'd known so long ago could show such ruthless behavior toward his own kind. Fangdarr was raised by the same mother as his light-hearted brother. Yet, his recent actions gave them reason to believe his mind had been lost due to solitude. His bloodlust had always been evident; however, this was no mere fixation.

Ironically, both Bitrayuul and Tormag had performed their share of relentless bloodshed. Though, in their mind, despite taking the lives of countless enemies, they always believed they were in the right—that their actions were just. How many orcs had Bitrayuul discarded for the favor of his dwarven god? And now he was criticizing Fangdarr. But such hypocrisy was lost on the pair, as it often is.

As they walked, Tormag decided to put words to his thoughts. "What do ye think made him go that far, Bit?"

The half-orc opened his mouth to speak but stopped abruptly. Tormag did the same, trusting the half-orc had heard something. Many moments passed as wind swept around the pair, their ears still perked. No sounds came.

Just as the tension in their muscles eased and the pair dropped their raised ears, a twig snapped behind them, followed by a quick gasp. Bitrayuul and Tormag spun around as one, weapons ready. Then the duo's shoulders relaxed as their eyes took in the curious sight.

Frightened blue eyes peeked from between disheveled blonde locks as the small girl noticed she had been spotted. In his twenty-two winters, Bitrayuul had seen fewer humans than years. Only the occasional emissary or tradesman from Wiston crossed his path. Nevertheless, he had developed an extensive interest in the race, as his birth mother was human, and he half the kind.

The girl shrank back in fear as the unlikely pair crept closer, hands extended in comfort. "P-please, don't kill me," she said, tears filling her eyes.

Bitrayuul's perplexed look caused Tormag to approach her first. "Oye, we're not goin' t' eat ye, girl. What're ye doin' out here with this mess?" the dwarf asked as his hand spread wide to address the blood-covered corpses behind them.

"I-I . . . heard yelling . . . and screaming. So, I came out to check what it was, but when I saw what was happening I had to hide or they would've killed me too!" she explained. As she spoke, her voice trembled as much as her body did.

The half-orc finally came out of his stupor and addressed the blue-eyed girl. "Child, what is your name? I am Bitrayuul and this is Tormag," he said, pointing to himself and the dwarf respectively. He gently extended his hand, palm upwards, toward the girl, begging for her own.

Moments passed as she stared at his blade-riddled, armored hand. Bitrayuul's skin could not be seen through the thin plates and interior chainmail. He noticed her hesitation and retracted his hand to remove his gauntlet, exposing his skin. It was thick and lightly browned on the exterior, but his palm remained the pinkish color of humans'. It was obvious she had never seen a hand like his before. Nevertheless, she quelled her fear and placed her soft hand in his outstretched palm.

"My name is Lilyana . . ." She paused as she got a clear look at the half-orc's discolored hand. "W-what are you?"

Bitrayuul gave a short chuckle, expecting the question. "Dear Lilyana, I am a half-orc. Part human, like you, and part orc, like them," he replied, pointing to the dead orcs Fangdarr had slain. As the young girl focused on the brutal, gory scene she cringed in horror.

Tormag watched the pain leave her face and looked back to the bodies. "Oye, Bit, let's get her out o' here. Ain't no place fer a wee one, don't ye doubt."

Bitrayuul nodded to his companion and gently kept hold of Lilyana's hand. She clutched his fingers lightly, drawing a warm smile from the half-orc. As they walked, her vibrant hair bounced with each step they took.

"Lilyana, how old are you? Where are your parents?" Bitrayuul asked calmly.

Shadows formed under her enthralling blue eyes as they drooped to sorrow-filled slits. "I'm seven winters. My pa was murdered, just the day before yesterday, at the hand of these orcs," Lilyana explained, nodding to the small party. "We were on our way to the dwarf city. My pa is . . . *was* . . . a fisherman. He takes a trip every moon cycle. I begged to come this time—to see the big city built into the mountain. Now . . . I just want him back."

"What happened?" asked Tormag.

"Everything was fine. We were four days into the trip from Port Tempest. He said we only had another day's ride to Tarabar. But he said he knew of a lake with rare fish that we couldn't get back home. So, we went into the forest. That's when they . . ." she could hardly continue. Her resolve was cracking more with each sentence. "They just attacked! We had no chance! I ran deeper into the forest. I had no idea where I was, or where to go. I just left!" She looked at Bitrayuul with desperation in her face. "How could I just leave him?" Her frantic thoughts caused her to hyperventilate as she relived the memories.

Bitrayuul knelt to her level, still tightly holding her hand. "It's alright, little one. You're safe now. Your father would have wanted you safe. That's all that would have mattered to him. I'm sorry you had to deal with that." He wanted to embrace her—to offer her comfort in her time of despair. If only his armor were not so unforgiving.

"What about your mother?" the half-orc pressed. "We can take you home to her."

Lilyana's eyes became distant and she sighed. "My mother left us. Four winters ago. My pa said she may be in Riveton, if I ever needed to find her."

Bitrayuul instinctively tightened his grip on her hand in comfort and stood to walk once more, Tormag close behind. "Well, Lily, it looks like we will have to take you to her. The forest is too dangerous for you to wander alone. Why did your mother leave you and your father?" he asked.

Another silent moment as pain filled her already-troubled young mind. "Well, she didn't tell me she was leaving. I woke up one morning and my pa told me she had gone. It wasn't until two years ago that he finally told me why," Lilyana explained, pausing to gather herself. "She had once been taken prisoner by the orcs down south, many years ago. Long before I was born. She said that something terrible happened when she was a prisoner, but she never even told my pa what it was—just that she needed to repay the orc who did it."

Bitrayuul's eyes ripped open at the possibility that suddenly raced through his mind as he was reminded of what his mother had told him of the night of his birth.

CHAPTER TWENTY-TWO
REFUTATION

Twigs and leaves crunched beneath their feet as they made their way deeper into the forest. The path had been filled with little excitement or danger over the last three days. The group had been able to enjoy each other's company in sincerity, practically begging an assault from one foolish enough to oppose the mighty trio.

Being one of the few dwarves who from time to time left the mountain's bosom, Cormac sang songs he had made on his former journeys through the forest. On this particular morning, the captain decided it would be a favorable day to fill the air with his raspy voice.

Oh, ye forest, Lithe be ye,
Out in yer woods, me legs be free.
O', great green forest,
Me eyes cannot rest.
Why not say ye?
Ain't no mountain over me.

Ye got no ores,
Nor willing whores,
What's a dwarf to do
In this big green zoo?
So, me lads, drop yer picks,
Get up, ye, grab some sticks,
Jus' start one fire
Hell, make a pyre!
Sure, this place be a tad bit pretty,
But, to a dwarf, seems just a wee bit shitty!

His singing brought an easygoing mood to the party, so they carried on at a brisk pace, springs in their steps, bouncing along eagerly toward their destination. The mountains where Crepusculus rested lay a full tenday ahead of them. They had already made it to the lesser of the Adder's Tongue rivers, which forked just east of Riveton. Bear charged happily down to the riverbed, rolling onto its back to let the water soak under its thick coat. Cormac and Fangdarr dropped their packs as they stepped to the edge of the water to refill their supply.

"Bothain's beard, Fang," Cormac started, before plopping down to his rear. "Me legs ain't been for much but standin' at a damned gate the past fifty years. Now ye got me runnin' around this blasted wood like a gnome on a rabbit!" He fell to his back as he spoke, groaning playfully with every feigned complaint.

The orc merely chuckled at his friend as he took his own seat. Fangdarr did not mind much the walk. Orcs were not known to be stationary creatures. While dwarves could sit in their holes for centuries, it was an orc's nature to patrol the nearby woods around their clan in search of possible conquests. Adding to his ease, were the enormous legs of the orc, nearly as tall as the entire frame of stout Cormac. For every pace Fangdarr took, the dwarf took three. Nevertheless, they were making good time.

The pair and, of course, Bear, ascended from their brief rest and crossed the eastern Tongue. After fording the slow, shallow water, the group strode through a thick brush, where thorns scratched and bit into their thick skin. Upon their emergence from the cumbersome foliage, Fangdarr and Cormac froze as they noticed what lay ahead—a small settlement outlined in tall logs sharpened at the top. A dozen human guards could be seen atop the structures, each armed with a long pike, a short sword, and a bow. The dwarf and orc stared at each other with more than a bit of concern on their faces.

"What do ye think, orc? Should we just go around?" asked Cormac, eyeing the guards closely.

Fangdarr's head dropped low as he looked toward the ground. His eyes turned helplessly to his dwarven companion.

"Aye, I know, I know. Ye want yer acceptance, Fang. Don't ye doubt, ye deserve it," he added, clearly acknowledging the orc's desire to approach the human village. Cormac thought to himself for a moment, weighing the risks. Going around meant tracking south, hugging the western—more violent—Tongue, which meant a brief jaunt through the Orclands. "Well, what're we waitin' for? I'm not for thinkin' they're gonna send out a chariot for us. Bahaha!"

The silly remark from Cormac brought a smile to the anxious orc. Ever the one to brighten the mood, that dwarf. Fangdarr nodded to his friend and beckoned his pet to stay close to his side. As one, the group started from the cover of greenery toward the village. Before they even made it ten paces, yells began streaming from the guards along the walls.

What started as a dozen men soon turned into nearly a hundred. Shouts continued echoing through the village, and still the pair slowly trod closer and closer. The party stopped far enough from the gate to show they had no intention of breaking it down as they waited for the humans to address them.

Moments passed with every guard and farmer with a makeshift weapon laying eyes upon Fangdarr. He simply stared back, not daring to let his emotions overwhelm him. All was silent as each side simply watched the other, questioning the other's intent. Before long a middle-aged man with a neatly trimmed goatee stepped up to the platform above the gate.

"Welcome, dwarf and . . . orc. What brings you to Adderhaven?" asked the man. It seemed he was the head of the guard. One hand held a standard and his cloak was much more extravagant than that of the other soldiers.

Fangdarr caught the man's distasteful tone, causing his bloodlusting rage to simmer. Luckily, his ever-faithful friend spoke in his stead.

"Well met, guardsmen of Adderhaven. Me name's Cormac—Captain of the Shield, honored guards of Tarabar. This here be Fangdarr, me friend and ally," began the dwarf, hopeful his soothing introduction of his monstrous partner would grant them some shred of leniency. The dwarf, always one to know exactly what to say to best fit a situation, began again. "We set out from Tarabar and are just passing through yer lands and we're hopin' ye can grant us a safe place to rest or passage."

The man waited a few long seconds, taking in the words of the distinctively odd group. "My name is Meilan, I'm captain here, as I'm sure you've noted," the guard said, drawing nods from both Fangdarr and Cormac. "I'd like to come down and speak with you personally, if it suits you both proper."

At that, Cormac sighed deeply, forcing his large friend to regard him with curiosity. The dwarf merely looked up at the black-skinned orc and gave a slight shake of his head. The notion sank Fangdarr's shoulders low—and his heart even lower. Cormac knew what that 'personal talk' meant. It was a captain's way of turning away threatening visitors. Even still, Cormac spoke again to the guard. "Aye, yer safe with us."

Meilan worked his way through the myriad guards and toward the locked gate. With naught but a whim, his fellows raised a narrow wooden doorway for him to proceed out toward the visitors. Murmurs crept in the air around him. The archers on the parapet lightly tugged back further on their bowstrings, anxiously waiting with nocked arrows. All the simple folk of the crude settlement had already determined the captain was heading directly to his doom.

As the sturdy man approached, Fangdarr and Cormac visibly relaxed. They took great caution to show they meant no harm to the man. Meilan stopped directly in front of the pair, staring at Fangdarr for a long while, his narrow, scrutinizing eyes just begging for the orc to advance as *any* movement would spell his end.

"Fangdarr, is it? Can you speak?" asked the man. He had never conversed with an orc before. For all he knew, the only words they could make were grunts and battle cries.

"Yes, human. I can speak," Fangdarr replied, keeping his simmering anger from boiling over.

Meilan nodded. "Good, then let me make this clear for I only wish to say it once. My village has been under constant attack by orcs for the past century. Surely you can understand our concern when one knocks on our gate. So, I'm in quite a predicament, you see. You are known to me, Cormac of Tarabar. As a fellow captain of guards, I respect you."

The dwarf rocked back on his heels a bit. No surprise came from being recognized. It was common to be known by other guard commanders of the realm. However, he knew that most conversations that began with kind remarks often were followed by unfortunate ones.

"And as such," the man continued, "I have reason to believe that this orc is no threat to me. However, my people are much less willing than I. An orc would create much more chaos than desired. Therefore, I cannot allow you entry into the village." While his words were direct and demeanor stoic, beads of sweat had already lined Meilan's forehead. His fear that the orc would be provoked into a frenzy had the man greatly on edge.

However, Fangdarr had already expected the outcome and respectfully bowed his head to the human—for the first time ever—understanding but truly distraught. "I wish I could be welcome. But reputation of orcs was earned, not assumed."

Cormac showed more fury than even his enormous friend. "Ye won't reconsider, Master Meilan?" asked the dwarf through gritted teeth.

The man shook his head. "Nay, I cannot."

Not having another word for the guard and fearful his anger would cloud his judgment, Fangdarr turned around and headed back toward the forest, leaving Cormac and Bear to follow quickly on his heels.

His anger had turned to sorrow by the time he reached the wood, and from the other side of the vegetation, the pair began setting their camp, dwarf and orc working together. Throughout the setup, Fangdarr remained silent, and Cormac decided it would be best to wait to discuss the event with his friend. But once the evening had seen the last gleam of sunlight and the pair were sitting around the fire, the old dwarf spoke up.

"Son, don't let the words of a single human get yer spirits low. There'll be other villages. Friendlier ones. These folks just live too close to the orcs down here. They're afraid of them, rightly so," Cormac stated.

The orc was relieved for his friend's words. His lament had built since they had left the village gate, and he could feel it tearing him apart.

"Humans do not like orcs, Cormac. I am orc. How will humans accept me?" he asked somberly.

The old dwarf could see the inner torment swelling within his companion. A hazy mist shrouded over the glowing yellow orbs that had seen so much bloodshed, and yet so much emptiness. A sense of guilt ran through Cormac, followed by doubt about his casual acceptance of the rejection of the ignorant humans. After all, this orc—the unlikeliest of creatures—had torn apart his own kind for him. Fangdarr had locked himself into a moral prison for the well-being of a dwarf he had met naught but a few days prior.

How could Cormac repay him, now that he was needed most? For all his stature and adamancy, did Cormac possess the strength to stand up for his friend, Fangdarr, greatest of chieftains, bearer of hundreds of scars, beholder of an unexpected warm heart fast becoming frozen by the cruelties of the world?

CHAPTER TWENTY-THREE

SERENITY

How sweet she seemed. Her innocence came through with each faint rise and fall of her chest, sending soft breaths and murmurs into Bitrayuul's ear as he lifted her serenely into his arms. His devastating armor was tucked tightly away within his travel pack, allowing him to embrace the cherubic girl without risk. Her blonde hair blew gently in the early morning breeze and draped over the half-orc's unarmored forearm.

Tormag finished packing up their camp, stuffing a few pieces of leftover mutton from the last night's fire into his mouth.

"So, what are we doin' with the girl?" he asked, his mouth packed to the point of suffocation, drawing a confused chuckle from Bitrayuul. Tormag, realizing he was incomprehensible, gave the half-orc a meat-filled smile. Bitrayuul had to stifle his laughter so as not to disturb the precious cargo sleeping in his arms. He could only grin in silence at the spectacle of a grumpy old dwarf running around the camp with cheeks bigger than a chipmunk's.

"What are you looking for?" he asked the now-frantic dwarf.

Tormag did not slow his search or look up, too determined to find whatever it was. Just as Bitrayuul started to turn his head away in a hopeless sigh, he saw his tunnel-visioned companion jam his toe on a large boulder. Seeing his friend's bloated cheeks meet up with tremendously wide eyes in sheer agony, the large half-orc could barely contain his laughter any longer.

"RGHHHHHHHHHHHHHHHHHHHH!" the dwarf exclaimed, tears in his eyes, as he hopped on one foot, holding the other tight before crashing down clumsily into the dirt—still grasping one foot. Bloated cheeks of meat prevented him from catching his breath. Tormag had no choice but to spit his breakfast out.

"BY THE GODS, DAMN THE DURNED THING T' THE NINE HELLS! Wasted me breakfast, I did! BAH!" he shouted, too enveloped in his rage to remember the sleeping Lilyana. Too irritated to see Bitrayuul's hurried shushing motions.

A yawn came from the startled child. Bitrayuul sighed in helplessness and Tormag simply gave him a guilty smile.

"Good morning, Lilyana," said the half-orc to the groggy-eyed youth. "Sorry to wake you so early. We were going to get an early start on the trip to Riveton."

She yawned the weariness away with child-like stretches. A sigh of relief curled her lips as her large, round, blue eyes shook away the last bits of slumber. "You don't have to take me to Riveton."

"Bah, what sort o' folk would let a wee lass such as yerself wander round by yer lonesome? Nay, girl. We be takin' ye t' yer rightful home, don't ye doubt. It be a dangerous forest, child."

"Well, if you insist, master dwarf. I don't want to be a burden," she replied meekly.

"Pay no mind, child. Bit and I are lookin' fer our friend, anyway. By the looks o' it, he was headin' t' Riveton, same as we. Ye just lost yer father. Don't think we're fer leavin' ye t' the wolves."

Lilyana was grateful for the kindness of her rescuers. Truly, she had resigned herself to her grief before the pair had intervened. After the loss of her father, she had accepted it was only a matter of time before her own life was taken one way or another.

"Thank you, both of you."

The pair waved the notion away and simply smiled. Bitrayuul and Tormag were kind-hearted and honorable beings. Even if their destination had been a tenday in the opposite direction, their honor would have allowed no less than to fulfill their moral demand. Luckily, in this case, Fangdarr appeared headed toward Riveton, though they could not be certain of the reason. He would obviously be rejected from entry.

Bitrayuul lowered Lilyana to the ground as he spoke, "We have a few days before we reach Riveton. Unfortunately, we have no horses, so it'll be a long walk. If you need us to carry you, you need only ask."

"I'll be okay!" she proudly exclaimed.

The half-orc smiled in return. He and Tormag completed their preparations to begin their trek. They were three days from Riveton and still a day behind Fangdarr.

As the day pressed on, the trio made good progress. Bitrayuul was proud of Lilyana's stubborn insistence that she continue without being carried. The girl just refused to be a burden to her saviors. However, despite her youth, she was dreadfully exhausted. When they stopped for a brief rest after the passing of mid-day, Lilyana slumped down against a tree with a heavy sigh of relief.

Bitrayuul and Tormag sat adjacent the girl and handed her a skin full of water. She grasped it vigorously and immediately started draining the cool liquid into her mouth. As they rested, the orc-kin decided to break the silence.

"Lily, what do you remember of your mother? Do you remember what she looks like?" he asked, hoping to obtain answers.

"Of course, I know what she looks like!" returned the girl, as if it was an unreasonable question. "Well, mostly. She looks just like me, only not as cute," she played. "But she was always somewhere else it seemed—like her mind was leagues away, even when she was there holding my hand." Sorrow had etched itself into the last few words, making Bitrayuul rethink his desire for knowledge. It was obvious her mother had been living a tormented life. If he was right about his assumption, that alone would be enough to break most anyone. However, it still seemed odd that she would start a new family, only to abandon them. His questions stopped there. He was both afraid of the answers and of pushing the girl too far into painful memories.

"How much farther?" asked Lilyana.

Tormag withdrew his map and pondered their route's progress for the day. "Eh, hard t' say. We made good progress today, don't ye doubt. I'd say we should come across the Adders tomorrow midday. We'll take a quick rest in Adderhaven t' ask if they've seen our friend. From there, it be only a half day's walk t' Riveton."

"Great! Well, we better get started."

The party continued their path, revitalized from their brief rest. As the light of the sun made its inevitable descent, Bitrayuul donned his armor once more. They were still outside the claimed territory of the Zharnik clan but did not want to risk being unprepared. After all, Lilyana and her father were attacked a half-day's travel outside the Orclands, and Bitrayuul and Tormag were well aware of the clan's rapid and continuous expansion. They feared that soon nearly all of the Lithe would be under orc control.

They set up camp one league east of the eastern Adder's Tongue river. They were all exhausted but had managed to go farther than they had intended and would reach Adderhaven the next morning before the sun reached its peak. Truly, they had made excellent progress; however, they were now forced to set camp later into the night. To light the area and keep warm, Tormag built a fire.

"Lass, stay by the fire. Bit and I will keep settin' camp," Tormag instructed Lilyana. It didn't matter, she was already deep into slumber. He chuckled as he continued planting stakes in the earth for a tent.

"I will go scrounge up more for the fire. Keep an eye on her, please," pleaded Bitrayuul. Without waiting for his adoptive father's nod of agreement, the half-orc slipped quietly into the wood, picking up dried leaves and dead twigs. The pitch-black emptiness of the lightless wood was unforgiving. Orcs have terrific sight in the darkness which grants them severe advantages over humans in nighttime ambushes. Fortunately, this was one of the rare blessings of his orcish blood, though limited. His eyes could see a short distance ahead, though not as well as Fangdarr would be able.

Dwarves, too, could see perfectly without light. A product of evolution from thousands of years of dwelling and mining deep into the mountains. As such Tormag would have fared much better searching the pitch-black wood. Bitrayuul cursed himself for volunteering to scavenge within the blackened forest.

Nevertheless, he did not fear. He took a deep breath of the cool midnight air and silenced his thoughts. Alone in the darkness, he perked his ears to listen to his surroundings. The Adder's Tongues could be heard, even from this far—tranquil water trickling over rock faces that brought a deep serenity to him. Just the subtle flowing of the river after it forked, splitting the rushing waters to the westernmost river and leaving the calm stream to the east.

Bitrayuul nearly got lost in the sound. The sweet, enticing stream relaxed his mind as his tired legs began to loosen. Moment after lingering moment passed until he was at complete peace. All of his worries fled. No concern for his foolish brother's impossible quest. No apprehension for the risks of war on his home. And, most of all, no regrets for the choices he had made. For just a brief instant, the burdens of his life became as weightless as his armor. His toughened body, hardened in dozens of battles with trolls, ogres, and monsters dwelling within the deep veins of the mountain now moved with no strain. It was in these moments he felt closest to Bothain, the god he had chosen to follow.

Bitrayuul's body became still. Not even the creatures screeching in the night nor the predator birds flapping in the sky as they searched for prey could shake him from his reverie. He was so lost in his meditation that he failed to notice the sound of boots crossing the river to his camp.

CHAPTER TWENTY-FOUR
HEADWAY

Fangdarr and Cormac walked on in silence the next day, picking their way slowly south through the thick woods of the Lithe. After taking a roundabout path south of Adderhaven so as not to alarm the townspeople, the trio made their way west near the rushing waters of the western Tongue, hugging the eastern bank, each still locked in their own thoughts from the night prior. The young orc kept to his wishes of acceptance, and the old dwarf questioned whether he deserved the devotion his new ally showed him. Darkness flooded the forest as the sun descended beyond the horizon. Of course, the pair could still see without issue, so they continued their walk as if nothing had changed. Bear nudged Fangdarr, signaling it was hungry, drawing the orc from his stupor.

A heavy sigh escaped Fangdarr as his large, blackened fingers, thick with calluses from a decade of swinging his beloved battle axe, found their way to Bear's soft, thick coat. "Ok, Bear. We stop," he stated, accompanying each word with an ear rub.

"Bothain's beard, orc. Me feet were starting to scream," puffed out Cormac. The dwarf picked a seat at the base of an old oak tree possessing a small concave pocket in its twisted and tangled roots for him to sit comfortably—relatively. They had been walking since morning without more than a few short rests. Now, night had fallen, and the group was a day's trek southwest of Adderhaven. Cormac was happy for any excuse to try to open a dialogue with his companion. But as the captain went about removing his magnificent shields, Fangdarr grimly set to work digging a fire pit, once again lost in thought of the previous events. It seemed the orc was not yet ready.

Only Bear seemed to be in a splendid mood, ignoring its companion's foul thoughts and corresponding expressions. The playful creature stampeded around the site in circles, giving tiny, excited jumps in between each stomp. Cormac just sat and watched the creature in its bliss. It brought a smile to his worn face, followed by a silence-shattering laugh. At the base of an adjacent oak Bear squished its head against the ground and flattened its back fully against the rough bark. The giant paws of its haunches dangled happily over its pudgy face. The creature was in complete ecstasy as it scratched its rear against the bramble bark. The slow rise and fall of its dangling paws, toes curled in pleasure, was truly a sight.

Watching the scene lifted Fangdarr's spirits. Bear always lightened his mood. He laughed aloud with Cormac, enjoying the clumsy beast's uncaring antics. The orc rose and stepped toward his pet to show affection. As he started to kneel toward the upside-down animal, he jumped back with a quick yelp, followed with a bellowing laugh that caused more than a few birds to flee the treetop above.

Cormac's curiosity got the best of him. "Oye, Fang, what're ye on about?" he asked as he proceeded toward his companions.

Fangdarr was still huddled over in unrelenting amusement. He tried to speak between laughs and breaths alike, "Bear . . . not what I thought. He not . . ." The giant orc could hardly force out the words. Bear, catching on to its master's amusement, flopped forward onto its belly with a loud crash. Fangdarr only laughed louder. "Bear not male!"

Cormac just stared blankly at the two for a few moments. His orc ally's boisterous outbursts were beginning to dwindle as he attempted to steady himself. "Ye didn't think to check that?" he asked.

With a smile as wide as ever, Fangdarr could only shrug in response. He never thought to check the beast. His assumption was that the animal was male, but he supposed he really had no idea. Cormac simply shook his head in bafflement. The pair returned to their encampment to prepare a meal, temporarily relieved from their stress. The fire was in full bloom, casting flickers of illumination all around as the skewers of shredded flesh lay suspended in the flames.

"Lad, I know it may not seem it now, but someday they'll accept ye. Wasn't long before I thought I would never clasp arms with an orc, meself. And yet, here we be, brothers on the road. And ye know I would die beside ye, fighting our way through a horde of enemies and not a regret on me mind. I trust ye, lad. And I won't be the only one to do so, don't ye doubt," Cormac explained from across the fire. He rubbed his hairless head as he spoke, only slightly uncomfortable with the personal nature of the discussion. He had been through many emotions after his son and wife were murdered, only hardening him to their sting.

Fangdarr smiled at his comrade. A genuine display of true happiness. "I respect you. I happy we joined. You trusted friend and great warrior," the orc went on, adding emphasis to the compliments, "I am lucky to have you with me; not judging me." His smile faded slowly as he again realized how much prejudice he would face in the coming years. "I am covered in scars, dwarf. All sizes. All weapons." He stretched his arms out to display his impressive scars. "Each one, story to tell. I am never afraid to get more scars. My legacy is here, on my body, but," he swallowed hard, pushing his ego as deep as it could go, "I am afraid. Rejection scars deep. I cannot display them." Fangdarr sighed and looked Cormac in the eye. "My instinct is to kill. Kill to survive. Kill to win. I cannot kill scars. Instead, I must break instinct. Or I will never be accepted. Have to break my nature and reject myself to be accepted by others."

There it was. The true reason for his lament. The orc knew that people would always see him for what he was and what he truly wanted to be: a conqueror. His pride and nature led him to believe that winning every fight was the goal—and it was. But his goal was also to be accepted. Which would he wish to give up more?

Cormac could only look at his companion in sympathy, unable to find the words that could help him through his struggle. "Lad . . . ye just got to—" he stopped mid-way, lifting his head to point his ears toward the northeast where he heard a noise. His one good eye scanned the forest, trying to discern a source for the ruckus.

By now Fangdarr had been tugged from his emotions, noticing something else had taken the dwarf's attention. Pointing his ears each way, he too searched for a distant commotion. A few more moments passed in silence. Fangdarr looked to Bear, whose mouth crept into a snarl and ears lay flattened against her head.

"Eh, maybe it was nothin'?" reasoned Cormac, returning to the fire, pulling each now over-cooked skewer of salted meat from the flames.

Fangdarr accepted a pair of skewers, and passed another pair to Bear, who had yet to pull her attention away from the noise. "Not nothing. Bear knows. Eat fast, we need to prepare."

They ate quickly in silence, even taking care to chew as quietly as possible. Too many of their kin had been slaughtered for campfire carelessness. The legend of Fangdarr would not be ended by some backstabbing marauder in the woods. After finishing the crispy chunks of meat, and prompting Bear to eat hers, they soundlessly eliminated the fire with surrounding dirt and stealthily repacked their supplies.

They made their way northeast, each step taking them closer to the noise. A hundred paces ahead, the screams and shouts of men, along with the guttural howls of orcs, could be heard.

Cormac recognized the distinctive sounds as easily as Fangdarr did. He looked to his comrade, wondering what the orc would do with the ethical dilemma. But Fangdarr was already in full sprint toward the battle, Driktarr in hand, adrenaline pumping through his veins. The orc could not contain his lust. Days had passed since he last tasted the sweetness of victory. Since his trusted weapon had cut through an enemy, bathing him in blood. This was his nature. All his previous thoughts and desires were eradicated. There was only the thrill of the hunt. The song of battle, drumming deep within his soul. Each step increased his speed along with his fury.

Fangdarr reached the encampment in no time, causing both humans and orcs to freeze in place. The humans stared in awed fear, mouths agape as they witnessed the impossibly-sized orc enter the clearing. Already they had been hard-pressed by the band of orcs. Friends lay dead or dying at their feet. Blood glistened over half the camp in the silvery light of the moon. But when they witnessed Fangdarr, they knew their hope of overcoming the ambush was at an end. His muscled body easily surpassed them, having thrice the girth of their strongest man, and he carried an axe half their weight. In their eyes, the monstrous orc could see the expression he loved most. Intimidation.

The orcs that had attacked the camp had ceased fighting as well. In truth, the humans fared better in the ambush then they had expected. The surprise attack had started with about twenty on each side, but the humans had retaliated, and now six remained for each. Each orc saw Fangdarr as the wave that would crash the stubborn rocks that resisted them. Their mouths stretched into crooked and sadistic grins, for now their task of mercilessly ending each human would go over much more smoothly.

Cormac watched from behind a nearby tree. He was unsure of what his comrade would do, but he clung to hope. However, if his optimism proved false, he would not play part in the slaughter of innocent men. But if the orcs saw him, then Fangdarr's choice would be made for him, of that the dwarf was confident. The orc would not let his kin harm the dwarf. Cormac was tempted to force Fangdarr to take the route of morality, ensuring he assist the humans. But he wanted the orc to make his own choice. He thought of how unfair this was to his friend. Would Cormac cut down fellow dwarves to save a few humans? He knew he would not—unless it was warranted. But was ambushing humans immoral to Fangdarr? Cormac knew that Fangdarr had acted in—even orchestrated and led—ravaging attacks on humans and dwarves alike. This was his norm, nature, and culture. Could he truly expect the great chieftain to rid himself of all he had known, simply because his own perspective of morality differed?

Driktarr remained tightly gripped in Fangdarr's calloused black hand as he slowly stepped toward the closest pair of orc and human. Moments earlier the two had been trading blow for blow, death granted to whoever made the first mistake. Fangdarr looked down at each of them with his imposing eyes. The man was immobilized in horror, afraid he would be ripped apart by the abnormally large hulk. The man's opponent still employed that stupid grin, imploring Fangdarr to kill the human.

Fangdarr pulled Driktarr back and held the blade tensely in the air, poised to strike. The man let out a whimper and peeked up at the orc every few seconds, wondering why he was still alive. The axe descended, diving straight for the man's shaggy-haired head. As it fell, the chieftain expertly diverted the attack.

The man heard the weapon scream through the air followed by a yelp and a groan. He looked up at Fangdarr, who stood watching him, speckled in blood. The man's fearful eyes then looked to the orc next to him. The grime-covered assailant was no longer standing. The hook of Driktarr was buried fully into the creature's torso.

Fangdarr, still holding onto his weapon, lifted the orc from the ground until his dying foe was suspended over him. The orc sputtered blackened-blood as his stupid grin washed from his face, painting the chieftain's face. Fangdarr pulled him closer. As he was examining his prey, a nearby man found his courage and charged the chieftain. Fangdarr rejected his mind's urge to defend as the man managed to bury his sword hilt-deep into his back, impaling his muscled abdomen.

CHAPTER TWENTY-FIVE
ADDERHAVEN

Lilyana's high-pitched shriek freed Bitrayuul from his trance. He privately cursed his carelessness as he rushed back toward their encampment. How could he be so inattentive? Here, in the middle of the pitch-black forest merely a day's stride from orc territory. His conscience sent unending messages of self-loathing as his legs carried him forward. Why had the girl not cried out once more? Bitrayuul forced away tormenting thoughts of the worst.

The half-orc finally broke through to the site without any regard for caution. His frantic eyes scanned the camp as he stampeded into the open. Over a dozen men encircled Bitrayuul's companions—scouts, he noted, by their attire and lack of formation. Each held a crudely-built spear of sharpened iron pointed directly toward his friends. His feet skidded to an abrupt halt across from the troop.

"What is your purpose here?" he asked through gritted teeth.

A member of the party stepped toward Bitrayuul, weapon at the ready. The militant orc-kin sized him up immediately. The man's clothing did not depict him as an appointed leader. Nor was his stance anything other than amateur. Even still, any fool can end a life.

"We would ask you the same," the scout replied.

Bitrayuul was at a disadvantage while his allies remained hostage. He visibly relaxed before giving an explanation. "We are simply seeking passage to Riveton."

The man seemed unconvinced. "Remove your helmet."

The half-orc groaned internally. As an orc hybrid, he knew he would be unwelcome in the eyes of these men. No amount of honor seemed to be able to wash away the sins of his ancestral blood. He sighed deeply as he removed his helmet.

Every man tightened his grip on his rudimentary weapon at the sight of Bitrayuul. The scouts surrounding Tormag and Lilyana stepped closer—one even touching Tormag with his spear tip. A scowl crept over the dwarf's face as he slowly moved his body to shield the girl from harm.

In front of Bitrayuul, the man's cautious demeanor turned to one of hatred and disgust in an instant. "Arms up, men! You, orc!" he called out to Bitrayuul—the mistaken assumption stinging the half-orc, as always. "To your knees!"

Bitrayuul's pride called for him to refuse, to lash out, anything. But he calmly obliged and fell to his knees. The sound of steel greaves crashing into the ground signified his obedience. It pained him more than he could admit. This was not the first time he had sacrificed his pride to accommodate another's faulty judgment. Nor would it be the last. Despite being ten times the superior to this man who now commanded him, he obeyed.

The scout seemed pleased with himself as Bitrayuul fell at his feet. With his spear tip a finger's length from the half-orc's eye, he said with malice, "You're coming with us, orc."

A while later, the company passed the threshold of Adderhaven, the captors still holding their hostages at the ends of their blades. Lilyana clung tightly to Tormag in fear, but the dwarf was a beacon of composure. Nearly a thousand years old, Tormag had been captured more times than he could remember—by friend and foe alike. He calmly reassured the frightened child that everything would be alright in the end.

Outside of a large tent that one could only assume was meant for a commanding officer, the troop halted. The man who had taken charge of Bitrayuul disappeared through the cloth flap. The half-orc looked to his dwarven ally in confirmation. Each was ready to fight to his last if the situation turned dire, especially if it meant protecting their precious companion.

After a short while, a man in an extravagant cloak exited the tent and approached. With his final step, he planted a standard bearing the insignia of Adderhaven deep into the earth. It stood erect next to the leader as he stared intently at the subjects presented to him by his subordinates. With a twist of his mustache, he spoke to the scouts without withdrawing his gaze from Bitrayuul. "Where did you find these people?"

"In the wood, Captain, not far east of the lesser Tongue."

The embellished man continued to fiddle with his facial hair as he pondered the situation. His eyes finally moved from Bitrayuul to Tormag. "You there, dwarf, what is your purpose here? Why do you travel with an orc? Speak quickly."

Tormag was clearly unamused at being ordered so. Nevertheless, he replied to the impatient brat, "Oye, we're naught but tryin' t' get t' Riveton. Just passin' through. Yer lads jumped us as we were settin' up our camp for the night. Oh, and he ain't no orc, Captain. He's a half-blood."

The guardsman did not fail to notice the dwarf's final insolent remark. He narrowed his eyes. "Master dwarf, if he is not an orc—and surely no threat—then you would gladly give me his name, and yours as well."

"Aye, I'm Tormag, commander o' the Dwarven Regime. This be Bitrayuul, me adopted son and general o' the army. The lass we picked up on the road outside o' Tarabar. Her father was killed by a band o' orcs in the Lithe. We found her alone in the wood. We're takin' her t' Riveton t' find her mother."

The man gripped the banner, still in the ground. "I am Meilan, captain of this town. You are known to me. My apologies for the abrupt display of power. We are on high alert for an orc attack in the nearby forest. Not even a day has passed since an orc and dwarf sought 'passage' through our humble village. Now, here you are, a dwarf and . . . *half*-orc . . . seeking 'passage' once more. Surely you can understand how we might see this as a possible precursor to an attack?"

Bitrayuul stepped forward at the mention of the previous visitors, prompting more than a few spears to glide across his armor. "Captain, this orc, was he large?" he asked with a bit too much eagerness.

Meilan considered his response. "Well, I believe even you are proof that those of orcish descent are of larger stature. But, yes, he was abnormal." His eyes narrowed with suspicion, "Do you know him?"

Bitrayuul calmed himself to avoid appearing aggressive. "Yes, he is the cause of our exodus from Tarabar. Fangdarr is his name. He is my brother."

Uneasy stares flickered between the guardsmen at the final statement. They inched closer toward their captives, waiting for the order to strike.

With an unnecessary flourish of his too-clean cloak, Meilan lifted his standard out of the ground and pointed the hidden blade atop the pole at Bitrayuul. "Why are you looking for him? And you, dwarf, is this orc your 'brother' as well?" Suspicion soaked into every word he spoke.

This time, Tormag spoke first. "Listen here, Meilan. I'll tell it t' ye true. We're pursuin' Fangdarr after he came t' see us in Tarabar. He came t' us fer help, and we refused. The next day we came t' our senses and took t' pursuit. We tracked him this far but lost the trail. We ain't part o' no damned orc raid, or scoutin' party, or anything else. I ain't fer knowin' which dwarf be with him, Bothain's truth. Once we're knowin' which way he went, we be out o' yer hair, don't ye doubt."

"Very well, Tormag," Meilan began, lowering his pole, causing his fellows to follow suit. "We will grant you passage, and trust on your honor that your words are true." Meilan turned to Bitrayuul. "Your *brother*, orc-kin," he added in disdain, "was denied entry yesterday. My scouts reported that he went south, though his original intention was Riveton before being turned away."

Bitrayuul thought to himself in silence for a moment before responding to the captain. "Thank you, Captain. It is our hope that our presence was not a hindrance to you or your people. You have our gratitude for aiding in our quest. Unfortunately, while our primary objective is to pursue Fangdarr, our current task is returning this girl safely to Riveton. Our honor demands no less."

Meilan seemed revolted at the notion of a half-orc speaking of honor. He ground his teeth in anger as he spoke. "Of course. You may rest here this night, for the sake of the child." At that, he turned rudely toward the village gate.

Curious eyes looked on at the strange party. The appearance of another orcish creature and dwarf stirred their suspicions as well. However, this time a young girl accompanied them. A *human* girl. As such, the villagers, though apprehensive, understood Meilan's decision not to banish them to the forest.

The remainder of the evening went without fuss as the trio settled into their room in the inn. Bitrayuul decided to remain in his armor during his slumber, should any disagreeing villagers decide to take to arms. While they were a bit wary, the comforting straw beds were far superior to the unforgiving ground of the forest. Bitrayuul's eyes weighed heavy as he watched the young girl sleeping in her bed—her care-free breaths a peaceful end to the day's stress. A smile found its way to his face as he continued watching over her until he drifted into slumber.

The next morning, as sunbeams broke through the latticed wood of their window, Tormag woke Lilyana gently. Already, he and Bitrayuul were fully prepared to continue their journey. Lilyana stretched, yawned, and shook away the last of the night's sleep. They could tell immediately that spending the night in shelter had done wonders for her mood. She greeted them with a chipper attitude, completely rid of the fear that had gripped her merely hours before. Racing down the stairs, she hopped onto a chair at the bar of the establishment. It was still too close to dawn for the innkeeper to be manning his post.

"Come, Lilyana. We will eat on the road. We do not want to overstay our welcome," Bitrayuul explained.

She gave a groan of disapproval, clutching her tummy. Nevertheless, she followed her friends as they exited the building. "Are we headed to Riveton, Bitrayuul?" she asked eagerly.

The half-orc could not help but notice that she was impatient to be off the road. However, his concern was on what came next. They still needed to find her mother. What if she was no longer residing in Riveton? Or even alive? He shook the thought away for another time. "First, we need to backtrack a bit. We left our essentials back at our camp last night."

"That won't be necessary."

They turned to see Meilan followed by two guards. Each man carried a bundle that they promptly dropped at the half-orc's feet without caution. "We took the liberty of fetching your supplies," Meilan said. "We wish you a fond farewell and a safe journey."

Tormag and Bitrayuul caught on quickly. This was not hospitality. Their supplies had been thoroughly searched for any conspicuous items that would give Meilan reason to imprison Bitrayuul. Once again, they were insulted at his lack of trust in their honor. But they understood. Some could not be reasoned away from their blind hatred. At least the gesture had spared them backtracking.

Careful to not push their luck, the half-orc remained silent and allowed Tormag to respond. "Thank ye, Captain Meilan. Yer kindness ain't t' be forgotten."

The man twiddled his goatee with his right hand, still holding his esteemed banner in the other. His pleasure at receiving gratitude from those he considered his lesser brought him great joy. With a final wave, he walked away as the guards escorted the group to the western gate.

As the gate closed behind them, they breathed a sigh of relief to be free from such a tense situation. It was places like Adderhaven that made Bitrayuul cherish his acceptance in Tarabar all the more. They put the town behind them and stepped forward, ready to continue their quest. It was a new day and Riveton was only a short distance ahead.

CHAPTER TWENTY-SIX

GRATITUDE

The treacherous beings fled at the first sight of the bloodied blade tip exposed through the abdomen of the hulking orc. Orcs lived for battle and possessed a nearly insatiable lust for spilling blood. However, seeing this monstrous beast impaled inspired better judgment. Immediately, Cormac charged toward the man who still clung to the sword imbedded in his ally. Fury spurred the dwarf into action.

Still entranced by the unlikelihood of his successful ambush, the man failed to notice the enraged dwarf barreling toward him. The opportunity wasn't wasted by the stout guard captain, though, as he unleashed a barrage of heavy fists into the man's face.

"H-hel—agh!" the man tried to call out before being interrupted by yet another punch to his cheekbone. The other soldiers looked on in confusion. "Help me!" the victim managed to cry out.

"Ye no-good-yella-bellied-stinkin'-human!" Cormac shouted at his victim, raining down a punch with each word. "He was just tryin' to help!"

The other soldiers moved toward the angry dwarf in caution. He noticed their approach and pushed off forcefully from his quarry. Armed with his shields now, he assumed a defensive stance in front of Fangdarr, who still stood in silence, sword securely stuck through his torso.

Tension filled the air as Cormac stood off against the slowly progressing men. He kept tossing sidelong glances to his friend, waiting for him to come to a decision. *Fight or yield*, he asked with his eyes. Fangdarr simply sighed—a resigned sigh of acceptance. He gripped the protruding tip of the blade and pushed it back through his body. The men watched in horror as their target showed no sign of pain while the wretched edges sliced through his internal organs once more.

Cormac smiled. Now, the answer would come—to retaliate against the men who had so wronged the orc or not. Cormac truly hoped for the latter, but did these men honestly deserve mercy? Fangdarr slowly reached his arm behind his back, gripping the sword once more. His hands were rugged and thick with callous, but still the blade cut through his enclosed fingers. Ever slowly, the blade slid out the rest of the way, before crashing to the cold ground. Blood poured steadily from the orc's wound—an unending stream of blackened red mixing with the dirt below.

"Fang, ye need to heal," his friend stated. His boot came down on the leg of the injured man he had beaten. "Use this one."

The man had no idea what the dwarf was talking about and it terrified him. He whimpered pathetically, begging his comrades to come to his aid. But it mattered not. They were completely immobilized by the horror of what they had just witnessed. No one should be able to function after such a grievous wound, let alone show no indication whatsoever of even the slightest inconvenience.

Fangdarr gripped the axe in his hand. His eyes were drawn to the quickly-drying blood from the orc he had skewered. The light from the beast's eyes had almost faded entirely, but not yet. Not entirely. With a flick of his wrist, he moved the immense weapon through the air and decapitated the motionless orc. Another orc felled by his blade. Further and further he strayed from his kin. He felt nauseous.

Fangdarr's wound stitched itself closed as his axe eagerly sapped the energy from the previous strike. Another tale for his legacy written into his skin. Fangdarr, the greatest of orcs to walk these lands, and proud chieftain of his people. Yet, here he stood, feeling like a pawn as if he was a feral beast going through the stages of domestication.

Cormac was glad his friend would be alright. Equally, he was proud of Fangdarr's choice. The old dwarf could not fathom the turmoil that was drowning his ally's emotions in that moment. All he knew was that the orc was safe for now. Cormac smashed his shields together and nudged Fangdarr to be ready in case it once again came to blows.

Fangdarr's distracted trance broke as the men shouted at each other and organizing a defense in the hopes of defeating this monster. This *immortal*, it seemed. The orc simply stood in silence, waiting for a verdict outside of his control. Cormac, though, spoke up.

"Bah, what're ye doin', men? We ain't here for a fight with ye!" the dwarf tried to reason. In response, the bloodied and beaten man beneath him scurried out of his grasp and toward his group. The men pressed on with swords and shields raised. "BAH, yer all dense!" the dwarf shouted.

Not more than two strides away, a man called for the troop to halt. He broke rank and stepped forward, drawing stares from the rest. It was the man that Fangdarr had first chose to save over the ambushing orc. His shield and sword fell to the earth in loud clangs. Fangdarr knew that sound. The ring of steel falling to the ground in submission.

"Orc," the man addressed Fangdarr, causing the mighty chieftain to turn his head toward him. Fangdarr grunted in acknowledgement, and knowing his presence was accepted, the human extended his hand to his monstrous adversary. "Thank you."

Fangdarr, Cormac, and even the man's own comrades could not help but go wide-eyed in surprise at the sudden turn of events. But as the man waited, hand extended, Fangdarr could not hide his smile of relief. He moved slowly, cautious of another unexpected assault. His hand—thrice the size of the man's—grasped the light-skinned palm and gave a small shake.

"You are welcome."

With that, the man released the orc's hand and turned to his allies. "Men, we are in no danger. Lower your weapons." They seemed uncomfortable with the request but nevertheless obliged after seeing the orc was amicable.

Cormac, pleased with the result, extended his own hand to his victim. "Eh, sorry, lad, for beatin' ye so hard," he offered to the still-whimpering man. The man did not accept the gesture, but Cormac simply shrugged it off. The man had no sense of fair trade. He had impaled his friend and in return only received a handful of bruises.

With the mood much lighter, the man who had clasped hands with Fangdarr spoke to the orc once more. "I apologize for your wound, though it seems you have miraculously recovered. I am Artemis, a member of the Adderhaven guard that patrols the forest near the Orclands. Thank you, truly, for your assistance in repelling the ambush." As if he had forgotten, the man looked around to see most of his comrades lying in pools of their own blood entwined with fallen orcs and grew somber at the realization. "These were good men. The orcs have been attacking much more frequently in the recent years. We have lost a lot of our kin."

Fangdarr and Cormac exchanged cursory glances. Cormac knew that Fangdarr was most likely the reason for the increased aggression of the orcs, though, he did not know that Fangdarr had personally raided this area numerous times before. Much had changed in the last tenday, the orc thought to himself.

"Aye, we would gladly help collect yer dead, that they may return to their home for a proper burial," the dwarf replied.

Artemis seemed happy with the sentiment and replied, "Master dwarf, I thank you for that. Won't you return with us to Adderhaven?"

This time, Fangdarr spoke first, "I wish to return with you—and be accepted by your people—but I cause fear there. I will remain on road to keep comfort with your people."

The man nodded in understanding. He did not need to ask for more of an explanation from the orc. Nor did he press the request. Both knew it was for the best. Fangdarr at least was glad to know that some minds—even just one—could be swayed. It was a minor thing, but a seed of hope had been planted. The impossible now only seemed improbable. That was all he could hope for.

After lending their assistance with gathering the bodies of the fallen, they watched as the few remaining men rode a cart northeast toward Adderhaven. Fangdarr and Cormac waved their final farewell as the cart faded into the thick wood of the forest. Once out of sight, the chieftain moved to the carnage of his kin and began dragging the orcs that fell in the ambush into a pile.

Cormac knew exactly what Fangdarr hoped to do and, in silence, wrapped his diminutive hands around the ankles of a nearby orc and dragged it to the pile. His friend gave a genuine smile. In silence, they carried the remaining orcs to the mound of bodies, now a dozen high, and set the corpses aflame.

"This, Cormac," he began, "how orcs respect fallen."

Cormac smiled at Fangdarr and rested a hand on the orc's hip. "Aye, lad. Honor the fallen."

CHAPTER TWENTY-SEVEN
RIVETON

The sun was beginning its ascent by the time they approached the gate, painting the sky with an extravagant splash of soft orange and bloodied pink. The gate was massive, yet plain. Only two guards stood outside the wooden doors, hardly paying attention to their party. It seemed odd to Bitrayuul that the second largest human settlement had such lax standards.

Almost as if on cue, Tormag piped in, "This here's a trade town, Bit. Ye've seen Wiston yer fair share and know it t' be marvelous. But Riveton ain't much the same. It ain't as accessible as Port Tempest or Wiston, but it's where everyone goes, don't ye doubt. All sorts o' folk come from around the world t' trade here. Ye might even see an elf; never know."

His mention of an elf caught the half-orc's attention. He was deeply intrigued in the race, but in his brief travels to Wiston, he had never caught glimpse of their kind. Dwarves did not welcome any elves into Tarabar due to a deep-rooted animosity tracing back millennia. The restriction only made Bitrayuul more curious. It was said that elves were the most long-lived race of their time—even surpassing dwarves. Due to their longevity, their prowess surpassed most other beings. In what way, he could not be sure. Any rumors about elves he overheard from dwarves he knew better than to take as accurate.

Lilyana chimed in with her own excitement, "An *elf*! That would be amazing!"

Tormag looked at her incredulously. "Bah! Yer daft, girl. Elves ain't nothin' but trouble."

She simply giggled in response, drawing a frown from the old dwarf for not being taken seriously. Bitrayuul smirked at the exchange.

The group continued further into town in silence before reaching a clearing lined with stalls. The market area was vast, expanding as far as the eye could see, even within the city walls. Merchants from all around the world—some of races Bitrayuul had never seen or heard tell of—were busily setting their wares out for view. Each cart bustled with activity, both from the owner eagerly preparing for the day's revenue and a watchful being scanning the area.

"Tormag, this is huge!" Bitrayuul remarked. "How many shops are there? I cannot even fathom. And where are all these beings from? How many ra—"

"Oye, oye, lad, simmer down. Ye ask too many questions, give me a damned minute, will ye?" Tormag huffed in irritation, forcing his ally into silence. "Riveton is massive—nearly the size o' Wiston—that ye can see fer yerself. I haven't got a clue as t' how many shops are here, don't ye doubt. Plenty, though. If ye ever need t' find somethin' in particular, this be the place t' look. Though, the price will be handsome, or I'm a gnome's uncle. Speakin' o' which, hope we don't see any gnomes . . . hate the infernal things . . ." he trailed off, going into a diatribe regarding all the negative qualities of gnomes. Bitrayuul, well aware of his adoptive father's 'passion' for gnomes, nudged Tormag to bring him back to reality.

"Eh! Sorry, Bit. Ye know how them gnomes be . . . Anyways, there are dozens o' races throughout the world. Only a handful reside on Crein, this region, o' course. Humans, dwarves, orcs, trolls, ogres, and what not. Elves and their other forest critters stick t' their twigs and moss on Y'thirya. I may be old, but even I don't know some o' these other types."

Lilyana seemed just as enthralled as Bitrayuul in the amalgamation before her. She stared intently at all the unknown races, studying them like each was a unique butterfly. However, her curiosity was truncated the moment her eyes fell on an astounding jewel. Without consideration for the others or her own safety, the youth trod forward in a trance, nearly getting trampled multiple times by the bustling merchants. Bitrayuul and Tormag ceased their conversation as they noted she was no longer stitched to their side. Panic struck each of them—Riveton was no place to lose a child.

They scanned the area in haste, careful not to call her name too loudly and draw attention. Riveton was home to plenty of criminals. Rapists, kidnappers, slave traders, and the like were all commonplace here. Luckily, they spotted her approaching a jewelry cart not far from where they were standing.

As the pair rushed to her, Lilyana's hand extended to the gemstone slowly. They would never make it in time. Tormag knew that in Riveton, touching wares without permission was considered theft, due to the sheer number of pickpockets and thieves roaming the market. If she made contact, her hand would be forfeit as punishment. But the gem called to the girl with an unbreakable will that she could never hope to escape. Her hand slid closer, her eyes glossed over in the reflection of the dazzling stone. Calling. Beckoning. Pleading to be taken. Tormag and Bitrayuul charged at maximum speed, but there was no hope. She was only a finger-length away now.

The shop owner took notice to her approach. His eyes narrowed, and his mouth twisted into a sinister grin. Merchants did not care for thieves and were only too happy to see a thief lose a hand, even if it was a young girl. As the merchant watched Lily about to clasp the jewel, he could not contain his wretched smile.

No one noticed as a wiry man crashed into the cart, knocking the gemstone from its perch and out of view. As soon as the bewitching jewel left her sight, Lilyana once again became lucid. She looked around with confused eyes, unaware of her new surroundings. A moment later, Tormag scooped her into his arms and clutched her tightly. Bitrayuul ran his hand over her hair in concern.

The hired man stationed at the cart picked the wiry man up by the mottled cloth he wore as a shirt and shoved him away before checking his master. By now, the merchant was in an unreasonable state of anger due to the beggar's distraction severing the girl's attention, though better judgment prevented him from placing the gemstone back on display for fear of someone discovering his true nature and intent.

Tormag caught it all. He made eye contact with the mercenary and gave a slight nod. The man responded in kind before tending to his employer once more. The old dwarf clutched the girl tighter in his arms as they pushed their way through the stalls until they reached an alley out of sight of the market.

"Tormag, what happened?" Bitrayuul inquired, sensing something amiss.

"Not here, lad. Soon." He looked down to Lilyana who still clung to him, no awareness of the near tragedy she had just experienced. "Oye, girl, we're meant t' be lookin' fer yer ma, right?" he asked.

She broke from her confused state and back to reality. "Yep! Where should we look?"

Tormag and Bitrayuul knew the market would be ideal as it drew the widest audience. But nothing in the world would force them back in that moment. Bitrayuul ran his hand through her blonde hair in comfort and said, "We'll start with the inns. But first, let's get something to eat."

The seasoned dwarf, vaguely familiar with the streets of Riveton, led the group to a nearby inn deeper in the heart of the city. Bitrayuul took note of the sign hanging from a rusted chain above the threshold. *The Stone Wood*, it read, gaining the half-orc's curiosity. Tormag failed to notice, pushing through the withered, wooden door to enter the tavern. Immediately Bitrayuul discerned the reason for his mentor's choice of establishment. Each table—and even the bar—was populated by dwarves.

Tormag led them to the last available table in the center of the inn. All commotion squelched at the sight of patrons of non-dwarven descent. Angry, beady dwarf eyes stared from beneath thick, furrowed brows at the unwelcome visitors.

"*Hal thild vant gar'thurim*," Tormag stated nonchalantly to the onlookers. As one, all turned their heads and continued their festivities. He simply smiled to his friends as he pulled a dwarf-sized stool from under the table.

Bitrayuul extracted the too-small seat from under the table. As he attempted to sit—legs wrapped around the outer rim of the wooden slab—he asked Tormag, "Father, what did you say to them?"

The gruff dwarf waved it away as if it was nothing. "Nothin', lad, just said ye lot was with me, more or less. Ye know, ye really need t' continue yer studies once we're settled back home." Bitrayuul knew he meant ancient dwarvish, the dialect his father had just spoken. Surely, with his life remaining in Tarabar, he had planned to learn. However, military duties were a constant. It seemed the invading trolls and the like were not fond of him learning the language of his adoptive kin.

"Oye, bar, three hots and two shots, if ye please!" Tormag called out to the dwarf behind the counter before turning to Bitrayuul. "This here is a dwarven spot, obviously. Ye see, Riveton is huge, lad, even though it ain't a port on the coast. Sure as stones, Port Tempest be vast. But Riveton used t' be the human capital long ago. Thousands o' years. So, this place has been used as a tradin' hub since. It's in a pretty inconvenient spot, don't ye doubt. But lots o' shady activity goes on here, boy. They use the cover o' the forest t' help . . . operations."

Bitrayuul looked at Lilyanna, who was just as fascinated by the place as he was and thought of the danger she had evaded in the market. "Tormag, that stone . . ." he began.

"Aye, that stone our wee lass took an interest in was enchanted. Riddled with dark magic, used t' enthrall unsuspectin' children. Once they get t' the cart, they're taken. Sold as slaves or worse in the underground market," he finished.

Bitrayuul sat in amazement and equal horror. "How is that possible? Worse yet, how is it known and not sought to end?"

Tormag's hands patted the air. "Easy, easy, lad. It *is* sought t' end. But the crime syndicates that run this place ain't no bumblin' fools. These be hardened criminals. Murderous dogs that kill any who snoop, as well as their family. Their brutality is what keeps 'em around. Folks are too scared t' get in the way, and rightly so, Bit. We got lucky the merchant's hired man saved her, or she'd have been lost. So, ye see, there are some still fightin'. But, takes a clever sort t' make a difference."

The orc-kin was baffled. He had little experience in the rest of the world outside of Tarabar. Even in his young years, he had known cruelty and seen it first-hand. But the suffering of the world he had known was always based in the lesser, more evil races. Never did he think that 'good' folk would ever resort to such action—against their own kind! It sobered him. To now know that cruelty extended to all realms. He cursed his own naivety.

As their meal plopped to their table, none of the group needed prodding to dive wholeheartedly into the savory lunch. After completing their meal, Lilyana was quick to ask, "Are we going to look for my ma now?"

"Aye, lass. We'll get started, don't ye doubt. It's a big place, sure as stones, but we'll start with all the inns and taverns."

Bitrayuul knew his father left some details unspoken. What if they did not find her, or hear of her? They could not leave her here alone. *No, not here*, he thought. Not this forsaken place where children were the target of the devious minds of many. But what was the alternative? Return to Tarabar? Abandon Fangdarr in his quest for the sake of a single human child who had simply stumbled upon misfortune? He could not bear the questions for which he had no answers. No, they *must* find her mother.

"Lily, what'd ye say yer ma's name was?" asked Tormag

"Alice! Her name is Alice."

CHAPTER TWENTY-EIGHT
MALICE

Riveton seemed to be on its last embers for the day. The streets were thinning, and all of the shops were in the midst of the tedious process of stowing away their wares. Tormag seemed not to notice. He approached a building with a single, dimly lit lantern flickering within. A small, broken, old man wearing a baker's apron stood in the entry portal to his similarly battered shop, sweeping with the pace of rolling cement.

"Oye, ye still open, Gramps?" grumbled the dwarf, exhausted from the day's search. Bitrayuul and a weary-eyed Lilyana trailed slowly behind, looking just as weary.

The decrepit baker slowly looked up from his broom, his own tired eyes ready to close in sleep—or death's sweet embrace, Tormag thought. His raspy voice came out slow and troubled, "I'm sorry, we're closed."

Tormag hardly even let him finish before giving a "Bah!" and walking on with a wave of his rough hand, off to seek food. A hungry dwarf is a mad dwarf. Four more shops gave the same reply, drawing more and more irritation from the ravenous dwarf. Lilyana and Bitrayuul just followed begrudgingly, peeking around corners for her mother and asking nearby, loitering citizens of her whereabouts. So far, none of the people of Riveton had ever heard of a woman named Alice. Inquiries were greeted only with shrugs.

"Tormag, go on and look for somewhere to eat," Bitrayuul offered. "Lilyana and I are going to try to find her mother before nightfall."

"Ye sure? Me belly be grumblin', don't ye doubt, but I'm well enough t' join ye."

"Yes, we'll be fine. You should return to *The Stone Wood* so that we might have a soft warm bed for the night. We will set out early on the morrow."

Tormag's eyes brightened at the notion of returning to the inn for hearth. The thought of a satiating meal in his grumbling stomach kicked his feet even higher.

Bitrayuul turned to Lilyana, "You're sure your mother came here? No one has even heard of her name, child."

Lily's head drooped down, causing her blonde locks to fall from her diminutive shoulders and sway in front of her face. "Yes, my pa told me she was here." Tears were already rolling down her face in glistening streaks. Another passerby crossed them. They too were unfamiliar with the name of her mother. On went their search, though their optimism diminished. Bitrayuul began to pity the girl. He knew they were at the brink of hopelessness. Before that, it had been rejected as they held fast to the faith in their efforts. But now, after speaking with so many and not a single flicker of recognition, they could not expect to beat back that beast much longer.

Meanwhile, on the other end of the district, the gleeful dwarf headed toward the familiar dwarven inn where their day had begun. However, whilst he traversed the dirty cobblestone street, his eyes were drawn to a lantern outside a worn building tucked between two others. It seemed they had missed this building as he did not recall its likeness. He noticed a sign hung above the door, oft the symbol of inns and taverns. He looked back to *The Stone Wood*, only a few hundred paces away. A heavy sigh escaped him. "Bah, damn it all t' hell!" the dwarf cursed as he turned toward the unknown tavern.

"Yer finest ale, lad," Tormag said to the young barkeep, a dusty-haired boy, as he slid onto a stool at the bar. Judging by how young he was, the old dwarf figured him to be the son of the innkeeper. "Oye, and a bowl o' whatever ye got that's steamin'."

"Yes, master dwarf," obediently replied the young chap. He put down the glass he was 'shining' with his soiled rag and scampered into the kitchen. It wasn't long before he returned with a steaming bowl of thick beef stew in one hand and a fresh burn on the other. Tormag privately sighed at the poor lad's clumsiness.

The bowl of stew was placed slowly on the counter, fearful of another burn, and slid even more slowly to the amused dwarf. Just as the boy was pulling his burned hand away, Tormag snatched it with his stubby fingers and looked it over. "What's yer name, boy?"

The frightened youth instinctively tried to pull away and replied, "Calus, master dwarf." After realizing he was no match for the dwarf's strength, the boy discontinued his feeble attempt to break the hold.

"Bit o' mustard on that there hand, Calus. Should clear up fine. Oye, and thanks t' ye fer me stew, and thanks t' ye in advance fer me ale." At that the barkeep's eyes lit up, remembering the dwarf's ale he had forgotten in the kitchen. He soon returned with ale in one hand and mustard on the other.

Tormag finally peeked down at his stew. His stomach clawed at him to dig in. He swirled the spoon through the hearty broth, uncovering pieces of beef and vegetables hiding below the surface. His eagerness betrayed him, however, as the first spoonful of the savory meal met his tongue with the searing heat of an open flame. Dwarves were known for their resilience; nonetheless, no such resilience resides on their tongues. Tormag's eyes filled with water as pride and stubbornness would not allow him to yelp in agony. Instead, a forced groan pushed out his brewing rage and pain, followed by a handful of hacking coughs. He blew a deep breath to settle himself and in went another spoonful of stew—searing his tongue yet again. Dwarves are known for their stubbornness.

With a belly full of steaming stew and a content smile on his face, Tormag sipped at his ale, wondering how Bitrayuul and Lilyana fared with their search. He had lost all hope of finding Lilyana's mother a while ago. No one had heard of an Alice around here. "Bah, damn it all t' hell. Suppose I might as well ask around while I'm here," he muttered to himself. He reluctantly slid off his tall seat at the bar, nearly falling over as he hit the ground. "Oye!" he began shouting to the few patrons of the inn, "Anyone here know a woman be named Alice?"

The few clients whispered amongst themselves, some shaking their heads. One man in the corner seemed to pull his cloak hood down, casting a deeper shadow over his face. Tormag's curiosity piqued. He decided it would be best to fetch Bitrayuul before approaching the hooded figure.

It didn't take the determined dwarf long to find his companion. After all, he stood out like a serpent among pondfish with his spiked armor amongst the diminished populace that wandered the streets so late in the day. Tormag waved them down and beckoned when they noticed him. The evening was in full bloom, and the dwarf could see the weariness on the girl's face as the pair shuffled over to him.

Tormag relayed the events at the tavern involving the hooded man, and Bitrayuul agreed it was worth investigation. After all, what alternative was there?

"Welcome back, master dwarf," stated Calus as the group entered the establishment. A gruff nod was all that he received as the party was too focused on the corner table, where the hooded man had been sitting.

"Hmm, empty," grumbled Tormag. "Boy, where'd that man in the corner go?" he asked, pointing.

"Uhh, I think he left naught but a minute ago, master dwarf," the boy replied with a shrug.

Bitrayuul and Tormag looked to each other questioningly. Each turned to the girl, but she had already been taken by slumber at the bar. Seated on the wood stool, her small, blonde head lay flat against the stained counter, a squished, rosy cheek already soaking in an accumulating puddle of drool. Bitrayuul could not help but smile. He had seen his share of dwarven children whilst staying at Tarabar the past few years. However, dwarven young were notably similar to adults, just smaller. The innocence in the human girl's face brought a profound sense of peace to the half-orc. Was it possible, by the most remote of chances, that this was his sister?

Tormag laid both hands on Bitrayuul's right arm, tugging at it, pulling the dazed half-orc out of his reverie. "Oye! What are ye doin'?" asked the frustrated dwarf.

"Sorry, I was away from myself."

"Aye, took a notice t' that," replied the impatient dwarf before addressing Calus. "Boy, can ye keep an eye on the girl?" he asked, pointing to Lilyana.

Calus looked puzzled. He followed the stubby finger to the heap of blonde hair and saliva on the counter. The poor boy must have been dopier than the dwarf had previously thought. Another puzzled look back to the dwarf, then he pointed to Lilyana, a question in his eyes.

"Aye, lad, that be a girl. Ye ever seen ye one o' 'em?" asked the increasingly frustrated dwarf. "Bah! Watch the damn girl, son! C'mon, Bit, we got some huntin' t' do." With that, the dwarf took a swig from a nearby sleeping patron's mug, draining it completely, and stomped out of the building, grumbling old dwarven curses.

Bitrayuul ran a hand over Lilyana's soft, dirty hair before exiting after his companion. "Keep her safe, boy!" he called out to Calus as he passed the threshold.

Once Bitrayuul and Tormag had departed, Calus looked at the sleeping girl with puzzlement. After a long moment to consider how to move Lilyana, he gently carried the girl to one of the rooms. Throwing a light, cloth blanket over her snoozing form, Calus closed the door behind him and returned to the bar, baffled at the night's events.

The pair bumped around the darkened alleys of Riveton, kicking disease-ridden rats as they scurried past. The town looked much dirtier at night, to be sure. Perhaps they were just in the unfavorable and forgotten part. The scents that filled their nostrils were of death and disease, making that section of town seem a rotting plague in comparison to the rest of the place. Nevertheless, they continued their path. A right turn around a corner in the tight alley, then a left. Three more rights, a dozen more lefts, and a dozen more rights. The place seemed a labyrinth of endless tucks and twists unaccompanied by any helpful landmarks.

"Bah! Damn the stones, son! We're lost!" shouted the dwarf. He crashed down against a wall in exhaustion, seeming to cause more harm to himself than intended. "Me bones are tired. What are we doin' anyhow? Goin' around chasin' shadows. Bah, it's late. I'm fer thinkin' it be time t' go back t' the inn and get some rest. Aye?"

Bitrayuul was similarly exhausted, though his curiosity was more than enough motivation to keep him going. This was their first shred of hope they had encountered in their efforts that day. The man they hunted knew something. He was sure of it. The half-orc turned to his father, "We ca—"

Tormag looked up. "We what? Bit? What are ye about?" he asked, following Bitrayuul's blank, open-mouthed stare to his right. "Oh."

Not ten strides away stood the cloaked figure in the middle of the narrow alley armed with a serrated sword in one hand and a curved dagger in the other. The blades stood out easily in the darkened lane as moonlight cast reflections on the cold steel. The man's hood was still pulled low to cover his face, so the pair could not determine his true intent, though they expected it was unfavorable. Tormag stood slowly, his eyes never leaving the dark figure. "Say, friend, what are ye about?" he asked.

The man's grip tightened around his notably magnificent weapons. A shallow breath escaped him. "Why do you follow me?" he asked in a soft but threatening tone. It was the menacing whisper of an assassin in his own killing grounds. Confidence poured from the man. These were *his* streets. The hunters had easily become the hunted, and they knew it.

Bitrayuul stepped forward, hoping not to cause more alarm. "We seek a woman called Alice, do you know of her?"

The cloaked man's grip tightened further, the muscles in his slight legs tensing.

"Uh oh . . ." Tormag said, knowing what was next.

The cloaked figure burst into motion. With a kick off the wall behind him, the assailant propelled toward them at near blinding speed, then maneuvering his slender form into a tuck, planted his deadly sword tip into the hard ground, causing his body to do two quick twists before reaching the dwarf. From the confusion of the swirling mass, the curved dagger came toward Tormag's face, nearly catching his right eye. In a single reflexive movement, the dwarf managed to bring his right war hammer into its path, deflecting the dagger toward the wall. The blade screeched against the stone flicking bright orange sparks into the dark alleyway.

Meanwhile, the skilled assailant flicked his sword from its planted position toward Bitrayuul's legs, aiming to hamstring the tall opponent. The half-orc attempted to jump back, but his focus was too concerned with Tormag's danger, costing him precious time. The serrated sword cut through his fine armor and made a shallow cut into the side of his left thigh. Beneath his encased helmet, Bitrayuul could not hide his surprise. His armor was of the finest dwarven steel, not easily dented or pierced.

Now that Bitrayuul and Tormag knew of the assailant's intent. They quickly composed themselves and formed defensive postures next to each other, war hammers and spiked gauntlets at the ready. The man stood tall with weapons relaxed toward the ground two spear-lengths away. The companions were staying prepared, not willing to be caught by surprise again.

Another few moments of silent anticipation from both parties, then it was the assailant who moved again. His domain, his advantage. The man began a sprinting charge toward his prey, weapons leading. As the assassin closed half the distance, he leapt into the air toward them, causing them to raise their weapons defensively by instinct. However, while in the air, the assassin simply vanished into nothingness—a faint cloud of black smoke left in his wake.

The pair instantly put their backs together. They scanned the area for any hint as to where their target went. Moments passed, but they knew not to let their guard down. That was what he was waiting for. Time crept by, seeming like an eternity, with not an inch of relent from the pair. Bitrayuul and Tormag were seasoned fighters who were disciplined in the art of warfare. Nevertheless, there is only so much tension a warrior can take. Paired with a contorted face, the dwarf's legs shifted, and out came a loud flatulence that only a dwarf could be proud of.

The dwarf could not hold his resolve. "Bahaha! That one might have been me!" As his claim concluded, the assassin appeared on the wall to his right, sword already accelerating toward his temple. But Tormag and Bitrayuul were ready for the assault. By the time the sword crashed into Tormag's intercepting hammer's dense head, Bitrayuul already had both hands around the assassin's dagger arm and left leg, pinning him to the wall.

"Oye, these be me favorite hammers, trickster. If there's a scratch on 'em ye'll be buffin' it out with yer teeth, aye?" he stated calmly, a castle's weight of seriousness in his voice. The dwarf headbutted the man for good measure, his steel helmet dazing his victim. Tormag then grabbed the man's sword arm and opposing leg before the assassin could regain his senses.

The pair held the struggling cloaked figure with strong hands, easily overpowering the slight-of-build man. They pushed him to the ground and Bitrayuul sat on his legs and chest while holding his struggling arms with ease. For each wiggle and writhe, the man only rend himself deeper on the blades of Bitrayuul's armor. Tormag tucked his weapons after kicking away the assassin's sinister, curved dagger and mildly bloodied, serrated sword. He leaned over the cloaked man, still unseen under the shadow of his hood, and yanked it up to glimpse the attacker in the moonlight.

Long blonde hair shined brightly in the dark of the alleyway—an illuminating presence in such an abysmal setting. Thin red lips twisted beneath angry, murderous eyes, showing the assassin for what *she* truly was.

"Bothain's beard! It's a lass! HAH! Say, Bit, we almost got fed t' the rats by a wee lass!" exclaimed the surprised and amused dwarf, ever the comic.

Bitrayuul had yet to move or make a sound as the surprise took him fully. For when he looked directly into the woman's face, beyond the murderous expression, past the strikingly sinister eyes, thin lips, and strong and determined attitude, it was behind those features that the half-orc saw a distinct resemblance to Lilyana.

"What is your name, woman?" asked Bitrayuul slowly, hardly able to form the words that fought the weight in his gut.

She stared back at him, still struggling, allowing her skin and clothing to be ripped asunder. Blood began to trickle down a dozen wounds, but her burning blue eyes never left his. He could see all the hate in the world in those blue orbs. Fires lit behind a glass ball, trapping the raging inferno for her disgust of him. She settled briefly, regaining her sinister composure. If she was to die, she would die with the pride of a murderer who instilled fear into those who heard her name. "Malice."

CHAPTER TWENTY-NINE

MATERNAL

Malice continued to struggle as the pair escorted her back to the tavern where Lilyana remained. Despite the woman's best attempts, the bonds that contained her could not be slipped or broken. Tormag threw her roughly into a chair in the corner of the room and tied her down as Bitrayuul retrieved two more stools for them to sit on in front of their captive.

Calus stood motionless behind the bar, equal parts confused and afraid. He began to mumble something barely audible before Tormag called out to him. "Aye, yer fine, lad. We found who we was lookin' fer. Don't worry, we won't be breakin' nothin'. How's the girl?"

From behind the bar, Calus simply pointed upstairs to the rooms.

Tormag nodded in response to the boy. He let out a grumble as he slid onto the stool and shifted his attention to Malice. "Bah, damned woman. Me feet are still achin'. All we were wantin' was t' talk."

The restrained woman spit at his feet. "So speak, dwarf!"

Tormag gave a hopeless sigh. "Bit, I'm beat, don't ye doubt. Ye ask the questions."

Bitrayuul had refrained from speaking since the alleyway encounter. He was too lost in his own thoughts that this might be his real mother. What were the odds? Was Bothain truly such a devious tormentor to put this on him? It hardly seemed real. Could this simply be a dream so vivid in its design that his emotions rubbed raw but prevented his rouse?

Tormag nudged him again to break his spell, drawing empty blinks from the confused half-orc. The dwarf prodded him again and eyed the woman.

"I-I . . ." Bitrayuul started uneasily, taking a deep breath to steady himself. "I need to know some things about you. We are not here to bring you any harm. Our purpose is not for ourselves, but for another. Will you answer?"

Malice narrowed her eyes menacingly, while underneath, her poisonous ocean of hate unraveled itself in secret curiosity. "Ask your questions."

"We are here because we encountered a young girl hidden alone in the Lithe, her father freshly slain by orcs before her own eyes. Lilyana is her name. She claims her mother, Alice, resides in Riveton, though she has not seen her for years." Bitrayuul studied her reaction with each word. Only at the mention of the girl's name did he catch a flicker of panic.

"I believe you to be that mother," he continued. "Our quest is elsewhere, and the girl sleeps naught but a room away. Will you care for—"

Malice could not control her emotions any longer. She broke out in outrage. "Who dares to ask such of Malice? You know not of what you speak! The woman for which you search is dead! Long lost to the horrors of this world. Her weakness knew no bounds. She was a frail, sorry excuse for a life wasted by the exploitations of others. Who *dares* to revive that pain!? I will carve the heart from your chest and swallow it whole! You know not of what you speak, you do not!"

Bitrayuul and Tormag were taken aback by the sudden onslaught. Prior to this, their captive had remained resolute in her silence. Now, her ceaseless stream of curses flowed with her tears as her secrets were brought to life. Her litany of insults finally came to a halt as her wailing mixed with screams of anger. Adrenaline coursed through her, nearly granting her the strength to break the twine binding her in place.

"Free me! Free me from this cage and see the strength that was born from that pain, captor! To know what it is to live in pain and humility, hoping each moment's breath be the last that ties you to this rotten and unforgiving world. I know nothing of what you speak, I cannot! That is dead! A final peace after unending torment that would fill a hundred lifetimes. Yet, you breathe life into a flame that you cannot hope to hold!"

Tormag had heard enough. He calmly rose from his chair and slid a rough hand over her mouth to silence her. Sympathetic eyes looked into hers. "Aye, we're knowin' yer pain, sure as stones, woman. This world ain't one o' pleasantries. Life be pain, ye know this t' be true. But, would ye not wish t' protect the girl from that pain?"

Her eyes drifted to the ground as her body went limp. What was once persistent wailing had simmered to occasional sobs. Her breathing eased until, finally, from her huddled position, she spoke lightly in remorse. "I cannot. Four years. Four long years. She has suffered or triumphed without me. I cannot bear the sight of her.

"Many years ago, I was taken by orcs. I was a prize presented to their chieftain, where I suffered his . . . brutality. Life within a cage, not knowing death, though I begged for it. To be the plaything of another. You could not wish such a fate on your gravest enemy. Such an existence . . ." she trailed off as the painful memories broke through her resolve for a moment. Her dagger eyes were now clenched shut in torment.

After the brief silence, she continued her story. "A son was born. A foul, mixed thing. Oft as a youth I heard the beauty that it is to be a mother. How such an act was truly the height of purpose. They were wrong. Such an act was not meant to be undertaken by force. By hopelessness of a fate not your own." Bitrayuul and Tormag noted her fingers were dug deep into her skin, drawing blood. It flowed easily, and as she continued, she tore at her flesh even more. But she had to go on, Bitrayuul thought. His hand clutched Tormag's to prevent him from stopping her torment. Tormag saw the pain and eagerness in his son's face, but he was nevertheless dismayed at his honorable companion's selfish persistence. He retracted his hand.

"It was that night I managed my escape. Broken. Weary. My disgusting child left behind with the pain I had suffered. One of the chieftain's own freed me from my prison. She had witnessed my nightly torment, only looking on unfazed. But, in that last night, at the height of my anguish, she freed me. Despite my weakened state, I ran. I ran until my legs could no longer carry me—all the way to the edge of the forest. There a man found me covered in blood and dirt. He carried me to his home where I was cleaned and cared for. He told me I entered an unshakable slumber for near a tenday. Yet, he cared for me.

"A woman he had never known. No kinship to tie us. Only that I was in pain and he sought to bring comfort. That man became my husband. And none, I believed, deserved my love more. Not only did he replenish my body, but also my mind. It was his hand that taught me the skills needed to defend myself. I came to know the sting of the blade as it cut into my skin, and the relish one could feel as it cut into another's. He was my teacher. My lover. My savior.

"Years after he found me, he set me on my path—toward actions that would truly grant me relief. Orcs. Hunting them. Killing them. Anything to bring woe to those who had brought it to me. I spent years gutting the beasts, picking them off one by one in the forest. Torturing them. Murdering them. Always with the same intent in mind, to repay my rapist. I sought him out for a decade with no luck. My blades claimed over a hundred orcs, yet none of the blood spilt belonged to the one I wished.

"It was after that time of hunting and 'healing' that I finally realized something. The man I was with had used me as a weapon. Not in the hopes of healing myself, but in playing out his own game. He had manipulated me, exploited my pain, so I could be his puppet. Pulling the strings of my heart and mind into his own design. He had whispered of a chance of regaining myself, and I had believed him. A fool, I was! As if I was some flirtatious child fancying her heart's first target. As if I deserved any more pain!"

The woman's audience was stunned into silence, especially the half-orc. His curiosity had served its purpose. This was his mother. He now knew the truth of his birth—and the truth of his mother's disgust for him. She had not perished at his entrance to this world, as he had been told. She had lived. Bitrayuul had so many questions, but he let her continue.

"I confronted him. After almost two decades. Lily was already in her third winter, and my pain had subsided to near nothingness. But when I discovered his true intent, I could not go on in silence. I had finally swept away the smoke of deceit and discovered his true nature. The betrayal stung, of course, but in a way, I was grateful. After all, I had healed. Did I care that my healing had been due to his scheme? Should I not pay homage to the man who had saved me?"

Once again, she steadied herself before continuing. "He was my captor—more so than the orc that had confined me for nearly a year. I was angry and disgusted at the beast and his brutality, but it was honest in its pain. This . . . my husband, the father of my child, the man who I cherished above all else was of the most devious kind. His assault was tenfold that of the orc. His was done as if I wished it upon myself. Tell me, would you rather an assailant stab you a hundred times, or be convinced to cut yourself a thousand as if it was your own desire?" she asked rhetorically.

"That was my downfall. A pain I could not bear, or so I thought. Instead, in my moment of uprising against him, finally breaking his spell, he made the final cut himself. The man I had trusted more than any other raped me. Not only did he make me realize the hidden pain he had inflicted on me over the years, he also forced me to relive the pain that had brought me to him. What luck I must have to draw such sadists toward me. You should have seen his eyes as he overpowered me. It wasn't an act of passion or anger. There was only the thrill. He had been waiting for this. Living in silence for all those years tormented him. He was the maestro that had created a masterpiece, only for it to never be seen in all its splendor. Then, in that moment, he knew I had finally noticed. He could not hold back his smile. Consummating his long torture of me brought him to ecstasy.

"After the act, he simply waved me away. I was a puppet that had fulfilled its purpose, he told me. Such an assault was unknown to me. The secret workings of a man so deviant that I could only feel horror. I thought of him, my life, and Lilyana and how it all was a fraud. I toyed with the notion of stealing Lilyana from him for fear of her suffering the same fate as I. However, in that moment, I did the only thing I knew. I ran. Vengeance did not cross my mind, only survival. Escape from the life I had suffered. I pleaded with myself to return to her. To save her from this demonic fiend, but each time I attempted to muster the courage, I could not. Even visualizing her face brought me to his. The pain was too close—too real.

"I did not have the strength in me to walk back into their life. To face my demons. To know I had been merely a pawn in a game that played out without my knowledge. So, I came here, to a place where I knew I could live unnoticed. Here, I could shed blood of any I wished. Here, I would 'heal' my sorrow in the only way I knew until I could finally muster the courage to break the chains of my past and reclaim Lilyana from her manipulative father. Tell me, is she safe? Is she sane?"

Bitrayuul spoke up first. "Yes, she is safe. As far as we could tell, no ill will befell her at his hand—only love. However, as you say, he weaves a story so deep that even the characters in place do not know the pages they fill. She needs her mother. As she once was—a beacon of hope and happiness. That is much to ask, I know. But will you forget all that was and share her life?"

A tear streamed down Malice's face. "I wish nothing more . . . But despite him being gone from this world, I *still* feel his claws in me. No, her life would be the worse for it. I would beg of you to leave her to her peace. She should not suffer as I—to know the true nature of the man she loved. Her memory of him should remain untainted. I am not fit to be a mother. I left her to the demon whilst I ran in my own selfish desire to survive. How can I be the one to care for her?" she whimpered.

The half-orc removed his helmet, allowing her to see him as he was. "Malice, you see my face?" he asked, watching her eyes instantly shift from quiet despair to pain-filled rage as she noticed his origin. "I am the son you left behind—the product of your misery. My whole life, I thought *I* was the cause of your demise. That pain I have lived with, but now sitting before you, I know it to be false. I hold no ill will against you. I was blessed with a mother and father," he said, gesturing toward Tormag, "who showed me love. Now, here I sit, a lifetime later, to tell you that Lilyana is in need of her mother. Unlike me, she knew you, if only in brief, though her memories of you fade. Nevertheless, that girl has no one else. Only you. This world is unkind, but there *is* kindness. If you truly believe the words you speak, we shall bring her to an orphanage or elsewhere in the hopes she will be given the love that you cannot. But, it is our hope that you will regain your will and reunite with her."

The woman's eyes still seethed with anger. Her conditioned hatred of orcs was too great to be broken. "You, half-orc, may be of my womb, but know that I cannot muster any feeling but hatred for you. That hatred may be unfair, unwarranted, and ill-received, but it is there. I am of the mind to kill you, though you have not wronged me. Even now, I heard almost no words of my daughter as I was intent only on how I could escape my bondage to bring an end to your life! That is the nature of the woman you would leave this girl to."

Bitrayuul gave a sigh and replaced his helmet, hiding his heritage once more. Instantly she visibly settled, confirming her deep-rooted stigma. "Nevertheless, Alice—"

"Malice! It is *Malice*!" she shouted, her heart racing in rage, though it calmed quickly.

Tormag tapped his ally on the shoulder, requesting a secret audience. Once out of earshot, he whispered, "Lad, are ye sure about this? She be broken, son. I know she be yer own mother but think o' the girl's safety. Is this the best choice?"

The half-orc looked back to Malice, straining to escape from her bindings. "I have to believe so. Otherwise, what else can we put faith in? Two people may be saved here, Tormag. Lilyana needs a guardian just as Malice needs to be free from her own suffering. I know it to be true that the girl is her only hope. I believe that if Lilyana was given the choice, she would give her mother a chance."

The old dwarf thought to himself for a moment before replying, "Well, let's test that theory." He strode to Malice and easily lifted her entire frame—still strapped to the chair—and started up the stairs. The woman shouted and cursed at him before being dropped to the floor. In her anger, she failed to notice that Tormag had taken her to a room. Her silence came abruptly as her eyes found the diminutive figure wrapped tightly in a blanket on the bed.

Quickly, she whispered, "No, no, no. Take me from this place, dwarf. I—" Her words trailed off as the girl stirred. The whole room froze in anticipation. Slowly, Lilyana's eyes groggily opened to take in the blurry sight. She raised a small hand to her face, lightly rubbing the night's glaze out of her eyes. Her adorable yawn was enough to bring tears and a smile to Malice's face. As they made eye contact, the girl was the first to speak.

"Mama?"

CHAPTER THIRTY
HOPELESS

"Keep a wary eye, lad," Cormac stated while lifting his widened nostrils into the air, "we're in orc territory now. I can smell 'em."

Fangdarr halted his march to take his own whiff. He stood sniffing in each direction but found nothing. His attention shifted to Bear, "Bear, you smell orcs?" The beast had already been testing the scents and in response, she fluffed her ears, tucked them against her head, and gave a low growl.

"We're downwind, so they shan't be too close, I'm thinkin'," Cormac added.

With a nod, Fangdarr trotted forward, sure to rub the taut ears of his companion as he passed her. As if given the cue that the threat was diminished, Bear instantly perked up and happily danced forward with her master. Cormac followed in line, continuing to sniff as he walked.

Despite the persistent looming scent of orcs, the group made good progress without interruption as they continued south along the western Adder's Tongue river. The sun was currently in the midst of its descent, warming the forest as it slid between the leaves of the trees.

"Fang, we should stop here for the night," Cormac said. The orc looked at his friend in puzzlement then scanned the surrounding wood for the reason. Noticing his confusion, Cormac continued. "We're on the outskirts of yer clan's border. The sun is settin', and the path ahead is treacherous and haunted, so it's said."

"Haunted?"

"Aye, if ye believe the stories. We're close to the Echoed Marshes, by my guessin'. Probably half a day's walk more. With the sun already goin' down, that's not a place we want to make camp, don't ye doubt."

Fangdarr sat against a nearby tree in momentary respite. "I have heard the name. Never been there. What in marshes?"

Cormac, too, dropped his pack and sat adjacent to the orc. "Naught but death and disease. It's a full day's walk just to pass, if we're quick. We could go around, deeper into the Orclands, but that would add a day to the journey and risk runnin' into yer clan. The marshes be treacherous, don't ye doubt. We're just on the border of Metridium Lake, which feeds the marsh. We can wash in the lake and take the evening to relax and plan our next move. If we leave early enough in the mornin', we should be able to push through the marsh before nightfall."

The orc contemplated the situation in silence. It was true, he did not wish to encounter more of his clan. He knew he would inevitably be forced to end more of his kind for, once they lay eyes on Cormac, their fate would be sealed. Their rage would drive them beyond reason—and truly, what reason could he give? There were no words he could offer that would convince an orc to spare the dwarf and leave them to their journey. No, he knew the outcome would always be the same. With that, he made his decision to remain outside the Orclands.

"What is on other side of marshes?" he asked Cormac.

The dwarf was taking off his worn boots when Fangdarr asked his question. He sighed in relief as the cool breeze blew on his sweaty, wiggling toes. "Let's see, accordin' to the map the Echoed Marshes extend widely. Streams spread out in every direction, it seems. A few even huggin' a human settlement and reachin' most of their way to the base of them mountains. We're needin' to reach Hell's Throat, right?"

Fangdarr nodded in confirmation.

"Right, so we can take three routes. First, through your territory," he started, but the orc was already shaking his head. "Figured as much. Next, we could attempt to swim through Metridium Lake. But, the lake is wide and deep. Folks seem to believe it houses a creature within its depths, hence why no humans have settled near it. It would be a long swim, Fang—a full day's worth. And I," he smacked his heavy plate armor and shields, "don't think I can float for long. Bahaha!"

The orc shook his head at his friend's everlasting humor. "And third? Through marsh?"

"Aye, through the marsh. It be thick with mud from the streams flowin' through it. However, it drifts west, toward the Coast." He passed the map to the orc. "As ye can see, if we stick to the east, the path should be less treacherous. Can't be forgettin' the humans to the west. Best to avoid them, I reckon."

Fangdarr looked the map over intently. The marshes were indeed vast. He was amazed at how accurately his clan's current borders had been depicted. It was obvious this map had been made recently and with special attention given to the Zharnik borders. Its accuracy was worrisome. He shook the care away—not the time or place, he thought. Focusing on the journey at hand, he scanned the map closely. The Orclands bordered all the way up to the eastern edge of the marsh. Fangdarr regretted not taking the time to traverse all his lands himself.

It was curious to him that his orcs had stopped their advancement at the marsh. Orcs were not known for their caution, especially regarding something so trivial as terrain. He recalled Cormac stating the path was treacherous, but orcs would not halt their pursuit of blood and glory due to mud. No, there had to be more cause for concern.

The orc tossed the map back to his friend, knowing the answer to be obvious—though unfavorable. "We rest here tonight. Tomorrow we stay in orc borders, avoid marsh."

Cormac nodded, knowing it was the smart choice. "We'll take it slow and keep caution. If we see any orcs, we'll try to avoid them."

Fangdarr smiled knowingly, ever surprised at the cherished relationship he shared with a dwarf he had only known for less than a moon cycle. Cormac understood him, and even more, he respected him. Respected his beliefs, his concerns, and his fears. The young orc could not have hoped for a better ally to join in his quest. With a quick jump to his feet that startled his animal companion, Fangdarr stretched long and hard. His hands tickled the underside of the leaves above, three times the height of Cormac.

After stretching his muscles, Fangdarr smiled and called to his friends, "Swim time!" His allies needed no convincing to join in the relaxing bath, despite Cormac's warning of fabled rumors. After rushing the few hundred strides to the shore of Metridium Lake, Fangdarr gently tossed Driktarr onto the shore, embedding the sturdy weapon in the earth. Bear splashed into the water first in merriment, having no provisions to discard.

Trailing behind on stubby legs, Cormac reached the shoreline a short while later. "Bah! Damned be the gods for the curse of dwarven legs!" he bantered, working slowly to remove his heavy shields from his arms. He removed one shield, then moments passed as he grew irritated with the buckle on the remaining piece. Impatience caused him to fumble even more as he listened to the joy of his companions. "BAH! Today be the day Cormac Shield-Slammer wishes he were known to be Cormac Dagger-Dropper!" He continued to curse himself, anger seething within him as he gripped the strap with his teeth in rage—only pulling it tighter.

Fangdarr laughed aloud at his friend's state of unrest. He watched in lighthearted humor as Cormac tried every which way to relinquish the strap's unrelenting grip to no avail. "Come, Cormac! Water feels—"

The old dwarf, too caught up with the stubborn leather that seemed to be the source of all the wickedness in the world, did not take notice to Fangdarr's sudden silence. It was Bear's whimpering that broke the dwarf's fury and brought his attention back to the water.

In an explosive instant, the enormous orc broke the surface of the water in a desperate gasp for air before disappearing below once more. Cormac could not tell if the orc was playing tricks or if something was amiss. Bear whined with more furor now, proving the latter. The dwarf charged into the water.

In the depths, Fangdarr struggled immensely. After the initial shock, he steeled his determination and peered into the murky water. He could only see blurred silhouettes of his assailant; nonetheless, he was gripped tightly by what seemed to be half a dozen long, rope-like appendages. They entwined his body entirely—putting even his impressive stature to shame—as they squeezed and dragged him further into the deep.

He fought against the strong tendrils with all his might. Each time he ripped one from his skin, tearing flesh with each removal, it simply rewound itself anew elsewhere on his body. Already he could feel a tightness in his lungs as his muscles consumed more and more oxygen in their struggle. The water around him grew cooler and darker the deeper he was pulled down.

Cormac splashed into the water and immediately noticed the steep drop off. His concern for Fangdarr became absolute for he knew he would be of no use past this point. The armor that served as his protection against steel and wood was merely a death sentence here. He could not hope to remove it in time, nor could he manage to swim against the pull of the armor's weight that would surely sink him to the bottom of the lake—wherever that may be. The dwarf shouted for his friend in panic. Long had it been since he experienced such helplessness. He could only watch in anxious horror, unknowing of the fate of his ally.

Bubbles formed a spear's throw from where he stood—surely air escaping from the trapped orc. Tears formed in Cormac's eyes. Each shout became louder than the last as he called to his friend. The despair of his uselessness hit him like an ogre's maul. Bear too whimpered for her master before diving into the darkened water, leaving the distraught captain to his madness. Not long after, she ascended and remained afloat, sending beckoning roars in the direction of the bubbles.

Fangdarr, still fully entangled in the monster's tentacles, was nearing his final breath. His vision dulled, bringing darkness ever closer. Sheer rage filled him with adrenaline. The legacy of Fangdarr would not be ended in a field such as this. In his last few breaths, his strategy changed. Rather than fighting the unyielding grip of the beast, he allowed himself to be pulled. Closer and closer he was dragged. Right up to the mouth of the monster. Now, within close quarters, Fangdarr began *his* assault.

Large hands clasped on each side of the beak-like mouth of the being now attempting to swallow him. Fighting through the restricting appendages, the hulking orc pulled, his enraged state granting him more power. Even though his muscles lacked oxygen, he managed an earth-shattering heave. Beneath the water, the cracking of bone echoed loudly as the maw of the creature pushed deep into its own brain. In an instant the relentless grip loosened around the orc, but still, he remained entangled as the suctioned limbs held fast, pulling him with only the limp weight of the beast now. The orc's rage subsided as quickly as it had come, unable to be sustained in his depleted form. His eyes blurred entirely, and Fangdarr's consciousness slipped away.

Cormac and Bear waited in anticipation. The dwarf was now kneeling in the waist-high water, sobbing uncontrollably. The glimmering memories of his mate and son flashed painfully through him. Though never forgotten, the pain of their deaths had buried itself deep within his mind in order to aid his survival of their passing. Now, those same memories which had roused him from countless nights of fitful sleep came crashing back. Only this time they were met with the doomed fate of Fangdarr, playing right in front of his eyes.

"Fangdarr!" he continued to shout as snot and saliva dripped from his nose and chin. Between his sobs, he never stopped shouting. He cared nothing for threats he may draw to himself in that moment from the surrounding wood. The dwarf only could stare intently at the bubbles slowly dying just out of reach.

Bear nudged the saddened dwarf with her wet nose. "Bah! Get away, ye damned beast! Why could ye not help him?! Ye can swim, ye blitherin' melon!" he berated her in anger, swatting harmlessly at the animal. Still, she nudged and whimpered, then lightly grabbed hold of his shield-less arm and gave a slight tug. "What!? What do ye want from me!?" Then his eyes were drawn to the water once more, where far out across the lake, he saw something floating—a hulking black mass that could only be an orc wrapped in the tentacles of a monster.

"FANGDARR!" Cormac called out. No movement came from the floating form. It continued to drift to the south. The dwarf hardened his resolve and addressed the animal still tugging at his arm. "Come, Bear!"

The pair rushed back to shore, pausing only to pick up his beloved shield as well as Driktarr. Against all instinct, he strapped his shield to his arm quickly. No fumbling this time. How he would ever manage to carry his shield and the axe that matched his own size while rushing through the thick foliage along the lake's shore was beyond him. But he had no choice.

Soon they were off, speeding through the forest along the edge of the lake while Cormac kept a watchful eye on the water in hopes of tracking the orc. He had already lost sight of the mass but knew the flow would carry him into the marshes. Night was nearly upon them, but the dwarf who previously had been immobilized in helplessness sped on. He would not be deterred.

CHAPTER THIRTY-ONE
MARSHES

Slowly his eyes opened. His mouth tasted of blood and mud, and around him, he could smell a clinging death. The scent lingered in his nose, drawing a wretched gag. As his vision began to restore, he felt the foreign embrace of objects clutched to his body. Faded memory of recent events eluded the orc until he looked below to see the tangled limbs of the creature wrapped loosely around him. Willing himself to move, he grimaced in pain as he roughly extracted the tendrils. Time had lessened their suction, yet still he could feel his skin being torn.

In his grogginess, he stood in the deep mud of the wet terrain. His confusion lifted as he pieced together his surroundings. Marshlands. The Tusks could be seen to the south, confirming his bearings. Fangdarr stretched his aching body and moaned in agony. Nearly half his skin had been ripped away by the monster that had dragged him to its domain, and blood flowed freely from the large wounds. As if on instinct, he searched for his treasured weapon to no avail. How he truly wished for its healing.

Each movement etched pain into his expression. The orc's anger simmered at the thought of showing such weakness. His yellow, glowing orbs looked over the creature that had sought to end him. Him. Fangdarr. To end his legacy beneath the murky waters of a lake! No field of glory. No carnage surrounding him as he finally fell to overwhelming odds. No. To a cowardly creature that hid in the shadow of an abyss, waiting for a misfortunate creature to stumble into its trap.

Fangdarr kicked the squishy bulbous mass that could only have been the creature's head. Again. And again. He kicked in rage at the monster that had tried to bring upon him an unacceptable fate. A fate that would dismiss all that he had claimed in conquest, as if a king were to fall by slipping on ice. His heavy foot crashed a dozen times into the flesh before finally breaking through. Black ooze and blood mixed with the sludge-like water of the marsh.

Pleased with himself, Fangdarr steadied himself once more. However, weariness had other plans for the exhausted orc. In his weakened state, his pride was not enough to support his towering frame, and he crashed into the earth onto his back. Fangdarr lay in the putrid liquid once more, chest heaving as it sought for breath. His memory had failed to recall that he had lost consciousness only a few moments prior. A heavy sigh blew past his lips and around his enlarged fangs as he accepted the rest.

*****

Cormac and Bear sped through the wood on the outskirts of the lake, continuing their sprint downstream in search of Fangdarr. The dwarf's burning muscles shot jolts of pain through his feet and legs begging him to stop. He paid no heed. Onward they traversed the foliage before finally reaching the edge of the Echoed Marshes.

"He has to be here somewhere, Bear," Cormac panted. Eerie fog swirled everywhere, making it impossible to see more than a few paces ahead of them. The dwarf laid a hand on the beast, making sure they did not become separated. From where they stood, the marshes spread into an ever-widening web. Their friend could be anywhere. A tenday could pass before they scoured the whole place, even more if the fog persisted. Cormac pushed away thoughts of the impossible task before them as they slowly pressed on.

*****

Stirring once more from the tar-like muck, Fangdarr rolled to his side while caressing his now-throbbing skull. Finally, the headache subsided and allowed him to see clearly. In his last recollection, it had been evening. Now, he sat alone in the pitch of night as low fog drifted over the water underneath the moon.

Fangdarr slowly groaned to his feet and once again assessed his wounds. The sight was grisly, to say the least. Pus seeped from the sores and infection had already begun to set in. A dozen leeches latched hungrily to his torn skin, feasting on his blood. His expression turned to disgust as he squashed one of the engorged parasites, causing it to explode bloodily in his hand. Fangdarr growled as he expelled the remaining bloodsuckers from their feast.

Nearly naked and weaponless, the orc considered his options. By his position in relation to the mountain range, he could tell he was not too far south of the Lake, though he could not determine how far east or west. He was not familiar with the marshlands, nor did he care for them. Making a trek in either direction was a risk that would either bring him to the edge of the harsh environment or deeper into its interior.

Heading south was the goal, but what of his allies? What if they came into the Echoed Marshes in search of him? Fangdarr could not risk the lives of his companions in such a fruitless search. It would be impossible for Cormac to track him in this watery muck. No. He must press on.

Fangdarr sniffed the air around him. It was thick with the smell of rotting carcasses—though that may have been the beast he just slew. The fog was thickening, sending an opaque shroud over the moonlight above. He hated this place. Isolation and emptiness were all he felt here. A chill ran down his spine shaking the proud chieftain from his normally unshakeable fearlessness—the beginning stitches of a blanket of terror. What if he fell in this desolate place?

Sheer stubbornness shook his thoughts away.

He shifted his attention to the noise that echoed in his ears. He had not noticed it before, but now he could hear it: a faint sound through the marsh. Fangdarr could not quite place it. It was both familiar and foreign. Warm and cold. Welcoming and warning. The seductive sound came from the south, from deep inside the marsh. Begging. Pleading.

Every instinct within Fangdarr tugged at him. *Flee! Escape this place!* Yet, the enchanting sound—naught but a whisper—told him to fight those instincts. And in his weakened state, Fangdarr could not deny the trance. His feet carried him slowly, deeper into the wasteland. With each step, the whisper gradually grew stronger.

He trudged through the muck for a few minutes, ignoring the drain on his legs as he was forced to pull his stuck limbs from the thickness. As he trudged closer to the sweet, embracing sound, it heightened as if his advancing presence increased its eagerness. Another song joined the first. Then a third. All melodies made identical promises to the mystified orc, echoing in his mind. Fangdarr found his eyelids growing heavy as he drifted closer to the origin of the nocturnal threnodies. In his narrow vision, he caught glimpses of rotted corpses riveted to the earth around him, nearly swallowed whole by the ravenous mud.

Dozens of them.

The orc's previous instincts that had begged for him to turn and run shouted ever louder now. *FLEE! NOW!* Fangdarr's enchantment wavered, and his eyes opened wider to inspect his environment. That single flicker of clarity was enough for him to catch sight of his assailants: a trio of withered beings drifting with ease ever nearer.

Their likeness seemed that of specters. Hollow, intangible, threatening. Yet, they were real. He knew it. Their songs grappled him with the strength of ten of the beasts of the depths—an unseen strength that the great orc could not hope to overpower or withstand. They drifted in and closed in on him. Fangdarr's yellow eyes had no luster anymore. They looked ahead—directly into the eyes of one the fiends—but saw nothing. Their enchantment had anchored him down and taken hold of his mind. The great chieftain could only remain immobilized as the maw of the bedeviled specter opened impossibly wide.

"GYAH!!!" Cormac shouted, slamming a shield heavily into the villain a moment before it consumed the head of his friend. Despite their apparent intangibility, the creature crashed into the sludge. "So, ye *are* real!" the dwarf exclaimed. "Well, that's unfortunate for ye." He punctuated his statement with a follow-up stab of his shield blade into the neck of the hollow monster. A shrill shriek escaped as bluish mist erupted around the steel with a hiss.

"Ye yella-bellied good-for-nothing specters sought to eat me friend!" Cormac shouted as he alternated each arm in vicious thrusts deep into the pinned fiend.

Bear let out a roar as she chased one of the remaining foes away from the battlefield. It wailed in fear as the beast nipped at its curtails. Careful not to drift too far from her comrades, Bear, once confident her enemy was disengaged from the fight, returned to her companions.

Fangdarr's befuddlement was immense as his mind returned to him. The echoing songs of his attackers had ceased due to more pressing matters. With the veil lifted from his consciousness, the orc took notice to Cormac and nearly jumped for joy.

"Cormac!" Fangdarr shouted to his friend. He watched as the dwarf angrily unleashed a flurry of stabs into the long-deceased target beneath him. The old dwarf's frenzy halted when he heard his friend's voice.

"Fang!" he turned toward the orc, blue blood dripping from every edge of his nose and jaw. "Bothain's beard, orc! I thought I'd never see ye again!"

The hulking orc could only smile.

Just then, the last remaining specter trampled into him with an unfathomable heft, considering its weightless appearance and tackled him into the muck, while biting down onto his shoulder. Now Fangdarr was angry. Never in his life had he been so pushed around as he had been that day. The rage filled him entirely as his hatred for the monster that had whispered incomprehensible, echoed promises broke to the surface. Brow furrowed, mouth agape, his large fangs exposed, he gave off a defiant roar before biting down onto the shoulder of the monster that likewise held him.

Now was his time. This specter could not hope to best him in a contest of strength. Fangdarr's jaw clamped down more tightly. Disgusting blue smoke and blood filled his mouth, but such distasteful liquid could not deter Fangdarr from his prey. It only added fuel to his rage. All the muscles in his body sent their force into the bite. The fiendish ghoul wailed in pain, breaking free from its own grip. Still, Fangdarr did not relent. He bit harder until, finally, the withered flesh gave way, spraying the surrounding area in blue carnage as the monster's shoulder shattered beneath Fangdarr's maw.

Fangs stained blue, the orc spit the large chunk of flesh into the sludge at his feet. Meanwhile, his foe rolled in spasms against the ground while fruitlessly trying to staunch the flow. Cormac appeared next to his ally, handing him his trusted axe. Fangdarr looked it over in appreciation, his eyes glimmering with gratitude. Never had he and his weapon been separated for so long, especially in such a dire moment. Fangdarr looked at his wounds. They still festered and oozed, but not for much longer.

As the ghoul flopped like a beached fish in the muck, clutching to its last few precious moments of life, the orc raised Driktarr high in the air. Never should the specters have sought to call to him. The thought of being ended by whispers in a desolate marshland only reinvigorated the orc's dwindling anger. His heavy, magical weapon slammed down with the weight of all the souls lost to the unbreakable song of these monsters. Even against the squishy, wet ground the axe had no trouble slicing through the entirety of the specter.

Fangdarr's torn flesh spit out the diseased corrosion that had already settled in his body before mending together. A hundred new scars formed, showing the pattern of the suction-cup tentacles of the abyssal creature that had rent him so. He had never healed such a disastrous number of wounds in a single instance before. The energy from the specter flowed through Driktarr's blood-thirsty blade and deep into his body, renewing him with an overwhelming surge of vitality and vigor.

The orc's fingers trembled as the final throes of the intense revival diminished. Oh, how truly good it felt. How he now yearned and craved for more of that rejuvenating power. He raised his weapon again before crashing it back down into the already dead villain that was slowly sinking deeper into the mud. Nothing. He cursed aloud. Again, his axe boomed down into the body of the specter but to no avail.

Fangdarr shouted at his prey, angry that its lifeforce had already fled from its physical form. He wanted to feed on it more—to feel that surge of life pulse through his veins again. Undeniable rage began to form in the orc once more, but before it could spark to flame, Cormac placed a hand on his friend's shoulder.

"Ye're done, lad. It's over."

The orc shot him a glare of flashing anger but calmed himself instantly. Seeing the blood-covered dwarf who had saved him from his most feared end brought him back to reality. He fell to his knees, disregarding the subsiding energy in his body, and tightly embraced Cormac. Tears streamed down his face as he hugged the friend he had come to love—the ally who stopped at nothing and risked all just to see to his well-being.

Cormac held him in return, hiding his own sobs. "There, there, lad. Yer safe now," the dwarf said, understanding the orc's fear. "This be not the place that Fangdarr the Great meets his doom. Ye had me scared sick, don't ye doubt. Bah! Never thought I'd hear meself say that for the sake of an orc."

CHAPTER THIRTY-TWO

CHAKAL

"Mama!" Lilyana exclaimed with excitement as she jumped from her straw bed and embraced her bound mother. Malice clutched her eyes shut in an attempt to staunch the flow of her tears. The young girl retracted and put her face directly in front of her mother's. Her tiny hands slowly reached up to slide over the woman's features, searching for familiarity.

A moment passed in silence as Malice remained frozen—not due to the ropes that bound her frame but due to the maelstrom of conflicting emotions crashing in her mind. Lilyana's eyes widened at finding a known pattern of freckles along the left temple of the captive. "It is you!"

Malice could not contain herself. Her sobs came harshly as she felt her daughter clutch her once more. Oh, how she wished to be free of her captivity to return that loving squeeze. Malice—no, in this moment she was Alice once more—could feel the slow progression of Lilyana's tiny fingers making their way up her face then across her brow to her hair. All the passionate hatred the woman had come to accept and know for the past four years simply drained away.

Lilyana giggled as her mother's golden hair tickled the innocent skin between her fingers. Another sob came out from Malice. How many of those giggles had she missed? How many scraped knees, curious questions, and tantrums had she let pass in her absence? Never again, the determined woman thought to herself. Her monstrous husband was gone. There was only the future—only this love she could now touch and cherish.

Malice closed her eyes in deep reflection as she tried to calmly let go of all her past pain. Knowing her sweet-hearted daughter was there was enough to start breaking the grip of her mental chains. But in her deep thought, she failed to notice Lilyana's hands stop their comforting scrape against her skin. Still locked in her mind, her eyes remained closed. That was until she heard the voice.

"Now you will finally play."

She knew that voice. Instinct triggered her response at the hidden character as she spat back in disgust, "Never! I have no mind for your antics!" Her angered eyes scanned the corners of the room for the intruder to no avail.

A small, evil chuckle came—seemingly from all directions—before he appeared in the window. "We'll see . . ." he replied with the most sinister grin ever formed on a face.

The woman spouted curses at him as he effortlessly dropped from the window to the cobblestone street below. Tormag was the first to act, rushing down the stairs and out onto the street in pursuit of the shadowy figure. It wasn't until he was in the empty street that Tormag heard the sound he knew would come. Wailing.

"Mama . . .?" Lilyana sputtered weakly as she lay strewn upon the bedroom floor, completely dissected at the waist, a pool of blood growing quickly beneath her. Malice screamed in anguish at the sight. Lilyana looked to her in confusion, uncertain as to why she could no longer move her legs. Bound tightly in her chair, Malice wailed non-stop. She could only watch on in horror as the life slowly drained from her daughter—the kind-hearted child that had instantly forgiven her for her past mistakes. At long last, they had been reunited and were looking toward a future together. But now . . .

Malice shook violently in her chair. Precious time was passing. "Release me!" she screamed at Bitrayuul. He was frozen solid, completely immobilized in shock. The half-orc's stare never broke contact with the girl as her eyes started to lose their luster. Truly, he did not know her long, and despite their kinship, he had no special bond with the poor girl, but he had grown especially fond of her during their journey to Riveton. No matter how seasoned he was, this was not war. This was not battle. His wits were not prepared to watch such innocence butchered, especially so close to those who would give their lives to protect her.

Seeing he would be of no use to her, Malice strained against her ropes even more. Now, Lilyana was aware of the situation and was pleading for her mother. "Mama, Mama! H-help me . . ."

The woman shrieked and cried incessantly. She had to break free. All her muscles tensed until . . . *Snap!* She was free! In an instant she was on the floor, her clothes soaking in the blood of her child. Despite the girl's state, Malice scooped up her upper half and clutched her tightly as her sobs and wails filled the room. It was pain like she had never known. She felt the light breaths growing even more faint against her neck. The gut-wrenching twist in her stomach only increased in those final moments.

Malice attempted to use her hand to push the escaping innards back into the girl's body, but she knew it was hopeless. There was too much blood. Malice took her hand away and let the organs fall. She took her eyes from the entrails sitting in the pool of blood and looked to her daughter's face, letting her bloodied fingers run through her daughter's similarly golden hair. "It's okay, it's okay. You'll be okay, Lily."

Tormag rushed into the room and let out a small sigh.

"Ma . . ." the girl started but could not find the strength to continue. Her eyes closed as she took her final fleeting breaths. One final embrace came from her mother as she squeezed her daughter tightly, pushing out even more gore.

"I'm so sorry. This is all my fault."

Tormag noticed Bitrayuul still had not broken eye contact and nudged him from his stupor. The half-orc's eyes blinked a dozen times as he once again took in the scene. He had watched it all unfold, but his mind had blocked the vision from his eyes to protect him from the horror. As he noticed Malice clutching his half-sister in the last moment of her life, gore all about, he could not stop the flow of tears that now made their way down his face. The large hybrid fell to his knees. Why did he freeze? Why did he not help her? What kind of man was he to simply look on with unseeing eyes as the girl pleaded for her life? No. Not a man. Only *half* a man, he thought. Bitrayuul's guilt was too extreme. He wished for naught but to go to the girl and hold her with her mother. But he did not deserve to.

A few more moments went by before Tormag walked lightly over to Malice. She still clutched tightly to Lilyana, though the girl had passed already. The mother's wails had died down to incoherent sobs, soundless except for the sporadic intake of air. The dwarf softly placed a rough hand on her shoulder. "It's time, lass."

Malice shoved him away, "No, no! She's not gone! Not yet . . ." Lilyana's head swung limply as her mother squeezed her once more, hoping to will the life back into her. Her yowls began anew as she realized it truly was over.

Tormag again placed a single hand against her in comfort before speaking softly. "Come, she needs t' be put t' rest." He knew she would not comply, of course, so he let her carry out her goodbye for as long as she needed.

As her cries of sorrow began to wane, the distraught woman slowly rose from the crimson puddle, her dark clothing and leather straps, dripping with the thick, viscous liquid. Her blood-soaked vestments caused each movement she made to make a small squelching sound. If she took notice, Malice gave no evidence of concern. All her attention was on picking up Lilyana's lifeless lower half and putting the two halves back together as if the girl could be whole once again.

Taking every precaution to not break apart the two parts of her daughter, Malice took minor steps toward the door of the room. Bitrayuul received a quick smack on the back of his arm from Tormag, breaking his grim stupor once again. "Bit! What are ye doin'? Are ye goin' t' help her or not?"

The distracted half-orc slowly turned his gaze to his father, his lip quivering uncontrollably as he attempted to speak. "I-I . . . j— . . . I-I . . ."

Tormag took keen notice of his son's level of distress and gave a heavy sigh before stating, "Son, if there be any part o' ye that thinks ye are t' blame fer this, ye'd be wrong. Hold fast t' the pain in yer heart. It be a villain who did this, not yerself. Ye best believe we're fer knowin' who that devil was. And we'll get our vengeance, don't ye doubt. Fer now, we need t' comfort Malice and put the wee lass t' rest. Aye?"

Bitrayuul, though still overwhelmed by guilt, gave a small unsteady sigh. "Father, what you say is true. But it does not erase the carnage painted in my mind forever, nor the guilt I will always feel for not protecting that girl. All I did was shepherd her to her end. My nightmares of this night will fill my dreams for more moons than I can predict. It is not death that brings me this pain, but shame."

The old dwarf could only do the same for his adopted son as he had done for Malice—the only thing he knew to do when words failed. His thick hand found its way to the blade-riddled shoulder of Bitrayuul. He had no helpful words. He could only be present.

Tormag and Bitrayuul slowly made their way out of the room behind Malice who had barely made it to the middle of the staircase. As they completed their mournful descent, Calus rose from the bar. "What in the hell happened!?"

The dwarf shot him an angry glare and raised a finger to his mouth for silence. Calus shrank back a bit but could not rip his eyes from the sight of the gore-covered woman carrying the limp form of the little girl who had slept at his bar that afternoon. When he realized it was Lilyana, he gave a soft gasp.

Malice and Bitrayuul continued out of the tavern slowly. Luckily, the woman had a firm hold on her daughter and did not expose the grievous dissection to Calus. Tormag trudged to the boy behind the bar and spoke lightly. "Son, an assassin attacked us. He came through the window and put an end t' that poor girl. Now, we know this looks bad. Don't ye doubt, we've had a hell o' a night. We need t' bury the girl, then we need t' be gone as soon as can be. There be a lot o' blood upstairs, boy. Normally, I'd never leave a mess behind at a tavern I be rentin' from. But I'll be blunt. None of us can stomach goin' in that room again. So . . ." he fumbled through his pockets briefly before producing a single gold coin and slapping it onto the countertop, "take this fer the trouble we've caused, and fer cleanin' the mess the villain left."

The young boy nodded somberly and with a pained smile, graciously accepted the coin. Though he had overpaid, Tormag felt sorry for what he was asking the boy to do. No amount of gold would erase the memories he was about to have after cleaning that room. Nonetheless, he took his leave and easily caught up to his friends outside of the tavern.

After nearly a long while, they reached the graveyard on the other side of the expansive town. By now, a light glow came from just below the horizon as the sun rose toward dawn. It was nearly morning and the city's residents were starting their routines for the new day.

Tormag led Malice to the undertaker who lay in the dirt next to three freshly dug holes in the ground. "Oye, these lots available?" he asked of the man.

The wiry man looked up from his reverie and gave a smile—with more than a few teeth rotted and others missing entirely. "They are not. A family slain the day before last has them claimed." His smile grew even wider at the mention of the fate of the family.

The gruff dwarf hated dealing with such folk. Those who took a perverted joy in the ill will of others sat wrong with him. "Aye, when are they due?"

"Hmm . . ." pondered the gravekeeper, feigning surprise as he looked at the brightening horizon. "My, my, they should be here any minute!"

This time Bitrayuul stepped forward and squared up against the dirty human, raising a bladed gauntlet to his neck. Instantly the man shrank back in fright and meekly stuttered, "O-okay! Th-they are not meant to b-be here until the afternoon!"

Tormag prodded the keeper with his finger. "Ye'll bury this poor lass for us, then, aye?" He handed the man a silver coin after his request, ever the honorable dwarf, even to beings who didn't deserve it. The worker nodded his head—as much as he could with a blade pressed to his neck—in acceptance and flashed another disgusting smile.

"Come, girl, bring her here," Tormag beckoned to Malice. Slowly she crept into the shallow grave and laid Lilyana onto the dirt below. She was careful to continue keeping both halves held together, but once her grip relinquished the girl fell apart slightly causing portions of her innards to fall out. The grime-covered undertaker could not hold in his smile as his degenerate thoughts took the mental image to mind. He noticed the dwarf watching him, and quickly hid his smile and produced a small, white, linen sheet from a pack of supplies he kept nearby. The man offered the cloth to the girl's mother, as was the custom.

Malice tenderly pushed the girl back together before wrapping the cloth over her diminutive form. It performed its purpose, though it too began instantly soaking up blood until it was stained crimson.

Tormag pulled both Bitrayuul and Malice to the side as the man started to fill the hole with loose earth. Each of the group members said a final silent farewell to the adolescent girl who left the world too soon for a purpose unknown.

Bitrayuul allowed a few moments to pass by in silence before asking the question he had been waiting to ask. "Malice, who was that assailant?" Tormag was curious as well but wished the half-orc had waited at least a while longer before putting such a difficult question on the woman.

She wiped the tears from her face and finally broke eye contract with the half-filled grave as the last bit of white linen was covered with dirt. "His name is Chakal."

"Why did he . . ." began the orc-kin before stopping mid-sentence.

She understood his meaning. "He killed Lilyana because I would not play his game."

"What game, lass?" asked Tormag.

She let out an exhausted sigh. "His twisted fantasy. He seeks to be the most notorious assassin to have ever lived. To do so, he demands other assassins to face him—once they begin to gain a shred of recognition. He has requested I face him a handful of occasions in the past, but I have always refused."

"Then why would he not simply kill you?" Bitrayuul asked.

"Because his ego knows no bounds. He *must* prove he is better. So, therefore, he must beat his competition in willful combat. I discovered this long ago, which is the only reason I have survived his stalking, though it was always borrowed time. My avoidance only increased his appetite and forced him to take measures to tempt me to accept his challenge."

"So, he killed Lilyana, simply to push you to fight him?"

"Yes." Her eyes closed as the words gave credence to her most painful thoughts. She was the reason her daughter had been killed. "He is brutal beyond words, as you have seen."

Tormag spoke up, "So, are ye plannin' on returnin' the favor?"

The woman seemed taken aback by the absurd comment. "Return the favor? Me? You think I can take him on?! You do not know this monster. He cannot be culled! He is a limitless demon sent to bring the end I have for so long wished for. You think I am not filled with rage and disgust at the thought of him? Of what he has done?! Of course I am! I will ever be! Yet, once again, you speak of that which you do not know. *You*, who has brought this ill fate to my doorstep by pulling my past to the present and informing the most brutal of enemies of the only weakness he could use against me in his sinister game.

"I *cannot* beat him. I could *never* beat him. I picked up a blade for the first time nearly twenty years ago and have used it sparingly compared to Chakal. He is over a thousand years old! A *thousand*! His wicked blades have ended more than all other assassins combined. Chakal *is* that which he seeks already. There are no others of our trade who could hope to compare. Yet, still he pursues us. Even now, I promise you he is watching us, waiting for me, hiding in plain view with his wicked grin. You think me capable? You are wrong.

"I feel the fire burning bright and ferociously inside me that I know would drive me to hunt him down for what he has done. I always will. But I will run. As I have always ran when conflict is at its thickest. As I ran after my imprisonment. As I ran after discovering the wickedness of my husband. I will run. I can only run. Do not think I care nothing for the fate of my Lilyana. Do not dare think that! But I will run. I will run until Chakal grows bored of me and leaves me to my life."

Tormag and Bitrayuul stood in silence, unsure of whether she would continue her tantrum. Her mind had been broken on numerous occasions, and it seemed the fragmented shards of her mentality caused her to take on two personalities. She easily fluctuated between rage and pain, especially in situations where she became stressed. Her range of emotions was extreme. They watched as her rage-filled tears flowed heavily down her face.

"You can come with us," Bitrayuul stated, drawing a wide-eyed expression from the old dwarf.

Tormag grumbled under his breath, "Oh, sure, not like we're already huntin' a damned *dragon*. Why not add the most brutal killer in the whole damned world while we're at it?" Bitrayuul heard him, and scowling under his mask, turned his helmeted head toward the dwarf. "Aye, ye can come," Tormag relented.

Malice wiped her face again, replacing the tears with streaks of blood from her stained hand. "Thank you. Where to?"

"T' the stables, me feet grow tired o' all this walkin'." Tormag replied.

CHAPTER THIRTY-THREE
DISHONOR

They slowed their mounts as they approached the western gate of Adderhaven. Their three horses had come at a fair price. Luckily, Tormag thought to bring enough coin for the journey's many unexpected expenses. Malice followed closely behind Bitrayuul and Cormac as the guards called down from their post.

"Who goes there? What is your business here?"

"We are Tormag and Bitrayuul. Our business is only to pass through." Bitrayuul announced their names with trepidation. Their first visit to this town was not a welcome one, and they had only been spared because of the presence of Lilyana. Now, she was gone. Would Meilan the Guard Captain be so generous this time? Tormag had suggested simply going around, but the town took up the entire expanse of land between the forking Adder's Tongue. To go around would be impossible without being spotted.

Meilan approached the gate with a sigh. He called down to the group with disdain in his voice. "Greetings, once more. I had thought we had said our final farewell on your most recent visit."

"Aye, same as we, don't ye doubt!" Tormag stated. "We're only passin' through, though. We considered goin' around but figured that would just cause suspicion. If ye'd like, with yer permission, we can still take that route."

The embellished man twisted his goatee in thought. He truly embraced the idea of them never stepping foot in his town but had to consider the downsides. After a few more moments of silence, he responded simply, "You may go around. Guards, the gate remains closed," before walking away smiling to himself.

Malice made a snide comment that only her companions could hear. "What'd you do to piss off that pompous peacock?"

Bitrayuul smiled from under his enclosed helmet but said nothing. Tormag, though, was sure to respond.

"Eh, he don't like girls." The dwarf could hardly contain his chuckling, especially after Bitrayuul burst out laughing. Malice, of course, was not accustomed to Tormag's sarcasm.

The group pecked their horses to continue around the walls of the town toward its southern end. As they were about to turn deeper into the forest, a guard approached from his post outside of the wall. "Hold, orc-kin," he called quietly to Bitrayuul, stepping slowly toward them, being careful not to draw the attention of his comrades.

"Oye, what now?" Tormag whined from his steed.

Bitrayuul simply shrugged as he waited for the man to approach. Once the gap between the two was closed, the man looked up at the half-orc. "You are the kin of Fangdarr, are you not?"

The half-orc readjusted in his saddle. Any human who knew his barbaric brother by name would most likely have vengeance in his mind. In any case, Bitrayuul remained calm and nodded in reply.

"Your brother is a good ma—," he began before correcting himself, "orc. He is a good orc. I owe him my life and hope he is well."

Bitrayuul was flabbergasted. *Fangdarr*? The kin he had known so recently to be aggressively expanding the borders of his clan, slaying all in his path? He could hardly believe his brother would save the life of a common guard. Was there some hidden motive? There was too much to speculate at the moment. He returned his attention to the man and asked, "What is your name, soldier?"

"Artemis, sir."

The half-orc nodded once more. "I shall relay the message to Fangdarr when I see him. He will be glad to hear of your kindness." The statement brought a smile to Artemis' face before he strode back to his post. Bitrayuul looked back to Tormag who only shrugged, similarly confused at the prospect of Fangdarr committing a merciful act.

From there, they broke off into the woods. First at a slow pace to avoid any cause for alarm from the guard tower, then increasing to a quick run as they turned into the Lithe heading south.

Tormag was beaming with excitement at their progress. Within half the day, they had already reached the border of the Orclands, just east of the northern point of Metridium Lake. Had they walked, it would have taken over a day, and his feet would have been aching. Dwarves were not overly fond of riding horses. They favored stouter beasts such as rams, goats, or even donkeys. Nevertheless, the old dwarf was glad in this case that he had made an exception for the benefits it brought to their journey.

With his feet unburdened, Tormag's rump now took the brunt of the battering from travel. He pulled the reins on his mount to slow it to a halt, and Bitrayuul and Malice followed suit, bringing their own steeds to rest. "Time fer a break, me thinks," the dwarf said as he awkwardly began to dismount the tall animal. After a few comical moments, Tormag finally managed to free himself from the saddle, crashing hard to the ground.

"Not fond of horses, dwarf?" Malice asked, laughing at his fate.

He jumped up with a groan and rubbed his sore rear. "What in the name o' Bothain's beard is the point o' such a tall creature? Might as well ride a damned dragon! This creature just be an ogre with hooves!" The woman laughed at his comments, rubbing the snout of her own horse.

Bitrayuul smiled at Malice's improved mood. She had—understandably—said little since Riveton. But now she smiled and laughed openly. It brought him comfort to know she was not dwelling too much on her pain. However, he suspected there could be a deeper underlying influence at play within her mind. No mother, even estranged, should overcome the death of her child so quickly, especially under the brutal circumstances that they had lost Lilyana. The half-orc was certain she was in such a broken state that she did not even recall the previous day's events. If that was true, Bitrayuul was envious of such a state of despair. He had not slept since before Lilyana's murder, too fearful of the vivid nightmares he would be forced to endure.

By the time the woman finished tying up all three horses, Tormag had a small fire started and was already pulling out his favorite cooking apparatus and setting it up. It was a simple thin sheet of steel, flattened to the width of a thick piece of cloth about the size of a hand. The dwarf shoved four sticks vertically into the earth in a rectangle around the small flame before gingerly setting the sheet atop the makeshift supports. Within a few moments, the steel glowed a dull red. His mouth salivated at the sight, knowing the meat he was pulling from his provisions would soon be cooked and in his eager stomach.

While the horses grazed happily on the thick grass and plentiful berry bushes nearby, Malice and Bitrayuul slumped to the dirt across the fire from their dwarven chef and watched him season the scraps of cooked meat with a small canister of accumulated spices.

"There we are, should be good t' go!" he said, pulling a piece from the steel plate and popping it directly into his mouth. "Ooooh, careful, the lads are still angry," Tormag added after searing his tongue. His allies shook their head at the obvious remark before pulling their own bites from the fire.

"Would you care if I were to join you?" came a voice from just behind Malice. The blood in her face instantly drained as if she had stared Death himself in the face. It was him.

Chakal lounged lazily against a tree in complete nonchalance, his hands resting easily atop his head, hiding some of the lustrous beauty of the white-golden hair that reached to his shoulder blades. Malice continued to shrink in fear, still having yet to turn to see him. In contrast, Bitrayuul and Tormag were both already up in arms ready to take on this relentless pursuer. The half-orc scanned the area and could not help but be intimidated. How did he find them? More to the point, how did he catch up to them? There were no hoofbeats, nor a steed in sight. They had not even heard him as he sat a short distance behind them. This elf's reputation seemed to have merit after all.

Chakal sighed deeply in feigned sadness, "I take that as a no?"

Bitrayuul and Tormag inched closer. Still the elf held his wicked grin, as if challenging them to make a move. Then, in an instant, it vanished, replaced by a genuinely friendly smile. "Oh, come now. I have no interest in you two. You are free to enjoy your meal. I am here for *her*," he said, pointing a finger to the huddled Malice, who now quivered in fear.

"Well you can't have her," Bitrayuul stated defiantly. "She's with us, nor does she wish to partake in your game, elf."

The previously friendly disposition of the elf changed to one of hatred, anger, and disgust. "It is not for her to choose!" he shouted menacingly. "Have I not proven the lengths of just how far I will go? Have I not been patient and fair until now? You tell me! I am here for one purpose. Her *beloved* daughter would still be alive had this woman not been so weak. Had she answered my challenge long ago, no blood would have been spilled. There are rules! Rules I do not break unless forced. It was *she* that forced my hand, this treacherous wench. All I want is for her to either prove her place in this world or lie in the earth where she belongs! Do *not* get in the way again, orc-kin!" As if on cue, his face returned to its wholesome smile and his tone pleasant. "So, please, allow her to answer my call."

Bitrayuul and Tormag held their resolve and refused to move. Each looked to the other before taking a step forward. Chakal sighed with annoyance as he jumped to his feet, brandishing his weapons in a single motion. Only a curved dagger and curved shortsword sat in his hands, both of elven craftsmanship, though otherwise unappealing. "Fine. I grow tired of your nuisance. Perhaps this time she will care enough for your corpses to take to the blade."

Chakal strode forward with his weapons at his sides, his confidence and wicked smile growing with each step he took. Bitrayuul and Tormag were both seasoned fighters—not ones that many would take on single-handedly, much less as a pair. But the elf simply glided forward as if he were tasked with cutting wheat. His eyes grew wide and lustful in anticipation as he was only paces away.

"I hope you know your deaths will be meaningless, but I will enjoy them nonetheless."

Bitrayuul was about charge forward with his gauntlets when he was halted by a hand lightly gripping his arm. Careful to keep an eye on Chakal, he glanced to see Malice standing behind them.

"I will fight him," she stated calmly, as if resigned to her fate.

Chakal stopped his smooth advance and smiled.

"Lass, ye don't have t' fight him alone! We're here with ye," Tormag assured her.

She was already shaking her head. "No. He will never stop. It has to be me." Tears welled up in her eyes as she put a hand on the shoulder of each of her new companions. "Lilyana must be avenged. It was my involvement that brought her end, and I am her mother." Malice steadied herself with a long exhale and her eyes shifted to the sky. "I'm just so tired. So very tired. Tired of running, of hiding, of living in fear. All I wanted was to be left alone. To simply stop my demons from chasing me. But they shall never relent, and I must either face them or succumb. Either I will be reunited with Lilyana, or, by some rare chance, this monster will be sent to oblivion in her name. But Malice will have no others die in her place." The woman's expression shifted from one of hopelessness to anger and determination as she stared down Chakal.

The elf started clapping after her speech, still wearing that stupid grin. "Bravo, my lady. An excellent choice of last words. I do enjoy listening to the final moments of my prey. You truly get to know their character. I am glad to know you will be accepting my challenge after so long. Now," his eyes widened to accompany his ferocious smile, "shall we begin?" Chakal's elven features contorted to sheer, vigorous glee as he charged forward.

Malice rushed past Bitrayuul and Tormag as she too drew her weapons. The half-orc attempted to press forward in assistance but was caught hard by his father. "No, lad. This ain't our fight." Bitrayuul looked back to his mother, almost pleading to be allowed to proceed. The dwarf's expression remained the same, rejecting his son's request. Bitrayuul relented. They could only watch as Malice and Chakal charged toward each other.

Assassins both, each combatant preferred the unseen blade on an oblivious target—well, Malice did, she could not speak for the insatiable ego of her opponent—as opposed to open field combat. However, neither were new to such a fight. The woman charged forward to meet her enemy, her weapons drawn. She growled as she advanced, hiding her intimidation well.

Chakal was a blur of motion. As he fell within arm's reach of Malice, he allowed her to swing her serrated sword downward toward his shoulder. Then his body twisted, using as slight a movement as necessary to let the weapon sweep down harmlessly a finger-width away. Already, in that first swing, Malice's assumption of being no match for the elf was confirmed.

She hid her surprise, though, as the curved dagger in her left hand pressed forward toward his exposed abdomen—a fast attack that would likely stick any common foe with ease. But Chakal was no common foe. The elf could have easily parried the strike; instead, he shot backwards. In the time it took her to extend her arm halfway, he had managed to spring nearly back to his original location. Elves were known for possessing heightened agility and strength, but this was much more than that.

Chakal's smile never left his face. "Come now, I have been waiting for this moment for years. Did you really think I would allow it to end so quickly?"

The woman screamed in frustration as she once again charged toward her foe. Her tactics would need to change, she knew. She needed something, *anything*, to catch him off guard. But what? How could she ever hope to defeat such an opponent? As she closed the distance, she opted out of a straightforward assault and dipped her sword into the ground. Sword planted into the earth, Malice shifted her momentum by tightly gripping the pommel of her imprisoned weapon, spun around it and kicked at the elf from his left side.

A rudimentary, flourishing attack—one more for flashiness and surprise than actual effectiveness. Chakal sighed as he simply raised a hand to intercept her foot, grabbing it in mid-air. Thrown off balance, Malice fell to the ground, the elf still holding her by the foot. "Is this what I have waited for?" he asked, growing irritated. "This is pathetic! More! Show me more!" he yelled as he shoved her foot away harshly.

Flipping onto her back then back onto her feet, Malice placed her hands on her hips as she scowled back at him. "Why? Do you *really* need the recognition that you are better than me? Is it not obvious? What is the point?"

Finally, his smug smile was wiped from his face. The assassin's shoulders slumped as his head drooped downward. Had she struck a nerve? A glimmer of hope flickered in her mind. Perhaps he would spare her? Chakal lifted his head slightly with a small inhale. "I can see now that you are indeed not worthy." His hands fell to his sides limply, still holding his curved weapons loosely in his grip.

She had done it!

Against all odds, Malice had survived the encounter. An internal scream of joy filled her mind as she fought back tears. Her eyes glanced over to Bitrayuul and Tormag who looked on in confusion, not knowing what had just occurred.

"Ahahahah! *Really?* You bought that?"

Malice quickly returned her gaze to the elf. Her eyes went wide in horror as she realized he had simply been toying with her emotions. Did his torment know no bounds? She let out a groan of frustration. "Just leave me alone!"

His stupid sneer was present again, this time even wider. How he enjoyed playing with his food. Chakal had devoted his life—*a thousand years*—to becoming the most lethal assassin the world would ever know. There was more than one way to bring fear and intimidation to an opponent than just your skill with a blade. His monstrous appetite knew plenty of ways to break the resolve of an enemy. That, he thought, was what made a true assassin. A knife in the back was just one simple way to end a life. No fun when there were so many deliciously brutal alternatives.

Chakal continued to laugh maniacally as he sprinted toward his prey with lightning quickness. Malice's dagger hardly had time to raise as he struck with his own dagger, glancing the blow to the side. "Fight!" he shouted as his sword sliced through the air directly toward her exposed neck. Still off balance from the sudden assault, Malice angled her sword tip to align with the incoming weapon.

Clang! The sound of steel rang through the air as his sword clashed with hers. His strength was too great. The force behind his swing caused her own blade to cut into her shoulder. She winced from the sharp pain, but she could tell the wound was superficial. "Survive!" Chakal yelled to her face through his grinning teeth, and with another swipe of his dagger, he cut the skin along her torso before she could raise her dagger to deflect.

The woman cried out in pain, fell back a step and quickly glanced to inspect the wound. Skin deep again. He was toying with her still! Her eyes turned to Chakal who stood—with that stupid smile! —staring at her as he licked her blood from his dagger.

"Not yet," he stated coldly.

His next attack came even faster than before. Another failed attempt to prevent the blade from tearing her skin followed by another yelp of pain. This time, he did not relent. "Bleed! Bleed! Bleed! *BLEED*! Paint the earth like your sweet Lilyana. Take up your brush and spread the strokes of crimson for all to see!" he shouted in his frenzy as his superficial slices cut through her skin at speeds she could never hope to parry. His onslaught was vicious. Malice could not even comprehend his movements. Each blinding cut made her wince in pain. Instinctively she shut her eyes for just a moment. By the time they opened, she had been cut twice more.

Blood dripped slowly down her arms and legs. She was not majorly harmed anywhere, but Malice knew her fate was sealed. There was no hope. Her hands fell limply to her sides as the air stung her wounds in bitter pain. She wondered why she was even here at all. If she had only continued to deny this monster his game she would have survived for longer. Memories of Lilyana flashed through her mind. No!

I cannot! She fought her inner struggle against the pain, the hopelessness, the guilt. The images that her mind had repressed flooded back with vigor.

She relived the moment that she had embraced her daughter as her entrails fell from her severed body. A girl of only seven winters, taken in a single brutal blow simply to tempt her to fight. Now, here she stood, fighting a hopeless battle with the very monster who had orchestrated her greatest despair.

Malice screamed in rage, fueled by her memories. The resource had finally been tapped. A sealed door within her conscience that had been bolted shut for the threatening substance inside was too volatile. But there was no choice. No other option. She had to break down the door and embrace the pain. She charged forward with her mental state nearly broken, striking swiftly in murderous abandon.

"Yes! There it is! The rage I knew was dwelling inside you! Let it out! Let it breathe life into this fight!" Chakal exclaimed. This is what he had been waiting for. This was the purpose for his pursuit. Malice often held to the pattern of running in fear from her conflicts. However, he knew she was capable of something else. He knew she had a nearly limitless source of rage within her due to the events of her past—one that granted her such a rush of adrenaline and lack of logic that her only instinct was to kill in order to survive.

Her assault came swiftly: sword slice, dagger thrust, sword thrust, dual slash. She battered forward in her fury, pushing Chakal back. Yet, in her state, she could not see him. All she saw was her own blinding rage as she continued swinging her weapons. Attack, attack, attack, attack! Malice's weapons whirred through the air as the gleams of steel were barely visible.

Back further and further the elf went as pure instinct kept her moving, guiding her rage and spurring her movements. But she could not see him. Nor could she see his smile growing wider than ever before.

"This is what I have been searching for!" he shouted loudly as she continued her assault. "Ahahaha! Finally! A true opponent!" Now that he had unleashed her full potential, he allowed her to remain on the offensive in order to gauge her. Above all else, he wanted to see her maximum performance, and he was not disappointed. Now was the time for the real challenge.

Chakal shifted his stance, flicking his weapons outward in a simultaneous parry of Malice's sword and dagger. With her torso unguarded, he thrust both of his weapons forward. Her sword managed to tilt inwards and deflect the elven sword from her body, but his dagger slipped through. His glee was apparent as he felt the blade sink deeply into the side of her stomach, just above the hip and below the kidney. His glee was short-lived, though, as her own dagger plunged through his right shoulder.

He gritted his teeth through the pain and cursed his own stupidity. How could he forget her current state of abandon? She felt no pain, only the emotional turmoil he had set free. Normally his strike would have stolen the strength from his enemy's counterattack. But without pain there was no interruption to her retaliation. Chakal pulled his dagger from her stomach and punched upwards with the pommel, striking her in the chin and breaking her balance.

Malice's dagger came away from his shoulder, dripping with the purplish blood of the elf. He kicked her leg just below the knee causing her to buckle. Her dagger hand fell to the ground to break her fall, allowing the elf to land a blow to her temple with the steel pommel of his dagger. Blood poured freely down her face and into her eye. Luckily, she had managed to tie up his left hand with her sword arm, preventing him from utilizing the longer weapon.

Her rage began to dwindle as the blow to her head disoriented her. Chakal could have ended the fight then and there with a stab to the head, but he could not. The elf *needed* to bring her back to sanity now. His wish to see and challenge her at her best had been fulfilled. Even more so, she had managed to strike him, something no other challengers he had faced could claim. It drove him mad to the point of hatred that one such as her could break through his defenses and draw blood. The assassin wanted nothing more in that moment than to bring a much-deserved end to her life. However, he could not. Not yet. First, he must bring her back to reality so that she may see, know, and feel the pain he was inflicting upon her. Without seeing his effect written upon the face of his targets, he felt no thrill.

The sadistic elf backed away as Malice blinked away the blood from her eye, breaking the disassociated concentration that fueled her emotions. No longer did she instinctively lash out in blind rage. Her head now pounded with the blunt trauma Chakal had inflicted to her skull, removing her ability to feed off of her memories. With that single blow, the limitless fountain of energy Malice had been using to improve her prowess had been sealed off once more.

"Wh-what happened?" she asked in a daze, showing no recollection of her previous trance. She looked around and saw Chakal standing in front of her. Rising to her feet, the woman gazed at her weapons. Purple blood dripped from her dagger. Elvish blood! "I cut you?" Malice asked incredulously.

Chakal's face turned to a scowl. "It seems I underestimated you. No matter. You have returned to your former self. Our duel has come to its final stage," he said coldly.

Confusion still swirled around her mind, but the assassin strode toward her. Two paces away. One pace away. The elf raised his sword over her head, ready to land the final blow. Malice held her weapons in her hands but could only offer a pitiful defense against the inevitable attack. The blood trapped beneath her skull from the large bruise pressed ever more forcefully against her brain. Her eyes clamped shut from the pain and fear of the blow.

Sword arm still raised, the assassin made sure to place the grin she so hated on his face again, despite her not looking at him. The small joy in knowing it would be the last face she would see made him happy. His arm began its descent, aimed directly for the top of her head, seeking to shatter the skull that contained her shattered mind. A fitting end, the elf thought.

Twang! Chakal growled in anger, his expression shifting to hatred once more as the arrow sank into his right pectoral muscle. His eyes went from the shaft of the arrow protruding from his chest to its source. Bitrayuul stood a spear's throw away with another arrow knocked on his large great-bow, Kwip.

"Grr . . . This is not your concern, orc-kin!" the elf shouted.

Another arrow flew toward him. This time, he caught the shaft in mid-air with his hand and threw it to the ground. Chakal's arm was still raised above the quivering woman's head. The assassin considered his next action before it was made for him. As the next arrow whistled in his direction, he simply vanished in a wisp of smoke.

Bitrayuul and Tormag were already running toward Malice when the elf's voice came from all directions, echoing off the trees. "It seems assassins are not the only warriors who lack honor," he taunted with a maniacal cackle. "You have interfered for the last time. I will hunt all of you until the end of my existence and send you one by one into the abyss. Next time, there will be no hesitation."

The dwarf scooped Malice up in his arms and carried her back toward the tied horses. Irritated, he said, "Way t' go, Bit. Now we got that madman after us, too!"

The half-orc knew it was not meant as harsh scolding, but he could not help but feel guilty. What had he just gotten them into? Did he seal a fate far worse than the one Malice had been about to receive? He could not help but be concerned with his decision. Nevertheless, the fact remained. "I had to save her, Tormag. She is my mother."

Knowing better than to argue, Tormag kept his tongue. He dropped the woman lightly to the ground as Bitrayuul untied the horses. Once down, Malice continued her quiet whimpering while Tormag gathered their supplies. He popped the last few pieces of meat in his mouth so as to not waste them and slid his favorite cooking sheet back into his pack.

Bitrayuul tied Malice's horse to his own and lifted his father quickly into a saddle. After getting situated, the half-orc lifted the woman to seat her in front of the dwarf. He would have preferred to have her sit with him, as he was more comfortable on a horse and his stature could easily see around her. However, it was not possible with his armor. She would have been shredded to pieces. He clicked his tongue to urge the horses to move. With a quick glance behind to check that his companions were well, he kicked his horse into a gallop, steering it toward the south in continuation of their search for Fangdarr.

After they had departed, Chakal stepped from behind a tree at the encampment. He gripped the arrow stuck in his chest with one hand and ripped it from his body. Within moments, the wound began to heal, as did the wound on his shoulder. The assassin turned to watch the party ride away and the smug grin returned to his face once more. "Hmm, back to the hunt, it seems."

CHAPTER THIRTY-FOUR
HUNGER

Though the night sky inundated their surroundings with an eerie blackness, Fangdarr, Cormac, and Bear managed to press through the remainder of the sopping marsh in a half day's forced march until morning. Thank the gods for gifting both races the keen ability to see in the dark. Exhaustion tugged at them from all angles. Their legs were weary from the long journey through the harsh terrain and even their feet were in pain from the constant strain of being pulled from the muck with each step. Still, they pressed on. They had to. Despite their own bodies' pleas, this was not a place to rest, they knew.

After finally reaching the clearing by late morning, all three companions crashed to the ground—happy to finally be on soft, *dry* grass again. Cormac managed to force a bit of humor. "Bothain's beard, orc, that's the most I've walked in over a century! Me bones are achin' somethin' fierce, don't ye doubt. I should've just swam down the Metridium with ye instead of runnin' me stubby legs all the way around the damned lake."

Fangdarr gave a chuckle, as best he could between his own labored breaths, and turned and lay face down in the thick grass. He wanted to savor the feel of the green on his face. How he had truly taken it for granted. After spending a whole day in the pestilence of that dreaded wasteland, the feel of this simple, warm grass against his face nearly brought tears to his eyes.

After a long while, the orc let out a groan and rolled onto his back. "You think this place safe to sleep? I want sleep . . ." he announced as his body continued to luxuriate in the downy surface.

Cormac—who was already snoring lightly—simply let out a fart in response. The orc took that as an affirmation and closed his own eyes. Bear let out a massive yawn from her gaping maw before slumping down onto her belly adjacent her master. Fangdarr felt her fur brush against his hand and rolled closer to her, embracing her with his enormous arms. "Night, Bear," he mumbled as sleep finally took hold.

By the time Fangdarr stirred again, it was nearly dawn of the following day. He wiped the grogginess from his eyes and looked to his companions who were still fast asleep. The orc at first could not tell how much time had passed, but judging by the placement of the moon, he knew the morning was not far off. Careful not to wake the others, he slowly stood from his impromptu bed next to his beast. He stretched his body to free himself of his restful aches and cringed at the loudness of his bones cracking.

"By the stones, Fang, ye might as well take up profession as an alarm to stir the nobles from their fat arses!" Cormac complained as he woke from the disruption.

"Sorry," the orc replied with a shameful smile.

"Bah, what time it be?"

"It almost dawn."

Cormac shot up painfully, not giving his stagnant body time to adjust. "*What?!* Ye mean to tell me we slept a *whole* day?!"

Fangdarr simply shrugged in response. "We were tired."

"Aye, ye ain't jestin'. Well, at least this spot was safe. The marshes must deter most anything from coming this way." The dwarf propped himself to his knee before rising, this time going more slowly to give himself time to adjust. He stretched as Fangdarr did, though, even with his hands reaching as high as they could, they still only came to Fangdarr's chest. "Right, we need breakfast." The dwarf started reaching for his pack to search for food but halted. "Ye know, I think I could go for some *real* food. Not the same scratch we've been livin' on for days. Aye?"

Fangdarr nodded happily in agreement. After the struggle through the marsh and their seemingly endless rest, he would welcome a fresh meal. "We hunt?" he asked the dwarf.

Cormac sat in contemplation for a moment before replying, "Aye, we certainly could. There is also a human village a half day's walk west of here, if ye want to risk that."

The orc pondered but denied the suggestion. "No, not in mood for humans today."

"Right, I'm with ye on that one." He tossed Fangdarr an unstrung bow from the pack and a string. Fangdarr quickly strung the crude bow and retrieved two arrows from the bag as well.

"Bear, wake up," the orc said lightly as he massaged his pet's fluffy ears with his free hand. The animal opened her eyes and looked at him in confusion. "It time to hunt." She rolled onto her back and splayed her limbs out, stretching them as far as they would go—drawing a hearty laugh from Cormac. As her stretch concluded, she shifted back to her legs and wiped her cold nose on Fangdarr's face in greeting.

"That beast sure is fond of ye, orc," Cormac stated, a hint of jealousy in his voice.

Fangdarr could only smile and rub her ears once more. "I fond of her, too. She good bear."

The dwarf chuckled and slung the pack over his shoulder before strapping his shields back onto his arms. "Right, best we get goin', I reckon."

They started south toward the mountains and back into the dense forest. They were much nearer today than two days before, that much was certain. By now, they could barely see the summits from their location. They still had much journeying, but Fangdarr was eager to be in sight of his goal. He kept his bow strung and an arrow nocked, ready to fire at the first sight of a walking meal.

Fangdarr led the party slowly through the wood, careful to place each footfall in silence. Despite his enormous stature, the orc could stalk noiselessly when he needed. Cormac, on the other hand, had a hard time hushing the constant scraping of the thick steel plates of his armor. Nevertheless, they continued their search certain that eventually their luck would change.

A long while passed with not even a squirrel, bird, or rabbit in sight. His stomach grumbling, Fangdarr turned to his early warning system. Cormac looked up at him and spoke first. "Eh, maybe I'm for thinkin' I should stay here. No critter is goin' to show its face with me makin' all this racket."

Fangdarr was glad Cormac had said it first. Truthfully, he wished it had been brought up much earlier. The orc was now ravenous. Already he could feel his muscles beginning to tire from lack of sustenance. Even still, he could not abandon his friend. They had been separated for too long during their last encounter, and Fangdarr aimed to keep the dwarf close.

"We try bit longer," he offered, much to Cormac's delight for not being left behind. "Look," Fangdarr said, wetting his finger and sticking it into the air beside him, "wind change direction. We downwind now. Our scent masked."

Cormac licked his own stubby finger and tested the air as well. "By the stones, you're right, Fang! HAH! Take that ye stinkin' critters! Even Cerenos wants ye in our tummies! Bahahah!"

The ignorant orc blinked curiously at his companion. "Cerenos?"

"Elven forest god. They think he be the cause of all nature, even the wind."

Fangdarr simply shrugged. He cared little for religion, though it drove so many. In his mind, there was only the here and now, where one must accomplish what he wished on his own through blood and combat. All other notions he considered false—or at least too complex to consider investing time in. His 'religion' was simple. *If I can kill it, I am better than it.* His mind reenacted the terrible scene of his dance with death under the depths, deep in the embrace of a creature so powerful and terrifying that he would easily assume *someone* must have considered it a god or demigod. Yet, Fangdarr emerged the victor. Therefore, he was superior. A smile found its way to his face.

They continued south through the forest, this time with wind as their ally. Fangdarr began to see woodland creatures fading from view much later than before. It wouldn't be long, now. Cormac and Bear could sense it as well, for they now crept even more quietly.

The dwarf spotted a fawn to his left that had strayed too far from its mother. His eyes were so riveted on the creature—mouth salivating to the point of dripping—he failed to notice Fangdarr stopped in front of him. Cormac bumped into the orc with a dull thud, "Oye! What ye stop for?"

A large black hard slowly patted the air in front of the dwarf's face, begging for silence. Cormac instantly hushed himself and took in his surroundings more keenly. "Ye smell that?" he asked after a few moments of sniffing.

The orc nodded. "We not alone."

"Aye, and if me nose be true, that's meat over a fire, or I'm a bearded gnome."

Fangdarr agreed. Even Bear started whimpering lightly at the smell of meat cooking upwind. The scent of searing flesh carried itself down to them, teasing their nostrils with succulent, juicy flavors that promised a full belly and content nap. "We get closer?" he asked.

Cormac pondered for a moment. "Hmm, a small party would have no need for that much meat. Though, they may be thinkin' to preserve it. On the other hand, a party that needs that much meat is . . ." he didn't need to finish the sentence. Both were well aware of that outcome. "But, me stomach is forcin' the answer to be yes. We get closer."

Once again Fangdarr nodded his agreement. Normally, they would not risk such an act, but their growing hunger propelled them forward. Sure, they could eat the provisions they had packed away, but they needed to save those for the mountains, if possible. There would be no dwelling squirrels or rabbits there.

The group continued forward in search of the origin of the smell that taunted and tantalized them so cruelly. Bear led the way now, too eager to remain at the back of their procession. Her speed increased progressively as the scent grew stronger.

"Bear, wait," Fangdarr whispered, but it was no use. The hungry beast trod along vigorously toward the meal to come. The orc increased his pace, as did Cormac, in an attempt to catch up to her. "Bear! Wait!" he half-whispered half-yelled to his companion. Unheeding, she accelerated even more, rushing nose first out of view. He cursed his luck at having such a voracious beast for a companion. It would have been so much easier to keep an eye on a turtle.

By the time Fangdarr and Cormac had made it to the point where Bear had disappeared, they stopped. The smell of the food was heavy now, and they were extremely close to whoever was cooking it. Fangdarr expected to hear yells or some sort of outcry as he could only assume Bear was now rampaging around in her pursuit. Yet despite his beast's possible need for assistance and his own stomach's moan, he chose to exercise caution, inching quietly toward the final layer of brush standing between them and the camp. Slowly, he poked his head through the brush to determine what they were dealing with.

The moment his face popped out of the vegetation and his eyes took in the view, Bear jumped directly into his face. Both crashed to the ground in a heaping mound of fur and flesh, drawing a groan from Fangdarr. Bear was up in an instant, happily wiggling her rear in anticipation. Cormac tried to hide a chuckle but failed, as always. In the mouth of their companion was the entire fawn that had been roasting over the fire. Even now, smoke still sizzled and steamed from the carcass as it made contact with the dewy leaves of the brush Bear had jumped through.

Cormac and Fangdarr simply looked to each other, then to Bear. A moment of quiet went by before the dwarf spoke. "Well, the deed is done, lad. Might as well dig in and take our leave." Cormac bent down and ripped a haunch from the charred carcass, and the orc, ignoring his previous apprehension, tore off his own piece of meat and took a bite. Ecstasy rushed through his body as the succulent meat shredded between his teeth and his tongue soaked the juicy wetness of the first fresh meal he had feasted on in days.

Bear now chomped down on the remaining carcass vigorously, ready to devour the entire animal. Each of their minds were too shrouded by the scrumptious meal that they failed to notice the enormous tree trunk swinging in from the side.

It crashed into Bear as she took her second bite. She landed a body's length away with a whimper.

"Git 'em!" a gruff voice shouted as Fangdarr and Cormac still had their mouths full of their third bite of meat. Four ogres of enormous magnitude rushed forward, toppling the small trees that surrounded the party. The supposed leader of the monsters held the tree which had bashed Bear out like a spear and threw it directly at Cormac. Unsuspecting and slowed by his lasting hunger, the dwarf hardly managed to put a shield arm up to intercept the projectile that tripled his height. He cursed as his arm could not brace against the impact with enough strength to fully deflect the blow. Fangdarr was too distracted by the other three charging foes to notice as his friend was knocked back near his animal companion with an *oof!*

The orc, also suffering heavily from lack of energy, instantly triggered his adrenaline and rage, granting him a slight amount of reserved strength. Driktarr found its way to his hand as he assumed his battle stance. Fangdarr defiantly roared into the face of the three enemies that were now only a few strides away. If they had any concern or felt any intimidation, it did not show. Instead, they met his challenge and returned the roar with one combined outcry that easily overtook his own threatening sound.

Fangdarr cared little. The roar was only meant to distract his attackers. Ogres were massive creatures, amounting to twice his height and girth, though lacking in intelligence. The orc was more thoughtful than the average battle-driven grunt. He knew they would return his challenge, and he also knew they would close their eyes to make their roar as loud as possible—while running straight toward him.

Driktarr cocked behind his shoulder at the ready, the orc eagerly waited for the perfect moment to swing. At the last possible moment, he unleashed his beloved axe in a single tremendous blow at the outermost monster while side-stepping further right to avoid the stampeding ogres.

The creature let out a horrendous groan of agony as the greataxe lodged deep into its abdomen. To Fangdarr's surprise the axe did not travel entirely through its stomach. Instead, its motion halted just after the navel before getting stuck. *Curse this exhaustion!* His rage and lust for the blood to be spilled was not enough to overcome the needs of his muscles. If only the ogres had attacked after he and the others had taken a few more bites. Luckily, Driktarr had taken in its fill of blood, transferring some of the energy back into him.

Fangdarr watched in concern for a moment as the two charging creatures turned toward Cormac and Bear, each carrying a sharpened pike made from thick branches in their hands, ready to skewer their prey. Fangdarr pulled with all his might, putting a heavy foot against the dying ogre, in order to free his axe, but it would not budge. The thick, mottled skin and bloodied organs of the beast had enclosed the axe, locking it in place. The orc knew he did not have the time to fuss with his weapon while three assailants remained.

Cormac was still disoriented from blocking the flying tree, but he noticed the two ogres rushing ferociously in his direction. He motioned for Bear to get behind the tree that stood arm's length behind them as he prepared for the assault. She whimpered at the thought of leaving him alone but complied. Truthfully, the dwarf would rather have her at his side, but she could never hope to prevent herself from being impaled by the makeshift pikes now coming toward them.

"Come then, ye stupid brutes!" he shouted from behind his raised shields, hoping to enrage the ogres.

The captain got his wish. Both now sped forward, closing the distance by bounds. Each took the most simplistic form of attack—stab the closest enemy! Cormac expected as much from ogres and held a sturdy shield in place, ready for each incoming spear. Both wooden spikes shattered instantly against his superior steel, but not without the force of the strike sending Cormac into the tree and knocking him unconscious.

Fangdarr howled and charged forward toward his fallen ally. His roar forced the nearest ogre to turn to face him while the other raised a meaty fist in the air, ready to pummel the motionless dwarf.

Bear sprung from behind the tree and latched her strong maw onto the calf of the monster who aimed to crush Cormac. The ogre let out a yelp of pain which quickly shifted to anger. It wrapped a massive hand around Bear's back leg and tried to pull her off. She bit down harder in stubbornness, refusing to relent. But her leg was starting to break—the monstrous creature possessed too much strength. Her jaw unclenched from the muscle of her prey with a whine. No longer latched, her attacker held her firmly by the leg and lifted her in the air, dangling her directly over its gaping mouth.

Fangdarr, still a few paces away, watched in horror. Unarmed, outnumbered, and with another ogre blocking his path, he could only stare in fear as his companion drifted closer and closer to the rotted teeth and stinking breath of the monster that intended to eat her alive.

From behind, he heard a cry of pain—one he could only assume came from an ogre. Still charging forward, he cast a quick glance back. His eyes widened in horror as he watched the lead ogre place its large, disgusting foot over the head of its ally and tug on Driktarr. It ripped the axe free from its companion, re-opening the wound that had sealed around the weapon. Blood and gore exploded with the unleashing of the axe. In the final pull, the monstrous foot of the ogre crushed down into the skull of his comrade. Shattered fragments of bone and a spray of squishy brain bits flung in every direction.

The orc took one more look behind him. As the sun crept past the horizon, its bright rays both outlined a figure and momentarily blinded Fangdarr. As his sight returned, the leader of the band of ogres could be seen slowly walking toward him, Driktarr in hand.

CHAPTER THIRTY-FIVE
NIGHTMARES

Bitrayuul turned his head to be certain Tormag and Malice still trailed behind. They had been riding hard for a while, fearful of being pursued by the unrelenting assassin. The sun was in its final descent. He knew the horses needed rest. The beasts had been pushed at a gallop since their departure.

The half-orc slowed the horses to a jog, then to a brisk trot, careful not to cramp their muscles with an immediate halt. Their breathing came in pants and gasps as they walked forward, eventually slowing to a halt. Bitrayuul dismounted tenderly to avoid cutting the animal with his sharp-edged armor. Once his feet were planted firmly on the ground, he rubbed the face of each beast in appreciation.

He had chosen a spot with a small pond, so his horse's tether in hand, the half-orc walked toward the glistening pool and allowed the beast to drink. Tormag and Malice caught up quickly on their own horse and followed suit. Malice seemed to be back to her former self. Her afflictions came and went but she did not look like someone who had just almost been executed. Bitrayuul eyed her curiously, wondering if she even remembered what had occurred.

"We will make camp here, then continue south before dawn," he said to his companions.

"Ye know this be Orclands?" Tormag questioned.

His son contemplated the warning then responded, "Just a short rest, the horses cannot continue. Then we will head south and west, away from the Zharnik village."

"Aye, but this be a water hole, Bit. Don't ye doubt we might not be the only visitors here tonight."

Malice chimed in quickly, "Orcs? I'm sure we can handle our own." Her pale hands instinctively gripped the pommels of her weapons at her waist. Bitrayuul had forgotten that she was so conditioned to attack orcs on instinct. He reminded himself to keep his helmet on.

"Let us hope none are thirsty," he added.

Within short order, the group had a minor encampment set up, though they built no fire. After allowing their mounts to drink their fill, they pulled the animals over to their camp a ways off from the pond.

Tormag passed around pieces of provisioned meat to his comrades, secretly missing the savory tender pieces that had entered his stomach earlier in the day. "Who be takin' first watch?" he asked as he finished handing out the scraps.

"I will," Bitrayuul responded. "I am still capable. Your ride together has left you both sore, I'm sure."

The dwarf had to admit Bitrayuul's words were true. Riding with a human woman twice his height in the same saddle was a trek accompanied by aches. Tormag laid his head on the soft grass. Despite being in his plate armor, the dwarf drifted to sleep within moments, snoring lightly.

Malice stepped over to Bitrayuul, taking a seat next to the half-orc. She sat in silence before quietly whispering, "Thank you."

Bitrayuul raised his eyebrow from beneath his helmet. He knew the pride of the woman and how hard it was for her to give voice to such words. The half-orc replied with a simple, "You are welcome." At least now he was certain she remembered some of the day's events.

The woman closed her eyes tightly in the hope that it would stop the tears she knew were coming. But it was futile. She sobbed lightly as her cheeks streaked with the warmth of her pain. Bitrayuul laid a hand gently on her shoulder, bringing forth a louder moan of sorrow.

"I-I could not avenge her, Bitrayuul. What kind of mother am I that I cannot take vengeance against the demon that brought her that awful fate?" she asked rhetorically. The half-orc simply sat in silence, swallowing his own sorrow.

"Believe me, I am thankful you saved me from his blade, if only to grant me another chance at him. But now I must live with this pain. The guilt of knowing Lilyana was . . ." Her words were interrupted by soft wails as she once again comprehended the reality of her daughter's demise. "My mind . . ." she began slowly, ". . . is cloudy. I know this, as I am sure you have taken note as well. It hides things from me. Painful things. It knows me in my truest form, better than any other, and deems me too weak to handle the truth. How am I to survive this world when my own body knows I am too weak to even fight myself?" Her words grew louder with each comment.

Her words perplexed Bitrayuul. He had never fathomed that his mother may actually be aware of her fractured mental state. He assumed she simply was a slave to its machinations. However, the half-orc also knew how volatile she was, especially when accessing the hidden knowledge she spoke of now. Already,

Bitrayuul could see her eyes were darting around in panic. She was starting to get lost in her painful memories once more. It was almost as if Malice was reading from a haunted book that had most of the words scratched away, and each word she uncovered only brought on more horror.

He found himself rubbing her back slightly, with her leaning toward him in comfort. A rush of confused emotions hit him as he was forced to push her—his birth mother—away from the protruding blades of his armor for her own safety. Bitrayuul wanted to embrace her in comfort but his wicked armor prevented such actions. The half-orc cursed the carapace that had served him so well, for it now served as a barrier—an obstacle to building a relationship with the woman who had brought him into this world.

"I am sorry, mother," he said softly. This time, she did not snap at him. Instead Malice simply let out a few more weak sobs as she laid her head on the earth before him. She was exhausted from the day, and her body needed to heal from the numerous wounds she had suffered at the hands of her tormentor.

Luckily, aside from the stab in her side, all of her wounds were minor or superficial. Bitrayuul wanted to dress the more severe injury but worried he would disturb her sleep. Even more, Malice's mental state would likely not hold up to being roused in the dark and having her clothing removed by one with orc blood.

The half-orc stood and retrieved a wool blanket from his pack and placed it lightly over his slumbering mother. With the evening still young and the sun down, Bitrayuul stared at his surroundings. The silence in the air was chilling. He heard nothing except the light snoring of the old dwarf near him. All three horses lay comfortably in the grass, resting to regain their strength after such an intense ride. Where domestic horses could only maintain a sprint for a short period of time, these horses had been bred specifically for long rides. Tormag had been around long enough to know it was worth paying extra for the special breed. Even still, the half-orc felt terrible for forcing them to continue at such a pace for so long. It put his mind at ease to see them so relaxed now.

With no sounds around and no companion to keep him entertained, Bitrayuul's mind played back images he had wished to forget. His own lack of sleep was starting to take its toll as his nightmares now broke free of the dream realm and began to haunt his waking thoughts. He slapped his hands against his helmet to rattle his head and stop the horrendous scenes from playing. A groan of frustration escaped him as it proved fruitless. Tears welled up in his eyes as he could not seek relief from the gory sight of Lilyana's severed body spilling to the ground.

In the scene, he could see himself standing there, watching, useless—immobilized by unseen chains that he should have broken. Why didn't he break them? He let the girl he had come to love in such a short time die in front of him.

Bitrayuul's mind twisted the memory in cruelly vivid detail. He cried audibly as he watched her nearly-lifeless eyes wilt and fade as her outstretched hand reached for his immobile replica in a last desperate plea for help. Yet the copy of him never moved. It sat in the shadows, watching the young girl bleed out, offering no comfort.

As the scene played out slowly, emphasizing each painful moment, it was as if he was there again, watching it all occur once more. Bitrayuul yelled in his mind to his inert likeness. "Go! Help her! You useless wretch! Take her hand, anything!"

Bitrayuul's focus on the ethereal clone became stronger with his angry pleading. The shadows around the face began to clear. He expected to see himself with his head hung low, accepting his shame. Instead, it was not his own face, but Chakal's. That wide-eyed smile of triumph and glee as the elf watched the girl die. The metaphor was not lost on Bitrayuul. If he could not even move a single muscle to help comfort the girl, was he really any better than her murderer?

The pain brought him back to reality. The half-orc sobbed harshly, drenching his face in tears and sweat. Off came his helmet. Bitrayuul threw it to the side and continued to sob as the scenes of his nightmare subsided. Looking around, he noticed much of the night had passed. A pang of guilt struck him for dozing off during his watch. "Always useless," he said to himself. With luck, his companions were in such a deep sleep that he had not woken them with his outcries. Luckier still, none had intruded on their camp and slain them in their slumber.

With renewed resolve, Bitrayuul managed to stay awake without any more nightmares—though his fear of their return did little to serve him. After a short while, he woke Tormag from his sleep and traded places. Many moments slipped by before fatigue finally grabbed hold of the half-orc and dragged him to a dreamless rest.

Bitrayuul awoke abruptly from his father shaking him. "Come, lad. It's time t' get movin'." The half-orc squinted and saw that it was morning. He was grateful the night had gone without conflict. He wiped his eyes before realizing that his helmet was still off. A flush of panic rushed through him as he searched around frantically.

Malice approached and made direct eye contact with his orcish face. He expected her to instantly snap to action and release an onslaught of attacks against his prone form. Instead, she held out his helmet and said, "Here, Bitrayuul."

Cautiously, he reached for the gear. Once in hand, he went to place it back on his head but then stopped. "Wait, you aren't going to attack me?" he asked.

She smiled slightly before replying, "No, son, I won't."

Bitrayuul beamed a smile back to her. Perhaps they had managed to form a bond last night after all. But that was not the real reason. Malice had awakened during the night and had heard his tormented cries for Lilyana. His guilt-driven pain at not comforting his sister in the final flickers of her life caused her to pity him.

Even with her acceptance, Bitrayuul still placed the helmet on his head out of habit and convenience before packing up camp with the others. Their moods were light as the previous day's events seemed, for the moment, in the past. In short time, the group was heading south toward the Tusks. The half-orc was uncertain how far Fangdarr might be ahead of them—or if he even lived—but Bitrayuul now knew that family meant everything to him. The passage that his brother would surely take was only a day's ride away. Soon he would be reunited with his kin.

CHAPTER THIRTY-SIX
SAVIORS

Fangdarr retracted his upper lip in a low grumble as he watched his axe sway back and forth with the ogre's movements. The orc's rage grew quickly; Driktarr was *his* to wield. His attention was pried elsewhere, though, as Bear let out a cry of fear. One of the other ogres, the monstrous cretin that stood between Fangdarr and his companion, chuckled at the unarmed orc, his disgusting teeth bared in a grotesque smile as it plodded toward its prey.

"Cuhmere, orcsy," it taunted with a giggle, arms outstretched, fingers waggling.

The orc rushed forward, directly at the monster. He knew he only had one shot for his plan to work; it relied explicitly on the clumsiness he had heard about regarding ogre-folk. As Fangdarr closed the gap between them, mere steps away from his target, the orc dropped to his hip and slid under the grasping reach of the ogre. The grass facilitated a slicker slide than he had anticipated, though, and he appeared on the other end of the beast.

In an instant, he rose from his prone position. He had to act before the confused creature turned to face him once more. With his feet planted, Fangdarr pivoted on his heel, spun to face the ogre, sending a balled fist directly into the groin of the beast as it completed its turn.

"Oof! Oooooooooooooooooooh!" Fangdarr's opponent howled, grabbing its groin with both hands. It fell to the ground in agony, still clutching and groaning in pain. As the incapacitated creature fell, the orc glanced to the two remaining ogres, determining the best course of action.

Time seemed to slow as his senses stood on end. Cormac still lay unconscious against the base of the tree. Bear still dangled dangerously close to the mouth of its captor, though her jailer had become momentarily distracted by its ally's sudden whimpering. Lastly, the leader, who wielded the axe—*his* axe—was now running for him. Within moments, Fangdarr would be at risk of being culled by his own favored token.

Fangdarr made his choice. Despite every selfish desire tugging at him, pulling him in the other direction, he broke off toward Bear. If he were to die by his own weapon in an attempt to save his companion, so be it. The orc knew he would never survive the guilt if, in choosing to retrieve his greataxe, the animal he had come to trust—and that had come to trust in him—was dropped into the gaping maw of the demon that held her. His mind would never let him sleep without reminding him of the crunching of her bones being shattered and ground to fragments as her dying whimpers of pain filled the forest air.

So, off Fangdarr went, both for her survival and his own. Anger added force to his pounding feet as he sprinted toward his pet. The ogre took notice of his charge. Though a stupid creature, it did not fail to discern the source of pain inflicted on its still-whimpering ally on the ground. It placed one hand over its groin as the other gripped Bear's leg tightly and swung her through the air like a club into the oncoming attacker. Fangdarr blocked the brunt of the blow, and the smell of fur and blood filled his nose as she swept past him, still in the grip of the ogre.

Ah, blood. If there was ever a word to the wise when dealing with orcs, it was this: Do not let them witness blood. Fangdarr tasted the irony black fluid that dripped down his face and over his thick upper lip. Instantly his pupils dilated in ecstasy as he lusted for more. Unarmed, outnumbered, the orc dashed forward under the next sweep of the makeshift bear club, his speed enhanced by the hunger he now needed to sate. Now at close quarters, the orc lunged forward and opened his mouth wide. His teeth sank deep into the upper thigh of the ogre and pressing with all the force the orc could muster, the large fangs of his bottom jaw tore both flesh and muscle.

With a scream of pain, the ogre reflexively dropped Bear to the ground and grabbed Fangdarr with both of its hands. No matter how hard it tried, it could not pry the orc from its leg. Instead, each tug only added to the agonizing pain. The ogre saw the oncoming leader of its gang only a step away. It whimpered and pushed out its leg toward the creature wielding Driktarr in plea.

"I git 'im!" the leader shouted, raising the greataxe.

Fangdarr was too lost in his bloodlust to notice. Feeling the blood drain from his foe's leg onto his salivating tongue had left the orc blinded in ecstasy. Bear barked to her master in warning but to no avail. She was too wounded from the twist to her leg at having been swung through the air. The animal whined and whimpered as the ogre swept the weapon downward toward Fangdarr's head.

The animal closed her eyes, refusing to watch the end of her savior. She waited in torment for the *thud* of the weapon entering the orc's skull, followed by a *thump* as his lifeless form fell to the grass. Yet, those sounds never came. When she peeked her eyes open, the ogre simply stood there looking odd, its ugly face twisted in confusion and pain as its eyes darted in every direction.

The other monster who still had Fangdarr ripping through its flesh groaned in pain and implored its leader. "Why no smash?!"

"I-I . . ." the creature began awkwardly. A whistling sound came as an arrow pierced the neck of the ogre, causing it to crash face-first into the ground. Once on its stomach, Bear noticed the other arrow protruding from the center of the creature's back. Blessed by luck, it must have severed the ogre's spine, immobilizing it completely just as it was bringing the axe down on Fangdarr.

From the source of the arrow came the sound of hooves. Thunderous clip-clops reaching closer and closer as the unexpected visitors arrived. Tormag hopped from his tall horse and rolled on the ground before reaching his feet, "Oye! Don't think ye can be killin' some nasty ogres without us! Bahaha!"

Behind the humorous dwarf came Malice, weapons drawn and still atop her mount. She stood at full height on her saddle, nearly the height of the ogres. Just as the incapacitated ogre was getting to its feet, the pain in its groin finally subsided, the assassin woman leapt from her perch wielding her gleaming weapons. She screamed in victory as she stabbed each blade into the eyes of her victim and finally into its brain. The explosion of blood that followed barely missed showering Malice as she flipped onto the skull of the fiend in a single fluid motion. She kept her balance while the creature toppled to the earth and collapsed into a lifeless heap.

By the time Malice felled her target, Tormag had reached the ogre still pulling at Fangdarr. Gross-smelling blood trickled down its entire right leg, also covering the front half of the orc. "Fang! *Fang*!" the old dwarf yelled. Nothing. Tormag sighed and raised his hammers as if to throw them.

The ogre blinked curiously at the dwarf before breaking into a childish cackle. "Hah! Dwarfsie think puny hammer hurt me? Hahah!"

As if on cue, Tormag launched one hammer followed by the other at a slightly lower angle. The first thudded squarely against the chin of his target, knocking the monster on its rear. The moment it landed, the second hammer struck in the same spot from the lowered sitting position, just as the old dwarf had planned. This was not the first giant-like creature who had underestimated Tormag. As the second weapon bashed into the ogre's already bruised chin, it broke through the weakened bone, shattering teeth.

"Well, would ye look at that, me 'puny hammer' did just fine, aye?" Tormag gloated. His stubby hands extended in front of him, and a tiny grin formed on his face as the ogre watched the devastating hammers fly back to his hands from their resting places on the ground. Eyes wide with horror, the ogre got up and turned to run—still with the ravenous orc attached to its leg. Tormag laughed maniacally as he threw hammer after hammer into the back of the creature as it tried to escape. Each *thud* followed with the weapon returning to his hand. His laughter could not be contained as he easily chased after the monster never ceasing his throwing.

Finally, after nearly two dozen assaults, the ogre fell to the earth. Bruises lined its back with a few trickles of blood from where the skin had broken. "Damn. C'mere, Bit. Ye think that looks like a chicken? Bahaha!" With the cretin gasping in pain, flat on its stomach against the grass, Bitrayuul approached. Indeed, the bruises that formed on its back did resemble a chicken, though he ignored the comment. The half-orc's attention was on the orc who was now trapped beneath the monster.

"Fangdarr? Are you alright?" he asked of his brother.

Within an instant, the orc's pupils returned to normal—the trance was broken. "Brother?" Fangdarr's incredulous face peered out from under the leg of the ogre. It was covered entirely in dark blood—a look Bitrayuul was not as used to as Fangdarr. A wide smile appeared on his face, "It is you!" With a hefty shove, the orc lifted the ogre's leg off his body and rushed to embrace Bitrayuul.

The half-orc quickly put a hand out to stop Fangdarr from nearly impaling himself on the sharpened armor. "Easy, Fang. Don't kill yourself the moment of our reunion." Bitrayuul removed his helmet and looked knowingly at his brother. Both smiled before clasping hands.

Fangdarr looked around before asking, "What happened?"

His brother looked at him in confusion. "You do not know?"

The orc simply shrugged in response. Though as he inspected the field around him, the pieces started forming. "Oh! Bear and Cormac! Come!" he begged his kin before rushing over to his animal companion.

As the pair rushed away, Tormag stood with his arms crossed over his chest. He raised them in the air in frustration. "Oye! What do ye want me t' do with this bloat-bellied beast?" he asked as his boot smacked against the face of the ogre. When no response came, he just sighed before using a simultaneous strike with both war hammers to cave in its skull. He scowled in disgust at the gore stuck to his beautifully engraved tools and attempted to awkwardly wipe the mess on the grass at his feet without much success. The irritated dwarf just groaned to himself as he walked back to the others.

Fangdarr reached his animal companion in short order and dropped to his knees to embrace her. His loving affection came as a surprise to Bitrayuul, who stood quietly watching the encounter. The orc's hands rubbed Bear's ears in comfort before moving down to inspect her haunch. After a while he said, "No break. Just sore from twisting." He walked over to their packs that had been dropped at the beginning of the ambush and produced a cloth bandage.

After the cloth was wound tightly around her ankle, Fangdarr helped Bear back to her feet. He watched in concern as she tested the weight on her foot. A few moments of tenderly pressing on the haunch passed before she resumed a normal stance and hopped excitedly at her master. The orc hugged her tightly once more, glad for her safety. His brother speculated that the love Fangdarr had for the beast had grown considerably since their last meeting. Bitrayuul was glad to see that his barbaric sibling was not only capable of death and ruin.

Fangdarr stood and faced his brother. "Now Cormac."

Bitrayuul nodded in acceptance as he allowed his kin to tend to his companions—as Bitrayuul would have done. Meanwhile, he turned his attention to the paralyzed ogre nearby. Its face still down in the dirt, the monster struggled for breath. Upon seeing the half-orc approach, it raised its eyes painfully.

"Kill me," it pleaded.

The half-orc was not unsympathetic of the disabled creature. Knowing the creature was immobilized, Bitrayuul sat next to the ogre. "I have questions. If you answer in truth, I will end your misery. Agreed?"

Teeth bared in anger at being manipulated, the ogre growled at its tormentor. "Agreed."

"You know of Crepusculus?"

A smile found its way to the fiend's face. He did not need to answer.

"Good. Now, where in the mountains does it rest?"

The smile faded instantly. "Dono," it replied.

Bitrayuul sighed. He pushed downward on the arrow protruding from the back of the ogre's neck. Blood squelched from the wound as the creature cried out in pain. "You're lying, monster."

With hatred in its eyes, the ogre clamped its teeth down onto its own tongue, severing it completely. The gray in its eyes became clouded by wetness as the pain overcame the beast.

"Where is the dragon?!" Bitrayuul shouted, pressing the arrow even more. The ogre only laughed, spewing blackened blood on the green grass beneath its mouth. It continued laughing until finally choking itself on its lifeblood. Gurgles and sputters escaped the monster as it struggled to breath. Groaning in frustration, Bitrayuul walked away in hopelessness.

Tormag and Malice stood waiting for him near the horses as Fangdarr carried Cormac from the tree where he had been lying. "Will he be alright, Fang?" his adoptive father asked.

The orc looked to his cargo before nodding in affirmation. Tormag was glad for that. Dwarves are a tightly-knitted race and look after their own. "Thank you for saving us," Fangdarr started, pausing for a moment to acknowledge each of his three saviors.

"What now?" Malice prodded impatiently. Though she did not show it, the woman struggled immensely to maintain self-control upon seeing Fangdarr—fighting back every conditioned response to gut him on sight. Nevertheless, the stress brought its fair share of agitation.

Bitrayuul handed Driktarr to his brother. He had stopped to gather the weapon while Fangdarr was occupied caring for his injured companions. The orc gripped the weapon in familiarity, pleased to hold it once again in his grasp. Bitrayuul spoke before Fangdarr had the chance, informing his brother of the reason for his appearance. "Now, we hunt a dragon."

CHAPTER THIRTY-SEVEN

PLAN

"Bothain's beard, ye sure are tall fer a dwarf," Tormag stated bluntly as he inspected Cormac. The younger dwarf, still groggy from being knocked out, peered at Tormag curiously as he came to.

"Wh-where am I? Who ye be?" he whispered from a dry mouth. Cormac's small hand reached up to rub the last remnants of weariness from his good eye. He could feel his bald skull resting on a folded blanket, though it did not help the throb in his head.

Tormag reached over and readjusted the makeshift pillow beneath the guard captain's head, drawing a nod of appreciation from the patient. "We're still in the forest, lad. Ye took quite a smashin' against them ogres. Me name's Tormag Double-Hammers. I'm with Fang's brother, Bitrayuul. Ye be Cormac, captain of the Shield, aye?" he asked.

Cormac nodded. "Aye, though, can't say me shields be used to blockin' damned *trees* used as clubs." His light chuckle seemed to appeal to the old dwarf as Tormag erupted in a boom of laughter.

Tormag then drew the Cormac's attention to Bitrayuul and Fangdarr who sat a few paces away, discussing something at length over a map. "What do ye reckon they're discussin'?" he asked.

The captain simply shrugged. "Probably tryin' to figure out which village to raid," he added with a smile that was soon interrupted by a cough.

"Bahahaha! Oh, lad, we're goin' t' get along just fine."

Malice tapped Tormag with her foot. The dwarf grunted in confusion at the woman until she nodded her head in the orcish siblings' direction. "They're coming over."

Walking side by side, the brothers approached their companions with determination, Bear close behind Fangdarr. Bitrayuul held his helmet in one hand and a rolled map in the other. He smiled, flashing the two bottom fangs that protruded twice the length of his human-like teeth, yet still only a quarter the size of Fangdarr's enlarged tusks. Apart from Tormag, this was the first time their companions had a chance to compare the two.

Though Bitrayuul's stature was large by human standards, the half-orc seemed dwarfed by his sibling—even in his heavy armor. The glow of Fangdarr's eyes was the only color that stood out from his black skin, which still managed to peek around the hundreds of white scars of varying dimension etched over his body. Malice forcibly restrained herself as the full-blooded orc approached, fighting every instinct she had to take to arms and eliminate the threat. Fangdarr shared some resemblance of his father—the source of her torment. It took every shred of her willpower to not cut him down.

"Friends, it seems we have our course," Bitrayuul stated as he set his helmet down and retied his long, black hair. "As you all know, we are nearly to the base of the Tusks," he added, extending his hand south to the nearby mountain range. "We will traverse around the base to the west, where we will encounter a river. We will then follow that river east through Hell's Throat, which will lead us up through the mountain."

Tormag's eyes grew wide at the name. "Hell's Throat? Are ye mad!?" he asked incredulously. All eyes shifted to him in curiosity. "Why do ye think it be named such? We won't be spottin' fairies and pixies, don't ye doubt!"

"What threat lies there?" Malice asked.

The old dwarf shook his head. "I only know stories, long since passed. One tale told o' trolls pickin' off caravans at the bridge, grantin' it the name 'Carrion Bridge'. Trolls would come down from their caves by the dozen; lyin' in wait, ready t' ambush any who crossed the bridge. There be a reason that map in yer hand ends there, do it not?"

Fangdarr grabbed the parchment from his brother and inspected the document. A low groan rolled in his throat. It was true. The orc handed the paper back to Bitrayuul who likewise confirmed the statement.

"Right," Tormag continued, "so anyway, the humans sent a battalion t' Hell's Throat nearly a thousand years ago. They were tired o' bein' picked off one by one, so they sent a small army t' eradicate the vermin." His head shook once more as he spoke. "Naught a single man left that passage, Bit. Now ye want us t' tempt the same?"

The group waited in silence for someone to speak. Malice, ever impatient, broke the tension. "Is there another way?"

"We could dig! Bahaha!" Cormac replied, though his laughter died quickly as his audience had no interest in humor, even Tormag.

"The mountain faces are all sheer, a climb would be impossible," Bitrayuul said. "There may be a more suitable path far to the east, though we cannot be certain. Even still, if we were to travel that far to scale a mountain, the task would remain to then backtrack over all the mountains we passed. No, it seems this is our only option," Bitrayuul said with a disappointing sigh.

Malice chimed in with sarcasm. "So, it's between certain death and a slow death. I, for one, prefer certain death."

Fangdarr did not catch on to her tone, but he agreed with the words. He pounded his chest in boastful pride. "I will take passage!"

The woman rolled her eyes at his obliviousness. "Why are we doing this again? Oh, right, to slay a dragon that has been terrorizing Crein for as long as any can remember and that has defeated any that have attempted to dispose of it." Her hands went up at the futility of their goal. It seemed an impossible task, to be sure.

As if on cue, the party started bickering amongst themselves. Finally, Cormac raised his hand to request calmness and motioned for everyone to sit down. The banter died down and everyone took a seat. Tormag removed a pipe from his bag to light a pinch of burnberry and nodded to his dwarf companion to speak.

"We need to be askin' the difficult questions," Cormac said. "All our lives be on the line here, Fangdarr. So, ask yerself, if the dragon be slain, what will ye do after? Will ye return to yer clan?"

Fangdarr wanted to shout in anger at the insulting nature of such a question. However, he kept his knee-jerk reaction in check and pondered it in silence, searching for what his honest answer was. In truth, the journey had come with more than a few obstacles that caused the orc to grow distant from his kind. Orc blood had been spilled by his hands in the protection of humans. What if he returned to his village only to learn they had discovered his actions? His first slumber would end with a knife to his throat.

Fangdarr exhaled painfully, "Don't know." He looked up at his allies. "That was plan. But . . . journey difficult. I have killed orcs. My own kind. I am always proud to be orc. But I do not think I can go back . . ." he stated plainly, as surprised to hear the words as the others.

"Where will you go?" Bitrayuul asked, hoping his sibling would choose to reside in Tarabar.

The orc took a steadying breath. "Not sure, Bit. I want to stay with Cormac and Bear." His dwarven friend smiled in response while Bear happily rested against a tree.

Tormag took it all in. He was glad to know that Fangdarr had developed much over his travels. However, he was keener on the finer details hidden in plain sight. "I'm proud o' ye, lad, don't ye doubt," he stated with a smile that was returned by his adoptive son. "However, ye all be forgettin' why Fangdarr came t' slay this beast in the first place. It was t' prevent the Zharnik clan from waging war on Wiston or Tarabar. If Fangdarr does not kill the drake or does not return t' steer the bloodthirsty orcs, another will simply take his place.

"Ye laid the pieces fer conquest, son. They've had a taste o' it. Next in line won't be so good-natured as ye, sure as stones." The old dwarf took a long draw from his pipe before blowing a ring of smoke into the air.

Fangdarr's eyes looked down in distress. "So . . . I *must* return?"

His half-blooded brother spoke up in vigor. "Wait, wait! No! They would kill him if his actions were discovered. In any case, Fangdarr, you said that the orcs do not have the strength to challenge either Wiston or Tarabar, right?" he pleaded, looking for any reason not to send his recently reunited kin to his death.

"Aye, that's what he said, Bit," Tormag added. "But don't be thinkin' that means they won't try. The orcs will devastate every village along the way before smashin' against the doors o' a city."

The realization of that fact hit Bitrayuul like a battering ram. He did not need Tormag to elaborate on the specifics. Was he really willing to let thousands die in the place of his kin? The half-orc's head pounded with the stress as he tried to think of a rebuttal, but he could not.

Luckily, it was Fangdarr who spoke for him. "I do not want innocent humans or dwarves to die for me." A proud smile stretched the cheeks of both dwarves, astounded at how the orc had grown. "I will return to my clan—alone—convince my people not to wage war."

"But what if they kill you!?" Bitrayuul shouted in frustration.

A scarred fist thumped against his pectoral, twice. "I am Fangdarr! Greatest chieftain of my clan. I will return dragging head of shadow dragon. My word never be challenged. I will be revered—God to my people!"

Moments of silence followed with no argument. It seemed incredibly stupid—suicide, even—though the logic seemed sound enough, at least when considering the average intelligence of orcs.

"To Hell's Throat, then?" Malice asked in irritation. Her patience had dwindled due to the needless bickering. As far as she was concerned, her life was forfeit already, so she cared little for the outcome.

Cormac groaned audibly, "Should just dig . . ." This time he drew a hearty laugh from the party. Even a Malice managed to crack a smile.

CHAPTER THIRTY-EIGHT
MEMORIES

Gray hues saturated the sky as the sun sank behind the relentless, unchanging clouds. As their party had increased in number, the horses were released. It was with reluctance that Tormag had to send them away, but the dwarf knew the tremendous steeds could never hope to traverse the mountains. To keep his mind from the returning stinging pain in his feet, Tormag clung near his new dwarven ally to share stories of their journey.

"Naked!?" the veteran commander barked in laughter as Cormac told of the first conflict he had faced in Fangdarr's company. "Aye, reckon the orcs would've at least spared yer . . .," Tormag started while pointing to his groin before breaking into another outburst of laughter.

Ahead, Bitrayuul and Fangdarr, too, shared the encounters each had faced. Mostly, the half-orc was curious as to the events that brought such a change about in his barbaric kin. Despite Fangdarr's reluctance to discuss the hateful rejection from humans, he explained all that had transpired. The half-orc sibling listened intently to every word.

Years had separated them; each following his own path. Bitrayuul considered his path to be more honorable, more *good.* In truth, Fangdarr's path had started as one driven by greed and a lust for power. Though he never spoke ill of his mother or her choices, the orc had been denied his youth within his culture. The draw to return to his kind—of blood, war, and pride—had been severe. However, once he had achieved his goal and sated his desire, Fangdarr realized the profound truth that Vrutnag and Bitrayuul had hoped to hide from him. His hands were stained with the blood of innocents. The orc had raided, murdered, raped, and so much more.

Bitrayuul walked in silence, listening with a mixture of eagerness, awe, and emotional tumult as his brother described the transformation of his former self into the orc he had become. Fangdarr was still one of orcish heritage and proud to be so. He still lusted for battle, glory, and the never-ending flow of blood from the wounds he inflicted upon his enemies. Yet, he no longer wished for his enemies to be undeserving. He felt no remorse for the ogres they had slain or even for the orcs he had culled, once his mind took the time to analyze his actions. Fangdarr told his attentive sibling—with more than a little hesitation and shame—that he simply wanted to know peace and to hold no regrets.

Bitrayuul felt that sentiment deeply. Once his kin had completed his tales, the conversation turned to the half-orc. He started with the easy events: encountering Lilyana, Meilan's prejudice—which Fangdarr was all too familiar with, and the splendor of Riveton. But eventually, his words slipped to unease as he relived the fate of the girl. Bitrayuul was brought to tears as he relayed the scene to Fangdarr.

The full-blood orc's eyes went wide as Bitrayuul spoke of his familial ties to the girl, and the woman walking behind them. A dozen questions instantly rushed to mind, though he hurriedly clamped his mouth shut to allow his brother to continue his story. With a sense of relief, Bitrayuul told of his shame—the guilt he felt for his actions, or lack thereof—and how it brought on an insomnia that only heightened his torment. How he feared sleep, knowing that the demons sat at the very precipice of the place he had to travel each night. Fangdarr nodded knowingly, for he had experienced a similar torment within the Echoed Marshes.

Bitrayuul's face was full of tears now, much to his shame. He wiped them away thinking himself weak compared to his brother, who maintained his stoic expression even when recalling his pain. At last, the half-orc stopped and cleared his throat.

"We shall stop here for the night," he called to the group.

Tormag and Cormac looked at their surroundings. They did not realize just how far their feet had carried them, too distracted they had been with their conversation. But night was thick within the forest with only slivers of moonlight piercing the overhead canopies. Following the base of the mountain, the party had made it all the way to the river. They could taste the moist air on their tongues, and in the distance, they caught the gleam of slow-moving water casting forth flickers of moonlight.

"Start setting camp, everyone. We are near Hell's Throat, and we should rest outside the passage while we are still able," Bitrayuul suggested. It was true, rest would not come easy in the mountains. Too many a foe crept around every stone, waiting to strike.

Malice sidled up to the half-orc. "I'm glad we're done walking. Orcs and dwarves talk much more than I imagined. I had a lovely conversation with the bear, though," she added sarcastically. As if she understood, Bear nudged the woman happily with her nose and licked at her face, causing Malice to laugh and swat at the beast. "Oh! You stupid animal! Gah!" Malice exclaimed as she wiped her face and rubbed Bear's ears. She could not help but smile at the innocent, carefree face before her.

After the encampment was in order, Fangdarr and Bitrayuul decided to take the first watch to continue their conversation. Once the others were asleep, the half-orc sat near his brother who simply stared out at the glistening, crystal-like surface of the river.

"Like rivers, do you?"

The orc blinked, but kept his eyes locked on the distant water. A silent nod was all he offered.

"Have you seen the ocean?" Bitrayuul asked.

Fangdarr raised an eyebrow, "Ocean?" He had heard tell of oceans, though he had never seen one. Orcs were not known for their interest in large bodies of water.

"Yes, the ocean," the half-orc started before producing a map from his bag. "See? Here," he pointed to the left edge of the map, west of Crein, "the Maelstrom Coast. It is named due to the constant storms that approach land. And here," his finger slid north-east, at the top of the parchment, "is the Monstrous Sea."

With intense curiosity, Fangdarr grabbed the document out of his brother's hands. As he inspected it in more detail he asked, "There are monsters in Monstrous Sea?"

"So the tales say. Though none have been seen for centuries."

Fangdarr continued his inspection. He had looked at dozens of maps and seen the seas listed before; however, the orc had never given it much thought. As the chieftain, he expected to stay within his plot of forest, never experiencing the wider world. But, now, this journey had shown him just how much he could experience. No longer did he feel confined within the borders of his clan. And this thought brought him distress as he realized his freedom would be revoked upon the resolution of their quest. Fangdarr did not wish to return, but he had no choice. How could he hope to call himself *good* if he did not sacrifice for the sake of the many?

Catching on to his change of mood, Bitrayuul took back the map and tucked it away. They sat in silence for many moments just staring at the water. After a while, Fangdarr forced himself to avert his eyes. He did not wish to give himself more pain by having beautiful images to remember once he returned to his people.

Seeing that his brother's trance was broken, Bitrayuul took the chance to speak about the purpose of their seclusion. "Fang, I have to inform you . . ."

The orc turned his head toward his brother to listen. ". . . the one who murdered Lilyana is hunting us. At first it was only Malice, but our interference has made us a target as well. He trails us even now, I am sure." With that final statement, Fangdarr looked to his surroundings as if Chakal would be standing a stone's throw away, waiting for an introduction.

"I tell you this because he is dangerous—deadly, rather. There has been no greater opponent in my experience, Fang. If he comes, you *must* not fight him."

"Why?" the orc asked. "Not scared of anyone."

Already Bitrayuul was shaking his head. "No, you must fear him. He is beyond us all. His games are brutal, yet he holds to his code. He will not seek you out unless you get in his way. You and Cormac both need to remain uninvolved or else Chakal may be the end of us all."

The orc scoffed in response. "You are target?"

His brother nodded, "All three of us."

Fangdarr did not hesitate before responding, "Then, I am involved."

CHAPTER THIRTY-NINE
BUNOVIR

Fangdarr woke to a gentle shake from Cormac. In the predawn darkness his instincts kicked in, causing the disturbed orc to jump to immediate alert.

"What happen?" he asked, struggling to blink the night's crust from his eyes. As he glanced around the camp, he saw his companions already up and prepared to continue. Without a word, Cormac handed Fangdarr his supply pack.

With a drawn-out groan, the orc stretched his stagnant muscles, shouldered his pack and strode to his waiting allies. Because of the rotating watches, they were as unrested as he was. Nonetheless, if the party had any hope of making it safely through Hell's Throat to the mountains in search of Crepusculus, they needed to start as early as possible. Trolls, ogres, and many more unknown monsters were known to traverse the Tusks; all of which one did not wish to encounter at night.

They trudged forward with purpose, though without songs or joyful conversation. Within a short time, they reached the slow-moving river that marked the passage. Fangdarr took the lead, tracing the river east toward the imposing path between the jagged points of rock ahead. The orc picked up his pace before Tormag called from behind.

"Look at that," the dwarf said as his finger pointed upriver.

From where they stood, the slow-flowing water was clear with occasional debris. However, the farther they followed the dwarf's finger upstream, the more tainted the crystalline liquid became, slowly transforming the clean fluid into a dull blackish-green. With each step they took, the opaquer the water became. They also began to see various bones buried into the earth beneath the glistening sheen.

"Seems we're in the right spot, bahah!" Cormac added lightheartedly. In truth, the scene was intimidating. At the base of the passage were a myriad of higher streams flowing together to form a viscous pool that spilled into the river. The pond was a spear's throw in diameter. Fangdarr led his allies to a tree near the edge of the pond, from where they took in the grisly sight.

The entirety of the pool was a deep black resembling the blood of many of the monsters that inhabited this environment. Bones of hundreds of skeletons littered the area in abandon. The stench was nearly unbearable. Rotting corpses and skeletal remains stripped of marrow by feasting bottom-feeders lay sprawled throughout the entire valley.

"Yeah, this be the right place indeed . . ." Tormag affirmed. Each of the gathered members had seen more than enough death, even the orc brothers who were still in early adulthood. But this . . . Even Fangdarr considered the implications of their task more clearly now. Not for himself, but for his dear friends.

For many more moments, they stood in awe, simply waiting. For what, none knew. But all were apprehensive to take another step forward—as if that next step was the deciding factor; they could not turn back once that determined foot touched the ground.

"Oh, gods," the woman gasped, drawing everyone's attention. She fell back a step, nearly tripping over Cormac's small form, her eyes never leaving the source of her dismay. Bitrayuul steadied his mother before looking for himself.

Across the pool, an enormous bipedal toad-like creature strode into view from the passage between the mountains. Its purple-black skin gleamed wetly over the rigid bumps that lined its body. Two bulbous eyes stretched on each side of its hideous face turning in every direction, as if searching for something. The party waited in silence beneath the cover of the tree, studying the monstrosity.

"That's a bunovir, if me memory serves," Tormag whispered with a shudder. "Nasty creatures, don't ye doubt."

They continued to look on in disgust and horror as the beast squished around its nesting. Then the silence broke with the sound of raspy screaming. Covered in slime and more than a few twigs, a troll cried out in fear as it was dragged across the ground by the abhorrent creature. It pounded weakly on the grasping digits of the bunovir, desperate to escape.

Fangdarr shuffled his feet. His tense shoulders tightened in angst while watching the helpless troll struggle. "We must help him," he stated to the rest of the party before taking a step forward.

His adoptive father gripped his shoulder to stay him. "Lad, there's no chance."

Fangdarr's expression quickly turned to anger and disappointment. "You would try if it dwarf or human!" he whispered harshly.

Bitrayuul immediately shushed his aggravated brother to avoid them being discovered. The orc scowled at him and turned to view the troll in dire need once more. More anguished screams echoed off the surrounding mountains. Bitrayuul retracted in shock at his brother's response. In that moment, he realized just how hypocritical his views were compared to Fangdarr's. The brother he considered barbaric and without moral sight was actually his superior in honor. The half-orc's *honor* only extended to the goodly races.

Seeing that Fangdarr was about to charge out recklessly, the old dwarf continued, "Son, this monster is not t' be tossed with." As if on cue, the bunovir tossed its prey to the edge of the blackened pool, splashing the fetid liquid in a spray. After a moment, the troll realized it had been released and moved to flee. Kicking water and bones alike, the creature rose to its feet, when a large hand extended from the bunovir, pushing it back into the pool face-first. An odd noise came from the monstrous toad, something akin to a bubbling grumble. It was laughter.

The orc clenched his fists tightly. Meanwhile, Tormag held tightly to his wrist urging him not to act. "Bit, help me!" the dwarf whispered, struggling to pull against the powerful orc's arm.

Bitrayuul, and even Cormac, helped grabbed ahold of Fangdarr. But his rage only heightened at being so restricted. His teeth bared, and his lip curled, further exposing his fangs. Luckily, the half-orc's gauntlets granted him a massive amount of strength that helped to restrict his sibling. Nevertheless, with Fangdarr's fury growing ever stronger, it was only a matter of time before he went berserk and overpowered the other three.

"It ain't . . . safe . . ." Cormac stated, hoping the sound of his voice would break through the rage-filled fixation. Desperately, he looked to Bear who sat in concerned confusion at the struggle between her comrades. She was nothing short of intelligent and had noted the three fighting to contain the massive orc's lust. Nevertheless, her fealty was to Fangdarr, first and foremost. The animal looked away in feigned distraction to avoid the dwarf's pleading gaze.

Across the pond, the troll remained held underwater, kicking and splashing in futility. The blood-stained liquid filled its lungs, slowly pushing out the oxygen. The bunovir stopped its guttural laughter. At the same time, a dozen tendrils peeled away from its arm. Each moved of its own accord, whipping around in search of a target until they found the troll. The helpless creature froze as the vines stabbed into him, and the party across the lake widened their eyes in horror as hundreds of small amber orbs travelled through the appendages and into their new host.

The bulbous eyes of the monster rolled back in ecstasy as eggs continued to fill the body of its captive. Fangdarr pulled with all his might now, despite the obvious fate of the defenseless creature he hoped to save. With the shock of the sight before them, his allies could no longer hold him. The enraged orc roared in triumph as his strong legs broke free then pushed him farther and faster into the putrid water and toward the object of his fury.

Bitrayuul immediately broke into a sprint after his brother for he held no hope that Fangdarr could conquer the monster alone. Each of his loyal companions—even Malice, with a groan of annoyance—chased after the siblings, all headed toward the wretched monstrosity that had now become aware of their presence. Unlike the orcish pair and Bear, though, the dwarves and Malice were forced to trace the edge of the deep pool.

Expressionless, the bunovir ripped away the tendrils that still pulsed in orgasmic spasms. Blood sprayed into the air, mixing its glimmering, blue hue into the blackened pool before diluting. The creature stood facing the oncoming intruders lacking all emotion. It set its wide eyes on Fangdarr, who was hardly slowed by the waist-high sewage. As if in slow motion, the bunovir shifted its foot forward into the ensanguined pond.

Driktarr came from his shoulder harness as Fangdarr closed the distance between himself and his foe. In his final strides, the chieftain let out a barbaric growl. Still the monster continued its dauntless progression.

"Bothain's beard . . ." Bitrayuul mumbled under his breath as he ran. Now that he was much closer, the true stature of the monster became apparent—it quintupled his own height; the half-orc only measured up to its knee. He cursed his brother's profound sense of honor, thinking it would surely be the end of them all. "Fangdarr, run!" Bitrayuul called out in urgency.

It was pointless. Lust for blood had consumed the orc fully—no fear, no hesitation, only unquestionable need. A heavy foot planted onto the exposed bone of what must have been an ogre. Using that, the chieftain kicked off and leapt high into the air, sailing through the splatter of black droplets, his face contorted in sheer anger. If expressions alone could kill, this one would have felled many. No expression came from the bunovir, though, even as Driktarr bit into the thick, armor-like skin of its left breast.

With Fangdarr still gripping the handle of his weapon, the nearest eye turned to the dangling orc. The chieftain was too blinded by rage to notice the impending outstretched hand reaching for his defenseless form.

Bitrayuul was still too far, still wading through the thick, imbrued pond. His hand reached back to pull Kwip from his its resting place and, as he had practiced countless times, strung it in one fluid motion. The half-orc loosed an arrow toward the bunovir's eye, hoping to distract it from its fixation on Fangdarr. However, the feathered fletching had become soaked in the fetid water, and Bitrayuul had to watch helplessly as the shot missed the mark and skated harmlessly over the monster's rigid flesh.

Not even noticing the glancing missile, the beast was near to closing its massive hand around the unsuspecting orc. With a defiant growl, Fangdarr pulled his beloved weapon from its prison and fell to the creature's feet with a loud splash. As the orc turned to face his opponent, Bear's intercepting form came into view, but so did a hammer-like fist from the creature that crashed into both of them, knocking them back a long distance. Luckily, the surface of the water softened the orc's tumble as he skipped along like a stone to the shoreline. Unfortunately, Bear took the brunt of the force, propelling her beyond the shoreline until she collided with the distant stone wall then rolled limply to the rotten ground in a heap. Fangdarr's allies were nearly to him at the water's edge. They had not missed the spectacle of the bunovir's heavy bash.

"Fang! We're comin', son!" Tormag yelled from a dozen strides away with Cormac and Malice in tow.

Fangdarr shook his head from the dizziness of the blow. As his vision cleared, he saw the troll lying next to him. Up close, the orc could see the oozing, puss-filled wounds left by the tendrils. He could not hide his disgust as the festering sores still pulsed like a heartbeat. The dwarves and Malice approached, checking the status of their companion first before noticing the reason for his twisted expression.

"My stones . . . what the . . ." Cormac started, too horrified to find the words. Malice puked a heap of bile onto the bloodstained grass, coughing and gagging at the smell. If the sight seemed unbearable, the stench was much worse. It resembled the smell of a carcass left to rot for a full moon cycle mixed with the excrement of a dozen ogres. The dwarf captain plugged his nose as he leaned close to better inspect the troll.

As if on cue, one of the pulsating pustules splattered, followed by a surging eruption of monstrous tadpoles. Cormac fell back and yelped in surprise. His heavy boots pushed him back as the hundreds of baby creatures flopped and flicked in his direction. Despite their size, long teeth could be seen protruding from the gaping maw of each as they bounced ever closer.

Tormag and Fangdarr lifted the prone dwarf to his feet with the woman still too incapacitated from her sickened state. Humans often did not have the stomach for such an assault on their senses.

Fangdarr's rage had dissipated from the bunovir's attack previously, though seeing the fate of the troll up close quickly rekindled the dying flame within him. His eyes glanced over to his animal companion, who still lay motionless against the wall. The enormous orc's muscles bulged in fury at the fate of his friend who had selflessly blocked the attack that certainly would have crippled him. But what immediately alarmed him was the monster had redirected its attention to Bitrayuul, who was pointlessly launching a steady stream of arrows at the beast—none successful.

Rage renewed, the orc flew back into the blackened liquid, once again leaving his friends behind. Tormag and Cormac stood motionless at the shore, pondering how to act. Meanwhile, Malice was in a fit of panic due to the unrelenting horde of miniscule creatures bounding toward them. The dwarf captain was aware of them too, but for the moment his eyes were on Bear's motionless form nearby. He had grown fond of the creature and longed to go to her aid. Unfortunately, he could not reach her, not until he assisted his allies. With a sigh, he looked at Tormag, and the dwarves simply shrugged to each other before starting to stomp, pound, and smash as many of the gnawing monsters they could.

There were so many. For each one they splattered, four took its place. A few dozen had already latched themselves to each of the seasoned warriors, drawing blood in trickles all over their bodies. Still, the pair held their ground and squished as many of the vile things as they could. Malice stepped forward to assist as well, though her thin, pale skin was not nearly as thick as the dwarves'. In no time, she was driven back from the immense pain of the tiny teeth and resorted to pounding the occasional stray.

From in the pool, Bitrayuul watched as his brother re-entered the fray, charging toward the bunovir once more, while their allies remained on the shore. From where he stood, the half-orc could not see what they were fighting. He could only hope it was more pressing than the behemoth that now stood only two paces from the mound of skulls where Bitrayuul remained.

Having unloaded nearly his entire quiver to no avail, Bitrayuul slung his bow over his shoulder and readied himself for the inevitable. Beyond, Fangdarr splashed loudly toward the monster, but the beast paid no attention. No, all its attention was focused solely on the nuisance that had released the missiles. The half-orc stood atop his heap, poised at the ready in a defensive stance, waiting for the bunovir to launch its next attack.

Fixated on the monstrous hands that still remained at the creature's flanks, the half-orc failed to notice the frontal assault—a disgusting, slime-covered tongue that shot out to him like an elastic band and stuck to his body. Before Bitrayuul could realize his mistake, the gummy saliva adhered to his armor. Quickly, he reached his arms around the thick muscle, hoping to extract the cord, but his eyes grew wide in shock as his arms also became cemented.

Upon seeing his brother attacked, the orc chieftain slammed the edge of his greataxe into the calf, knee, and ankle of the fiend. Nothing. The bunovir's skin was too thick. Fangdarr stomped the water in frustration. Even his massive, trust-worthy weapon had failed him. He looked up to his trapped sibling as the tongue started to retract, pulling Bitrayuul straight toward the stretched maw of the monster. No teeth could be seen—only a small pocket which must have served as a tomb for many.

In that last moment, Bitrayuul called below to his brother, "The eyes, Fangdarr! The eyes!" before vanishing behind the closed gate of the demon's jaw.

Fangdarr froze. His mind raced after watching his only surviving kin be swallowed whole in front of him. From the shoreline, Tormag had also glanced up in that final fleeting moment, just as the son he had come to love and call his own fell victim to the horrific fate. The dwarf, like Fangdarr, ceased all movement; the world seemed to have paused its never-ending turn. All thoughts of current dangers fled Tormag. There was only that last gut-wrenching image. It played over and over in his mind painfully. His lip quivered with profound despair. The distraught commander slowly extended his hand to the monster, almost silently begging the return of his boy.

In his state, Tormag paid no attention to the growing number of parasites that had latched to his body in those few desperate moments. Meanwhile, Cormac worked furiously—smashing, squelching, bashing, stabbing—to clear the vermin-like horde.

Seeing what was happening to his entranced dwarf ally, Cormac tucked his shield-covered shoulder and charged forward. He barreled into Tormag, forcing the aggrieved commander to roll to the ground. With his concentration on Bitrayuul's fate fortunately broken, Tormag snapped back to reality, took a final look to Fangdarr and the bunovir, then turned back to clear the last remaining creatures. With a shout of anger, the dwarf ripped the pestering monsters from his arms and legs. His hammers swung faster than before as the distracting stream of offspring still poured from the nearly consumed troll carcass.

Filled with insurmountable rage—more than had ever consumed him previously—Fangdarr bellowed in pain and monumental fury. His bulging muscles pumped with the intense swell of adrenaline. The orc replaced Driktarr in its harness before climbing the rigid skin of the monster, that was currently focused on squeezing and suffocating the prey in its mouth. Fangdarr was nearly to the creature's shoulder when a billowing flap of skin stretched drastically at the creature's neck. The sac spread wide as it ballooned with air. The orc stared in disgust. As he was about to resume his climb, his eye was drawn to movement beneath the cloudy, thin skin from the stretched canvas. It was a hand. *Bitrayuul's* hand!

The sight of the moving hand spurred Fangdarr on. His powerful legs pushed him over the rounded shoulders, granting the enraged orc a clear vantage point to the nearest eye. Rather than become encumbered by his axe's size, Fangdarr chose to take a crude assault. He balled a fist and sailed it the short distance to the toad-like monster's left eye. All the orc's fury, lust for blood, vengeance, and pain propelled that swing. The disgusting squelch that followed as his hand broke through the orb's spongey layer was terrifying. Liquid trapped within the thin lens exploded over Fangdarr, and sickening goo flung into his open mouth filling it with bitter vile. He did not relent. He pushed deeper into the iris until, from around his fist, the bunovir released a mixture of a loud croaking and painful moaning.

Fangdarr spat out the distasteful gore directly back into the creature's eye as he extracted his arm. He paid no mind to the filth that lined his limb; instead, he clambered onto the head of the creature to reach the other eye. The orc's mind flickered to his lost kin for a fleeting moment. Bitrayuul had given him the strategy for this fight, he knew. His barbaric tactics would surely have ended in his death. Fangdarr growled away the thought as it created too much tumult in his mind and distracted from his necessary rage.

It would not matter. Before he managed to reach the remaining eye, a monstrous hand gripped his torso. Instantly his hands reached for anything they could grab ahold of. As the bunovir dragged him over its head, Fangdarr's grip tightened over the nostrils of the beast. With all of his might, the orc pulled; however, despite his anger and pain, Fangdarr was losing the battle. He shouted in defiance into the creature's face, as he hung directly over the gaping mouth of the humanoid abomination. No, *no*! It would not end here. It could not. Bitrayuul must be avenged. The chieftain increased his rage and pulled harder. Between the exertion and the rough grasp of the hand that clutched his torso, Fangdarr's blood vessels started to burst one by one. Sweat poured from his body profusely, screaming to end the pain his muscles were suffering.

"Nooo!" the orc screamed as his energy could no longer sustain the hold, and the bunovir pulled Fangdarr away from its face.

For a moment, Fangdarr hung limply in his foe's grip. It was a temporary relief to not be dangling helplessly over the same jaws that had swallowed his brother. Then again, he would not mind dying beside his kin. Memories swarmed in his mind of their past. How fitting, this would be the end of their story.

At last, the bunovir shifted the orc back over its mouth, and the chieftain felt its large fingers loosen around his torso. It was time. He closed his eyes, shutting away the glowing yellow orbs that were so often filled with the fires of rage. Not this time. His bloodlust had failed him. No fire remained beyond the lens, only acceptance for what was to come.

Back on the shore, Tormag and Cormac watched the scene in horror. They had finally managed to quell the endless torrent of parasitic monsters, but now the effort seemed in vain. Both rushed into the water, uncaring for the depth or the weight of their armor. Tears streamed down Tormag's face as he charged in desperation. "Not again . . . Please, Bothain . . ." he prayed as his body splashed through the shoulder-high water. Both knew it would be impossible to fight in the water. Nonetheless, they pressed on. Even Malice followed behind, for what choice did she have? With the hunter that pursued her, her death was certain anyway, so she might as well die here, of her own volition.

Though their loyalty was admirable beyond compare, it was hopeless. The bunovir's fingers released fully, and Fangdarr's companions watched helplessly as Fangdarr, feared chieftain of the Zharnik clan, who surpassed even his father's great legacy and drove his kind to new heights, fell toward the waiting maw.

CHAPTER FORTY

HELL

Cormac froze in shock at the realization that his friend had been lost to the monster's foul pit. He cared not for the cesspool he stood in, nearly as deep as the dwarf was tall. Nor for the infections he would possibly develop from the putrid liquid entering the miniscule bite wounds left by the tadpole creatures. What was the point? Cormac wondered as his tear-filled gaze could not be averted from the fiend that had swallowed Fangdarr and Bitrayuul.

Tormag, too, was immobilized in despair. Why was he being so punished? He screamed ancient dwarven curses in his mind to his god for abandoning him. Had the old dwarf angered Bothain to bring this fate on himself—to be forced to watch both of the boys he had raised as his own perish just beyond his grasp. What could have brought such a fate to his sons? A hundred dark questions shrouded his mind. Had it not been for the fetid pool nearly consuming the dwarf, he would have fallen to his knees. Instead, he hunched his head and wept.

Despite the loud, unrestrained wails of the dwarves, Malice remained silent, keeping her feelings bottled deep inside, as she had oft learned to do. For all of her might, a single tear rolled down her pale cheek. She had recently discovered her bond to the half-orc, but she had only begun to build that connection. In truth, the woman did feel remorse for Bitrayuul—though the same could not be said for Fangdarr. Nevertheless, a lifetime of pain had numbed her to most everything.

As the trio remain motionless in the pond, the bunovir turned to face them. Though a monstrous creature, it was sentient. A gurgling, croaked laugh escaped the behemoth as it watched the despair come over the faces of its victim's companions. From within its gullet, the muscles tightened to crush and suffocate its meal.

* * * * *

Inside the mouth, Fangdarr felt the squeeze of the tight quarters drawing closer, followed by sharp pain all over the front of his body. Luckily, even in his tired form, the orc was too muscular to be crushed by the internal pocket in which he lay.

However, no amount of muscle would prevent him from suffocating. His eyes turned downward to determine what was causing the continuous stinging. Something metal was cutting into Fangdarr's torso, arms, legs, everywhere! A large hand pushed aside the bit of flexible muscle between him and the metal, revealing the cause. *Bitrayuul!*

His brother sat limply inside the tomb with him, covered entirely in the disgusting saliva that lined the internal tissue around them. Fangdarr shook Bitrayuul lightly to stir him. Nothing. The large orc embraced his sibling in a tight hug. If this was to be their end, he would go with his kin. The spines lining Bitrayuul's razor-like armor bit deeper, drawing blood instantly. Fangdarr growled in frustration. All he wished was to be with his sibling in their final moments. This stupid armor was such a nuisance! *Wait!*

The chieftain had an idea—one he knew his tactical brother would be proud of. Slowly, in the airtight chamber that continued to constrict them, Fangdarr began shifting. With each shift, Bitrayuul's weaponized shell sliced his scarred skin more and more. But it also cut deep into the tissue lining their living casket. Purple-tinted blood started trickling from a few dozen points where the spines had pierced. Fangdarr smiled intensely through the pain; his plan was working.

* * * * *

Another step forward. The bunovir stood only ten paces away now, progressing slowly toward the three before it. Tauntingly. It relished in the hopeless expressions of those that had intruded on its domain. The neck sac ballooned with air, followed by a long, deep croak. It almost sounded like it was trying to speak, though obviously none could understand the rotten language of its kind. Billowing with each vocalization, the bubble of stretched skin under the fiend's chin grew larger.

While the dwarves were lost to their emotions, Malice stared down the beast. Her eyes shifted to the troll. Such a fate was not one she wished to be subjected to. However, could the bunovir truly fit another in its gullet? Two large beings of orcish heritage certainly must have filled the space. Connecting the dots, the assassin knew what that meant. The next victim would follow the fate of the deceased troll. From the shoreline, its body had been almost entirely consumed. Only bones and scraps of tattered organs remain of the carcass. The sight horrified her. It was not the decrepit corpse that vexed her, rather the thought of the monster bulging her body with a thousand eggs only to be eaten from within. Malice shuddered at the thought.

Her eyes were drawn to the approaching abomination. With each inflation of the sac, Malice noticed that more and more blood had started to fill it. Could it be from its wounded eye?

* * * * *

Fangdarr growled in agony as his flesh was rent. Muscle and skin alike were torn apart, though only to a short depth. The last of his strength was nearly spent. Blood—from the bunovir and Fangdarr each—had filled their tomb to nearly half. The air was empty, offering no relief for his tiring muscles or pounding lungs. Still, as his vision began to fade from lack of oxygen and blood, he gripped his brother's body, once again utilizing the makeshift weapon.

*****

"Look!" Malice shouted to the dwarves, who still struggled against their urge to simply fall beneath the water's surface and embrace their own deaths. Each looked up through teary eyes, and a glimmer of hope immediately surged through both as they noticed the woman's cause for exclamation. The sac had filled entirely with blood and the creature had started to swoon. It lumbered forward on uneasy footing until finally it toppled onto its side into the cesspool with a groan.

Tormag stared intently at the monster's neck which had remained inflated despite the fall. "There they are!" he shouted, swimming forward as fast as his armor would allow. From within the pouch, Fangdarr's foot could be seen pressed against the stretched skin—still moving. Cormac and Malice followed quickly, reaching the writhing monster after a short swim.

Tormag was shouting curse after curse at the monster as he clambered to the top of its sidelong skull. He raised his war hammers and pounded both simultaneously into its last remaining eye. The orb burst beneath the blow with a whimper from the victim, and gooey liquid oozed onto its face. Cormac followed suit, crawling into the monster's limply open maw, fearless of the possibility that the monster may recover. Nothing would stop him in that moment—not with hope so close and real.

Each of the captain's bladed shields went to work furiously, cutting away muscle, tendons, tissue, and all the other encumbering inner workings of the monster's throat that stood in his path. His body became covered in the purplish blood of the bunovir as he sliced deeper and deeper. Outside, Malice pierced a hole into the sac, releasing a torrent of blood. The disgusting filth flew into her mouth, and the woman fought the urge to gag as she cut the stretched canvas, allowing air to re-enter the pocket.

They could hear Fangdarr's muffled coughs as the influx of air revitalized his lungs. "We're comin', lad!" Cormac yelled as he continued to cut away tissue. The monster writhed in pain as it was carved from the inside. Finally, the dwarf cleared away the last layer of muscle, and his eyes refilled with tears as the bald head of the orc came into view. It was the same feeling as watching his own son come into the world all those years ago. "Fang?"

The orc, covered head to toe in gore—much his own—craned his neck to look up to his friend. A weak grin found its way to his face. How Cormac loved that large-fanged grin. The dwarf had thought he would never see it again. His stubby arms worked to cut away more muscle in order to widen the gap. Once complete, Cormac reached down and grabbed hold of Fangdarr's shoulders. He pulled with every fiber of his considerable strength, but he could only move him a short distance.

Thankfully, Tormag hopped down from his perch and crawled into the carved tunnel to help. With both dwarves tugging, the siblings slowly were extracted from the beast's throat. Cormac and Tormag continued to drag the pair out of the beast and into the water. They noticed Fangdarr's shredded body with concern, though he still clung tightly to his brother.

"Ch-check Bit," the orc demanded weakly before rolling away. It pained him greatly to relinquish his hold, though he knew they needed room to inspect Bitrayuul. With dreadful agony, Fangdarr rose to his feet. The blackened liquid from the pool and devilish, purple blood of the bunovir spilled from inside his wounds as he stood. The proud orc swooned uneasily before steadying himself with gritted teeth. To his surprise, Malice appeared under his arm, hoisting him for support.

She allowed the chieftain to lead as they slowly waded toward his axe. It had fallen into the pond when the monster had yanked Fangdarr from its face. With luck, the blade had embedded into the earth lining the bottom of the pond, causing the pommel to glimmer just above the surface. Agony surged through Fangdarr's body as he bent to retrieve the weapon. His mighty hand could hardly hold it due to his lack of strength. Malice pressed forward, struggling to support the orc as he grew more sluggish.

As Cormac rushed back to the shore to check on Bear, Tormag tip-toed over to Bitrayuul. The poor dwarf could hardly breathe as he took his son into his arms, the spines of the half-orc's carapace cutting deep into his toughened hands. He paid the discomfort no mind. All that mattered was his adopted kin's health. He gently removed Bitrayuul's helmet and stroked his face tenderly. Tormag begged forgiveness from his deity for the stream of curses he had unleashed to the heavens only moments before. With whispers and light taps on the half-orc's face, he attempted to stir the young warrior.

Across the water, Fangdarr and Malice returned to the bunovir's dying form. The monster's elastic tongue floated at the top of the pool, uncurled to nearly its full length. Fangdarr breathed heavily with exhaustion and tenderly pushed the woman aside for her own safety. Malice watched for a moment as Fangdarr struggled to lift his greataxe high enough for a strike before offering aid once more. Never did she think to support an orc in his cause, especially one who was the full-blooded son of the brute who imprisoned her—the monster who had taken the sanctity of her womb, night after night, while she cried out in terror and pain. Her stoic face refused to show the inner struggle she fought as her hands pushed Fangdarr's arm and Driktarr higher into the air.

Gravity brought the blade down onto the limp appendage. It was a slow fall, but the weight of the weapon and its sharpened edge managed to cut deeply into the listless tongue. Fangdarr absorbed the brief surge of vitality. It wasn't much, not nearly enough. Nevertheless, the orc now had just enough strength to hold the weapon on his own. With more vigor, he lifted the weapon again before crashing it down to slice through the original cut.

Malice backed away as Fangdarr's shredded flesh began to mend before her eyes. Immediately her mind started to crack under the confirmation of what she had suspected since joining Bitrayuul's search for his sibling. The axe was the same that had been carried by her tormentor. She thought she had recognized its shape. But design can be faked. Now, seeing it stitch the grievous wounds, Malice had no doubt. Too many times she had watched from her cage in shock as Brutigarr returned from a successful raid and healed the wounds he had suffered at the cost of one of the other prisoners. The woman shut her eyes in mental agony. This could be her chance to end the line of Brutigarr. Every thought screamed to stab the orc in his back—to carve out his heart in vengeance!

Yet, she did not. Two days prior, she would have gladly done so without a second thought. However, the woman had formed a bond with Bitrayuul that screamed even louder than her instincts. *Do not break his trust*, her mind cried out to her through the fragments. The command resounded continuously within her. Malice's fingers loosened their grip on the dagger she did not even notice had appeared in her hand. Still, the fight was not yet won. So, she opened her eyes and forced herself to stare Fangdarr in the face. She scanned every detail, cementing the image in her mind. Dare Malice sacrifice all to be rid of Fangdarr due to the sins of his father? For several moments, Malice stood motionless, grappling with the thought, her eyes wide from the turmoil raging inside.

Fangdarr, now almost fully healed, finally noticed the pale assassin staring intensely at his face—the dagger still loosely clutched in her hand. The orc lowered his weapon, turned cautiously toward the woman, and dropped Driktarr into the pool. He then stretched out his arms wide, offering her that which she craved. Lost within her raging subconscious, Malice's hand tightened around the curved blade.

Seeing Fangdarr stand with arms splayed wide, the remaining members of the party turned their attention to the pair. Cormac was returning from the shore with Bear and when the limping animal saw Malice holding a dagger to her companion, she took off running as best as her leg would allow. With an imposing snarl, the animal charged headlong into the water to protect her master.

Arms still out wide, Fangdarr decided to take a risk. He took one slow step forward, but Malice's practiced hand instinctively gripped tighter around the worn handle of her blade. Her eyes remained glued open, allowing not a single blink for many moments. Unbeknownst to the orc, the woman was losing the battle in her mind. The fragments were just too great. Too many years of seething hatred had bloomed inside her, waiting for the moment to end Brutigarr. Unfortunately, with his passing, Fangdarr was the next best option. Oh, how every bone in her body yearned for Malice to sink that dagger into this beast's chest. The resolution to her long torment was finally here. It even stood in acceptance of its fate, waiting with its arms spread wide for her to exact her revenge.

"Mother, no!" Bitrayuul called out, now standing in the pool.

The assassin's resolve shattered the instant the word *mother* rang out with its piercing chime, muddying all the other roaring screams in her head. She blinked a dozen times, restoring the moisture to her dried eyes. The half-orc strode forward, still weak from his recent resuscitation. Tears welled in the woman's eyes as she looked upon his serene face. Her son's face. Mother. *Mother.* ***Mother!*** The dagger fell into the black liquid at her waist as Malice broke down into uncontrollable sobs. No, no! Now was the time! How could she pass this up? Did she not wish for vengeance? How could she be so weak as to let her tormenter go unpunished?!

Vision blurred by tears, the woman hardly noticed as she was embraced roughly. In her mind, she willed him not to speak. The woman knew he would talk about how proud he was of her restraint. How she had managed to fight away her sorrow and deep-rooted pain for his sake. But he would be wrong. In that moment of strength, Malice had won. Though Bitrayuul had stayed her hand in that moment, he could not know the relentless approach of her vengeance. It would return at a time of its choosing and there was no guarantee today's outcome would be repeated. Her wails were muffled as she buried her face and pounded her fist against the chest of her partner. She wanted to tell him of his faulty faith in her. Of how one day she may very well succumb to her deepest desires and eliminate his kin.

But as she wiped away the tears in her eyes and locked eyes with him, Malice realized it was not Bitrayuul who was holding her. Those yellow orbs knowingly glared into her own. But there was no blame. No anger or fear. Not even sorrow or confusion. Instead, there was only acceptance. Within that gaze she found relief, and for however brief of a period, her pain washed away. All the misguided voices in her mind ceased their whispers and screams. Wrapped in his tight embrace, Malice felt only the innocence of Fangdarr's true nature. He was ashamed by the brutality his predecessor had inflicted upon her. She knew without a doubt that, after that moment, there would be no more pain at the sight of the orc's face. No longer would his face be seen as a resemblance of her captor. Rather, he would be seen for himself and all that he was.

The woman relaxed as all the stress left her muscles. Finally, she was free from her anguish. Fangdarr held her limp form tightly against his chest. After a few long moments, the orc broke into a wide smile as he felt Malice lightly return the embrace in gratitude. Slowly, he lowered the woman to her feet—she had not even noticed she had been suspended. Fangdarr smiled at her—a genuine smile as the pair's bond had been cemented in that single moment.

Bitrayuul watched it all in envy. Despite the positive outcome, his expression turned to distaste at the bond formed between the two most unlikely of allies.

Minorly agitated, the half-orc stomped over to the bunovir. It struggled to breath its last breaths as blood poured freely from the grievous wounds it had suffered. How the monster had survived this long was a feat in itself. Bitrayuul stooped low and crawled back into its mouth. He shifted his orientation to position himself toward the creature's brain before unleashing a plunging strike with his bladed gauntlet. A light moan escaped the fiend. Another blow. Another. And another. His arms pumped as the half-orc sank his blades deep into the bunovir's brain. Bitrayuul sighed in relief at having his frustration played out. He did not wish to hold Fangdarr and Malice's bond against them. It was a good thing, in truth. The son of the assassin simply wished his own mother could form such a bond with him as well.

Having released his emotions, the half-orc crawled out from the maw of the corpse, covered in gore. Fangdarr was strapping Driktarr to his back as Malice returned her dropped dagger to its scabbard. With all the allies gathered together, mostly unharmed, Tormag could not pass the opportunity to speak. "Told ye it wasn't safe." The assembled group laughed heartily as they blissfully ignored just how close to death they had come.

CHAPTER FORTY-ONE

RAZ'JA

Bear nudged her master's leg for reassurance. As the animal scanned the area, she could not miss the heaping mass of mutilated bunovir that had knocked her unconscious. Her mood was lightened by the full-bodied laughter of her companions, though it confused her. Fangdarr and Cormac were completely covered in a foul-tasting liquid that her tongue could only guess was the blood of the monster they had slain. The dwarves also were covered in tiny trickles of their own blood, it seemed. Bear's nose reared up, and she groaned in disgust at the blend of scents coming off the warriors. The incoming waves of putrid vapors from her companions and the area alike were almost too much for her.

Noticing his friend was whimpering now, Fangdarr knelt down to rub her ears. "Do not worry, Bear. We all safe now. Thank you for protecting me." His arms wrapped mightily around the large grizzly in a loving embrace. The beast visibly relaxed. She trusted her master beyond doubt. After the orc was certain her growing discomfort had lifted, he released his grip and stared her in the eye. "I love you, Bear," the prideful chieftain said with a smile. As if the intelligent animal understood, she licked his face in happiness, forgetting the slime and gore that clung to his skin.

"Well, now what?" Tormag asked, taking another look at the deceased monster as well as their expected path.

All remained silent. For many moments, none would speak. Even Malice, with her typical irritable comments, simply sat quietly to herself on the shore in reflection. The storm that had been raging in her mind for years had been quelled, it seemed. The woman relished in the tranquility that now took its place. Emptiness had never felt so full. No longer did the assassin believe her mind would be constantly tormented by an internal enemy that she could not hope to cull. No, she felt free.

Finally, Cormac replied gruffly, "Eh, to be honest, I'm not sure how much more difficult a dragon may be in comparison to what we just wiggled away from."

"Aye, that be true, don't ye doubt. Ain't never thought I'd come face t' face with a bunovir, sure as stones. Just like dragons, they're the stuff o' legends. But . . ." the old dwarf paused to inspect the damage of their foe, "seems we did alright. Bahaha!"

Cormac returned the sentiment, joining in his ally's laughter. Bitrayuul strode to Fangdarr's position. The chieftain did not need to hear the words or even meet his gaze. He sighed as he extended to full height before turning to his companions. "We should turn around," the orc stated plainly.

The dwarves turned to one another in confusion. Their voices rose over each other's refusals, clambering to be heard. Fangdarr was already shaking his head. "I can't control myself. I get you killed."

Bitrayuul chimed in with agreement, "He is right. This task may be beyond us. We are only at the precipice of these forsaken lands, and we were almost wiped out before we even stepped foot into the mountains."

"But what about Fangdarr? Without the dragon, the orcs will only take action," Cormac responded.

"Aye, and we just knocked the innards from that there beast," Tormag added, pointing a short finger to the fallen bunovir's corpse. "Ye mean t' tell me ye think we can't take on a drake?"

The half-orc sighed in frustration. Did they not see he only cared for their safety? "Fang, we can—" Bitrayuul stopped in confusion as Tormag slung his pack over his broad, plated shoulder and started walking to the passage. "Wait— where are you going?!"

His father offered no words, only the heavy stomps of his boots. Before long, Cormac reached his cupped hands into the water and splashed away all of the accumulated gore that had dried to his skin. A funny thing, to wash away the blood of a beast with tainted water mixed with the blood of countless others. Nevertheless, with his face 'clean' the dwarf took off after Tormag without a word.

Bitrayuul looked to Fangdarr expectantly, as if demanding he say something to halt them from marching toward their own doom. Instead, his brother gathered his own supplies and smugly whispered, "Dwarves be dwarves." The half-orc groaned in his growing frustration before following his companions, each step paired with a grumble under his breath about the bull-headed nature of dwarves.

Seeing her group leave, Malice rose from her seat and skipped lightly past Bitrayuul. Her sudden lighthearted demeanor left her son speechless, though not from happiness. Seeing the fragility of the woman's mind first-hand, the half-orc was concerned for the longevity of her state. In any case, he did manage a smile beneath his helmet as his mother seemed to be free of her affliction—for now.

The procession walked quietly, cautious of drawing unwanted attention. It made sense given the passage was littered with the remains of other unsuspecting creatures that had stumbled upon the bunovir's lair. Countless troll corpses had been picked clean after being left for the carrion pickers. As they continued further east and higher into the mountain, the bones became more scarce. Finally, they came to a narrow gap in the passage.

Tormag dropped his pack to the ground. "We'll take a break here and get cleaned up. This is a defensible position," he added as his eyes scanned their surroundings.

The dwarf did not speak falsely. Only the path behind served for poor defense, while the gap in front of them was hardly big enough for Fangdarr to squeeze through, meaning no surprise attacks from large monsters. In addition, due to the enclosed stone over their heads a small pool of clean water had accumulated along one side of the area. It wasn't much, but it was enough to fill their waterskins and wash away the filth. And free from the sun's heat, the gathered water would not evaporate any time soon.

The old dwarf removed the map from his bag and marked their position, both to track their progress as well as mark the location should they need it again. With all of the companions wiped free of fetid grime, they each sat against the stone walls of the shelter. "Should we camp here, father?" Bitrayuul asked.

Rolling the map before stuffing it into his pouch, the gruff dwarf exhaled loudly. "Well, we could. There won't be many more opportunities like this one. No fires, though."

Bitrayuul nodded knowingly; they were in the realm of evil now, best not to draw attention. "Malice and I will take the first watch, followed by the dwarves. Fangdarr and Bear, you can take the last." The small pangs of envy still stood present in his mind as he continued to dwell on Malice's bond with his brother. The half-orc decided now was the time to act. If she would not make the effort to strengthen their relationship, then Bitrayuul must force it.

With the remainder of the party resting, as much as they could in such a cold, treacherous environment, Bitrayuul fell to his rear next to his mother near the small opening through the passage. To his relief, her blue eyes scrunched slightly as a genuine smile found its way across her fair-skinned face. For a fraction of a moment, the half-orc froze in panic, as seeing the woman's kind-hearted smile beneath those shining sapphires drew him back to Lilyana. He tried to shake away the painful memory without notice, but it was hopeless. Bitrayuul could not forcibly remove the vivid remembrance of the young girl, bouncing around happily in his mind. Nor did he want to. Nevertheless, this was neither the time nor the place.

"I miss her too," came the soft whisper from his mother. In surprise, Bitrayuul turned to face Malice. She still sat motionless with that smile glued to her face. Had she gone mad? "But . . ." the woman continued, this time with a hint of sobriety, "the past is gone. All we can do is remember and press on." Her final statement caught Bitrayuul off guard as her tone had once again heightened to a chipper mood.

The half-orc pondered for a moment, unsure of how to continue. He was nearly certain her mind remained broken, and now the conversation was taking a risky turn. In their location, Bitrayuul could not chance prodding his mother to gauge her stability. With a sigh, he simply nodded in reply, deciding not to unleash the slew of questions, arguments, and chastisements that begged to be given voice. His bond with the woman would be hard to strengthen in her current state. The half-orc swallowed his growing aggravation, and their watch went by uneventful and devoid of any dialogue thereafter, though the smile never left Malice's face.

Shifts rotated to the grumbling dwarves who were not fond of being stirred from their slumber. Their dreams had taken them far away to blissful recreations of their stone and kin that served far better company than the constant risk of monsters and demons bedeviling this uncharted land. Nevertheless, once fully roused, Tormag and Cormac took to their watch without further complaint.

Tormag watched in curiosity as his son stomped off to sleep without any more words. The old dwarf had been around Bitrayuul long enough to know when he was irritated. Even so, he simply shrugged it off and hoped a rest would relieve whatever tension the half-orc clung to. His attention returned to Cormac who was already buzzing with conversation. Tormag joined his dwarven ally in the lighthearted topic to speed the time.

Later, a rough hand tapped Fangdarr on his shoulder, drawing him from his sleep. "Oye, yer turn, lad," Cormac softly whispered to his friend. The orc rolled to his side and scanned the area. At least they seemed safe enough. With a *hmph* he was on his feet and ready to start the watch. Before waking Bear, the orc grabbed a small handful of dried meat from his provisions to settle the rumble in his stomach.

Chewing on some of the meat, Fangdarr walked over to Bear and gave her a soft shake. Nothing except the lazy snoozing of her snout came in response. He shook her more forcefully now, still to no avail. The orc rolled his eyes, knowing exactly what the playful beast was doing, but in truth, Fangdarr loved her childish games. With a large piece of the salted meat held tight within his outstretched hand, he inched it closer and closer to her nose.

Fangdarr smiled past his large tusks as Bear's nose wiggled with more vigor, sensing the meal to come. Just as her maw opened to take in the slab, the orc retracted it. Without hesitation, his companion softly whimpered, only widening the orc's smile. But Fangdarr could no longer torment the poor creature. With a small chuckle, he slid the meat into her mouth where it was devoured instantly. In response, Bear sprang to life and rubbed her cold, wet nose all over the giggling orc's bare thighs.

Cormac and Tormag simply looked at each other with incredulous expressions at the ridiculousness of their company. Then the two dwarves rolled onto their backs, flat against the stone before returning to their imaginary paradises within their minds.

After feeding Bear a few more pieces, Fangdarr strode to their watch point at the threshold. He looked out beyond the gap for any threats but saw none—only the ceaseless view of sharpened stone and rough terrain leading to the many mountains beyond. Despite the near impossibility of a sighting, the orc scanned all he could see in search of the dragon. He scoffed at the notion of it flying about without a care. But pondering the thought more, Fangdarr realized it was not such an impossibility. This was Crepusculus' domain, after all. The drake must have lived here for hundreds or thousands of years. Fangdarr recalled the tales of dragons Tormag had told them as boys and contemplated how this one was different.

Unlike a red dragon, Crepusculus held no care for gold, glory, or pride. And, unlike a black, it did not seem to want to remain sleeping in its pit forever due to a profound self-awareness of its own godlike prowess that made all life seem meaningless. Unfortunately, not much was known about shadow dragons—only that one or two had been seen over the last few thousand years—and never with a positive outcome. They were said to be devious and foreboding creatures, capable of terrible things. Like most others of its kind, shadow dragons spent the vast majority of their life hidden away from view. The ageless monsters simply waited, biding their time; waiting for an era where dragons ruled over all other races once more.

Fangdarr retreated into the small cavern and plopped to his rear. Bear, ever loyal, nudged against his chest before laying over the top of the orc's legs. For many moments, Fangdarr remained prone under his companion, running large, calloused fingers through the animal's thick coat. Bear blissfully exhaled to show her contentment, inching ever closer until she was sprawled over Fangdarr's chest entirely.

Though the orc was happy to be cuddled up with his soft, warm companion, Bear's weight made it a strain for him to breathe. After a handful more of loving pets, Fangdarr exhaled and lifted the hulking mass of beast off his chest. She opened her eyes in confusion, wanting to know the reason for her comfort's interruption.

"I need to go," he stated plainly, signifying his need to urinate. Bear rose with Fangdarr, but when the orc noticed her trailing him, he turned to add, "No, Bear. *I* need to go. You stay. I just be through there." Her glistening nose followed his pointing finger through the passage gap. Bear gave a low whimper; whether for her lack of a cuddle partner or concern for his well-being, Fangdarr could not be certain. In any case, the orc wanted to get some fresh air for a moment. His hand rubbed her head in comfort before turning to exit the cavern.

Passing through the threshold felt liberating as the wind bit into Fangdarr's skin. It was the blooming season, so warm days that still held their moisture were the norm. However, up here in the mountains, the seasons were entirely altered. The heat that rose from the forest below got caught up with the winds against the high, jutting summits, causing it to cool. They were about half way up the mountain, where the wind was just beginning to get that slight edge to it, just enough to chill the orc's skin. Fangdarr closed his eyes and stretched his arms out wide, embracing the whipping gusts.

He stood for what seemed a lifetime—arms extended, fingers spread, allowing the chill to bring bumps to his blackened skin. Fangdarr took a large inhale and blew it out slowly, enjoying the crispness in his lungs. As the orc opened his eyes to scan the mountainous surroundings, his gaze locked on to a figure leaning loosely against a boulder a short distance away.

"Beautiful view is it not?" stated the creature. Fangdarr instantly knew it for a troll due to the accent; the vocal flair of 'is it' sounded more like '*eez eet*'. The orc turned to face the intruder with caution.

Before his journey, Fangdarr gladly named trolls his allies. They were vicious fighters capable of lethal action. However, this was the Tusk Mountains—labeled as such for the sheer number of trolls that inhabited its spine—and his party were now the intruders. The chieftain was torn between his own desired response and that which his band of companions would expect. Were they here with him, they would have demanded Fangdarr eliminate the threat of one from such an *evil* race. These were not necessarily false labels, but the orc wished to see past that as he hoped others would one day do the same for orcs.

Unable to form words that would satisfy both perspectives, Fangdarr nodded his agreement. The creature walked forward slowly, nonchalantly, and though his protective instincts told him otherwise, the orc stopped himself from reaching for his weapon strapped across his back. He would at least allow this to play out. As the troll warrior came into view, Fangdarr spread a smile. "Raz'ja!" he exclaimed in eagerness. Never did he expect to encounter the troll chieftain this far from his home. Fangdarr extended a forearm in greeting.

"Ah, Fangdarr, is that you?" Raz'ja asked in his distinctive dialect as he clasped arms with the orc. "What you doin' here, chief?"

Fangdarr still held the smile to his face, truly joyed to see his old ally. "Out for walk, you?" He did not want to be entirely honest with the troll just yet.

Raz'ja continued without hesitation, "Ah, you know, lost me necklace!" The ensuing laughter at his own joke mixed with the joke's obvious absurdity forced the orc to break out in hilarity as well. The troll's neck already had nearly a dozen necklaces. Each were made of a mixture of bones, teeth, fingers, or ears; trophies from worthy kills. Fangdarr could pick out the different races based on the removed extremities—dwarven fingers, elven ears, and the like.

Seeing the chieftain again reminded Fangdarr of how skilled Raz'ja truly was. They had fought together side-by-side on a handful of raids of the human lands. The troll was certainly a force you would rather have as an aid than an obstacle. His savagery seemed limitless. Fangdarr used to watch as his ally would skitter around the battlefield agilely cutting the hearts from innocent villagers and taking bites from them before the life finished leaving his victim's eyes. Prior to his change of conscience, Fangdarr had been proud to call Raz'ja his friend—and even more so his ally.

The orc briefly pondered in silence before deciding it would prove useful to have the troll aid in their quest, but before Fangdarr could speak, the troll leader cut in. "Fangdarr, the time has finally come . . ." Fangdarr tilted his head curiously and gave the troll a puzzled expression. Raz'ja continued, slightly irritated that elaboration was necessary. "We will attack soon."

Taken aback by the sudden news, Fangdarr's mind raced with questions and concerns. "What? When?" The act his counterpart spoke of now left a dense weight in the orc's stomach, and Fangdarr's bright yellow eyes could not hide his concern—a fact the troll was certain not to miss.

Despite the orc chieftain's unexpected reaction, Raz'ja continued. "Our numbers are great. We follow a leader—one who would see our races rulers of this land. Finally, we will be rid of the greedy fingers of man's endless grasp. No longer will we hear the incessant strikin' of dwarven pickaxes in the mountains beneath our feet. Can you imagine, Fangdarr? Bein' able to walk this land freely without fear of annihilation simply because of the color of our skin or shape of our teeth?"

Fangdarr listened intently as the troll rambled on in excitement. Each word he spoke only heightened his enthusiasm. By the end of Raz'ja's response, the troll was nearly sweating in his fervor. The orc allowed his old ally to settle before asking, "Who this leader you follow?"

At that, the troll's wide mouth stretched to a sinister grin, revealing dark rows of sharpened teeth. The large curved tusks of his jaw became more exposed as Raz'ja's lips curled back in glee. "We follow the Shadow One. Crepusculus."

CHAPTER FORTY-TWO
CONSEQUENCES

Fangdarr's eyes grew wide in shock. *Crepusculus*?! The same drake his party now hunted? How could Raz'ja seek to follow such an unholy beast? The orc knew trolls, by reputation, were ill received, yet even he found this barbaric.

"The dragon?! For what purpose?" the orc asked.

Still sporting that wicked grin, Raz'ja happily provided answers. "It called to me, Fangdarr, O' Mighty One. Even now, I hear his whispers in me ears." The troll began pacing as his hands made exaggerated movements while recalling the story. "We trolls have always sought our rightful place in this world—above the weak humans and cowardly dwarves that hide in their caves. The Shadow One called to me and said, '*You are strong. You are savage. Yet, you are the roots that remain unseen, holdin' the towerin' growth above on your shoulders. Do you wish to become immortal?*' So, of course, Raz'ja accepts his servitude. Crepusculus has promised us this land—agreed to be the guide to our fate and spread the plague that will erode the goodly races from this place, directly into our waiting hands.

"Fangdarr, it has told me of your strength—that you stared the Shadow One in the face and roared in defiance. Such a feat! Raz'ja is strong, but even he cowers under the gaze of Crepusculus. I ask you, will you join us? Will you lead the orcs of the Zharnik clan to become the rulers of Crein? Our legend will be made immortal through the fables told by the few survivors that are left in our wake!" As Raz'ja finalized his pitch, he extended his arm toward Fangdarr.

The orc chieftain was torn completely. His companions were relying on him—had even put their *lives* on the line for his impossible task. How could he even consider betraying them? But, Fangdarr's gaze drew toward the three wide fingers now extended to him. All he had ever wanted for his people was there for the taking. Fangdarr only needed to serve.

"Why hesitate?" Raz'ja asked, narrowing his eyes at the orc's uncharacteristic reluctance. "You do not wish to bring your people the glory they desire?"

"I would see my people rise!" Fangdarr growled back. "This decision not easy. Orcs not meant to serve."

"Ah, that's right. You're not meant to serve—only to be forced into the corner of the forest, hiding in your shame, beggin' the humans to not swarm your clan and eradicate what is left of you. That is preferable to serving? I see. I see," the troll taunted.

Fangdarr growled in his face with growing anger. "Yes!"

There it was. His decision had been made without the orc even knowing. Fangdarr immediately pondered his response and the possible consequences. Could he really bring about an era where orcs were considered equals on his own? Fangdarr clamped his eyes shut tightly. Did he just turn away the one opportunity in his lifetime that would turn the advantage and grant that wish?

The orc was so distracted by the stress overtaking his mind, he hardly noticed Raz'ja extracting the sharpened stone dagger from his side. The orc looked down at the rush of blood and back to the one who had stabbed him. The expression on the troll's face was not one of anger or hatred but disappointment. Raz'ja had truly wished for Fangdarr and his orcs to join the cause.

Fangdarr grasped the wound with his left hand and reached for Driktarr with his right. In response, Raz'ja reached into a small animal skin pouch at his waist and flung an unknown substance into Fangdarr's unsuspecting eyes. As the blinded orc fell back, he could feel the burning sensation of another dagger strike tearing into his thigh. Wiping the substance from his eyes, Fangdarr growled angrily as both wounds continued to bleed without relent. He scanned the area, but the troll was nowhere in sight.

The orc chieftain's thoughts turned from rage to concern as he realized his companions were sleeping a short distance behind him. Clutching both wounds tightly to staunch the flow, Fangdarr slowly marched back to the cavern with determination. As he closed the distance, the ring of clashing steel and hooting shouts of savage trolls could be heard. Fangdarr disregarded his own safety now as he removed his hands from the wounds to aid in speeding his charge.

"Get a fire goin'! They regenerate immediately if ye don't burn the wounds!" Fangdarr heard Tormag yell as he passed through the gap he was meant to defend. Already, he could see Bitrayuul dousing a small handful of sticks with oil in the center of the camp as their remaining allies held the attacking trolls at bay.

"Fangdarr!" Bitrayuul called out upon seeing his brother return. The half-orc did not fail to notice the blood glistening on his sibling's skin. As if in reply, Fangdarr removed his greataxe from its strap and charged toward the nearest foe.

With the fire lit, the surrounding cavern became illuminated with the flickers of the dancing flames. Shadows stretched along the face of the walls around them.

Gods, there were so many of them. With the faint light now granting a wider range of vision, a hundred pairs of eyes could be seen. They were completely surrounded. Even the path Fangdarr had passed through was now hemorrhaging trolls; each bearing their tusks in anticipation, ready to sink their sharpened stone weapons into the flesh of the intruders. This was their domain.

Despite the overwhelming odds, the companions had managed to hold their own thus far. But the fire still had not been made. Each troll that was felled simply regenerated. Severed limbs grew back, and even decapitated enemies, after a few moments, rose to fight once more.

"Agh!" Malice let out a yelp of pain as the six trolls she fought simultaneously managed to slip through her defenses to land a deep cut on her arm. Fortunately, Bitrayuul had just finished lighting the torches and handed one to Malice and each of the other allies—excluding Fangdarr and Bear—as they fought off the endless wave of enemies.

Finally, the first troll fell as its oily skin instantly immolated in a raging inferno. Their strength was also their weakness, it seemed. While the hellish race could regenerate beyond comprehension, it came at the cost of producing an oily substance whenever their body became wounded—a highly flammable oil.

Fangdarr found a place alongside his friends, between Bear and Bitrayuul's position, and armed with their torches, the allies held back the tide. The makeshift fire to their backs, they formed a tight-knit circle to protect each other's flanks while the flames behind served to dissuade any from attacking their rear.

Bitrayuul cut through the trolls flawlessly. His armor served as a perfect tool against the creatures as the half-orc only needed to make minor cuts to cause the flammable liquid to excrete at the wound. Once his armor gashed their skin, he swiftly followed with the torch conflagrating the screaming troll. Fangdarr's weapon, on the other hand, was less suited for the encounter. Despite his quick cuts that would cleanly dissect each troll's softened skin, they would simply rejuvenate. Though the irritated orc's wounds had healed through the magic of his weapon, he had yet to fell any of the multiple trolls that had engaged him.

Meanwhile, the dwarves were masterfully disposing of trolls at every turn. Being of the mountain, they were well accustomed to culling the filthy monsters that sought to infest their caves. Cormac held a torch in each hand from behind the blades that protruded from his shield. The moment the sharpened point pierced the skin, the torch immediately made contact and set the wound alight. Tormag took a less cumbersome approach. The dwarf simply doused both of his war hammers in oil and dipped them into the flames. Burning bright with orange and yellow flickers of light, the commander launched his hammers endlessly at the surrounding trolls. As each made contact, it immediately broke through the skin just enough to force the wound to fill with the flammable substance before igniting it in the same moment. He laughed all the while as his trusted weapons returned to his grip after each new inferno.

Already the dwarves had managed to eliminate over three dozen trolls on their own, proving their efficiency. Trolls who witnessed the prowess of the pair chose to direct their attention to the human woman who was quickly becoming overwhelmed. And it was true. Adjacent to Cormac, Malice continued to be on the defensive. Her pale skin shone brightly against the dark environment, only bringing more attention to the many cuts she had suffered. Her expertise was more aligned with the shadows, picking off unsuspecting targets one-by-one. This was the first encounter she had experienced of this magnitude, and despite the woman's best efforts, Malice could not hold back the wave of enemies that flung themselves against her with increasing abandon.

Watching his mother be pressed back, inching closer and closer to the growing flames at her back, Bitrayuul broke formation to come to her aid. With Bear now alone on the flank, there was no way to prevent trolls from pressing the weakened defense. She swiped with heavy paws, claws rending flesh apart with a spray of blue blood in every direction. However, like her master, the animal's weapons were ineffective. To make matters worse, she had no torch. Even if she had held one in her mouth, the awkward position would only have served to expose her neck more. Nevertheless, the clever beast found a way.

With powerful jaws, Bear grabbed at the nearest troll who aimed to attack Bitrayuul's backside, clamped down tightly, drawing blood, and launched the troll behind her into the pit of flames. The fire roared in ecstasy as its flames grew higher and higher consuming the dying creature, the troll's screams shrieking loudly off the cavern walls.

Tormag and Cormac, those sudden machinations of death whose sole purpose seemed to be to remove all trolls from existence, chanted happily and boasted with laughter. This almost seemed a game to them, and in truth, as veterans of the dwarven military, it likely was.

In their joyous state, however, neither had noticed the breach of formation at their rear. Malice and Bitrayuul were hard at work regaining the ground that had been lost while Bear and Fangdarr struggled to keep their targets at bay. All the orc and his companion could do was keep fighting while they waited for their allies to come to their aid.

Bear growled in concern as a troll jumped past her and through the flames to arrive at Tormag's back. Due to his reliance on the monsters being too afraid of fire to approach from behind, the unsuspecting dwarf continued merrily in his slaughtering. Fangdarr took a moment to glance behind after hearing Bear's lament.

In that minor glimpse, the orc recognized the troll instantly. Raz'ja stood behind the dwarf, each of his three-fingered hands wielding sharpened stone daggers. That sinister grin Fangdarr encountered before was pasted on the troll chieftain's face once more.

"Tormag!" cried the orc in desperation. "Turn around!"

With luck, the dwarven warrior managed to hear Fangdarr's plea over the cacophony of clashing steel and the constant guttural howls of the trolls and turned to face Raz'ja. But it was too late. The vicious troll's weapons were already sailing toward the dwarf's neck, seeking to end him in a single strike. Tormag was a skilled warrior, but even he could not hope to lift his weapons to parry in time.

The round, brown eyes of the dwarf never closed; Tormag would not grant the troll the satisfaction. Instead, he stared determinedly into the blood-thirsty gaze of Raz'ja and accepted his fate. The troll stretched his maw into a salivating grin, savoring the kill to come. How he yearned to feel his daggers puncture through the thick skin of the dwarf. Raz'ja was so enthralled by the prospect that he failed to notice the glimmer of shining steel coming toward him.

It passed through the troll's neck in an instant, completely halting the leaping troll's momentum. Raz'ja's decapitated head retained its grin as it rolled into the fire. Despite being severed completely from his body, Raz'ja's face still bore his lucid expressions. It contorted from wickedness to shock before finally settling on agony as the flames consumed him.

Chakal kicked against the troll's torso hard, pushing it into the pit of flames, the roaring inferno howling voraciously as it engulfed the fallen corpse. The kick allowed the spry elf to launch himself into the remaining fray of trolls. Immediately, the assassin was surrounded by a dozen of them.

Tormag watched in confusion at the turn of events before turning back to focus on the enemy at hand. Upon seeing their leader being corroded away by the flames and hearing his piercing screeches of agony, the creatures spurred forward enraged. If they had been formidable before, they were twice so now. Their blind fury at the loss of Raz'ja spurred their attacks to blitzing speeds that greatly surpassed their previous skills.

Each of the companions were pressed back by the aggressive assault, causing their circle to tighten once more. Even both dwarves were now on the defensive, unable to retaliate. However, Tormag had a clear view of the elf who had saved the dwarf from his fate. Still, Chakal remained surrounded by the tumultuous wave of fiendish creatures, but his dagger and short-sword worked expertly at a level the commander had never before witnessed. Not a single attack penetrated the elf's perfect defenses. Always were they brushed aside at the last moment with a sweeping glance of his elven blades or dodged by Chakal's agile movements.

The spectacle was both inspiring and terrifying to watch at the same time. Tormag knew this to be the hunter who sought to end them all. But if that were so, why would the elf save him? To that extent, the dwarf's honor would allow no less than to return the favor. Granted, Chakal did not, at the moment, seem to need saving, but Tormag would settle for a bit of assistance. As the dwarf repelled the opponents in front of him with a heavy shove, his right-handed hammer poised back for a throw. The flames on the weapon had nearly died away entirely as the oil had been consumed—only the bits of troll flesh on the head kept the flames alive. The throw would be difficult—many intersecting trolls stood in its path—but he had to try.

As the flaming weapon soared through the air, trolls ducked away in fear as it sailed overhead. They had seen enough of those rampaging hammers being thrown into the bodies of their allies to know to avoid contact. With a loud *thud*, the hammer found its mark, and the troll nearest the elf assassin burst into flames. With fire in his eyes, the elf's face shifted to sheer thrill, and the assassin savagely sliced away limbs, heads, and even cleaved bodies in half, sending them all into the burning pillar. Within mere moments, Chakal's pit of fire grew thrice the size of the other as it chewed away at the dozen trolls in its grasp.

Chakal conquered his enemies without so much a scratch. By the time the elf had disposed of the first dozen, the remaining half wanted no part of this impossible warrior. There was no hope for them. The elf sprinted after each as they clambered away, clawing at the stone in an attempt to flee up the walls around them. The remaining trolls all turned their attention toward the screams of fear. Watching their kin get slaughtered brutally by a single enemy caused them to lose their resolve and those out of his reach fell back into the shadows.

Fangdarr and Bitrayuul watched the creatures retreat, glad to finally reach the conclusion of the skirmish. They looked to each other, breathing heavily from the assault. As Bitrayuul was about to speak, he heard Malice scream.

"What is *HE* doing here?! No! *No*! Leave us!"

Confused, the half-orc followed her gaze and found Chakal nonchalantly striding toward them. The elf's attire was covered head to toe in blue-tinted blood, making him hardly recognizable. But for Malice, there was no mistaking the monster that had haunted her—and would forever more.

The woman instantly charged forward with unintelligible screams, weapons raised. Tormag lunged forward and grabbed hold of her by the waist. "Wait, wait! He saved me. Us!" Malice heard nothing he said. She cried out in a mix of emotions. She thought her mind had been restored, but the elf's appearance proved it was all an illusion. There was no chance for renewal. She crumpled to the ground and wept as the realization hit her like an ogre's maul. Would she ever be free from herself?

Bitrayuul, however, was not of such a broken state of mind. He strode forward accusingly before also being stopped by Tormag. "Lad, no! Me life is owed t' him today."

The half-orc seethed with anger at the presence of their stalker, but he could not dispute his father's claim. It was an unspoken rule among the honorable that a life saved was a debt to be repaid. Bitrayuul growled from beneath his helmet but remained in place.

Fangdarr, Cormac, and Bear had not encountered Chakal before; they had only heard of their allies' recounting of the assassin. As a result, they were not as concerned by the threat at hand. As far as they knew, here stood a single elf, one who had helped them, no less. Bear, though, growled with a furled snarl at the assassin.

"Listen, elf," Tormag began, turning toward Chakal, who stood smiling awkwardly. "Me honor demands that I thank ye fer what ye did fer me, and so I shall. On me life, I thank ye." All eyes were on the dwarf as he thanked the same devil who had threatened their lives and had brought about the destruction of the young girl three of them had come to love. Malice continued shrieking and wailing in mental agony, refusing to look at the elf.

With an almost negligible shift, the elf pushed both of his curved weapons into the dwarf's chest around the plates of his armor. Bitrayuul gasped in shock as the tip of the elf's sword punctured through his father's back. Chakal proceeded to lift Tormag's dying form high into the air with strength that seemed impossible for his slim frame. The assassin held the dwarf suspended as he inspected his prey as if he were a piece of meat. No expression. Nothing. Tormag's mouth sputtered blood. His beloved magical hammers fell to the earth with dull thumps.

"It was not his kill to claim," Chakal stated coldly before kicking the dwarf's lifeless form free from his blades directly into the fire.

Each of the companions were frozen in shock. Bitrayuul and Fangdarr watched as their adoptive father's corpse lay atop the blistered carcasses of the trolls beneath. Tormag's eyes still hung placidly open, peering right at them—a sight that would haunt them all the rest of their days, they knew. Even Cormac, who had grown attached to Tormag over their short time together, was pained heavily by the loss. Though, seeing a dwarf treated as such by an elf caused his grief to be eclipsed by anger. The captain charged forward with a yell. As he reached Chakal, the dwarf stabbed forward with both shield-blades, but the assassin's face turned to a grin as he chuckled and faded into nothingness as the weapons passed through. Sparks flickered as the blades skittered across the stone. Cormac looked around confused. How could he simply be gone?

The chuckle came again, this time louder and from all directions. "One by one, each of you are mine. I have sated my lust for now. Go, fight your dragon. Know that I will be waiting for you thereafter, so do not fall." As soon as it came, the sound was gone, leaving them with only the sound of Malice's terrorized sobs and Bitrayuul's joining cries. Fangdarr, too stubborn to allow himself to show vulnerability in front of his kin, placed a hand atop Bitrayuul's shoulder in comfort.

Cormac quickly jogged back to his companions. His thick hands reached over the heaping mass of charred corpses to pull Tormag out of the fire. Luckily, thanks to dwarven skin being so thick, Tormag's corpse did not suffer too heavily from the flames, though most of his beard and hair had withered away. The captain patted down his friend for good measure, stamping out any wisps of smoke that had started to form.

Bitrayuul reached forward to grab the lifeless hand of his father, bringing about renewed tears as he felt no squeeze in response. Fangdarr reached down gently and closed Tormag's eyes for all of their sakes. Bear stumbled away quietly before returning in short order, holding the pair of war hammers in her mouth for the half-orc. Bitrayuul took them from her with a smile, glad to have a part of the dwarf to keep with him.

The party sat in silence, deep in their thoughts, each lamenting the loss in his or her own way. However, they did not get to wallow in their grief for long before an odd noise came out of the distance. The party looked to each other, thinking the sound had been imagined. Yet, all searched for the source, confirming it was real. It came again, closer now. They scanned the area unable to find the origin. Then it came again—this time unmistakable.

A dragon's roar.

CHAPTER FORTY-THREE

DEFIANCE

Far off in the distance, just below the smog-like clouds that shrouded the mountain peaks, Fangdarr could see the drake's billowing silhouette. Powerful wings spread wide as the beast came for them. Yet the orc showed no fear. He would scream into its face just as he had done before. With all he had been through, he was ready to face this greatest of challenges without regret.

The proud chieftain's companions were not so resilient. After all, this was *Fangdarr's* quest, not theirs. Seeing the wisps of abysmal black and purple trailing off the wingspan of the monster, glittering in its wake, nearly broke their resolve. Closer it came. Another shriek. Bear nudged against her master in support, though the others may have needed it more.

"You ready, Bear?" the chieftain asked of his beloved ally with a smile that stood contradictory to the task at hand.

As if she understood, the animal huffed in confirmation before sending up a defiant roar. Fangdarr had never been more proud to call her his companion than in that moment. Opening his jaw wide, Fangdarr joined in Bear's howl at their enemy.

Despite their crippling grief and fear, the remaining members of the group took confidence in the defiant outcry of the pair. Bitrayuul rose from his father's corpse, anger burning inside him. A vicious flood of rage, the likes of which he had rarely felt, surged through his veins. His *orcish* veins. Bitrayuul had seen the effects of such fury on his brother. He had watched as it granted him impossible strength, far surpassing Fangdarr's already impressive capabilities. The half-orc knew that without control, such a blind berserk state could spell his own doom. Nevertheless, Bitrayuul allowed the warm, embracing emotion to permeate his body. Tying Tormag's small, thick war hammers onto his belt, Bitrayuul strode forward to join his sibling.

Cormac needed less convincing, though the dwarf could not deny his fear. He could not abandon Fangdarr. Too strong was their bond. He simply mumbled a small message to his long-lost wife and child waiting for him in Bothain's Mines. "I may be joinin' ye sooner than ye thought," he said before his shortened legs pressed him forward until he was standing next to the roaring warriors. With his most boastful voice, the dwarf let out his own cry into the wind.

Malice watched as the final companion left her to join the cause. Even now, her paranoia over Chakal continued. His presence was nowhere to be seen, but she knew the assassin was there. Watching. Waiting. She thought to end it there and then. Rid herself of her pain and fear and join her lost daughter. *Oh, sweet Lilyana.* The memories of running her fingers through the child's soft golden hair, cuddling up with her at night, and watching her play in the grass all flooded through the frightened woman. How she yearned to be reunited with the girl. Malice knew the regret would stain her for the rest of her days. The woman looked to her friends—the ones who had risked their own lives, and even lost it, for the sake of hers—and to her son, who now needed her more than ever. Without realizing her actions, Malice rose to her feet. This was one regret that would not be added to her list.

With all of the party assembled on the rock, they watched in awe as the dragon's hulking form continued to grow in size. By the gods, it was vast. Only Fangdarr had seen the beast in all its splendor before. And such a wondrous, terrible sight it was. Even if this were their last battle, it would be one few others could claim—a small consolation in the face of the prospect of being melted alive by the shadow dragon's acidic breath or being crushed by its tremendous jaws.

The dragon screeched again. It would be upon them soon, they knew. There was almost no time to plan after wasting so much time answering the challenge. Immediately, Bitrayuul hopped down from their perch to inspect the field.

"The trolls are still littered everywhere, we have uneven footing, and little cover." As the half-orc peered at their surroundings, he couldn't help but notice just how unfavorable this location was for engaging a dragon. The encasing walls of their shelter would serve as their tomb should the dragon think to unleash its breath within. Bitrayuul had never encountered a dragon before, but he suspected they were not unintelligent monsters.

Cormac jumped to the lower level as well, scanning each direction. His eyes lit up as he remembered a more suitable location. "Come, come!" the dwarf called to everyone, urging them to follow. Friends in tow, Cormac traversed the small gap through the shelter and into the open passage once more, to the place Fangdarr had first met Raz'ja.

"This is good. This will do well," Bitrayuul complimented him.

The area proved much more beneficial than the last. Here, the group had a clear view of the sky should the drake remain in flight. Even more so, many tall, jutting rock formations sprouted all around to stand as barriers to the acidic breath of their enemy. Additionally, there was plenty of space for the dragon to land once they were hidden, forcing it to come after them within range of retaliation. They took their positions in anticipation.

From Bitrayuul's spot, he could still see through the gap into the sheltered hovel that had served as his father's demise. The half-orc could just barely make out the dwarf's body. He drew rage from that vision and let the anger rush through him.

The dragon's roar came, this time closer than ever. Bitrayuul watched as Crepusculus blew its corrosive breath in a line directly over Tormag's corpse, adding insult to injury. His eyes went wide in horror as his father's body began melting away from the burning acid. Furious, the half-orc warrior rose to charge. Yet, just as Bitrayuul was about to step into the open, he halted. *This is what it wants.* The dragon wanted to draw them out into favorable ground. Bitrayuul growled from beneath his helmet. Indeed, the beast was not unintelligent.

After three final slow passes above, Crepusculus grew bored. With a roar that pierced the mountains and stabbed at their ears, it landed. Each of the group peeked around their stone barriers to gaze at the awesome figure.

"Bothain's beard . . ." Cormac whispered with an open-mouthed, awestruck expression.

Indeed, now that the Shadow One was in their presence, its sheer magnitude could be appreciated. It dwarfed the bunovir nearly five times over, standing nearly the size of a small castle. Its purple scales caught the little moonlight that remained. However, instead of sparkling, as most dragons were said to do, this shadow dragon emitted wisps of blackened smoke—a dark smog that spilled ever more shadows from its body. What a spectacle it was, to see the purple and black swirl together in a mix of pure beauty.

Crepusculus raised its head with dignity as it 'spoke' to the party telepathically. *I am the Shadow One. The greater god of death and sorrow. You stand before a might you cannot hope to suppress. Join me and we shall know the likes of immortality.*

Bitrayuul and Cormac looked to each other, unfazed by the empty promises of an evil being. Malice, too used to the many voices in her clouded mind, paid no mind to the words as she could not even recognize they were the dragon's and not her own. The orc chieftain glanced at his companions to be certain none were interested in taking Crepusculus up on the offer as Raz'ja had done. He smiled as his expectations were confirmed. It would take more than the whispers of their enemy to halt them. In response, Fangdarr stepped out from behind his cover.

The dragon's eyes narrowed as it recognized the orc. *Ah, I remember you, Roaring One. To know that you stared a god in the eye and roared was a rush I had not witnessed in thousands of years. It took all my will to resist the desire to end you in that fateful moment. To allow you to feel the crunch of my jaw. The agony of my 'fire'. Instead, you proved your strength before me, signifying your worthiness. You will serve as commander of my armies and be ruler of these lands once we have scorched them and wiped out all our enemies! Come to me, child, that we may bend these cowards to our will.*

Fangdarr stepped forward slowly, as if accepting the great dragon's promise of fortune. His allies sat and watched, fearful the orc may have been swayed. But, in their hearts, they knew otherwise. He would not abandon them. Not now. The chieftain continued his unthreatening approach toward the godly creature. Crepusculus gave a moaned grumble deep within its throat, pleased that Fangdarr would join its apocalyptic cause.

He stopped directly below the beast's maw, still high in the air. Fangdarr looked skyward to the creature of doom before calling out, "Crepusculus! Shadow One! Deity of fallen and cleanser of land. Fangdarr Blood-drinker stand before you to eradicate those who oppose. Stare me in the eye once more, that I may prove my worth!"

Displeased to be ordered by such a lesser being, Crepusculus exposed its sharpened teeth with a low growl. Nevertheless, it lowered its head in respect toward the orc who remained unafraid in its wake. Finally, the shadow dragon's enormous head stood across from Fangdarr, standing twice the orc's height. The vibrant, yellow hue of its eyes contradicted heavily against the deep, dark purple scales that emitted black smog. With the light of day not yet upon them, the smoke nearly concealed the gargantuan figure. But the chieftain could not help but stare in awe at the raw beauty of the drake.

Beautiful, am I not? Crepusculus stated as if reading his mind. Fangdarr simply nodded in response and took a step closer with his hand outstretched to touch the glittering blackness of its maw, drawing a growl from the dragon. The orc continued unfazed, hoping to place a thick palm against the plated armor. The dragon once again seemed displeased at the insubordination but allowed Fangdarr to continue. While the great drakes of the ancient world were marvelous and powerful beings, they were prone to vanity. The dragon's yellow eyes closed for a moment, reveling in the feeling of knowing it was so magnificent that one would risk their own demise to simply touch its jeweled hide.

CLINK!

Fangdarr stared incredulously at Driktarr in his hands, then back to the maw of the beast. His strike had landed cleanly against the edge of the dragon's mouth with as much strength as the orc could muster in a single blow. Yet, not even a scratch was visible. Without a moment's hesitation, Fangdarr turned around and sprinted for cover just as Crepusculus gave a mighty shriek that pierced their ears with such force they nearly bled.

"Fangdarr, run!" Bitrayuul called out from his shelter. Already he had knocked an arrow and let it fly toward the drake's face in an attempt to stall the monster. It skittered harmlessly off the scales before ricocheting to the ground.

You dare strike me?! I shall consume you, rip you, melt you! Before this night is done, you shall know my wrath. You shall know nothing but fear and pain. Come, face me, coward! Stare into my face once more, orc. The words screamed through their minds with blinding pitch. They *felt* the dragon's rage in their bones as its words hissed in their head with such venom. Crepusculus reared its head and neck, preparing to unleash a torrent of corrosive, tar-like liquid onto Fangdarr's retreating form. Out it came, glowing bright like purple flames in the dim light of pre-dawn. The orc sprinted at full speed, nearly reaching a rock that would serve as a shield for the impending stream of death that rushed toward him.

Crepusculus barreled forward into the rocky arena, still breathing acidic fire with each step, creating a line of melting rock between the dragon and Fangdarr's location. The party watched in shock as even the resilient stone of the mountain began to sizzle and wither away. It seemed neither armor nor shield would serve any purpose here. And, after watching Fangdarr's giant axe bounce harmlessly off the drake's impervious hide, they realized the folly of their task. But it was too late. The Shadow One had been stirred and would not relent until it had consumed all those who opposed it.

The stone behind Fangdarr hissed in protest before shriveling beneath the liquid. If he could only reach the barrier in time, he would be safe. Powerful bounds of his legs carried him swiftly forward as the air behind him trickled like electricity and the flickers of the flame licked at his backside. In the final moment, Fangdarr lunged behind the rocky outcropping to safety. He watched as his previous path was covered in the tar-like substance and sighed with relief. However, his solace was short-lived as Crepusculus continued charging in Fangdarr's direction at full speed. The mountain shook beneath its clawed feet with each stomp, serving as drumbeats of doom for the orc. At each step, the chieftain felt the vibrations shake ever more beneath him.

Bitrayuul continued to launch arrows, though he knew it was pointless. Cormac, Malice, and Bear could only watch in immobilized horror. How could they ever hope to defeat such a creature? The bunovir had been barely culled by their team with Tormag by their side, and this devil equaled ten of those monstrous fiends! In what world did they ever think their goal could be achieved?

Cormac looked to Bitrayuul. With absolute certainty that left no room for question, the dwarf stated, "Bitrayuul, we must flee."

The half-orc looked to the dragon and his trapped kin. He would not abandon Fangdarr, but the dwarf was right. This was a battle that would only end in their demise. Bitrayuul nodded in agreement, but added, "Not without Fangdarr."

The dwarf did not argue. He had no intention of leaving his friend behind. Cormac called out loudly to the orc, "Fangdarr! It's time to leave! Get out of there!"

Fangdarr wanted to reject the command. He wanted—with every proud cell in his body—to stay and complete his task. For himself. For his people. For all. This was no longer just a personal task to dissuade his clan from war. He knew Crepusculus was on the verge of something tremendously terrible and could not be left unanswered. Alas, Fangdarr knew he did not hold the strength to quell the drake. The orc's axe was no match for the dragon's hide. That resounding sound of Driktarr reflecting against the armored flesh of his foe would ring forever. In that single blow, Fangdarr had felt more diminutive and fallible than ever before.

Peering past the quickly-withering stone that stood as the sole obstacle between himself and imminent death, Fangdarr waited. The pounding strides of the shadow dragon were quick and nearly upon him. There would only be one chance to escape the charge of the mobile beast. Its forelegs were as wide as the orc was tall, each ending in razor-like talons that would surely cut through his flesh without even slowing. Three paces away. Two. *Now*!

As Crepusculus appeared over the rock barrier, its left claw came whistling through the air. Fangdarr dove under the dragon's arm with hardly a breath of room to spare, scraping skin against the cold stone, and smiled as his opponent's arm whizzed harmlessly overhead. Rising to his feet once more, Fangdarr was up within a moment and sprinting toward his companions. The expression on his face turned to confusion as they all began pointing behind him with concern. The orc turned back to see the source of their attention, just as he was met by an incredible force.

After the drake's claw swipe had failed, the mace-shaped tail had whipped heavily into the orc, bashing Fangdarr into the nearby face of the mountain. His heavy form paired with the strength of the attack managed to shatter the surrounding stone around the orc's prone form and cracked more than a few of his bones.

Bitrayuul raised his useless bow again and pointlessly began launching arrow after arrow toward the drake's head—even into its gaping maw—as it reared its head in preparation. Tears began forming in Bitrayuul's eyes as the bright purple liquid could be seen deep inside the throat of its long neck, ascending quickly toward the open mouth of the dragon. Cormac, and even Malice, cried out in protest as they, too, watched in horror at the coming fate of their friend. Bear whimpered and whined incessantly, knowing what was about to occur.

Fangdarr still lay upright against the stone, blood trickling down his jaw from internal bleeding. He took note of the expression on each of his friend's faces. The orc felt at peace knowing his presence would be missed. The proud chieftain hoped they would only carry fond memories of him. The warrior's yellow eyes glowed purple as the dragon's devastating flame broke free from its passage through the beast's throat and out into the open air. Fangdarr strained to move even though his mind had accepted what was to come. Still, instinct took over and forced his limbs to wiggle. There were only moments before the flames would be upon Fangdarr, disintegrating him.

One arm broke free from its stone prison. With luck, the orc was not too injured. A handful of cracked bones, some bruising, and some very sore muscles on his backside were all that Fangdarr had suffered from being hurled into the mountainside. Another arm free. His eyes turned upward to see the growing light as it was only two spear-lengths away. Not enough time. Fangdarr roared as both legs simultaneously came free from the wall. This was it. He could not escape. The orc screamed out in a ferocious roar of defiance, refusing the be culled without his pride—his damned pride. Fangdarr's body glowed bright purple, reflecting the illuminating beam of acidic fire as it drew closer. No escape.

CHAPTER FORTY-FOUR

SECRECY

Bitrayuul clamped his eyes shut. He refused to add another awful scene to the growing bank of nightmares that would be sure to haunt him for years to come. Bitrayuul especially could not bear to witness this ending. To watch his proud brother's bold frame stand vigilant against the torrential blast before crumpling away to dust was too much to endure.

Each of the half-orc's friends had the same idea. All hid the spectacle from their view. Cormac gave a loud, guttural whimper that grated against the stones. The poor dwarf tried so hard to convince his legs to move—to charge into the line of fire and die in Fangdarr's place—but he could not. Survival instincts kept Cormac rooted firmly where he stood. Crying out loud, the captain put his thick hands over his ears to muffle the impending sound of the orc's demise.

In the final moment, Fangdarr looked to his friends once more. Only Bear had her eyes up to witness his passing. A smile formed in the corner of his mouth as he locked his gaze with hers. There was no fear in him—only acceptance. Fangdarr knew he had brought this fate upon himself. He turned from Bear's gaze and stared directly into the stream of acidic fire that was now just out of arm's reach. The orc's pride would allow no less than to meet his death head-on.

The purple, flicking flames gave way to a pitch-black darkness that started just before him and spread immediately in all directions. Is this death? Had Fangdarr become so overwhelmed by pain that he could comprehend no agony? His vision was entirely devoid of color. It was all . . . nothingness—an unending abyss. The orc looked down at his arms—still fine. Fangdarr's confusion was immense. He was not religious and so put no stock in an afterlife. Perhaps this was the realm of emptiness between life and death, and he would simply remain in this blackened void forever.

Almost as quick as it came, the pitch-colored void retreated. As it shrank away to nothing, Fangdarr realized this was no other realm, for Fangdarr stood in opposition to Crepusculus once more, who looked as puzzled as he. In a circle around the orc, the stone had been melted and still bubbled with the corrosive liquid that had been spewed in his direction.

How can this be? Asked the shadow dragon with eyes narrowed. It watched as Fangdarr looked around just as surprised as it, verifying the suspicion that the orc had no part in the black globe that had saved his life.

Despite averting death and being across from one of the realm's most terrible creations, Fangdarr simply shrugged in response. Bitrayuul, Cormac, and Malice each opened their eyes upon hearing the dragon halt its breath, expecting to see nothing left of Fangdarr but a corpse.

"Fangdarr?!" the half-orc warrior yelled in surprise, followed by a cheer from Cormac.

Bear was just as excited that her master had been unharmed. However, she was the only one who had witnessed the spectacle and thus had seen the origin of the abyssal blackness that had blocked the drake's attack. The beast let out a small groan and strode forward reluctantly. Thinking the animal aimed to rejoin Fangdarr, the three remaining companions started to pursue her. Their movement caught the dragon's attention.

"Look out!" Malice cried out as she pointed to the reared head forcing yet another torrent through its throat.

Fangdarr watched as his friends took up defensive positions behind their barriers again. His eyes glanced between his draconian opponent and his friends. The orc wondered if he should attempt to go back on the offensive, or simply hide with them. Both seemed futile. What sort of assault could he hope to unleash against an enemy of this magnitude? More so, how long would they be able to hide before the entire field was littered with a layer of melted stone, preventing their retreat? A decision needed to be made. Now.

Just as the chieftain started to open his mouth to command the group to run away, a large, stygian spear launched itself toward Crepusculus' open maw. This was no ordinary spear, however, as it forced the dragon's jaw to clamp shut and knocked it back a step. Fangdarr's eyes went wide with surprise at the tremendous force behind that seemingly magical blackness.

Rahh! Show yourself, fiend! Crepusculus shouted telepathically. *Come. Face death!*

As if in response to the taunt, another spear of pitch-black magic soared through the air before connecting against the scaled torso of the monster. This time, the dragon was prepared and hardly budged behind the force of the blow. The spear-like shape was enormous, yet the beast managed to shrug it off without concern. By the gods, could this creature not be killed? Was it truly immortal?

Seeing that the dragon's flame would no longer be unleashed, Bear barked to signify her continuation. Fangdarr leapt over the swirled mass of melting rocks at his feet and ran the remaining distance between himself and the party.

"What's going on?" Bitrayuul asked impatiently. His orc-blooded kin could only shrug in confusion as well, for he, too, remain flummoxed by the mysterious interference.

Bear kept howling as she trotted forward at a light jog, beckoning the group to follow. They took off in pursuit of their furry companion as she ran along the wall of the mountain. The ground turned to an incline as they followed the stone face, leading them toward the summit. From above, they could hear the frustrated roar of their enemy as it continued to be the target of magical spears. After a short while, the group managed to come to a flat section where their eyes came across something they never expected to see.

A white-robed elf stood in front of the assembled troop. His long, golden hair whipped viciously in the wind caused by the swirling abyss in his hands. With grace that defied the result, the elf joined the two raging voids in his hands and pulled them apart to form a giant spear—the same spears that had been assaulting the dragon. Once produced, the elf stretched out a single hand. With his hair and robe violently pummeled by the rushing winds of his creation, the spear shot out from its suspended location without any movement from the elf. The group watched as it screamed through the air before colliding against the dragon's head.

"What are you?" Fangdarr asked incredulously. In truth, it was obvious. The elf was some sort of magician—something the chieftain was not overly familiar or fond of.

"He is a necromancer—a warlock, if you will," came the reply from the side. It was a voice Fangdarr had never heard before, though it rang oddly familiar. The orc and his companions turned their heads to see a female elf standing beside them, watching the necromancer. All caught by surprise, they backed away. Elves were known to be tricky creatures, only caring for their own lives. Too well did they know the relationship between elves and dwarves and orcs were not friendly.

Fangdarr looked around in confusion, making sure all of his friends were safe. As he inspected the area, the orc started to panic. "Where Bear?" he asked of Bitrayuul.

"*I* am Bear, Fangdarr," responded the elf woman. The orc looked up at her in confusion, clearly refusing to believe the elf was a bear. *His* bear. But her hair was black, matching the color of Bear's fur exactly. In addition, while the necromancer donned robes, this elf wore only simple leather clothing. "Well, my name is not 'Bear'," she continued, "It is Aesthéa."

"Yes, yes. Perhaps this is not the time," came the frustrated call from the elvish necromancer, still launching spear after spear.

The orc chieftain and his companions were completely bewildered. After all this time, Bear was an elf? Fangdarr could hardly believe that he could have been so blinded by the trickery of an elf!

It was Cormac who cut off his thoughts. "Aye, lad. We need to take care of that dragon, don't ye doubt."

Fangdarr broke from his mental irritation to focus on the threat at hand. He managed to make the connection that the warlock had saved him from the dragon's flames that surely would have brought his end. With a huff of annoyance, Fangdarr agreed. He watched as the necromancer weaved a field of blackness in front of them, blocking yet another stream of flames from Crepusculus.

You will suffer! Anguish! Torment!

"It's time to change strategies," the elf male stated. The group watched as his robe opened to expose his torso, and his body dropped hundreds of rotting bones to the ground—in total, three corpses worth—revealing the elf's slim frame. Though slim, he was covered in swirling black tattoos that appeared to move. His skin was painted with the same abyssal blackness of his magic, though it was embedded deep into his flesh.

With a yelp from Malice, the three corpses began to assemble themselves before rising to their feet. It became apparent almost immediately that they too had once been elves judging by the height of their cheekbones and slim stature. "Go, my brothers! Go, now!"

All three ghouls rushed to the edge of the cliff before jumping down. The drop was taller than the height of the dragon; the fall would have surely killed any living creature, though, these were not living creatures. They were the raised dead—immortal beings frozen in time, ready to be called upon at their master's whim.

Cormac peered over the edge to see the risen warriors sprinting toward the dragon. "By the stones, they're fast!"

The dwarf's allies peeked as well, watching the ghouls climb up the dragon's coarse, beautiful scales toward its face and wings. The necromancer, confident in his minions, began flinging more spears. Crepusculus growled in rage as the summoned creatures tore the film from its wings, little by little, and scratched at its eyes.

RAHH! You think these pawns can deter me?

With a flick of its tail, the beast brushed away the one ghoul on its head. Once it hit the ground, it crumpled back into a pile of bones before immediately reanimating and charging back in. Such efficient fighters, the dead. Roaring in anger once more at the incessant scraping of the summoned minions on its body, Crepusculus spread its wings wide.

"Ah, finally," stated the necromancer.

Bitrayuul and Fangdarr watched the elf in amazement. After all, he was single-handedly holding a *dragon* at bay. Moments before, their only hope had been to flee. Now, it seemed that winning may actually be possible. With the dragon's wings spread wide in the air, reflecting the light of the rising sun, the elf smiled. He had been waiting for this.

Crepusculus kicked off the ground heavily, taking to the air. It rose higher and higher into the sky, now level with their position. *I have you now, Elf. Do not think I have never faced one of your kind before,* the dragon chuckled under its breath with ground-shaking heaviness. No response came from the necromancer, only a knowing smile in return. With both hands outstretched, a dozen spears rose in the air and pointed directly at the hovering drake. The raging wind from the elf's magic blew wildly, nearly ripping the robe from his person. The elf's eyes went wide with madness as he screamed in ecstasy, unleashing his spears.

The dragon tried to turn in an attempt to dodge the impending magical attack. However, in its ignorance, Crepusculus failed to notice just how much damage the ghouls had already done—and were still doing—to the skin of its wings. Tattered and ripped in a few places, the drake could not get enough control to spin out of the way. Instead, the shadow dragon could only flail about awkwardly in the sky. A dozen crashing sounds came as the spears all made contact. The elf had been aiming for its already-weakened wings, though only half of the spikes hit their mark. The rest crashed heavily into the armored hide of the drake with little effect.

Slowly, Crepusculus began descending as the wind holding up its wings now blew through the gaping holes that had been ripped by the black magic. The dragon roared in anger. *Curse you, Elf! You are too late. I shall be the ruler of this world before long. My acid will melt your precious tree and consume all that you love.* It growled in frustration before tucking its wings together more tightly. With them tucked, the dragon could not fly, though the holes were covered enough to allow it to glide away. The party watched as Crepusculus retreated deeper into the mountains.

Cormac could not help but laugh as he watched the three ghouls jump from the dragon's back and fall onto the ground far below in a heap of shattered bones. They instantly reanimated and began sprinting back toward their master, though it would take them some time to return. "Whoa, I got to get me some of them! Bahahaha!"

As the dragon faded from view to retreat to its hole, the assembled warriors visibly relaxed. Fangdarr was the first to approach the necromancer and Aesthéa. His eyes narrowed in reproach as they made contact with the female elf who had been hiding at his side all this time. Aesthéa looked away, unable to endure the orc's glare as he approached. Fangdarr switched his attention to the male before speaking. "Thank you, elf. I owe you my life."

A minor flash of disgust appeared on the warlock's face. "You are welcome, orc," he spat through gritted teeth, "though, do not count on the favor to be repeated. This is the first time in my long life to have saved an orc—a fact that does not please me."

Fangdarr nodded despite his irritation at the quick prejudice that came from their unlikely savior. The chieftain turned to Aesthéa. No words were necessary. His harsh stare clearly demanded answers.

"I am sorry for hiding my true self from you. As you can see," her arms spread to expose her frame, "*this* is what I am. An elf. I am a druid, which allows me to take on the form of the animal my spirit has become linked to—in this case, a bear. I had t—" she stopped, interrupted by the male elf.

"There is no need to explain yourself to an orc! Come, you are needed back home." The necromancer had already begun walking away.

"No, Elethain!" Aesthéa cried out in protest, stopping him in his tracks.

He stopped and turned to her. "No? The king demands it. He sent *me* across the entirety of Crein to come look for you! You were instructed to stay in Jesmera, yet you disobeyed to pursue this orc on your own." The party inched closer with intense curiosity and confusion. "Oh? You haven't told them?" Elethain let out a small chuckle at the fact he found amusing.

"Told us what?" asked Bitrayuul, stepping forward. Malice and Cormac, too, now invested in the conversation, joined as well.

The druid sighed in hopelessness, looking to Fangdarr as she spoke. "The elves took note of your expansion, Fangdarr. I asked that we eliminate the threat immediately before it spread further. However, my uncle, the king, refused. Elves do not often concern themselves in the matters of the other races. We are to remain secluded on Jesmera and watch from afar. So, I . . ." she paused and shut her eyes, remembering her actions.

"You attacked me," Fangdarr replied.

Aesthéa nodded in confirmation. "I aimed to eliminate you on my own. Though, I was easily overwhelmed. All we have heard of orcs only told of your brutality, stubbornness, and stupidity—that you were just dumb creatures easily overwhelmed yet imposing when enraged. Once beaten, I expected my life to be forfeit for such a stupid mistake—for being so bullheaded. Instead, you spared me. Cared for me. So, I remained at your side, waiting for an opportunity to return the debt. Meanwhile I could keep a close eye on you and report back to my people."

"You saved me. Many times. The debt is paid."

She nodded in response. "Indeed, it is. But I have stayed for other reasons." Her eyes closed lightly as she spoke. "I grew attached. You were not the brute I was told you would be. Nor was your goal one of treachery. You are actively avoiding a war, rather than waging one. I see now that you wish for orcs to simply have a home in the realms and to not be looked down upon."

Elethain scoffed at the notion in disgust. Fangdarr and Aesthéa ignored him.

"Then why you stay hidden? Why not show your true form?" the orc pressed.

"I could not risk being known as an elf. A party of orcs and dwarves? Hah! I did not think I would be received well. Our races are not known for being fond of one another. In addition, I was acting on my behalf alone. I could not make it seem the elves were involved. Contrarily, they were adamant as to *not* become involved."

Bitrayuul stepped forward. "Wait, wait! You mean this entire time, you could have shifted back to an elf at any time? Used magic? Are druids not capable of manipulating nature around them?" Aesthéa nodded in response, pushing the half-orc to an instant shift to anger. "You could have saved him!" he yelled.

The druid remained stoic despite the half-orc's anger. "No, it would not have been possible. I can utilize nature, plants, to be more precise—a gift from Cerenos, the Forest God. Do you see any such nature here?" she responded calmly.

The half-orc could not hide his tears as the vision of watching his father be murdered by Chakal played again in his mind. "You! You can revive him! Necromancers can bring back the dead, can't they?"

"No, *orcblood*," Elethain shot back with disdain. "Necromancers cannot simply bring back the dead. There are rituals. *Rules*. Besides, he was covered in the dragon's fire. There is nothing left of him to bring back. Even still, I would not bring back the likes of a *dwarf* at the behest of an *orc*!"

Bitrayuul could not contain his anger any longer. The cold superiority of the necromancer had touched one nerve too many. He removed his helmet forcefully and threw it directly at the elf while screaming, "*Half*-orc! Half!"

Elethain nonchalantly conjured a clawed hand of black magic thrice the size of his own to catch the helmet. His slanted eyes narrowed with hatred. The abyssal markings on his pale skin began to shift in eagerness. "Careful, orcblood. Do not try my patience."

Aesthéa stepped between the two with a hand raised to each. "Now is neither the time nor place. We need to get moving. Trolls will be swarming us soon, and I would rather not be here when they arrive. Crepusculus went east, deeper into the Tusks."

"East? I think not. *You* are returning to your uncle. They may do as they wish," the warlock replied forcefully.

"I will not."

A wrinkle appeared on Elethain's fair skin as he scowled. "You *will*. The king demands it."

"Then you shall have to subdue me. My place is here, at least until the dragon has fallen."

The elf rubbed his temples in frustration before sighing heavily. "Then you will return home?"

Aesthéa looked to Fangdarr, though the disgruntled orc quickly averted his gaze. Her head drooped low, shrouding her angular face behind locks of hair. She could not form the words. Doing so would make it real. She faced a struggle she had never known—torn between her duty and her heart. Elethain—and her uncle, no doubt—was deep-rooted in his prejudice. Aesthéa could not make her wishes known, for surely it would only end in disaster. With a nod, the elf confirmed her agreement.

"Fine, then we set off for Crepusculus."

CHAPTER FORTY-FIVE
TRUTH

Fangdarr, even more determined to pursue his goal now that it no longer seemed impossible, fell in line behind Elethain. Being led by an elf left a fowl taste in his mouth, but this was the only way. The orc could not deny the prowess of the warlock. Without him, their task would never prove successful. Accordingly, the chieftain swallowed his pride. He turned to see Malice and Cormac following as well, though Bitrayuul remained frozen in place.

"You coming, Bit?" Fangdarr asked.

Broken from his angry trance, the half-orc bent to retrieve his helmet. Fangdarr had never seen him so irritated. Without saying a word, Bitrayuul donned his bladed helmet harshly and looked back to his father's resting place—now only a steaming remnant of ash and tar-like liquid. He moved past his kin in line with the others, too angry to speak.

The assembled party trudged forward, beginning the search for the dragon's lair. The sun was well above the horizon now though hardly piercing the gloom of the clouds overhead. Cormac called out to the procession, "Once we're clear of our last site, we should make camp. It's been a rough night, don't ye doubt, and we will need to rest before encounterin' the drake again."

Cormac's assessment came with no arguments. In truth, they were all exhausted, even Elethain. Once the king had discovered Aesthéa's insubordinate departure, Elethain had been commanded to retrieve her. As one of the royal advisors, compliance was mandatory. Since then, Elethain had scoured nearly the entire forest in search of the young druid. Torturing orcs and questioning humans had kept the warlock on her trail. It was not until he had come upon their battle with Crepusculus that the elf finally realized she was no longer following Fangdarr, but *with* him. Though, whether her intention came from her duty to the king or herself, he could not know.

After walking through the harsh mountain pass for quite a while longer, the group finally stopped to make camp. With luck, they managed to find a secluded location that was both safe from view and the elements alike. Cormac built a fire using kindling that Malice collected while the orc kin prepared the food. The captain produced his favorite cooking tool, the thin sheet of metal that served as a hot plate with which to cook the dried meat.

Fangdarr handed a skewer of meat to Elethain, though he quickly rejected the offer. "Elves do not eat meat, orc. Except for some," he said, nodding toward Aesthéa. "Her shapeshifting capabilities are not simply a trick of magic. She is wholly linked to the spirit of a bear, which means she must take on certain qualities, including eating meat. Her skin is even thicker than normal, though it still retains the softness of an elf's. Luckily," he added, turning to the young female, "she does not hibernate."

"Bahahah! Could ye imagine, Fang? Just walking along one winter and seein' a sleeping elf, fat for the winter?" Cormac couldn't help but pipe in with his usual humor. Despite his stoic attitude, even Elethain managed to crack a minimal smile.

"So, Aesthéa tells me you ran into Chakal, is that so?" the necromancer asked, shifting to a less whimsical topic.

Almost immediately, a somber silence enveloped the campsite. Only the sound of the crackling fire was heard for many moments, yet Elethain still peered around expectantly. The druid lightly laid a hand on his shoulder and shook her head, signifying it was not a subject to broach. Clearly irritated with the group's inability to discuss harsh subjects, the warlock disregarded her concern and pressed further. "His presence is known to us, as are his . . . tactics." Aesthéa could only bow her head in shame at his persistence. Even being acquainted with him in that moment left a sour taste in her mouth. She hated Elethain's prejudiced nature and complete lack of empathy.

Despite the incredulous looks the elf was receiving from Malice and Bitrayuul, the elf continued to speak in his matter-of-fact tone. "Chakal was once of Jesmera, as most elves are. He was banished long ago for his murderous antics. We elves are a race of tranquility, especially in our home. That elf is an imposing force, to be sure. His—"

"Enough!" Bitrayuul cut off the elf angrily. Malice lay curled up in a ball, sobbing profusely, reliving the horrors her stalker had inflicted upon her and her kin.

Elethain's thin, angled brows bent inward to form a frown. "If you cannot even *speak* of the assassin, what hope do you have to stand against him?" His disgust was evident, adding bitterness to each word that came from his mouth. "Such inferior beings . . . You know how to defeat such an enemy, don't you? It is obvious." The necromancer paused, waiting for the confirmation of his superiority from Bitrayuul.

Even though the half-orc's irritation begged him not to, Bitrayuul knew he needed to allow the elf to continue. It was true, he did not have any idea of how to conquer such a limitless foe. To spare Malice, himself, all of them, Bitrayuul would have to swallow his pride. He breathed deeply to settle his heightened agitation. "How?"

A snide, arrogant grin etched itself upon the elf's face. "It is simple, really. Deny him. Ignore him. Chakal is a powerful warrior, that much cannot be disputed. But he is emotional. It is his greatest weakness. He cannot break his own rules: no killing a target that will not return the fight, only killing one target at a time—in *most* cases—things like that. These commandments are not of another's will but his own. He *must* follow them. To disregard them would prove disastrous for his mind. There are more ways to fell an enemy than by blade."

Bitrayuul remained silent, refusing to give Elethain the satisfaction of his appreciation. In truth, Bitrayuul had edged on a similar conclusion back in the forest during their first true confrontation with the elf. He remembered how the assassin had acted when Malice had first refused to fight. And Chakal had hunted Malice for years without ever causing harm simply due to her refusal to play his game. It was true. So long as he was denied, he was harmless. But then Bitrayuul thought of the murderous elf's escalation. Once Chakal had learned of Lilyana, an advantage had presented itself. It was true one could survive the assassin's blades if they could ignore him, however, could Bitrayuul ignore the assassin knowing that it would lead to the death of all those he loved?

The half-orc rolled to his side. In any case, now was not the time to concern himself with the stalker on their outskirts. A much larger task was at hand. Crepusculus would not simply allow them to stride into its lair and end its life. They needed to keep their wits. Bitrayuul placed a calming hand on his mother's arm to comfort her light sobs. Before long, the pair were fast asleep near the warmth of the fire. Cormac curled up near them as well. The old dwarf had dealt with elves occasionally over the years, ambassadors and traders mostly. He was accustomed to the snobby nature of the woodland creatures, though Elethain's prejudice was particularly irritating. Rather than allow emotion to take over, the captain elected to rest.

The encampment remained quiet for a long while with only the elves and Fangdarr remaining awake. Elethain's ghouls had returned to his side some time ago, standing motionless at the mouth of the cave staring with lifeless eyes. The orc could not help but inspect them in wonder. No breathing, no blinking, no moving. They were truly lifeless, it seemed. What useful tools, Fangdarr thought. The ghouls ensured the elf could rest whenever necessary despite embarking on his journey alone. Even so, used to the necessity of rotating shifts, the orc, out of habit, remained awake watching over the camp. Some habits are not easy to break.

Elethain noticed Fangdarr eyeing his creations and smiled. How he wished to boast of their creation. The obnoxious elf hated to miss the opportunity to display his superiority to an orc, but he was very tired. He leaned back against the stone to relax and shut his eyes. While Elethain was a powerful spellweaver, pressing a dragon back was no easy task. Each spell drained his stamina, little by little. Over time, magical beings grow stronger and can use more magic at one time, and indeed, the elf was powerful, though still nowhere near the capabilities of others of his race. He began practicing magic over two-thousand years ago when he was very 'young'. Elves could live for nearly ten-thousand at their longest, though most passed into Cerenos' Forest at half that. There were elves within their kingdom that had twice the experience and strength that Elethain possessed. Due to magic having a direct correlation between strength and the amount of time spent learning, practicing, and building more stamina, it was not often a human—or orc, for that matter—that could compare to an elven or dwarven spellcaster. Their short life spans simply put a limit on what could be mastered over their years.

Aesthéa quietly rose from her seat near the fire and walked toward Fangdarr. The orc watched her calmly, knowing she might attempt to talk. As she sat next to him, he could not help but see her for the first time in her true form. When first she revealed her elven nature, Fangdarr was too taken aback to focus on her features. Now, sitting next to his not-so-furry companion, the chieftain could not help but notice her beauty. Chakal, Elethain, and Aesthéa were the first elves the orc had encountered. He had read descriptions of them, all of which described them as fair-skinned and beautiful creatures, and it was not false.

She looked up at him with tears in her eyes, those familiar brown orbs gleaming vibrantly behind the glaze. The elf could hardly form words, each attempt only brought a meek noise from the amount of shame she carried. "I-I . . . so . . ." Fangdarr's eyes met hers. He was calm with no sign of anger or distrust, no sign of anything. "I'm so . . . sorry, Fangdarr," the druid managed to get out between gentle sobs.

The orc placed a large hand on her back, realizing that it covered half of it due to her slender build. "I feel betrayed," he began slowly, drawing another sob from the distraught elf. Fangdarr moved a finger to below her chin to force her to look into his eyes. "I am betrayed you not tell me, not that you are elf. I understand why you hide. But," he paused to wipe the tears from her eyes, "I would have accepted you no matter what. Should not have lied to me."

"I'm sorry, Fangdarr. I was afraid you would turn me away."

He chuckled in response. "You took bite from my arm," Fangdarr raised his left arm to reveal the maw-shaped scar Aesthéa had left in their first encounter, "and you afraid I turn you away? Who would help make brutal scars then?" A smile formed on his face in playfulness as the elf let out a quick outburst of laughter before covering her mouth. With the mood lightened, the orc asked the question he wished to ask previously. "Why *you* not leave?"

She sighed, knowing he had called her earlier bluff about gathering information for her kingdom. "You know the answer to that, Fangdarr." The elf turned her face away, unable to meet his gaze in that moment. Yet the orc was relentless.

"Why?" he asked again softly.

Still not looking at him, she answered, "Because my heart demanded it."

Fangdarr brushed the black strands of hair that had fallen in front of her face away with a finger, as gentle as an orc could muster. Once again, he lightly steered Aesthéa's face toward his. "Now you know why I not turn you away," the proud chieftain said quietly. The druid's eyes lit up in an instant. To the orc's surprise, the elf lunged forward and pressed her thin lips against his with deep passion. All her accumulated feelings that she had forced to remain hidden since the start of their journey were channeled into that single moment. The orc had never been kissed before, not even by his mother. It was a foreign act in the realm of orc culture. Yet, Fangdarr needed no explanation of what to do. His body and mind made the decisions for him, returning her passion in kind. Unlike Aesthéa, his feelings had been immediate with the discovery of her true form. Nonetheless, Fangdarr's love was real and immense, overtaking all thoughts completely. In that moment, there was no dragon. There was no clan conflict. No death. There was only her.

As the elf's face retracted from Fangdarr's, both had tears streaming down their faces. It was the first time the orc had shed a tear since his mother died. For her part, Aesthéa did not need to give explanation to her tears. Too long had she waited for this moment with the pent-up tension of not being able to express herself despite the object of her love being near her every day. Now that the elf could finally release the emotions she had kept locked in the coffer of her heart every waking moment, it overwhelmed her. She felt the passion channel through every muscle in her body, pushing her closer to him.

"Why are you crying?" Aesthéa asked, wiping the tears from his cheeks. Fangdarr turned his face, too proud to show his vulnerability once it had been noted. She took his face in her small hand, turning him back to face her just as the orc had done.

Fangdarr sighed hopelessly, letting his guard down for the first time in his life. "This all I ever wanted."

The elf leaned forward and kissed him once more before lying down against his torso. Her diminutive frame seemed so small compared to Fangdarr's. Just over half his height and a fraction of his stature, the druid embraced him tightly, unwilling to let the moment she had been waiting for end. The orc placed his arm over her body, nearly covering her entirely. Another tear fell down his face as Fangdarr watched Aesthéa drift off to sleep, her gentle breaths lightly tickling his side. He smiled and closed his eyes. But then his thoughts turned to the morrow and to the dreadful experience they would have to face. The realization that this moment would end, only to be replaced by the risk of death, shook Fangdarr more than he was used to. With his goal of being loved finally accomplished, the true despair of what that meant hit him like a hammer. Now that he had it, he could lose it. The orc shook away the thoughts and tried to force sleep. He could not afford a restless night.

Only a few paces away, Elethain clenched his fists and bit his lip with enough forceful anger to draw blood. *The indecency of it!* Even so, he would not dare cause a scene now or risk attacking Fangdarr. Elethain could not openly dispute the personal life of a member of the royal family—though her relation was somewhat distant from the crown. Instead, the elf was forced to seethe and boil in his rage at the sounds of their embrace. The verbal confirmations of their affections brought bile to his throat. *Such filth and disgust!* Yet it was not his place to interfere. Still, while the elf lay against the cold stone in feigned sleep, he considered the possibility that Fangdarr may fall to Crepusculus in their next skirmish—by the dragon's hand . . . or another's.

CHAPTER FORTY-SIX
JOINED

Fangdarr awoke startled, his heart pounding against his chest in panic. The orc scanned the area with blurry eyes, not yet realizing the nightmare was over. Visions of Crepusculus had poisoned his mind. Scorching. Ripping. Murdering. Within that apparition, the chieftain had been forced to watch Aesthéa perish before his eyes. Remnants of the dream flickered through his mind as Fangdarr stirred awake and settled back against the boulder with a sigh of relief. Still under his arm, Aesthéa slumbered peacefully. Fangdarr recalled the previous night: the confession, the passionate embrace, and the feeling of finally having one to call his own. The orc could not help but laugh at the ridiculousness of how it had all come to pass. Never in his lifetime did he ever expect to find romance, much less start a romance with what he had before assumed was a bear—a beast of the wild. Yet, there he lay with her beside him.

A finger traced the impressions of the muscle on her arm. Despite her small frame, he admired how strong she was. Perhaps one of the byproducts of linking her spirit with a bear? Fangdarr's hand continued to slide over Aesthéa's smooth skin. It was not rough, nor hairy, but felt somehow thicker. Yet, it was tremendously soft. The elf's black hair reflected the shining light of the campfire, drawing the orc's eyes from her body. His thick fingers pushed their way through her hair. Fangdarr could not believe the feel of the silk-like strands over his hand and between his fingers. While the chieftain may have been bald, he knew what orc hair felt like. It was coarse and dry, nothing but a stringy nuisance. Running his callused hands through Aesthéa's locks soothed Fangdarr immensely.

From the gentle rubbing, the elf stirred from beneath the orc's arm. She opened her bright, brown eyes and looked at Fangdarr. Aesthéa immediately smiled and squeezed his abdomen in greeting. "Morning," she yawned.

Fangdarr chuckled happily. "Morning, Bear."

The elf giggled at him, eyes still closed in grogginess. "It is Aesthéa. '*ess-thay-uh*'," she pronounced for him.

"Esstayuh," he replied, botching the pronunciation. His tongue was not used to the intricacies of elvish articulation. Fangdarr frowned at his failed attempt, repeating different variations of her name—all incorrectly.

She giggled at him again. "Bear will suffice," Aesthéa said with a smile. After all, 'Bear' was not a false name for a druid who shared her spirit with such a beast. The elf stretched from beneath the orc's arm, still not able to reach his full height, even with her arms fully extended and toes pointed. She pulled herself from his embrace and stood, straightening her leather jerkin. Aesthéa looked down at the orc and smiled wide—a beautiful expression that Fangdarr could not avert his gaze from.

Fangdarr watched as his companion reached out for him with a small hand. "No more secrets," she said softly. He smiled tenderly at her before taking her hand. Of course, his own dwarfed hers five times over, so as he stood, she slid her hand over his to wrap her arm around the chieftain's thick wrist. Together, they walked over to the entrance of the cave where their companions were just starting to rouse. The fire still danced with life, though it had become obsolete with the encroaching sunlight beaming through the mouth of their abode. The pair remained joined while looking out of their mountain hole. Elethain's ghouls still stood motionless, ever vigilant for any threat that might come.

Cormac rose, rubbing his shoulder beneath the plates of his armor. "Ughh . . . Mornin'. Never thought I'd say I regret sleepin' on stone, don't ye doubt." A deep yawn escaped him before being interrupted by another groan of pain. The captain rubbed his hip while adding, "Orc, yer damned forest dirt has made me soft."

The dwarf strolled over to the entrance and disappeared around the edge of the rock face out of view. After a short while, he returned grumbling as he struggled to lash together the belt that held his trousers and plated girdle up. With a grunt, Cormac finally managed to accomplish his task. He stood directly in front of both Fangdarr and Aesthéa and looked at them curiously. Fangdarr chuckled lightly. In truth, the orc was nervous of how Cormac—and more so, Bitrayuul—would receive the news of his new companionship.

The dwarf was no simpleton. He could see the beaming happiness on the elf's face and the nervous expression painted on his ally's. It was as if Fangdarr was asking the elf king himself for her hand. Cormac feigned a sigh of disappointment, but quickly shifted it to a genuine, wide smile. "Aye, I'm happy for ye, lad. I truly am."

Relief washed over the orc immediately. Fangdarr had not realized he had been holding his breath in anticipation, waiting to be judged for his actions. Now that he had his friend's approval, all the stored air in his lungs finally broke free in a blast of surprise. Aesthéa giggled at him and his stupid nervousness. Cormac watched as the elf wrapped her arms as far around Fangdarr's waist as they could go and kissed his chest. A smile returned to his face, and the dwarf simply laughed and turned away. "Yer in for a whole new world, Fang. Nothin' prepares ye for what yer in for, bahaha!"

The orc's expression shifted to confusion, but he waved away his friend's comment. His attention was drawn back to Aesthéa. Fangdarr loved the way she looked at him, as if he brought her more pride and security than anything else possibly could. Those almond, brown eyes that glittered vibrantly atop her playful grin could stop the orc dead in his tracks. He could not believe the feelings that rushed through him. A constant turmoil of love, passion, exhilaration, and panic. She made him feel it all but tying all those feelings together was a with a vivid sense of freedom. As if his life had been trapped in a prison, hidden from the elements, only to now be broken free and experiencing the outside world for the first time. Even more startling was how quickly the feelings came. Only the previous day had Fangdarr discovered her true nature.

It didn't matter. Aesthéa was with him, and the orc wished to be nowhere else. The only reason his gaze was forced away was due to Bitrayuul calling out to him—and not for the first time. "Fangdarr! Are you listening?" his brother asked with more than a hint of irritation in his voice.

With his half-orc kin behind him, Fangdarr realized Bitrayuul could not see Aesthéa hidden behind his frame. Both turned together to face their visitor who reacted in shock. "Oh, I did not . . . Uh, good morning."

Seeing his brother taken aback brought the chieftain back into the realm of nervousness. "Morning, Bit. This is . . . okay?" he asked hopefully. Unfortunately, his brother's expression remained secret beneath his helmet, leading Fangdarr to wonder at his reaction.

Bitrayuul sighed. Not at what he saw, but of the deeper meaning. As always, the half-orc was more calculating than his brother. First, he felt saddened that Fangdarr was worried he would disapprove. On the contrary, Bitrayuul shared the same notion as Cormac. However, he also realized the complications that would lie ahead. Aesthéa was not only an elf, but a relative to the king. It seemed unlikely her commitment to an orc would be tolerated. Nevertheless, it would not be he who cast the stone against them. "Yes, Fangdarr. This is okay," the half-orc responded, clasping a hand on the orc's shoulder, immediately bringing a smile to Fangdarr's lips.

"Do I have to marry the dwarf now?" Malice asked nonchalantly.

Cormac instantly froze and dropped his sack of supplies to the ground in a loud crash. "Ye what!?" Seeing her dead-pan expression that proved her remark was sarcastic, the captain released an eruption of laughter. "Bahahah! Whew, lad. For a second there I thought we was about to turn this cave into a banquet hall." He continued laughing to himself as he cleaned the spilled products, placing them back into the pack.

The dwarf's wholesome laughter was halted immediately, however, once Elethain stepped into view. All fell silent, waiting for the judgmental warlock to speak his mind. Visibly irritated, the elf simply continued walking until he reached the entrance of their shelter. Without a word, the three animated warriors fell into a half-circle formation at their commander's sides and rear. Their bones scraped against the cold stone as they walked, softened only by what little pieces of tattered skin remained attached. The tattoos on Elethain's skin danced violently, giving proof to his discomfort.

Fangdarr half-expected the necromancer to turn on him then and there, in front of everyone, Crepusculus be damned. With the elf being so old and powerful, the orc could not fathom how he could hold onto such hatred. Over *two-thousand* years of pure hatred for his kind.

"We should get going," stated the elf to the group's surprise. The magical etchings that covered his body were still raging from within their cage. Tensions ran high as no one wanted to point out the obvious—not against such a powerful ally on the day they hoped to cull a dragon.

Aesthéa motioned to Elethain, requesting a private conversation. Irritated, but bound by duty, he reluctantly complied. Fangdarr started to proceed toward the elves as well before Bitrayuul stopped him. "Not now, Fang."

The large orc did not press further. He stood and watched as his new love began trading words with the disapproving necromancer.

"Elethain, this is not for you to decide," Aesthéa spoke calmly.

Already the elf's eyes had grown wide as his true emotions came forth. "It is not, but it is my responsibility to *advise*. And I *advise* that you stop this disgusti—"

"Mind your tongue! Do not forget who serves whom, warlock. You will show respect!" she snapped back. His eyes fell to the floor in shame for a moment before looking up once more.

"My lady, you are young. You are unfamiliar with the world and therefore easily swayed. You have not yet spent enough time around elven men. *Real* men. Your people. I, and the rest of the kingdom, would see you linked to one of your own kind rather than . . . an *orc*." His distaste was clear. The way he spat the word 'orc' from his poison-filled mouth brought Aesthéa closer to anger.

The druid raised her hand to calm her raging ally, still spewing his insults regarding the orc-blooded beings. "Fangdarr is with me. You will respect that. In addition," she started forcefully with a commanding voice, "*you* will do all that you can to ensure the dragon is defeated and everyone is kept alive. *Everyone.*"

Elethain narrowed his eyes at her. The elf realized that Aesthéa had already considered the possibility he would attempt to remove Fangdarr during the battle to prevent any possibility of her relationship going further. After considering all the options and alternatives in his head, the warlock simply bowed his head slightly. "As my lady commands." He continued his bow as she smiled in return before turning to walk away. Elethain's eyes remained narrow, watching her happily skip back into Fangdarr's arms. Sometimes advisors must go against their commands for what is right for the kingdom, he thought. With that notion in his mind, the magical markings on his skin went from a raging storm to a settled sleep.

Cormac, eager to break the tension, beckoned for everyone to leave. Fully rested, they all walked out of the cave ready to continue their search for the shadow dragon's lair. The dwarf took up the vanguard, with Bitrayuul and Malice following. Behind them was the new couple, eager to stay near the other but not needing to remain in contact. Not now. The task at hand could not afford such distractions. Elethain took the rear, visualizing pushing a magical spear deep into the orc chieftain's exposed back. The elf smiled at the visions, feeling the satisfaction at the prospect of bringing about the end of the orc that sought to undermine the elven kingdom with his manipulation of the young druid. He believed there was no way the orc could have wooed one such as Aesthéa without some form of treachery or force.

As the sun hit its peak, the party realized they had travelled for quite a while. It did not matter. They had to find the lair today. Too close to the dragon's hidden location, the party could not stop for another night or risk being ambushed again.

At one spot on the path, Cormac stopped, placed his ear against the stone and gave it a hard tap with one of Tormag's hammers—as he had done at several points throughout the afternoon. Listening to the resounding vibrations through the mountain, he could draw a rough idea of the layout in his head. Luckily, they were searching for a dragon, so this would not be a small dwelling. As such, the dwarf was waiting to hear the resounding chime of a large open space—one big enough to fit their godly opponent. No luck. The captain handed the weapon back to Bitrayuul before continuing on their path.

On the jagged horizon, the sun had nearly completed its descent. The party had been sure to move slowly but efficiently throughout the day in order to conserve energy. Unfortunately, none had expected it to take this long to find the drake's cave. But the Tusks were vast, expanding the entire southern and eastern edges of Crein. All they could hope for was that Crepusculus had not taken habitation far.

With a sigh, Cormac turned to request the hammer once more. Bitrayuul already had it extended before the dwarf even had to ask.

"Aye, thanks, lad." He lifted the hammer lightly, no longer caring enough to give a hard pound against the stone. Nor did the captain put his ear against the rocks. He just tapped the hammer lightly, not expecting to find any sign of a large cave underneath. By the time the steel clanged he was already walking away; however, his dwarven ears twitched when he heard that familiar sound. Countless years of working with stone and living within a mountain made it unmistakable. The dwarf immediately returned to the boulder and placed an ear against it. His lips curled into an incredulous smile.

"Oh?" Cormac pondered to the stone as much as to himself. The hammer raised high before crashing down into the rock, followed by his ear. His eyes lit up and his smile grew wider. "Ahah! We're here, lads!"

"Finally!" Malice groaned, leaning against a rock.

"Are you sure?" Bitrayuul asked the dwarf. Cormac's face twisted to an absurd expression, as if he was offended by such a question. "Alright, so how we do get in?"

The dwarf tapped once more, closing his eyes to draw the layout in his mind. "There's an entrance to the east, big enough for the drake to fly in."

Knowing their target was close renewed their motivation. Each was ready to finally bring the journey to a close. However, they could not call the journey resolved just yet. There still remained the largest task yet, and whether it would be successful remained to be seen. Nevertheless, they moved forward with eagerness. In short order, the group managed to find the cave entrance. It was immensely large, able to fully compensate for the dragon's entire wingspan and formidable size. They stood in the threshold, remembering just how massive Crepusculus was. Fangdarr turned away from the hole to look at the valley below.

The orc's eyes gazed at the view; a desolate wasteland for as far as one could see. Curious, he asked the party, "What is this place?"

Elethain laughed openly, mocking the orc's ignorance. "Elves call it Ifildé, meaning wasteland. In the common tongue, it is known as the Hollowed Vale. It is a vile place, filled with disgusting creatures."

Fangdarr grew annoyed with the elf's condescending attitude. He turned back toward the entrance. As the orc was about to step inside, Bitrayuul stopped him. "Fangdarr, wait."

His brother looked at him in confusion.

"We can't just go in blind," the half-orc continued. "We need a plan."

CHAPTER FORTY-SEVEN
DESTINY

Bitrayuul wrapped a stray bone in oiled linens and presented it to his mother. "Here, you are the only one who's eyes cannot shift." She cast him an angry glare as if the half-orc had just insulted her before grabbing the torch.

"Will the dragon not be alerted to our presence with the light?" she asked.

"Normally, you would be right. Though, I do not believe Crepusculus has any trouble seeing in the dark."

The assassin remained silent. Part of her wished to remain outside the cave. Malice was widely outside of her comfort zone. Picking off orcs and drunkards in the cover of forest or the midnight alleyways of Riveton was where her strength lay. Fumbling around in the pitch of caverns hosting a demonic fiend resembling a god among mortals hardly seemed like her skillset. Internal debates ran rampant in her mind as she considered abandoning her companions to prolong her own safety. After all, how much assistance would she be? A human with a pair of blades and eyes that begged for more light. Would she not simply be a burden . . . or bait?

Malice watched as the group discussed their plans together, arguing over the best tactics. She considered leaving then and there, simply slipping away and never returning. The woman nearly gasped audibly as her foot started to step away of its own accord. Then another. Was she really doing this? Her mind scrambled. Malice could no longer think straight, though her feet continued.

No!

The steps ceased with her mental outcry. Despite only taking a few steps, Malice was heaving heavy breaths from the struggle. After a moment, she realized that *she* had commanded herself to stop. All became a blur. So much confusion clouded her mind that she could hardly stand.

NO!

Her eyes shot wide open in a moment of clarity. Malice had finally found a resonating truth that halted her retreat. She needed her allies. Without them, her blood would have soaked into the earth—deep within the Lithe, where Chakal would have spread his gleeful smile and resigned sigh at a task finally achieved. No. That wicked glee had been denied due to her companions. Her son. Malice owed Bitrayuul her life. Even more, without the party, how long would it be before Chakal simply collected on the debt? A day? A tenday?

Bitrayuul stood, the plans completed. He watched as his mother walked back toward them, clearly disheveled. "Are you alright?" he asked. She smiled nonchalantly and gave a nod. The half-orc doubted the sincerity of her response, but this was neither the time nor place.

"Let's move," Elethain stated, already walking into the cavern. Fangdarr and Aesthéa followed closely behind, tailed by Cormac—after dropping the excess supplies. There would be little need for his cooking sheet or rolled blanket where they were headed.

Bitrayuul followed suit. He listened intently as Malice paused in hesitation for a moment, confirming his suspicions. To his surprise, the sound of light footfalls picked up to his rear. As they passed the threshold of the cave and continued deeper, the woman struck the torch, illuminating the area around them with flickering light. The light was limited, granting her only a short field of vision, though anything was superior to nothing.

The cavern was vast. Tunnel entrances that more than likely housed other creatures of the dark were everywhere—and not just on the ground but placed along the rock wall and high into the air. The party all looked on in unison as the large path they took opened into an expansive arena, where hundreds more openings lined the walls. Bitrayuul glanced around. He expected there to be trolls. Anything, really. Yet, the cavern seemed empty.

Ahh, you are here. I was beginning to wonder . . .

Immediately the group was on the defensive, all except Elethain who simply strode forward to the ledge. He peered below to where the shadow dragon lay. It resembled a cat who had just stirred from its nap. The drake raised a curious head up toward the lingering elf.

Won't you come down, Elethain?

A small shiver shook through the necromancer at the mention of his name. In truth, he had expected such a thing. Dragons were terrible creatures capable of mysterious power. The elf rubbed a pendant that hung at his neck. Inside the small orb appeared the image of another dragon. In a moment's notice, Elethain turned to the group and asked, "Well, what are we waiting for?"

The group gasped as the elf jumped off the ledge. They rushed to see him hurtling downward, followed by the three servant ghouls. To their surprise, wings of black magic sprung from the back of the warlock, slowing his fall. Elethain hovered toward the ground before landing lightly on his feet with a smug smile. Breaking the moment's glory, the abominable minions crashed heavily next to him. With an annoyed sigh, he willfully commanded them to rise, reanimating them as if nothing had happened.

"D-did ye know he could do that?" Cormac asked Aesthéa in awe, though she was already shaking her head. Bitrayuul, on the other hand, could only be irritated at the elf's complete disregard for their planned assault. Their complex plan had been completely altered by the necromancer's plunge into the pit. Fangdarr looked around for a path down. Unfortunately, it was unlikely the orc would sprout wings any time soon. The chieftain took off running along a path that lined the wall of the giant amphitheater. Soon, all his companions were in pursuit, rushing to catch up to the foolish elf.

It seems you may be part dragon as well, elf, Crepusculus chuckled. *It will be a shame th—*

Immediately, Elethain launched a barrage of magical, boulder-like masses at the drake's head, interrupting its comment. "Oh, you talk too much."

The dragon roared in outrage at the blatant disrespect. Such an awesome beast should be looked at in fear and devotion by the peasants beneath! How dare this elf elect to disregard its power? *I shall enjoy ending the ego of Elethain!* It opened its maw and spat its bright purple flames of burning acid toward the elf. Elethain simply waved a hand in a slicing motion, bringing an angled wall of magic directly in front of him. The breath diverted harmlessly to each side as it struck the barrier.

Unbeknownst to Crepusculus, as the necromancer was launching masses at its face, he was also conjuring a massive spear-like pyramid above its body. More and more blackness coagulated into form, adding to its size. Elethain's eyes smiled wider as the strength of the mass grew. His manic mind began to show as the trait of the black magic started to take its toll. The elf began laughing hysterically as his hands continued to move, faster and faster. The dragon was keenly familiar with the magics of the world. Black magic temporarily cursed the mind of the wielder when stronger magic was utilized. The small masses that were colliding with its face were not enough to bring such an aggressive response from the necromancer.

Crepusculus narrowed its eyes as it looked up at the pyramid above it, cursing its own foolishness. Just as the dragon noticed the danger, a loud gleeful scream came from the elf. His whole body extended as far as it could reach into the air. Elethain's eyes were impossibly wide as it seemed his hands gripped an enormous imaginary object. "HYUUUUUUUGHHHHHHHHHHHHHH!" His arms pulled down with such force that his body crumbled to the ground. With the motion came the reciprocated movement of the pyramid, driving downward toward the drake's spine.

Fangdarr and Aesthéa ran ahead, not noticing that the others behind them had halted to watch the spectacle. They were completely immobilized; awestruck by the sight before them. Cormac could not help but mumble, "Bothain's beard . . ." as the mass hurtled downward with incredible force.

Nonchalantly, Crepusculus opened its maw as the physical form reached it. A risky endeavor, to say the least, though the godlike beast saw no risk. Catching the weapon directly in its gaping jaws, the dragon stopped the massive shape before the point could pierce its throat. Elethain screamed ever louder as he pulled with all his might toward the cavern floor. To his credit, the pyramid pushed slightly deeper into the drake's mouth, though not enough. Time seemed to freeze. Only the sound of Elethain's grunts, Fangdarr and Aesthéa's sprinting footsteps, and the low groan of pressure being transferred into the shape could be heard. Then, came the boom.

Every companion was blown from their feet and crashed into the walls behind them from the sheer force of Crepusculus shattering the mass between its jaws. The amount of compacted magical energy within that weapon released in a shockwave along with thousands of shard-like pieces of magic crystal. Their ears rang and bled from the painful shriek of the blast. Through the muffled noises, Bitrayuul peered down to see the dragon roaring, but he could hardly hear anything.

The dragon looked to Elethain's collapsed form across the cavern. With a prideful exclamation at conquering the largest threat, Crepusculus charged forward toward the prone elf. *What is the matter, elf? Can you not muster the strength? Did you not consider that your feeble form could never hope to defeat the god of death and sorrow!?* The elf shifted weakly as the drake came closer. *Now is the end of Elethain the Fool!* Crepusculus mentally yelled as it opened its mouth to swallow him.

A blinding light pierced the cavern, along with the sound of something small shattering. The rushing beast halted its charge as the light grew fiercer. *What trick is this? Why prolong the inevitable?* From the illuminating pillar came the jaws of another monster, clamping down on Crepusculus' exposed neck. The disarming light faded to reveal a glowing, golden dragon. The Shadow One shrieked in pain as its new opponent pierced through the plated scales covering its body. With a powerful kick, Crepusculus raked at the golden torso, causing enough pain to break its hold.

Each dragon stood facing the other in the cavern. Elethain's dragon shined with beauty, giving light to the entire area with its imposing presence. However, the light it emitted could not penetrate the dismal, black swirling mist that came from Crepusculus. *Aurum. It has been a long time.*

The golden dragon snorted a quick wisp of steam at the mention of its name. *Indeed, Crepusculus.*

It seems you have fallen. By the likes of this faded creature? The shadow dragon asked, indicating the still form of Elethain at Aurum's feet. Upon closer inspection,

Crepusculus took note of the large gaping wound behind the golden being's right horn—a grievous sight and clearly the source of the proud drake's fall. *You let a mere* ***mortal*** *pierce your hide!? You are a disgrace to our kind!*

There were others to accompany him, Aurum replied. *Do not underestimate the mortals, brother. We have very differing perspectives on what brings shame to our kind. Stop this pursuit of power. We immortals are not meant to influence the world, only oversee.*

Crepusculus laughed at the remark. *Stop? Now? When I am at the very cusp of glory? I am not like you, Aurum. I am strong. I will not sit and watch as the millennia pass by like snows on the mountain! We are the rulers of this world. Can you not see?* ***This*** *is our destiny.* ***My*** *destiny!*

The shadow dragon kicked off, rushing through the air toward Aurum. The animated golden dragon roared in response before launching a torrent of fire toward Crepusculus. The raging inferno flow harmlessly over its target due to its natural immunity to fire. Cursing its stupid choice of action and loss of precious time, Aurum leapt into the air to join its enemy. By the time it had reached the same elevation, the shadow dragon had already prepared its counterattack. Crepusculus bit down onto the golden limb of Aurum's wing, drawing a roar of pain. As it clamped its jaws tightly, acid breath poured from its mouth and into the wound. Aurum's painful shriek pierced the cavern as it felt the corrosive liquid melting its limb from the inside.

Despite the pain, the shining drake tried to bite at Crepusculus but was too restricted due to its captured wing. The shadow dragon held the golden beast dangling in the air like a worm caught by a hawk. Bitrayuul, Tormag, and Malice all watched in horror as even their new dragon ally was quickly overwhelmed. Fangdarr and Aesthéa were still running, though seeing how long of a trek remained brought them to a light jog. The path wound around the entirety of the cavern in a single spiral path, and they were not even halfway to reaching the ground level. The druid slowed to a distracted walk as she watched Aurum helplessly try to ward off its opponent. She was aware of the imprisoned fate of the drake by Elethain, as all elves were, though, there was a story to tell there. She knew Aurum to be a kind being, dissimilar to the likes of Crepusculus.

Kicking and biting with abandon, the golden dragon could not break free. The luminous limb of its left wing had begun to wither, dying from the inside. What was once glittering and bright had now faded to a poisoned gray. Satisfied, Crepusculus twisted its neck before launching Aurum into the cavern wall near Bitrayuul and his companions. The rocks shattered beneath the beast's weight, causing a rockslide that destroyed three levels of pathway. Now, they had no way to get down to the ground floor. It was all up to Aurum, the elves, and Fangdarr.

Bitrayuul ran forward toward the golden dragon. It looked weakly to him before channeling its mental voice. *Run, mortal. It is . . . too strong. Run. Do not submit to its will.* Its chest heaved with exhaustion, trying to keep its wounds from spreading. Once its eyes re-opened, they went wide immediately. *Run!* The half-orc did not realize the shadow dragon had fluttered to their location. Its maw spread wide to consume the half-orc. Bitrayuul nearly tripped over himself in his surprise; his footing was not secure enough to react in time.

As Crepusculus' mighty jaws lined with razor teeth were about to shut around his form, Bitrayuul was shoved out of the way. His eyes caught only a glimpse of his savior as he fell to the ground. In that single glance, the warrior watched his mother's smile fade from sight as the dragon's teeth crushed down onto her in an explosion of blood. Malice's hand and part of her left leg fell to the ground at Bitrayuul's feet. His eyes shut tightly as he could hear Crepusculus crunch down once more. He tried to block out the sound of bones snapping and organs bursting, though it was too late. The vision had been seared into Bitrayuul's mind. He saw it all. The drake's mouth opened just enough to readjust her body within, unleashing a wave of blood that had been trapped behind its ivory cage, his mother's lifeless eyes staring at him from within that hell—the smile gone from her face. The half-orc's ears could not block out the sounds. He whimpered quietly as the gulping noise of his mother's decimated form slid down the demon's throat.

CHAPTER FORTY-EIGHT

MIND

Shaken to the core. Bitrayuul could only clench his eyes as the new memory played over and over in his mind. His mother was dead, and it was his fault. She had died in *his* place. Crepusculus turned a gleeful smile to the terrorized half-orc. *Know anguish, orcblood. Know, too, that the same fate will befall you all.* The ensuing horrific chuckling rumbled through the warrior's mind. How could they win? What hope was there?

The dragon opened its maw wide, aiming to consume Bitrayuul as well. The half-orc begged his limbs to move. Now was the time to react! Please! But they would not budge. With a dwarven shout, Cormac launched himself onto the demon's face. "Take this, ye smelly bat!" he yelled as his right shield blade plunged into the dragon's eye. Bitrayuul watched as Crepusculus reeled in pain. Actual pain! More than that, Cormac had risked himself as Malice had done in order to save him. He was bringing their fate to them. It was *him*. The half-orc steeled his resolve. No longer would he be their harbinger of doom.

The drake was flailing wildly to shake off the dwarf, roaring in agony. With a harsh shake, the captain was thrown free. Bitrayuul gasped in surprise as he saw Cormac's form sailing through the air with nothing but the pit below to catch him. The dwarf, accepting his fate, called out as he fell. "Yer hammers, lad! Yer father's hammers!"

The half-orc responded immediately, quickly removing Tormag's enchanted weapons and launching each down toward the descending captain. With luck, the first connected with Cormac, who caught it. The second whizzed past the mark. Despite only having one, they had to try. Bitrayuul mentally called out to the hammers to return. One came back in haste, having nothing attached. The second, however, made only slow progress due to being gripped by Cormac.

The smile on the captain's face was genuine as his descent slowed and reversed. He realized he may yet not fall to his death. He cradled the floating weapon with all of his might, careful to not slip to the depths below. It was then that the dwarf took note of the flailing drake getting dangerously close. Cormac tried to paddle through the air in an attempt to steer clear of the rampaging beast, but he could not. The weapon may have been magical, but it was mindless. It performed its function perfectly, and only that. Its path toward its owner could not waver or be altered. The dwarf braced for impact as the monster's heavy tail swatted at him. To his credit, the dwarf managed to hold on by a few fingers. His armor protected most of his body from the blow, though the exposed part of his face was bruised terribly.

Almost there. Just a bit longer. The magical hammer had sluggishly drifted more than half of the distance back to Bitrayuul. The half-orc waited eagerly at the ledge, ready to pull in his ally. Crepusculus roared again, this time in less chaotic fury and more in focused anger. It had regained control of its actions once more and saw the dwarf hovering directly in front of it like a piece of meat. Cormac watched as the dragon's throat started to shine bright purple from the base of its neck, rising as it went. The dwarf looked to Bitrayuul. "Good luck, lad. Ye keep Fangdarr safe."

The half-orc's eyes went wide as he listened to the dwarf's final words. Even wider still as he watched the captain deliberately release his hold on the magical weapon. The hammer immediately hastened to return to his grasp, just as the acidic flames blew from behind it. Bitrayuul leaned as far over the ledge as possible to watch Cormac's small form growing smaller. "No! Cormac!" he shouted helplessly. He did not wish to watch the dwarf that had saved him fall to his death, but this time, Bitrayuul forced his gaze to remain open. The dwarf's honor deserved no less than to have his valiant death witnessed.

Cormac's form grew smaller and smaller as he plummeted toward the cavern floor below. Such a long drop—even without plate mail—would surely kill any creature. The orc-blooded warrior watched, preparing for the final splat of the dwarf. Instead, the captain vanished into darkness. Bitrayuul blinked in confusion. Did the cavern go even farther than his eyes could see? Was there a deep pit in the ground that led to an even further descent? The half-orc waited for the sound. A splat, a scream, a thud, anything. Instead, the dwarf came back into view. This time, he was running toward Elethain. Ah! The necromancer had saved him! As Cormac's body was about to crash into the stone below, Elethain used what little strength he had left to summon the magic that eased his fall. Bitrayuul gave a gleeful shout of triumph before noticing he had drawn the attention of the confounded shadow dragon.

Launching both hammers, Bitrayuul aimed to distract Crepusculus enough to run away. But where would he even go? The spiraling ramp on the levels below was shattered. Only the exit was left, and he would not abandon his companions. He glanced over the ledge once more to see that Fangdarr and Aesthéa had finally reached the cavern floor and were carrying Elethain to a safer location. Bitrayuul saw the dragon aiming to breathe fire at him, hoping to burn and eat away at his flesh.

Come, orcblood. Do you not wish to join your dwarf?

The half-orc narrowed his eyes in anger at the mention of Tormag. The orcish blood within his veins began to boil in anger. Despite the dragon's throat glowing purple, Bitrayuul leapt from the ledge toward the demon in the air just as the flames barraged his location on the ramp and clipped his boot midflight. There was no time to pay heed. Distracted by releasing its torrent of acid, Crepusculus did not notice Bitrayuul climbing quickly over its scales to reach the closest wing. The half-orc steadied himself, then jumped directly onto the film of the webbing. The sharpened blades of his armor allowed him to cut into the membrane and hold on despite having nothing to grab. Bitrayuul started climbing all around the wing, ripping and shredding the thin material as he went.

Crepusculus roared in agony as it felt the skin between the fingers of its wing being torn. It turned to face Bitrayuul, who still continued to rend as much as possible. The half-orc did not care if his actions brought his own death. Surely, he deserved that by now. He only thought to cripple the godlike being enough to prevent it from escaping, should they fail. The dragon took aim to bite at him. However, Aurum struck first.

Given the advantage of surprise, the ancient, golden dragon bit deeply into the back of its opponent. All three started to fall, each dragon with an unusable wing to sustain it. Bitrayuul clung to the shadow dragon's membranous wing while Crepusculus raked with its right claws, cutting through Aurums glorious scales. Each grievous wound turned the glittering scales from gold to gray as the area died off.

Finally, as they were about to crash into the ground, Crepusculus arched its neck harshly to bite at Aurum's head. Its teeth ripped through the only wound that had culled the golden drake in life, reaching deep into its brain. With a quick turn after Aurum's hold relinquished, the shadow dragon spun to be on top. Bitrayuul jumped free of its wing in the last moment, tumbling along the ground with the impact. Despite being much less of a fall, the wind was still knocked from his lungs and more than a few of the spines along his armor broke off upon contact with the stone. He maintained his resolve, however, and remembered to kick off his boot. The acid had just barely eaten through the steel with only a few drops on his skin. Though the drops were small, he groaned in agony as the liquid continued to push through the skin and into bone and sinew.

Fangdarr appeared, lifting his brother entirely from the ground and carrying his prone form to the others. Bitrayuul opened his eyes to see Elethain still taking heaving breaths from the strain of his enormous magical attack. Thankfully, Cormac, Fangdarr, and Aesthéa were all in good health, though the same could not be said of their spirit. Each turned in unison at the roar behind them—a victorious exclamation from Crepusculus who stood atop the bloodied and broken form of Aurum. They watched the cavern grow dim as the golden light emitting from Aurum's luxurious scales faded away. All that remained was the pitch blackness of the cavern.

Ah, that's better. Now I can see. Came the mental words from the remaining drake, despite its wounded eye. It chuckled and spread its grin wide, baring those teeth that could be seen even in the darkness. The party pondered silently as to how they could conquer such a beast. Elethain was completely depleted and of no use, and all they had remaining were the blades of steel on their person.

Cormac nudged Fangdarr slowly, careful not to draw attention. "Oye, Fang. Ye remember what Tormag told ye about shadow dragons?"

Fangdarr tried to recollect his memories of that day—the fateful day that had started it all—and his eyes grew wide as his mind replayed the discussion that had taken place within Tormag's home.

'Lad, ye be careful. If yer thinkin' o' takin' on the drake, best ye should be knowin' that shadow dragons have a weak spot. Right in the back o' their blasted head. Ain't much, but their scales will shrug off even yer axe. No scale on the back o' their head, so be sure t' bring a dagger.'

"Do ye got a dagger?" Cormac asked quietly.

Fangdarr nodded and produced a dagger in his hand.

"We'll distract the beast, ye find a way to the back of its head." The dwarf made eye contact with Bitrayuul and Aesthéa. Both signified their agreement before all three took off charging toward Crepusculus.

The chieftain slid the dagger back into the loop on his belted loincloth. After a moment to grant his allies time to divert their opponent's gaze, the orc jogged toward the dragon. He was forced to watch in agonizing fear as the three beings he loved more than all else rushed to face a fate that could very well spell their doom. But he had to go on. For Tormag. For Malice. For his people. For all of Crein. Fangdarr's companions knew the risk and that this was indeed larger than them. If they did not succeed, how long would Crein last before being covered in ash and flame? The orc tucked his head down and increased his speed.

Bitrayuul was the first to reach Crepusculus, thanks to his orcish stature. With a boot missing, his balance wavered, though the warrior showed no sign of discomfort. He pulled Kwip from his back and launched one of the last two remaining arrows in his quiver. It glanced harmlessly off the scales of the dragon's face as all others had before.

When will you learn, orcblood? the beast chuckled. *My armor is beyond your pointed sticks and sharpened metal. Your necromancer has fallen. Aurum, your last hope of survival, has left this world for the second time.* Crepusculus shot a distasteful glance to the dulled corpse at its feet. *Come, meet your doom!*

The half-orc planted his foot the moment the dragon began inhaling in order to have enough time to outrun the wide blast. Cormac and Aesthéa were already well on the opposite flank, waiting for the moment to strike. They remained tucked behind a rock as Fangdarr took advantage of the drake's vision going skyward as it inhaled and sprinted past the beast. The flames came shortly after, illuminating the blackened cave in that ominous purple light. Sounds of melting rocks and sizzling acid filled the echoing chamber as Crepusculus continued to unleash the devastating liquid.

Now that it was distracted, Fangdarr clambered up the dragon's leg. Luckily, the armor that served the beast so well seemed to prevent the feel of the orc's body against the demon's own. The orc was half-way up the drake's enormous frame when the flames halted.

You think I do not see you, Roaring One? Or smell you? Crepusculus turned its head around to face Fangdarr. *But you are not the Riding One, are you?* it asked with a grin. *Why do you continue? What hope is there for you?*

Fangdarr paused and remained silent. He was still a fair distance from the back of the dragon's skull where the vulnerable spot was, but even now the orc could spot it. It was obvious the dragon would not allow him to continue the climb. *Think. Think. Think!* Nothing. The demon was right. A god of death walked among them. How could they compare? Nevertheless, Fangdarr had his response. The proud chieftain did the only thing he knew to do in that moment. Baring the large fangs of his bottom jaw, Fangdarr roared with as much rage and power as he could muster—directly into the shadow dragon's grinning face.

Very good, orc. You would have served me well. Such a pity . . .

"Fangdarr!" Bitrayuul called as he threw one war hammer after the other at the dragon's turned face. Immediately after making contact, the magical weapons returned to his grasp before being launched again and again.

Ugh, the annoyed beast turned away from the orc on its side to face the nuisance. *Stop, mortal. Why do you persist?* Its words came out slowly and with growing agitation as the heavy steel continued to collide with its head. Irritated beyond words, Crepusculus roared and charged after the half-orc. *This time, I shall not spare you with fire, orcblood! You shall know the fate of the woman who spared you.*

At that, Bitrayuul wavered as flashes of his mother's chewed and lifeless form appeared in his mind, causing the half-orc to trip over a stone. He gasped as the wind was again knocked from his lungs.

Fangdarr noticed as the living mountain he scaled grew more excited at the ill fate of its prey. The orc moved frantically, nearly upon Crepusculus' skull. His hands shook nervously, knowing Bitrayuul's fate was held within them. Fangdarr reached to his waist in order to retrieve the dagger. Never before had his hands fumbled so badly. It was as if the digits had never been used until this moment. They seemed to disobey his commands. The orc's uneasiness only increased by the moment. The beast was nearly upon his kin and he needed to hurry. Cormac and Aesthéa were shouting on the periphery of his vision in an attempt to draw the dragon's attention, but to no avail. Fangdarr groaned in frustration as he finally managed to extract the blade from his loincloth. However, as his hand swung forward, the blade scraped against the orc's leg and fell from his grasp.

Clang, cling, tink.

The chieftain watched in terror as the gleaming blade bounced down the scales of the demon he rode before hitting the ground. He screamed in outrage and helplessness at his foolishness. How could he not simply grab the dagger? Fangdarr's fists pounded against the base of the drake's skull directly into the fleshy spot. The thick membrane jiggled like a gelatinous blob beneath his fists. His rage increased as he realized just how close to his goal he had failed.

Bitrayuul was able to stand, finally, and began limping away toward the cavern wall. He knew he would not make it. However, at least he could offer Fangdarr a few more precious moments. Crepusculus was only a short distance away.

Cormac and Aesthéa continued to throw stones and shout insults to the proud dragon. Normally, such a beast would never tolerate such disrespect. However, with its prey so close in sight, it cared not.

The shadow dragon bared its terrible teeth as it drew nearer, sending one more mental communication to Bitrayuul and his companions. *Now, you will finally know the folly of your task. In what world did you ever ho—*

Bitrayuul looked up in shock to see his enemy halt with a curious expression on its face. The dwarf and druid threw one more stone each before realizing the monster was no longer charging toward the prone half-orc.

Crepusculus arched its head up slowly before turning it. It felt odd, as if a bug were chewing on its skin. Indeed, as the dragon turned its head in the opposite direction, the companions noticed that Fangdarr was now face-down in the membranous spot on the drake's skull, ferociously ripping and gnawing away with fury, using his large fangs as daggers in place of the one he had dropped.

"Go, lad!" Cormac called out in excitement, but it didn't matter. The orc heard nothing at that moment, too driven by his rage.

Fangdarr's face was covered in the squishy material and blood as he finally surfaced for air. It seemed he had finally broken through the outer layer and was now digging deeper. The orc slid down into the hole he had made, clawing and pummeling the next layer of flesh out of the way. He had no idea how far the monster's brain would be, but he didn't care. The orc planned to rake, bite, and tear until the demon fell dead.

What are you doing?! Crepusculus called out in horror. Its eyes widened and twitched as it felt the tiny gnawing of the orc's hands and teeth inside its head. *No, no! Get out!* it roared in outrage and fear. Quickly, the dragon began slamming its head into the stone walls in the hope of ejecting the orcish parasite within. Instead, the chieftain remained safely tucked inside, protected by the monster's own scales. He felt nothing. Crepusculus wiggled and rolled in discomfort, disgust and terror. *Out, mortal! My body will not be tainted by your filth!* Again and again it wailed and smashed itself into the cavern walls.

Fangdarr's fury only grew as he delved deeper. Purple blood now covered his entire body as he slid through the inner tissue. Suddenly his hand hit against a spongey material. This was it! With vigor, the orc went into a frenzy, ripping his way through until he reached the brain.

The dragon's eyes began blinking impossibly fast and rolling in random directions as the orc in its skull began clawing away at its brain. In a last effort, Crepusculus inhaled to prepare for another torrent of flame. Whether it was an attempt to eliminate the companions on the cavern floor or burn out Fangdarr, none could be certain. The torrent came, though, a pitiful beam compared to those it had managed previously. It sprayed in every direction, though mercifully nowhere near Bitrayuul or his allies.

From within the monster's skull, Fangdarr's body started to feel the drastic heat. His body sweated profusely as the flames passed a short distance below him through the drake's throat and mouth, nearly cooking him. Still, he managed to continue.

Reeling in agony, the dragon put its face directly into a small opening in the wall. It was a simple concave indentation, nothing more. With its head fully in the cave, Crepusculus launched another beam of acidic flames. This time, the flames filled the entire small opening, enshrouding the beast's entire head.

Bitrayuul looked to his friends in concern as they heard painful yells, though faint, from within the dragon.

Fangdarr screamed in agony as the liquid acid poured through the hole he had created before reaching his legs. He clawed more and more in rage as the acid continued to pour down to his torso, melting his skin. The orc struggled to remove Driktarr from his back to avoid it being eaten away by the devastating viscous liquid. Slowly, he pushed away enough mass to get a small amount of room to push the weapon forward into the monster's brain. He felt the echo of the dragon roaring in pain beneath his strikes as he unleashed another assault. His body slowly started to heal, only to be eaten away again due to the pool he lay in. But Fangdarr's rage was relentless. He struck again, and the dragon's blood poured freely into his mouth, reinvigorating him.

No, you cannot! Crepusculus cried out in pain. But it was hopeless. There was no way to get Fangdarr free from inside its head. The dragon knew its fate was sealed. However, the spiteful demon of death would not allow the deed to go unpunished. It was not certain how the orc had survived its breath. Certainly, the acid was eating away at its own flesh now that it had poured into the opening, causing the dragon to wail in pain and fear. But now that it had accepted its fate, its only goal was to bring the orc with it. None would ever hear this low beast's claim to culling the great Crepusculus.

Most of the drake's limbs would no longer move from the brain damage it had suffered. Almost all of its body had lost function. Crepusculus did the only thing it could. Within the small confines of the cave, it bashed its head upward into the low ceiling. Again. Again. Finally, the stone broke free and plummeted down onto its head. In its final act and with its dying breath, Crepusculus had interred its head in a rocky tomb.

As well as sealing Fangdarr inside.

CHAPTER FORTY-NINE
BLOOD

Bitrayuul was the first to rush toward the trapped dragon, yelling Fangdarr's name all the while. Shortly after, Cormac and Aesthéa appeared by his side to join in calling out for their ally. They took care to steer clear of Crepusculus, fearing it may still be able to kick at them or flick its deadly tail. However, their caution was soon dismissed as the vibrant purple scales began to dull. The half-orc watched as the black smoke that had previously emitted from the drake's marvelous body wafted away. Just as Aurum had deteriorated to a faded husk of its former self, so too did their enemy.

"Fangdarr!" the elf druid continued, terrified for her beloved. Tears had already filled her eyes as she feared the worst.

Cormac groaned in effort as he attempted to use his powerful arms to shove a boulder free but to no avail. The dragon had performed its final act expertly.

"Aesthéa, see to Elethain. Perhaps he has the strength left to help us," Bitrayuul suggested. Her eyes brightened with the idea as she took off running toward the cubby, where the necromancer had been hidden. After watching her go, the half-orc turned to Cormac. "How does it look?" he whispered.

The dwarf shook his head somberly. "Not good, lad. There be a chance. But half a mountain fell on him, don't ye doubt."

"The stones cannot be moved?"

Cormac pondered for a moment. "Mm, they might, if the Necromancer is up to it. But . . ."

"It may bring down the rest of the cave or crush him even more," the half-orc finished, drawing a nod from the captain.

The pair of elves returned, but Elethain looked no more improved than his previous state. His golden hair was matted to his face and neck from sweat. The magical tattoos covering his body moved dreadfully slow, if at all. It was obvious the warlock was exhausted, though the moment Elethain's eyes made contact with Crepusculus' hulking corpse, they grew wide with excitement.

"You did it! Cerenos be praised, the dragon has fallen!" The elf's smile was wide and genuine, though his eyes were nearly manic. He pushed free of Aesthéa and stumbled forward before crawling toward the faded drake. "Now. Now I can . . ."

Aesthéa pushed him to the ground quickly, catching Bitrayuul and Cormac off guard. "Elethain, no! Not yet."

"What's going on?" Bitrayuul asked curiously.

"He aims to enslave Crepusculus as he did Aurum—with Fangdarr trapped inside!" She could hardly contain the excited necromancer as he clawed forward fervently.

Elethain began mumbling a chant under his breath, tapping into the last of his strength to begin sealing the shadow dragon into the magical realm. Luckily, Cormac fell on top of him, disrupting the spell. The elf stared daggers at the dwarf in response, showing naught but pure hatred in that moment.

The captain showed no concern as he tore a piece of cloth from the elf's robe and stuffed it into the necromancer's mouth. "Listen, ye can have yer damned drake. *After* Fangdarr is free. Deal?"

The pinned elf frowned in outrage at being commanded so by a dwarf. However, he knew he did not have the strength in that moment to fight back. In addition, he believed the captain would honor his word. All Elethain wished for was the dragon. He nodded his agreement before settling.

"Can ye hold him, lass?" Cormac asked of the druid.

She nodded firmly. Aesthéa had no intention of allowing Elethain to rid her of Fangdarr.

* * * * *

Fangdarr groaned in pain. After cutting deep into the dragon's brain, he had felt the powerful vibrations and crashing sounds surrounding him that could only be falling rocks. The shock of their impact had shaken him violently and put a lot of pressure on the already tight space he was in. The orc now could hardly breathe. Dead flesh squeezed his body from all angles, restricting his movement. Luckily, most of the acid that had pooled in the small opening where he lay had carved its way through the dragon's muscles and no longer burned his skin.

The chieftain contemplated what to do next. His entryway was now sealed tightly by a massive boulder that he could not hope to remove. He let out a heavy sigh to steady his breathing. It seemed his best option would be to try to cut his way to the dragon's mouth and go down its throat. At least then he could navigate a passage rather than be forced to cut through endless amounts of flesh and sinew. With the decision made, Fangdarr began cutting downward until he reached what he assumed was the roof of the monster's mouth. The palate was exceedingly durable, however, and it took a great many strikes to cut through with Driktarr. Luckily, despite perishing into the afterlife, the dragon's body retained enough vital energy to be stolen by the enchanted weapon. With each minor cut, Fangdarr's energy remained topped off.

After what seemed to be an eternity, the orc finally broke through the palate and fell into the beast's mouth. He nearly gasped in terror as he truly realized where he was. The serpent-like tongue under his rear stank of rotten flesh and blood, and perfectly in his view were the tall ivory blades that served as the dragon's teeth. Fangdarr wished he could extract one to use as a trophy and dagger. However, none were smaller than a dwarf's height and all looked firmly rooted deep into the jaw bone. The orc turned toward the opening at the back of the mouth, knowing he could never break through those razor jaws. Never in his life did he expect to purposely enter the throat of a dragon, dead or alive.

Steeling his resolve, Fangdarr dove head-first into the entry. The passage was much slicker than he anticipated. He slid quickly down the throat despite his feeble attempts to slow his movement. The smell only worsened the deeper Fangdarr traveled. It was almost enough to knock him unconscious. The orc could see the tunnel end and a pit of bubbling fluid below. He frantically tried to catch on to something, but there was nothing. Finally, in the last moment, he pushed the hook-end of Driktarr deep into the throat's lining. It continued to rip for a short distance before bringing him to a halt just before the opening.

Fangdarr breathed a sigh of relief. His eyes were drawn to the disgusting pool below. It was hard to see between the water in his eyes from the heat and stench and the heated liquid releasing its light layer of steam. However, the orc caught a glimpse of something out of place. As much as possible, Fangdarr leaned forward and squinted his eyes to see. Once recognized, the chieftain nearly lost his grip in shock. He could not avert his gaze, no matter how much the orc wished it. Below, floating in the fetid pool of stomach acid, Malice's shredded face stared back at him—a lifeless stare with one eye dangling freely at the end of its fibrous tendon. Fangdarr was not aware that she had been consumed by their enemy, and he hardly recognized her from the damage that had been done by the stomach acid. Reddened and boiled, her skin was nearly falling apart. Staring directly into her torn apart form, his thoughts could only shift to guilt for bringing such a fate upon the woman.

Finally, the orc managed to pull his vision away and his thoughts turned to his discussions with Bitrayuul regarding the half-orc's nightmares that plagued him every day—visions that played over and over in his mind when his body floated in the dream realm. Fangdarr knew he would soon know that experience from seeing

Malice's face, here, of all places. The orc shook free the distracting thoughts. He had to continue.

He pushed a long arm through the hole in the lining, reaching for anything he could latch onto. With luck, thick muscles were lined along one side, allowing Fangdarr to secure a hold and pull his body through the gap to safety. Once again, he was trapped inside the small confines of flesh and muscle. Yet, anything was better than falling into that disgusting pool to rot beside his kin's mother. The orc took a moment to breath and ponder his location. He was near the stomach, which had to be somewhere in the center of the drake, though he couldn't be sure exactly where. Fangdarr now had no idea how he could escape. The armor-like scales could not be pierced, even from the inside. For a moment he pondered going out the dragon's waste trail before laughing at the ridiculousness of such a notion. He was much too proud for that. Death seemed a better fate than climbing out the sphincter of a dead dragon.

In any case, Fangdarr could not simply dawdle. The beast was enormous. He could spend days traversing the disgusting flesh before dying slowly. The direction did not matter. What was important was that he needed to keep moving until an escape route presented itself.

Fangdarr cut his way through more and more. Flesh, muscles, veins, arteries, anything and everything. His body was ever more covered in the purple-tinted blood of the fallen creature, but such a thing did not bother Fangdarr. He enjoyed being painted in the lifeblood of his enemy.

After a long time, the orc felt warmth up ahead. He paused for a moment in caution. The heat could be coming from the sac of acidic fire stored within the dragon's body. If it was, and he punctured the sac, his body would be immediately overrun with the liquid and he would be melted alive. With dreadful slowness, Fangdarr cut tiny slits through the last bit of sinew. No purple light came through. It was not the flame sac. He breathed heavily in relief. Once he had finished cutting a gap, Fangdarr felt the surge of warmth increase. The orc pushed himself through, falling into a sort of chamber large enough for him to stand.

His eyes widened immediately.

*****

Bitrayuul and Cormac sat with the elves. By now Elethain had calmed to his former self, though they still had him gagged and bound. A large amount of time had passed since the dragon had fallen. Almost too long, they all thought. However, they clung to hope.

"What do we want to do, Bit?" the dwarf asked.

The half-orc remained silent. He was not ready to put words to his thoughts yet. It seemed obvious; either they would continue to wait for a miracle or they would not. Bitrayuul searched his mind for alternatives until his eyes lit up with a random thought. "Elethain, can your ghouls traverse the inside of the dragon?"

Elethain replied with a scowl before shaking his head. The half-orc already knew the real answer. Even if they could, the prejudiced elf would not risk even his reanimated corpses for the likes of an orc.

"What if we could extract a tooth from Aurum? Could we use it to puncture the dragon's scales?" Aesthéa questioned.

"Ye'd probably have an easier time movin' the stone," the captain responded.

So, with no alternative, they all remained seated in silence, begging their gods for a miracle. None, except Elethain, were willing to part with their trapped companion yet. They still had no knowledge of whether Fangdarr was alive or dead. Nevertheless, they had to hope.

* * * * *

He was drawn to it. The marvel. The strength.

Something within him called out, demanding he touch it. Fangdarr reached out hesitantly, as if it was some sort of cursed thing, but once his hand made contact, a warm sensation surged through his body, and Fangdarr could not contain his smile.

The heart.

Even though it no longer pulsed with life, it *felt* alive. It made sense. A dragon's heart must be such a wondrous thing for such a 'small' organ to be the driving power behind a mortal deity. Fangdarr touched it in his hands and felt the life emanating from it. The bulbous organ was nearly as large as the orc with a handful of thick arteries connecting to and from the suspended structure.

It called to him.

Immediately, Fangdarr bit into bloody heart with as much force as he could. Blood instantly filled his mouth as he sucked forcefully. Taking gulp after gulp of the purple liquid down his throat, his eyes rolled back in ecstasy. It felt as if the room was getting smaller. In reality, Fangdarr was getting bigger. His already impressive stature grew as he drank, and the surge of power through his body was so addicting, he could not stop consuming. Gaining strength.

A small voice in his mind screamed for him to stop. Pleading. Begging. *No more!* Despite his craving demanding he continue, the orc managed to pull away with a gasp. Blood poured from his mouth. How long had it been since his last breath? His chest heaved from the lack of air. Fangdarr looked down to his body. His muscles were nearly bursting through his skin. The veins that lined his arms were pulsing with vitality. He stood once more to his full height. However, now he could not extend fully. Fangdarr had grown nearly a quarter of his previous stature in both size and girth.

The orc clenched his fists, feeling the new life within them. He felt limitless, as if his body was hardly able to contain the amount of strength he now possessed. Fangdarr looked to the heart. It had shriveled to nearly half its size, now a decrepit thing. He could hardly fathom that his mouth had done such a thing. Still, the chieftain could not deny the gift he had been granted. Driktarr in hand, Fangdarr cut through the opposing side of the chamber. It was time to leave.

CHAPTER FIFTY
HORDE

Elethain groaned, clearly frustrated and bored. Bitrayuul sighed and finally removed the elf's gag.

"Finally! You stupid half—" the irritated necromancer began, until his captor started moving the gag back toward his mouth, "Wait, wait!" Bitrayuul paused, torn cloth at the ready. After steadying himself, the elf began again with caution, though with a distasteful glare. "Thank you. We have been sitting here for too long. How long must we push our luck?"

"What do ye mean, elf?" Cormac chimed in.

Elethain rolled his eyes with exaggeration. "Crepusculus claimed to have armies. Look around," his head motioned to the large cavern they sat in. "Where do you think we are?"

Cormac looked to Bitrayuul in concern. "Elf's got a point. It be odd that we ain't been swarmed yet."

"Odd, yes. But I will take the blessings the gods have granted us for now." Bitrayuul exhaled slowly. "Alright, let's consider our course of action. Say what you would like to do, each of you." He turned to Aesthéa first.

"I will not leave until I know of Fangdarr's state."

The half-orc nodded in appreciation. How incredible, he thought, that his kin had ensnared the love of such an unusual companion. Bitrayuul next motioned to Elethain—though he already knew the response.

Remaining calm as he spoke, Elethain offered his suggestion. "I wish to enslave the dragon, so that it may be used as a tool later, as I see fit. Then I suggest we leave immediately, with or without the orc."

Bitrayuul nodded again in appreciation for the necromancer's honesty. At least there seemed to be no malice in his voice this time. That was an improvement. The half-orc turned to Cormac.

"I'm not one for a horde of trolls, don't ye doubt," the captain started, bringing a smile to Elethain's face, "but I can't leave him." The elf's expression quickly shifted to a disappointing scowl, just as a smile came over Aesthéa's face. Cormac looked to each of them and shrugged in half-apology.

"Right, I agree that our stay here being uninterrupted is a blessing that may be short-lived. However, I do not wish to leave my brother. Yet, Fangdarr knew the risks and took it upon himself to eliminate the threat. I believe he would not wish that we sacrifi—" the half-orc was interrupted by a dull thud behind him.

The party looked to each other in suspicion, wondering if they were the only one who heard it. Puzzled expressions confirmed that the sound was real.

Thud.

There it was again! Immediately, they were all up in arms, save for the bound necromancer who struggled and complained to be released.

Thud.

Bitrayuul cut Elethain free. "Prepare yourself, elf."

Immediately, the warlock began chanting. The half-orc watched as the air around the dragon began to vibrate slightly. He was trying to enslave the dragon! "Elethain!" Bitrayuul shouted.

The elf smiled as if no other response were needed before being tackled to the ground once more by Cormac.

"Damned elf! Can ye not just wait a few moments?"

Thud.

"No! There is no time, I must complete the ritual," Elethain said with strain as the dwarf pushed his face into the cold stone.

Thud. Thud.

"Whatever it is, its progressing," Aesthéa stated. She took a few steps forward, allowing her keen senses to lead her. Within a moment, the druid had shifted into her bestial form and was sniffing the air with ears perked. Another few steps forward. Her ears continued to shift in each direction, waiting for the sound.

Thud!

The bear's head instantly shot up. She knew where the sound was coming from.

With a final booming sound, one of Crepusculus' dulled scales broke free of its body and fell to the ground. The companions all stared up at the place the scale had been just as an extremely gory orc slid out and fell to the ground with a crash. Almost immediately, Fangdarr was met by Aesthéa's embrace, already back in her true form.

"I thought I lost you . . ." the elf said softly in his ear.

Fangdarr, still covered in blood and shredded bits of dragon flesh, returned the embrace. He had to be careful not to squeeze the life out of her, though, as his new stature was much more capable.

As if on cue, she retracted in awe. "Fangdarr, what happened to you? You've grown somehow."

He smiled in response as Bitrayuul and Cormac walked over with glee spread across their faces. "I am much stronger now. Dragon blood."

The dwarf gave the orc's bicep a squeeze. "Bothain's beard, lad. Yer a damned ogre now! Bahaha!" he laughed as his short arms could not even begin to wrap around his lost friend's waist. Cormac backed away as Bitrayuul made eye contact with his kin.

"Bit, you okay?" Fangdarr asked with concern.

"Am *I* okay?" he laughed at such a ridiculous question. "Well, I have to say, it's been a bit uncomfortable sitting in this cave. I wish I had a *dragon* to relax in!" he said with a laugh.

The orc smiled at his brother as they clasped forearms. Fangdarr's smile quickly vanished, however, as his memory recalled the sight he witnessed in the pit of the demon's stomach. "Bit. Sorry for Malice."

Bitrayuul's smile faded. All he could offer was a simple nod of appreciation for the sentiment. In truth, the half-orc had tried to keep that painful memory at bay. Now, it completely enveloped him with fresh thoughts of guilt and remorse. With renewed mourning, he watched as Fangdarr returned happily to his reunion with Aesthéa and Cormac.

While the dwarf and druid launched a thousand questions at the fate of the orc, the dragon's hulking corpse began twisting and turning. All watched as the lifeless form began caving in on itself over and over until finally becoming the size of a gold coin. It floated effortlessly to Elethain's waiting hand where a new glass-like orb had been conjured out of black magic to capture the miniature beast. Once inside the orb, the minor version of Crepusculus came to life and immediately began spewing purple flames against the barrier. Luckily, it was contained completely. Even as the drake bashed its small head into the magical walls, only a small *tink*-ing sound could be heard.

"Just like that?" Bitrayuul asked.

"Just like that," the necromancer replied, securing the orb to a finely-crafted twine around his neck.

It all seemed so unreal. They had traversed the long journey to get here, lost friends and family along the way, in order to eliminate a dragon, only to see it brought back to life in miniature by an elf. Fangdarr could hardly believe all he had witnessed and experienced over the last moon cycle. He had slain a *dragon*! Never again would his power be questioned. His legacy would live on for all time amongst the people of his clan. With that in mind, he turned to his friends. "Let's go home."

After a long trek up the winding ramp along the cavern walls, with the required assistance of the necromancer's magic to create a path over the broken sections, the group finally made it outside. By now, the sun had fallen below the horizon. They were all exhausted and required a rest. Figuring the entrance to the dragon's cave was as good a place as any, they made a small encampment. Elethain's ghouls took watch as they slept. None had the strength remaining to stay awake for long. Even the necromancer ignored the sight of Aesthéa cuddled beneath the thick arm of the orc, as she slept against his chest.

Morning came quickly, or so it felt to the weary band. They still pondered their great string of luck at not being encountered by trolls this far into the mountains. Nevertheless, they were in no mood to linger, so they continued along the mountain passage, grateful for every step they took without conflict. After half a day of walking, they could finally see north through the tall stone around them.

"Come quick!" Cormac yelled, his gaze riveted north toward the Lithe Forest.

The elves and orcs stepped over, curious as to what had the dwarf in such a fuss. Their mouths all fell slack in shock at the sight. Though they could see little through the small gap between the mountains, enough could be determined. An army of nearly unlimited magnitude was blazing through the woods, leaving a razed and gouged land in its wake. Fire and pillars of smoke were everywhere. Though they could not see more than a short width, it seemed evident that the horde of enemies must have numbered near a million. A dark, foreboding wave was sweeping through Crein, killing everything in its path.

This was Crepusculus' goal, they knew. Despite killing the dragon, the preparations had already been made long before they entered the cavern. The deity had organized the single greatest army that ever walked the land, and now it was destroying everything. It all made sense now. Crepusculus wished to upset the balance—to turn the tables—to help the lesser, monstrous races take over and send the goodly races to the depths.

Fangdarr watched in horror. All they had done seemed for naught. They had culled the ringleader of the threat, yet its machinations had already come to pass. They were too late. A voice screeched in his head, a mix between a whisper and scream. *Now, do you see what you could have been a part of? This would have been* ***your*** *legacy, Fangdarr Blood-drinker.*

www.ingramcontent.com/pod-product-compliance
Lightning Source LLC
Chambersburg PA
CBHW030621310726
48979CB00003B/820

* 9 7 8 1 7 3 2 7 6 0 7 3 8 *